Thomas Hewlings Stockton

The Book Above All

The Holy Bible the only sensible, infallible and divine authority on earth

Thomas Hewlings Stockton

The Book Above All
The Holy Bible the only sensible, infallible and divine authority on earth

ISBN/EAN: 9783337780517

Printed in Europe, USA, Canada, Australia, Japan

Cover: Foto ©Andreas Hilbeck / pixelio.de

More available books at **www.hansebooks.com**

THE

BOOK ABOVE ALL;

OR,

THE HOLY BIBLE

THE ONLY SENSIBLE, INFALLIBLE AND DIVINE AUTHORITY
ON EARTH.

A SERIES OF DISCOURSES.

BY THE LATE T. H. STOCKTON, D.D.,
LATE CHAPLAIN TO THE U. S. HOUSE OF REPRESENTATIVES.

ON THE TEXT,

"Thou hast magnified thy word above all thy name."—PSALM cxxxviii. 2.

PHILADELPHIA:
CLAXTON, REMSEN & HAFFELFINGER,
Nos. 819 & 821 MARKET STREET.
1871.

PREFACE.

"THE times seem to call, with unusual emphasis and interest, for something of this kind. Sceptical developments, even among ecclesiastical and collegiate authorities, make it painfully evident that the true character of the Bible is misunderstood by many of its professional teachers. With these mischievous perverters of great providential advantages, it is too plain to be longer doubted that 'science, falsely so called,' has absorbed the attention and confidence due only to the Records of Divine Inspiration."

Several years since, the author of these sermons having in view their immediate publication, wrote the above sentence, but was prevented from accomplishing his design by reason of sickness, which terminated in death. It therefore becomes a duty for others to perform—not only of loving affection to the departed, but also of supplying one of the great wants of the living—of meeting one of the great necessities of the times. If this want was felt years ago, because of the existing antagonism to the Word of God; surely, much more must it be felt now, in view of the recent developments in our own country, especially regarding the bitter hostility of the Roman Catholic Church against its use in our own schools.

Well would it be for us to know, that this first demand

of the Church of Rome upon Protestant United States, is but the beginning of a series of demands of similar import, which refer not only to the Public Schools, but to all other Public Institutions, including the various State Legislatures, the Army and Navy, the United States Senate and the House of Representatives—requiring the suppression of the Bible and the dismissal of the Chaplains, and thus the total abolition of all public religious observances, unless performed under the direction of the Pope at Rome. And this same Roman Catholic Church, which would exclude the Bible from the public institutions of a Protestant Country, would just as cheerfully sweep it away from the entire land, and substitute the darkness and despotism that have marked her entire history, and which are essential elements in her government.

It will be observed that the last sermon in this series, the tenth, is composed of three parts. It was the intention of the author to condense these into the limits of one sermon, but this was too much for his feeble health, and lest an attempt by other hands to accomplish the same object, should fail in anywise, and as each one contains valuable information that could not easily be dispensed with, it has been decided to present the three parts separately. Lastly, all the additional matter has been in constant demand for years, and cannot be now obtained excepting in the present volume.

T. H. S.

PHILADELPHIA, 1870.

CONTENTS.

1*   v

SERMON I.

THE BIBLE AND OTHER CURRENT AUTHORITIES.

"Thou hast magnified thy word above all thy name.
Ps. cxxxviii. 2.

THE great questions of the age relate to government. This important fact is equally prominent
and impressive in church and state, among rulers
and people, in all the world. To the contem-
plative Christian it is a fact hopefully significant
of the speedy approach of predicted and happier
times,—the times of Him who is "the blessed and
only Potentate, the King of kings and Lord of
lords,"—the one perfect and immortal Sovereign,
who, even though many of them know it not, con-
centres in Himself "the desire of all nations."

Allow me to state and answer a few of the
questions referred to, in simple expression of my
own convictions, in respectful assumption of your
sanction, and as suitably introductory to the dis-

1

cussion of the proposition which I shall afterward affirm.

Is man capable of self-government? Not at all. Is he, therefore, of necessity subject to authority? This is the only alternative theory. The philosophy of our nature and the history of the world abundantly sustain these assertions.

By what authority, then, ought man to be governed? By Divine authority alone; and this for reasons both absolute and relative. It is the authority of Him who made man,—on whom he is dependent, and to whom he is responsible. Moreover, it is the only duly-qualified authority.

But has this authority been proclaimed? It has been proclaimed. Where does it reside? In the Bible. How is it exercised? Through private judgment, or the conscience of its subjects. What is its tendency? To personal and social improvement,—to entire and eternal redemption.

What, then, are its essential and formal characteristics? Essentially, as proceeding from God, it is infallible; formally, as adapted to man, it is sensible.

These last particulars bring us directly to the special theme selected for this occasion.

Here, then, I affirm—as a fact susceptible of

easy demonstration and most useful employment—that

THE BIBLE IS THE ONLY SENSIBLE, INFALLIBLE,
AND DIVINE AUTHORITY ON EARTH; *i.e.* THE ONLY
AUTHORITY COMBINING THESE DISTINCTIONS.

By AUTHORITY, I mean—a *rule of government,*—a
standard of personal and social life.

By SENSIBLE authority, I mean—an authority in
a *material form,* and which, therefore, addresses its
subjects through the bodily senses.

By INFALLIBLE authority, I mean—an authority
so constituted as to be, and so guarded as to remain, *unerring in its decisions.*

By DIVINE authority, I mean—an authority *duly
attested* as a *revelation from God.*

By the COMBINATION of these *three distinctions* in
this authority, I mean—not only to show that in
this consists the *peculiarity* of the Bible, but also—
to imply, as the great consequence of this peculiarity, the *superiority* of the Bible to every *other
authority,* making it fit to be confessed as the
PROPER AND SUPREME CONSTITUTION AND LAW OF THE
WORLD.

FOUR OTHER AUTHORITIES.

Now, there are four other agencies, which, to
some extent, may be acknowledged as authorities,

and which, indeed, on account of their combining
two of the three distinctions just noticed, are regarded by many as rivals of the Bible, and by
others are preferred to the Bible. They are
sensible authorities. They are, more or less,
Divine authorities. But they are not infallible
authorities. Their original condition, the original
condition of man himself, and, consequently, the
relations between them and man, have been so
changed, that they can no longer be reasonably
considered, either separately or jointly, as entitled
to sovereign control.

These four authorities are of two classes:—
natural and social; two in each class. The natural are—creation and providence; the social—
the church and the state. The two former are
wholly Divine; the two latter, partly Divine and
partly human. That these solemn and imposing
institutions may not be treated too lightly,—as
well as in justice to the exclusive proposition
which has been submitted for demonstration,—
it is necessary to review their character and
claims. Their character involves both their constitution and condition. Their claims are of
interest chiefly in relation to the single point
of infallibility. Let us now look at their character.

I. THE CHARACTER OF CREATION.

What, then, is the true notion of creation? What is the ideal of its constitution? Let me try to give a fair answer.

Created things compose two classes:—the *unliving*, or the worlds and their purely physical developments; and the *living*, or the animal and intellectual orders.

From the first class, separately considered, it is impossible to educe a design which seems worthy of the Creator. For of what advantage could it be to the Deity to fill the solitude of His infinite spiritual glory with merely material forms and motions, sounds and colorings? And, if no advantage to Him, it could have been of no advantage at all; for the lifeless elements would have felt no thrill of joy.

In like manner, from the simple animal existence of the second class we are at a loss to infer a becoming purpose. For, again, what adequate pleasure could the Almighty have found in presiding over an endless succession of creatures so humble?—eternally unconscious of His being and unimprovable by His care? And if it be supposed that their own enjoyment was a sufficient reason for their existence, still, it may be asked,

But why the manner of their existence? Why their occupancy of a system so lavishly supplied beyond all their wants and so magnificently expanded beyond their little comprehension? What to them would have been the roll of the sea, the rise of the mountains, the meteors of the air, the changes of the moon, the apparitions of the comets, and the boundless sweep of the sun with all its train among the innumerable stars? In a word, take from the universe the intellect which illustrates it far more than the blaze of all its fadeless fires, and there is nothing left, in the bare contemplation of senseless spheres and thoughtless ephemera, at all correspondent with the implied dignity of creative exertion.

The true notion of creation, therefore, is derived from its spiritual connections. It is the splendid ideal of a spiritual universe to which the material universe should be subordinate and subservient. The spiritual was to come between the Divine and the natural; to vindicate the former and elevate the latter. It was to be constitutionally allied to both, conscious of its relations to both, and thoroughly sympathetic with the attributes of both.

Now, it is not irrational or irreverent to suppose that God would take pleasure in the existence of spiritual beings. They were to be like Himself; to be His children; and to be His heirs. They were to think as He thinks, feel as He feels, and act as He acts. Moreover, while thus capable of direct communion with Him, they were also to commune with Him indirectly. Because of the difference between the finite and the infinite, because of their equality and sympathy with each other, and because of their investiture, more or less refined, with material forms, they might derive advantage and pleasure from the whole inferior creation; not only perceiving and admiring its physical beauty, sublimity, and variety, but also understanding and appreciating its nobler moral significancy. To them, every opening blossom, every flying bird, every floating cloud, every rolling world, was to express some thought, some sentiment, some law, of its Maker; and so all nature was to be suspended around them as a grand gallery of instruction, a vast artistic system of permanent symbols of the Divine perfections.

And here it is that the great principle of infallible authority first becomes sensibly impressive. For no error can be properly supposed, either in the original significancy of natural objects, or in the unperverted interpretation of their observers; and, of course, no imperfection can be admitted in the obligations of whatever truth or duty might be so revealed. With particular reference to our own race, it may be added, that this notion of creation necessarily includes the original perfect adaptation of the human constitution to the study of this symbolic system, and to the enjoyment of all its harmonious felicities.

But what is the current condition of creation? Does it answer to the notion, does it realize the ideal, thus described? Certainly, so far as our relations extend, *it does not.* What then? Has not the earth been changed? Has not man been changed? And have not, consequently, their relations been changed? If we deny a change, then, arguing from facts as they are, we must conclude that the ideal never was realized; that perfection never existed; that God himself is imperfect, or else that, being perfect, He preferred an imperfect to a perfect world, a distorted image of Himself to a faithful reflection, and the error and wretchedness of His children to their knowledge and bliss. If, on the other hand, a change be admitted,—and surely we all agree in this admission,—then the inference is easy and the truth is plain. We need not pause to inquire whether this change has chiefly affected the symbol or the observer. Be this as it may, the result is the same. Creation, to us, is no longer a source of infallible authority.

Since the change referred to, every student of nature has erred, both because of the defects of his authority and because of his own incompetency. As long as the influence of that change remains, every student must continue to err. That nature still teaches some truth, and that man, impaired as are his powers, may yet learn it, are suggestions not at all at variance with these statements. That many and ample systems of natural history, natural science, natural philosophy, natural law, and natural religion, have been compiled from accessible and appreciable facts, are remembrances of no force against the argument. *Some* truth is not what we want. We want all the truth that properly belongs to the form of revelation we are studying, and that without any admixture of error.

And as for the ample systems just alluded to, what are they, even at the best, but representations, more or less exact, of things as they *are?* They have neither history nor prophecy of a better estate. They supply no deficiency, they remedy no incompetency; their whole character is determined by the facts and principles of the condition in which they originate. They have no power to change the condition. They do not create facts, but investigate them; they do not inspire principles, but develop them. Besides, even the facts which they do investigate are not such, generally speaking, as involve our highest interests; neither are the principles which they develop those which enable us to secure these interests. Nor only so; but, even within the inferior range to which they are limited, their facts and principles, to a great extent, are perversions of the original intention. And so it comes out, that the seeming demonstrations of the fulness and certainty of natural wisdom are the real demonstrations of its uncertainty and emptiness. For natural history has no beginning; and natural science, no end; and natural philosophy, no explanation; and natural law, no force; and natural religion, no salvation.

II. THE CHARACTER OF PROVIDENCE.

What, then, is the true notion of providence? What is the ideal of its constitution? Here, also, I seek a fair answer.

Creation shows us God in action thousands of years ago, and does not forbid the thought that He has been at rest, afar off, ever since. But providence brings Him near to us, and keeps Him always with us and always employed in our behalf.

The true notion of providence may be thus stated :—It is an agency which includes thorough knowledge of the two great classes of created things, and the disposition and ability to make the best possible use of this knowledge; that is, it knows all the wants of all living things, and all the resources of all unliving things, and how to make these resources supply those wants, and is actually engaged every moment in the universal application of this knowledge, according to circumstances, in all wisdom, power, and grace.

Animal wants supplied, the notion rises to the supply of spiritual wants. It contemplates the perpetual, interchanging display of all the phenomena of creation; heightening their symbolic character, varying their relative uses, and in every way multiplying their power. In regard to this world, the moral impressiveness of providence is confined to our own race. Whether the particular instrument it employs be small or great,—a dew-drop or an ocean, a pebble or a continent, a bubble or a sky; and whether it affect a flower or a fleet, a child or a nation, a worm or a world,—by man alone its intellectual indications are dis-

2*

cerned, and on him alone is exerted its most important influence.

There can be no doubt that providence was designed to be a ministry of bliss. Not only— for it is always this — was it intended to be a ministry of love. We have learned from another source that "God is love;" and, therefore, that, in chastening as well as in reward, His providence is proof of His love. But it was originally designed to be the ministry of love to the *sinless;* and, of course, to be the ministry of joy alone. Had this design escaped interruption, then, with no symbolic error, no administrative error, and no error in observation, from sun to sun, from sabbath to sabbath, from moon to moon, from harvest to harvest, and from the universal fulness of one perfect year to that of the next, this glorious superintendency would have continued to this day the practical demonstrations of its infallible authority. Like the unclouded light of the sun, the wisdom of God would have shone on all things; like the unchilled heat of the sun, the goodness of God would have glowed in all things; and as the sun, generous as it is, does not lose its light or heat, but sees them glorified in all growth, and bloom, and life, so all the Divine perfections, already illustrated in the stabilities of creation, would have disclosed new charms and dispersed new delights by means of the ceaseless alternations of providence.

But what is the condition of providence now? Certainly it has been changed. It is not correspondent with its constitutional ideal. Its ministry has become, to a great extent, a ministry of desolation and woe.

True, it is still easy to refer to fair and attractive scenes. That eye must be dim indeed which does not flash as it turns toward them; that ear must be dull indeed which does not ring with their blended music; and that heart must be cold indeed which does not quicken with their myriad living sympathies. But that is poor philosophy, as well as poor poetry, which, in its devotion to abstract good, overlooks or denies the relative contrast of evil. In this world there can be little light, or no beauty, where there is no shadow. The desert is exceedingly illustrious; but, in the paradise, every hill, and tree, and flower, has its shade as well as its sheen. What sort of a painter would he be who should leave out the shadows?

In all cases it is unwise to disregard distinguishing facts. In this case it is peculiarly so. The ministry of providence is no longer an exclusive

ministry of bliss. We must admit a change.
This is not in the qualifications of providence.
Providence knows all wants as well as ever.
Providence knows all resources as well as ever.
Providence is as able to adapt the latter to the
supply of the former as ever. Providence is as
full of love as ever. The change is in the mode
of operation, and is occasioned by moral causes.
Wants are only partially supplied. Resources are
only partially employed. Love often assumes the
appearance of wrath. Punishment is as common
as reward. Sometimes virtue seems to be punished
and vice rewarded; for the good suffer and the
evil rejoice. Impressions, therefore, are contradictory, and the mind is perplexed. Even with
the aid of revelation, it is acknowledged to be
difficult to understand providence. To say the
least that can be said, it is far from being an
infallible authority.

III. THE CHARACTER OF THE CHURCH.

What, then, is the true notion of the church?
What is the ideal of its constitution?

I answer,—The church is a religious society,
governed by Divine revelation alone. This statement, in my judgment, embodies all that is essential to the constitution of the church. I will not

say that there cannot be a church without certain articles, officers, or ordinances. Neither will I say that any association must be a church which has certain articles, officers, or ordinances. But this I do say,—that no society can be a church unless it be a religious society, governed by Divine revelation, and by this alone; and, further, that every *such* society must be a church. There never was, is not now, and never can be, any other true church than one of this description. Nor can I hesitate a moment to add, that, when I speak of its being governed by Divine revelation alone, I mean by *its own understanding* of that revelation; only requiring that it exercise its understanding, with due reverence toward God and due respect for the whole Christian brotherhood, in ardent, patient, studious, prayerful, practical desire to be led into all truth by the Spirit of truth. All this, indeed, is logically and philosophically involved in the proposition itself.

To me it is clear that the original intention was that the whole human race should constitute the one undivided membership of the church. Church and state, if designed to be separately and dif· ferently organized, were always to exist in close union and perfect harmony. Their separation, however expedient now, could not have been demanded by the primitive condition of things. This expediency is an effect of the introduction of evil. Revelation, in whatever form furnished and to whatever organs restricted, would have qualified these organs for the exercise of infallible authority. The multiplying generations, with no tendency to error in themselves, with nothing to suggest it in creation or providence, and with nothing to occasion it among their social instructors, would have continued forever to enlarge their acquaintance with truth, and to enrich their character and estate with the blessings of obedience. Every birth into the world would have been a birth into the church. The prattle of the child of a year or two old would have been readily inspired with the worshipful spirit of the patriarch of a thousand years, and the softest lisping of its all-believing love might have been more touching to the heart of God than the sublimest anthem of angels ever sung before His throne.

But what is the condition of the church now? How does it compare with the ideal of its constitution?

Its whole history is a history of change. Once and again, and again and again,—to say nothing of human changes,—God himself has changed it; not, indeed, the principle of it, but the form of it. The principle of it—the sole sovereignty of revelation —is as much identified with His own honor and the good of the church as ever, and, of course, is cherished by Him as sacredly as ever; and all the formal changes alluded to have had a progressive tendency, as, indeed, the influence of them still has, toward the universal and everlasting establishment of this principle.

At present, however, after all the struggles of nearly six thousand years, the most extended boundaries of the church, instead of including the whole current generation, comprise only a small minority. Instead of being closely united with the state, the very theory of such union has to contend with increasing prejudices, occasioned by the offensiveness of the miserable caricature unions of apostate churches with apostate states; and, therefore, the best practical condition of the church is that of entire separation from the state. Again: instead of being united in its own membership, the church is broken into almost innumerable sharp-edged fragments, nearly every one of which it is dangerous to handle, even in a charitable effort to restore them to their proper connections and original integrity. But the saddest part of the answer is that which accounts for all that has gone before.   I mean that the church, as a general fact, is not governed by Divine revelation; *i.e.* not by Divine revelation *alone*.

Certainly it has no immediate, personal inspiration,—no peculiar, official prerogative, in virtue of which it can independently ascertain the Divine will.   In a word, it has no infallible authority apart from the Bible; and it is not governed by the Bible alone.   In some cases it trusts to its own understanding, without due efforts to secure a correct understanding; in others, it alternates between its understanding and its authorities; and in others, it confides implicitly in its authorities without any understanding.   In all these cases it falls into manifest and egregious errors; demonstrating that it is not itself infallible, either in whole or in part, and, moreover, that it has neglected, misunderstood, or perverted, the infallible authority of the Bible.

IV. THE CHARACTER OF THE STATE.

What, then, is the true notion of the state? What is its constitutional ideal?

I answer,—The state is a secular society, governed by Divine revelation alone.   It has been already intimated, that church and state, if at all intended originally as separate institutions, were nevertheless designed for close sympathetic union. It is doubtful, indeed, whether a separate state organization would be necessary, or could even conveniently exist, in a perfectly holy and happy condition.   Rather, it is probable that such an institution would not exist under such circumstances.

There is no intimation of a separate state organization in heaven.   There "the King in his beauty" is, at the same time, the "Head of the church, which is his body, the fulness of him that filleth all in all."

Dominion was given to Adam, indeed, even before the Sabbath was instituted.   The sceptre was placed in his hand before the censer.   But this dominion was not that of a man over men. It was dominion over the inferior orders.   Still, it is remarkable that the existence of the animal races in association with man—especially as affected by the introduction of sin and death into our world—is among the chief facts, to say the least of it, which render a modification of sovereignty necessary here, which, in the absence of such facts, is not necessary in heaven.   In a multitude of ways and to a greatly-controlling extent, these inferior creatures, both living and dead,— from the cochineal-insect up to the elephant and

the whale,—enter into state affairs. What would
the arts and sciences, the agriculture, manufactures, and commerce of the world be without
them? And what would the state be without
these arts and sciences?—without agriculture,
manufactures, and commerce ?

But there is no such dominion in heaven.
Imagination has transferred many earthly things
to that blissful region, but none of these. A sky
is there, with only one cloud, and that merely to
shade the throne and show the rainbow. Mountains are there for sublimity, hills for picturesque
variety, and vales for beauty. A city is there
with innumerable mansions for eternal homes.
A paradise is there with inexhaustible resources
of perpetual delights, with living winds, living
waters, living trees, and living flowers, blowing,
and flowing, and waving, and breathing forever.
But, not to degrade the allusion, it is enough to
say that, except man himself, imagination leaves
the living things of earth where it finds them. A
pagan or a Mohammedan heaven, indeed, may
not be so select; but the Christian heaven is infinitely higher and purer than theirs. No mock-
ing-bird sings on the Tree of Life; no gold-fish
gleams in the River of Life; and no lion overlooks, from any tufted lair, the Plains of Life.

Not even a lamb is there,—the symbol of Jesus. Not even a dove is there,—the symbol of the Holy Ghost. Heaven is the home of intellect. Heaven is the home of affection. Heaven is the home of knowledge and wisdom, of holiness and joy. Nothing less than a saint or an angel treads the golden pavement, traces the fadeless paradise, approaches the throne of glory, or flies away from it, on missions of mercy and peace, to other worlds. There, at least,—if such distinctive names are not utterly unknown,—the church and state are one.

But what is the condition of the state here? What is it in comparison with its proper constitutional ideal?

It has become almost entirely separate from revelation. I cannot, indeed, say that the history of the state, in this connection, has been a history of change. There never was but one fair instance of the state's conjunction with and dependence upon Divine revelation. I allude, of course, to the Jewish theocracy; and that was neither of great duration or great expansion. With this exception, the state has generally remained aloof from revelation, and has been only indirectly influenced by it.

One reason—perhaps the chief reason—of the

separation of nominally-Christian states from revelation is to be found in their general union with what are properly enough called the state churches. These churches have come between the state and the Bible. They have eclipsed the Bible, and, by so doing, have darkened the states. The fact that no such union exists in our own free and happy country is one of the greatest blessings we enjoy. Here there is no eclipsing apostasy. I will not say that there is no dark orb, astray from an older and melancholy firmament, which would fain intrude between our new heavens and earth. But, so far, there is nothing to prevent the Bible from shining in all its glory on all our State. So— thank God!—it does shine! So, God grant that it may continue to shine forever! And, as God himself is in this light, may all the nation rejoice to walk in the light, loving and serving Him who gives it!

The main difference between the church and state, in this connection, is this :—that, while the acknowledgment of revelation is *essential* to the *existence* of the church, it is *not* essential to the *existence*, but merely to the *perfection*, of the state. There have always been states without revelation.

So there are now. True, this condition will not always remain. The state, according to prophecy, is to be brought up, in some form, to its proper intention. For the time-being, however, it seems to be the plan of God, in His government of the world, to employ the two institutions for the accomplishment of purposes which neither of them could fulfil alone. I mean, that the church, instructed by revelation, is bound to teach what *ought* to be and *will* be; while the state, in partial separateness from revelation, shows what *is*, and, for a time, *must* be. At present, the state, generally speaking, has no wisdom but human wisdom. Of course, it has no infallible authority. It needs to be taught itself.

In hopeful conclusion of this topic, however, let me submit these statements. The Bible shows God's way alone; the church shows God's way and man's way united; the state shows man's way alone. The result will be the triumph of God's way. The Bible will secure its due supremacy. The church will abandon all false authority, obeying and exemplifying the Bible. The state will be merged in the church, or the two institutions act as departments of the same agency. And so, as first the star, and then the moon, hide themselves in the sunrise, thus state authority, and church authority, as now exercised, will be lost in the boundless simplicity and glory of the infallible authority of the Bible.

SERMON II.

THE BIBLE AND OTHER CURRENT AUTHORITIES.

"Thou hast magnified thy word above all thy name."
Ps. cxxxviii. 2.

In the former sermon I commenced a review of
the character and claims of the four current authorities which are variously but vainly brought
into competition with the Bible. The manner in
which their *character* was then noticed renders it
the less necessary now to expatiate largely on their
claims. Let us treat them in the same order.

I. THE CLAIMS OF CREATION.

Creation presents no claim to infallibility,—
except in one relation, which no change can essentially effect. I mean, the doctrine of the Divine existence, power, and sovereignty. Whatever the condition of nature may be, though it
descend from perfection through all degrees of

25

imperfection, this doctrine remains unimpaired,—
an absolute, universal, and perpetual demonstration. The existence of evil, as well as of good,
implies the existence of a Creator; and creation,
whether of good or evil, implies infinite power and
sovereignty. A demonstration, however, though
perfect in itself, does not necessarily imply the
ability of observers to comprehend it.

It is a remarkable fact that Revelation, the vindicator and interpreter of Creation, makes no
claim for it beyond this. Natural theology claims
more; but herein is the deadly vice of natural
theology. Not natural theologians, who are often
the mere imitators of ancient heathen philosophers or modern scientific skeptics, but spiritual
theologians, the sanctified oracles of the Holy
Ghost, are our authorities.

The nineteenth Psalm may be cited as condens-
ing the instruction of the Old Testament on this
subject. Its statements are wonderfully distinctive and decisive. It consists of two parts,—the
first referring to Creation and the second to Revelation; the former claiming all that can be justly
claimed in behalf of nature, and the latter proving
that God has magnified His word above nature.
The first part opens thus:—

"The heavens declare the *glory* of GOD: and the firmament showeth his *handiwork*."

That is all! The sky is contemplated in its two chief conditions; both demonstrating the existence of God, but each peculiar in its testimony to His character:—the day-heavens, full of one common and all-commanding glory, declaring His sole and omnipotent sovereignty; and the night-firmament, myriadly variegated by milder splendors, showing the diversity and delicacy of His wisdom and skill. The succeeding verses say no more. They merely amplify this opening:—

"Day unto day uttereth speech, and night unto night showeth knowledge."

The days are eloquent; the nights silent. The days speak; the nights show. But what do the days speak? The same that "the heavens declare." And what do the nights show? The same that "the firmament showeth." And yet, this is not mere repetition: but "day *unto* day uttereth [this] speech;" and "night *unto* night showeth [this] knowledge,"—so that every day learns it, and every night learns it; and every day teaches it, and every night teaches it; and thus the sublime tradition is perpetuated, without a moment's intermission, from age to age.

"There is no speech nor language, where their

voice is not heard.   Their line is gone out through all the earth, and their words to the end of the world."

That is, the testimony, whether properly understood or not, is as universal as it is perpetual. Still, however, it is the same,—everywhere the same.   There is nowhere any addition to it.   So, in what follows, of the sun :—

"In them hath he set a tabernacle for the sun; which is as a bridegroom coming out of his chamber, and rejoiceth as a strong man to run a race. His going forth is from the end of the heaven, and his circuit unto the ends of it; and there is nothing hid from the heat thereof."

The sun appears gay and brilliant as a bridegroom, strong and swift as a racer, and with the whole circuit of heaven and earth before him ; but he does not appear as a witness to any further truth in regard to the Divine character.   The testimony remains precisely as it was,—the magnificent tribute of creation to the being, power, and skill of the Creator, but nothing more.

Now see how differently the second part of the Psalm opens.   It quits the range of nature, and comes within the limits of inspiration.   It drops the name of God, and substitutes that of the LORD or JEHOVAH,—a name that nature never knew, a name peculiar to revelation and redemption. It drops, also, all natural symbols, and brings us at once to the living word. And thus it magnifies the word:—

"The *law* of the LORD is perfect, converting the soul:

"The *testimony* of the LORD is sure, making wise the simple:

"The *statutes* of the LORD are right, rejoicing the heart:

"The *commandment* of the LORD is pure, enlightening the eyes:

"The *fear* of the LORD is clean, enduring forever:

"The *judgments* of the LORD are true and righteous altogether.

"More to be desired are they than gold, yea, than much fine gold; sweeter also than honey and the honey-comb."

Richer than the treasures, and more delightful than the pleasures, of nature! And so the Psalm proceeds, closing with the prayer:—

"Let the words of my mouth, and the meditation of my heart, be acceptable in thy sight, O LORD, my strength and *my redeemer.*"

The two spheres are entirely different; and the superiority of the spiritual must be instantly and

impressively evident. Here, both the moral character and redeeming purposes of God are disclosed. The perfections of the law reflect His
own perfections. Its objects are His objects.
Infinitely holy and happy in Himself, He seeks
the holiness and happiness of mankind. All this
is apart from nature, and above it. The heavens,
glorious as they are, declare it not; and the firmament, beautiful as it is, shows it not. Day unto
day uttereth *no* speech, and night unto night showeth *no* knowledge, like this. Through all the
earth, to the end of the world, there is no speech
nor language where *this* voice *is* heard; nor does
the sun, in all his circuit, searching as are his
beams, discover any thing resembling it, except
the developments of its own extending influence.

In like manner, the first chapter of the Epistle
to the Romans may be cited, as concentrating the
intelligence of the New Testament, in this connection. Here, also, as in the Psalm just noticed,
we distinguish two parts, but in reversed order,—
the spiritual first, and then the natural. In the
former, the apostle proclaims the excellency of
revelation; asserting, in particular, that he is
"not ashamed of the gospel of Christ,"—which
is the sum of all revelation,—because "it is the
power of God *unto salvation;*" that is, the power

of God as displayed not in creation, but in redemption; not by nature, but by grace. In the
latter part, he opens the awful contrast to this,—
claiming for creation, indeed, all that ought to be
claimed for it, but at the same time confessing its
insufficiency, and proving the absolute necessity
of revelation :—

"*For the wrath of God is revealed from heaven*
against all ungodliness and unrighteousness of
men who *hold the truth* in unrighteousness; because
that which may be known of God is manifest in
[or to] them; for God hath showed it unto them.
For the invisible things of him from the creation
of the world are clearly seen, being understood
by the things that are made, *even his eternal power
and godhead ;* so that they are without excuse."

Now, what *is* "the truth" which men in their
best condition, under the natural system alone,
may be said to "hold"? Plainly, according to
the apostle's statement, it is the doctrine of the
existence, power, and sovereignty of God,—this,
and no more! And *how* do they hold it? In
unrighteousness; in all impiety and iniquity;
gradually losing their original clear perception of
it; perverting and abusing it; descending, as
described in the conclusion of the chapter, to
the lowest depths of idolatry and immorality,

4

and becoming unutterably vile and abominable.
Against all this ungodliness and unrighteousness
of men God reveals His wrath from heaven.
Speaking with all reverence, He appears not as He
would, but as He must; not in love, but in anger;
not with good, but with evil. This is the current
presentation of nature. Not only is it true that
"the heavens declare the glory of God, and the
firmament showeth his handiwork," but it is
equally true that they declare and show, by day
and night, all round the globe, His omnipotence
in vengeance for the sins of our race. Just as sin
is everywhere, so sorrow is everywhere and death
is everywhere. The disguise of God is terrible.
If we would see Him without disguise, see Him
as He is, and as He desires to be universally
known, we must turn back from creation to revelation, from nature to grace, from the wrathful
heavens to "the gospel of Christ," from His power
in restraint or punishment of sin to the same
power in deliverance from sin.

In short, in all that relates to the moral character of God, the testimony of creation, in its
present estate, is defective, disturbed, and con-
fused. Moreover, as, if necessary, might also be
shown at large, in all that relates to human history, duty, and destiny, it is nearly silent. From

the time of the first great change, no nation, tribe, or person has ever acquired clear and full knowledge of either God or man from nature alone.

II. THE CLAIMS OF PROVIDENCE.

The study of Providence leads to the same result. Its action, in great part, is sensible; but it does not always reveal the principles on which it acts. Its movements are so constant, complicated, numerous, and various,—sometimes so unexpected and seemingly contradictory,—that it is utterly impossible to understand the system without a supernatural teacher. Like creation, it presents no claim to infallible authority on its own part; and revelation, which is its vindicator and interpreter also, makes no such claim for it. The strongest inspired affirmation is this:—that God, who "in times past suffered all nations to walk in their own ways, nevertheless left not himself without *witness*, in that he *did good, and gave us rain from heaven, and fruitful seasons, filling our hearts with food and gladness.*" That is, "in wrath" He remembered "mercy,"—wherever practicable, preferring the administration of good to that of evil. We cannot indeed resist the impression of goodness produced by the general regularity and rich supplies of the seasons. Bad as man is, he has never yet been abandoned to a whole year of winter. Relenting a little at the pleasantness of the thought, it may be remarked that summer has never for so long a time bidden farewell to Cape Farewell, nor withdrawn for such an interval her cornucopia from Cape Horn. Within the tropics, however, thousands of years of summer have been known. And, as to the temperate zones, our fine old world, ever vibrating northward and southward, has continued to bowl around the sun, expanding its belts of white and green and red and yellow, in all the significant diversity and loveliness of ever-changing repose and revival, bloom and growth. The heaven has not withheld its rain, nor the earth its fruit. Our bodies have been nourished by the abounding food, and our spirits refreshed by the abounding gladness. To indulge a little further in familiar figures:—spring is as welcome as a virgin sister, half tears and half smiles, yet ever full of wit and love and joy and grace and health and beauty. Summer is as welcome as a thoughtful and skilful mother, glowing over many a wholesome and grateful preparation, and crowding every nook of home with stores for future comfort. Autumn is as welcome as a prudent father, who,

by long-continued toil and care, has completed
the accumulations which he now soberly contemplates, and by which he perfects the ingatherings
of his younger and fairer partner. And even winter is as welcome as a historical and prophetical
grandfather,—outwardly severe and frosty, but
inwardly warm and cheerful; remembering well
that the world is not as it was in the spring, but
foreseeing as clearly that another spring is coming, and so abiding in hope, prompt with sage
advice and maxims often proved. Still, returning
to more important and literal truth, it must be
considered that all this is partial testimony; that
even the seasons themselves often give counter-
statements; that many providential movements,
gentle as well as violent, are most mysteriously
and awfully destructive; and that, in a word, the
system neither directly nor indirectly claims the
office of infallible instruction.

III. THE CLAIMS OF CHURCH AND STATE.

Having thus glanced at the fact that the two
great natural authorities do *not* claim infallibility,
I prefer, for the sake of general and brief statements, to notice the remaining fact—that the two
great social authorities *do* claim infallibility—without division of topics.

4*

It is not too much to say, that both Church and State often, perhaps generally, if not indeed always, claim infallibility. Nor only so; but they claim it as Divine. They do not pretend that mere human wisdom is infallible. They assert a Divine gift, an official prerogative. They are infallible in virtue of their origin, and as essential to their office.

Even a slight acquaintance with civil and ecclesiastical history is sufficient to assure us that the fact is as thus reported. In some cases, the assumption is formally prominent; in all, substantially observable.

In civil history it stands thus,—representing monarchies, aristocracies, and republics or democracies:—

1. The voice of the *king* is the voice of GOD!

2. The voice of the *nobles* is the voice of GOD!

3. The voice of the *people* is the voice of GOD!

In ecclesiastical history it may be found thus,— representing Roman and Greek Catholics, the Protestant State Establishments and dissenters from them, and the coequal denominations and congregations of our own country:—

1. The voice of the *pope* is the voice of GOD!

2. The voice of the *council* is the voice of GOD!

3. The voice of *the church* is the voice of GOD!

4. The voice of *our church* is the voice of God!

That is, the voice of the present power, whatever it may be, is the voice of God! All parties, to a greater or less extent, challenge this same high regency. The unrelenting rigor of their governments, the severity of their administrations, the technical obstinacy of their creeds and statutes, the pains and penalties they have inflicted and still inflict, their uncompromising controversies about things of little interest, their wilful neglect of other things of greatest moment, their undervaluation of manly freedom and brotherly charity, their overvaluation of slavish and unimprovable conformity and uniformity,—these and innumerable other evidences are all confirmatory of this actual characteristic or prevailing tendency.

In all these connections, the agents, however externally diversified, compose but two classes, which are easily distinguished. They are either believers or unbelievers, zealots or hypocrites, fanatics or impostors: or, in the first class, those who are *honest* in their claims, however deluded; and, in the second, those who are either above or below delusion, deliberately and selfishly *dishonest*. Whether, however, honest or dishonest,—sadly, in either case, as they are unfit for the office,—these,

too often, nay, generally, are the leaders of the
world,—either its tyrants or deceivers, the fool-
makers or slave-makers of the rest of the race.

Notwithstanding the obvious fact, that these
authorities do, formally or virtually, urge this
claim, it is still more obvious, if possible, that it
is not to be justified, has no proper sanction, is a
miserable and abominable imposition.

The state infallible! Put the history of monarchies under the title,—the voice of the king is
the voice of God. Put the history of aristocracies
under the title,—the voice of the nobles is the
voice of God. Put the history of republics or
democracies under the title,—the voice of the
people is the voice of God. And what blasphemy
is here!

So it is with the church. The church infallible!
Put the history of Roman or Greek Catholicism
under the motto,—the voice of the pope, or patriarch, or council, is the voice of God. Put the history of *the* church, in any of its forms, or the history of *our* church, in any of *its* forms, under the
vaunted vanity,—its voice is the voice of God.
And who that has any reverence for God,—
Father, Son, and Holy Ghost; who that has any
love for truth or righteousness; who that has any
respect for himself, or sympathy with mankind,

can suppress the kindlings of indignation, or withhold the burning utterance of intensest wrath and scorn? Away with such absurdities and cruelties!—away with them, at once and forever!

One test is enough,—one incomparable historic illustration,—infinitely solemn and forever decisive. On some occasion, when it was said, The voice of the people is the voice of God! it was replied, Not so: for, when the Son of God came into the world, the people cried, Away with Him! Let Him be crucified! But, admirable as this reply was, the case in whole is more significant and impressive than it thus appears. The truth is, that case brings to the test and condemns all the classes and claims of which I have spoken.

Behold the scene! The trial of Christ is the trial of the world. To justify the world were to condemn Christ; to justify Christ condemns the world.

All civil authorities are here represented:—monarchy, (though not in person,) by Cæsar; aristocracy, by Pilate and Herod; and democracy, by the masses of the people. In like manner, all ecclesiastical authorities are here represented:—the pope or patriarch, by the high priest; the council, by the Sanhedrim; *the* church, by the

Pharisees; and *our* church, by the Sadducees and others.

Here they stand, circle within circle, rank above rank, in mighty, multitudinous, and tumultuous pressure. And here stands, in the midst of all and apparent to all, the only-begotten and dearly-beloved Son of God, the gracious Redeemer and glorious Sovereign of the world.

And are not the angels, of all orders, here? And are not the saints, of all ages, here? And is not God, himself, here?

And what is the voice of God? To the angels "he saith, And let all the angels of God worship him!" And lo! they do worship Him, more profoundly and solemnly, if not more readily, than when He first came into the world. And to the saints, and to the world, God saith, "This is my beloved Son, in whom I am well pleased: hear ye him." And the saints do hear Him, though the world will not hear. "But unto the Son he saith, Thy throne, O God, is forever and ever: a sceptre of righteousness is the sceptre of thy kingdom: thou hast loved righteousness and hated iniquity; therefore God, even thy God, hath anointed thee with the oil of gladness above thy fellows."

But what is the voice of the Church? And

what is the voice of the State? The grandest
occasion in the history of the world has now
come for the demonstration of their consonance
with the voice of God. Let them speak. And
hark!

The voice of the High Priest, or pope, is, Crucify
him!

And the voice of the Sanhedrim, or council, is,
Crucify him!

And the voice of the Pharisees, or *the* church,
is, Crucify him!

And the voice of the Sadducees, or *our* church,
is, Crucify him!

And so, the voice of Cæsar, or the king, is,
Crucify him!

And the voice of Herod and Pilate, or the
nobles, is, Crucify him!

And the voice of the masses of the people is,
Away with him! away with him! crucify him!
crucify him!

And so, directly, having meekly endured all
passing indignities and pains, there hangs, on the
cross of Calvary, the cold corpse of Him whose
proper place is in the glory of the throne and the
glow of the bosom of God.

How often, since then, have popes, councils, and
churches, kings, nobles, and peoples, "crucified

the Lord afresh and put Him to an open shame"!
Alas for their pretensions to infallibility! Alas
for the servility of persons who submit to such
pretensions!

SERMON III.

"Thou hast magnified thy word above all thy name."
Ps. cxxxviii. 2.

Is there any scene on earth so sublime as this? Not one. Architectural provision may be vastly more magnificent. Instrumental accessories may be far more attractive. The assemblage of persons may be innumerably greater. The official organization may be incomparably more imposing. And the common object may seem to command a higher interest. But, in reality, there is no such scene as this. What are the halls of art and science, of philosophy and literature; what are the courts of civic rule; what are the cathedrals of ecclesiastic superstition; what are they— with all their charming appointments, and all their enthusiast crowds, and all their splendid hierarchies, and all their fugitive aims, and all the

5   43

traditional, conventional, conflicting, and ever-
changing authorities which control and dishonor
them,—what are they all, in comparison with this
or any similar congregation, made solemn by the
dignity, liberty, and sympathy of assured and
earnest immortality; worshipping God, in the
Spirit of God, around the open word of God, looking, longing, and laboring only for the coming and
the greeting of the kingdom of God! Do I mistake
you, my friends? God forbid. Surely He smiles
on such a scene! And, hark! it is the *Bath Kol*—
the daughter of the voice—the call from heaven:
"*O earth, earth, earth, hear the word of the Lord!*"

On former occasions, the proposition was submitted for demonstration, that the Bible is the
only sensible, infallible, and Divine authority on
earth: *i.e.* the only authority combining these distinctions. On those occasions, I reviewed the
character and claims of four other authorities,
which are variously brought into competition with
the Bible,—viz.: Creation and Providence, the
Church and the State. It was acknowledged, of
course, that these are sensible authorities; and,
moreover, that, to a greater or less extent, they
are Divine authorities. But I trust it was demonstrated that they are not infallible authorities.

They possess, therefore, only two of the three distinctions attributed to the Bible; and, lacking the third, they leave the Bible, as affirmed in its behalf, alone in its glory.

In order to make the demonstration the more complete, I now design to notice these facts:—

1. That there have been other authorities which combined the three distinctions of the Bible; but,

2. That all these other authorities have been withdrawn from the world, still leaving the Bible in sole supremacy.

I. ANCIENT SENSIBLE, INFALLIBLE, AND DIVINE AUTHORITIES.

The very existence of the Bible presupposes these. Its character was determined by them. It is itself, indeed, in part at least, the record of them. And it is to this record, of course, that we are indebted for our knowledge of them. They occupied the whole interval from the creation of Adam to the end of the first century of the Christian era. I allude to elect men, to angels, and to Christ,—the one Mediator.

Elect men have held this high position:—patriarchs, priests, prophets, apostles, and evangelists, —some of them regularly, in virtue of their rank; others occasionally, without regard to rank, to meet special exigencies. They received their inspiration by means of duly-modified natural dreams; or supernatural open visions; or silent spiritual suggestions; or outward intelligible voices; or other appointed and reliable modes. Now, I do not say of them that, under all circumstances, and merely as men, they were free from error. The doctrine itself implies the opposite fact. But, as elect men, as inspired men, when they acted *officially*,—when they spoke or wrote *as* prophets, *as* apostles, as the anointed orators or amanuenses of the Holy Ghost,—*then* they were infallible. The Divine omniscience was exercised through them without hinderance and without mistake. In the saintly meekness, in the sacred sublimity of their sanctified persons, they stood forth, in the presence of the church and the world, in visible, audible, infallible administration of the authority of God.

Elect angels, also, have been employed in the same way. Their general ministry I need not notice. Quick as thought, wide as space, and perpetual as time, it must be indeed a grand and mighty agency. But here I speak of their special ministry,—their *manifested* ministry. The philosophy of it, I pass. It is enough for my purpose to treat it as a conceded fact. The instances of it are too numerous to be cited. The manner of their appearance and disappearance seems to have been as easy and changeable as volition. In most cases, they wore the guise of men and acted like men, though apparently superior in countenance, bearing, and speech. In some cases, personal names are applied to them. In others, their social orders are designated. In all, their mission, both in purpose and performance, is worthy of their nature and relations. Let this suffice; or, if a more poetic reminiscence be desirable, it is enough to add, as somewhat significant of the fairer ideal, that, with the bloom of unfading beauty on their cheeks; with the light of tearless joy in their eyes; with the music of immutable truth on their tongues; with the pulse and the impulse of eternal life and love in their hearts; and with the glory of heaven's highest noon still lingering among their pinions and flashing from their plumes,—often, more swiftly and brightly than the sunbeams, have they made the descent from their world of bliss to our world of woe, in sensible and infallible revelation of the authority of God.

Not only so: but, now, it becomes us to notice the more important and impressive fact, that One, different from the prophets, different from the apostles, different from the angels,—above them all, as well as different from all,—having "obtained by inheritance a more excellent name than they,"; even the name of "the only-begotten Son of God," —that He, "the Christ," the "one Mediator between God and men," has Himself filled, and to a great extent fulfilled, in a manner peculiar, incomparable, redeeming, and adorable, the same gracious office.

I introduced these ancient infallible authorities with the remark that they occupied the interval from the creation of Adam to the close of the first century of the Christian era. But now it is necessary to specify and distinguish the fact that it was Christ alone who personally and regularly maintained this position during that long lapse of four thousand years. Even the oldest of the patriarchs did not reach one thousand years. The priests and prophets of the Jewish economy, and the apostles and evangelists of our own, belonged to generations as rapid in their succession as the present. The angels, indeed, were immortal. They lived through the whole time. It is possible that the same groups which sang over Eden chanted still more joyously over Bethlehem. But the angels, as subordinate agents, were only employed occasionally and interchangeably in sensible visitations. For aught we know, the angel that delivered Peter from prison was never on earth before. But Christ—and this is the great fact I desire to state clearly and surely,—Christ, as the Supreme Agent, lord alike of angels and men, having in charge both the work of creation and the work of redemption, superintended the entire progress of affairs, and manifested Himself, at His own will, whenever, wherever, and however He pleased.

What *is* the Bible? Pre-eminently, it is the BOOK OF CHRIST. What is the Old Testament in particular? It is the history of the manifestations of Christ *without the flesh.* And what is the New Testament in particular? It is the history of the manifestation of Christ *in the flesh.*

Who was the God that walked and talked with Adam among the sinless bowers of Paradise?— and with Enoch, before his translation?—and with Noah, both before and after the flood?—and with Abraham, Isaac, and Jacob, in their pious migrations and worshipful repose? Who was it that so thrillingly called to Moses from the burning bush and revealed Himself, not only as "the God of thy father, the God of Abraham, the God of Isaac, and the God of Jacob," but, also, as the "I Am"? Who was it that so awfully announced from the midst of the fires of Sinai the precepts of the Decalogue,—that First Sermon on the Mount, of which the one in the New Testament contains the proper exposition and illustration? Who was it that shaded Moses in the cleft of the rock, and passed before him in the cloud, and proclaimed His name and the meaning of His name—the standard statement of His character, for common confidence and appeal—to all succeeding generations? Who was it that responded to the priests in the oracles of the Sanctuary and the Shekinah during the ages of the Tabernacle and the Temple? Who was it that, by all the sensible methods which have been alluded to, qualified the long series of prophets for their surpassingly eloquent and subduing challenges to rulers and people:—"Thus saith the Lord!" and again, "Therefore saith the Lord, the Lord of hosts, the Mighty One of Israel;" and again, "Hear, O heavens; and give ear, O earth; for the Lord hath spoken"?

Who was it? Does any one answer, "It was the Father"? Then, what is the meaning of St. John's assertion:—"No man hath seen God at any time: the only-begotten Son, which is in the bosom of the Father, he hath declared him"? Christ was seen—both seen and heard, seen and heard as God —at many times, in various forms, and on various occasions. All this was in fulfilment of His Mediatorial Office. But the Father was never seen: neither seen or heard. I do not remember that the Old Testament contains any intimation, even of the existence of the Father,—whether by distinction of persons between the Father and the Son, or in any other way,—that is not plainly a revelation of the Father by means of the Son!

For instance, the 2d Psalm is supposed to distinguish the Father and the Son: the Father giving, and the Son receiving, univefsal dominion. But who is it that makes the revelation? Certainly, it is the Son. "*I* will declare the decree: the Lord hath said unto ME, Thou art my Son; this day have I begotten thee," &c. So in the 110th Psalm, which, indeed, Christ applies to Himself in the New Testament, David says, "The Lord said unto my Lord, Sit thou at my right hand, until I make thine enemies thy footstool." Now, how did Dàvid know what the Father said unto the Son? Did he hear him say it? Not at all. But, as in the former instance, the Son Himself revealed it unto him. This is sufficiently intimated by the fact that David styles the Son "*my* Lord:" *i.e.* the Mediator, with whom alone (and not with the Father) the Psalmist held communication, and by whose spirit or voice he was instructed or inspired. In a word, it seems that the

revelation of the Father, which was generally
withheld from men and angels, was intentionally
reserved to glorify the ministry of the Son, in
the flesh. "All things are delivered unto me of
my Father," said Christ, "and no man knoweth
the Son, but the Father; neither knoweth any
man the Father, save the Son, and he to whom-
soever the Son will reveal him." So it had been
from the beginning: the Son was the revealer;
not the Father. "Ye have neither heard his
voice at any time, nor seen his shape," said the
Son, to the Jews. It was His own voice which
had been heard; and His own shape which had
been seen.

It will not do, therefore, to say that it was the
Father who appeared to the patriarchs and prophets. Nay; it was His Mediatorial Son. And
this view is in strict accordance with all the language of Christ and His apostles.

What said Jesus? Hear His assertion of His
pre-existence:—"Your father Abraham rejoiced
to see my day: and he saw it, and was glad.
Then said the Jews unto him, Thou art not yet
fifty years old; and hast thou seen Abraham?
Jesus said unto them, Verily, verily, I say unto
you, Before Abraham was, I am." This statement, you perceive, antedates, in its reference, the

very origin of the Bible. Abraham died some three centuries before Moses wrote the first sentence of the Bible. But Christ said, "*Before* Abraham was, I am." How long before? At the time of Noah, of Enoch, of Adam? Certainly, before all; but how long before the first man, nor man nor angel may presume to tell. Who shall compute the generation of Him who calls Himself the "I am?"—importing that He never was less, and can never be more, than He now is: a saying, indeed, which is only expanded in one of His last claims in the last chapter of the Bible:— "I am Alpha and Omega, the Beginning and the End, the First and the Last;" and, especially, the Alpha and Omega, the Beginning and the End, the First and the Last, of the Bible.

But come within the limits of the composition of the Old Testament, and you will see that it is distinctively and peculiarly devoted to the Son, rather than to the Father. Hear the reference of Christ to the author of its first five books:—"Had ye believed Moses, ye would have believed me: for *he wrote of me.*" See that!—Moses wrote, *not* of the *Father*, but, of Christ. Surely, this is not an allusion to any one passage alone; but to all the writings of Moses. His communion was with the Son; and therefore he wrote of the Son. On other occasions, our Lord just as distinctly claimed all the other writers of the Old Testament as His special witnesses. So it is said, "Beginning at Moses, and all the prophets, he expounded unto them in *all the Scriptures* the things *concerning himself*." And again: "All things must be fulfilled, which were written in the law of Moses, and in the prophets, and in the psalms, *concerning me*." And again: "Search the Scriptures; for in them ye think ye have eternal life, and they are they which *testify of me*." True, it may be said, that some of these allusions are merely to predictions of the New Dispensation, rather than to actions performed under the Old: but the fact is, the predictions involve actions; for it was Christ who gave the predictions to the prophets, before the prophets gave them to the nation and to the world.

And here the language of the apostles becomes doubly corroborative; for they not only declared, again and again, that "all the prophets" had foretold the occurrences of their days: that to Christ gave "all the prophets witness:" that "the testimony of Jesus is the spirit of prophecy,"—*i.e.* the sum and substance, the very life and glory, of it: but they also declared, that it was "*the spirit of Christ*" himself "which was *in*" the prophets, and "testified beforehand the sufferings of Christ, and the glory that should follow." They did not, therefore, hesitate to style Him, in accordance with all these intimations,—"Jesus Christ, the same yesterday, and to-day, and forever,"—*i.e.* the same in all the past, the present, and the future!

But now let us turn from the many manifestations of Christ *without the flesh*, to His one, open, and prolonged manifestation *in the flesh.*

I do not now inquire, Who was the *God* that walked and talked with Adam among the sinless bowers of Paradise? But—the new-born Babe, that slept in the manger, at Bethlehem: the young child, so hastily carried into Egypt, to save its life: the sprightly prattler, so cautiously brought back, and secluded in Nazareth: the marvellous boy of twelve, who confounded the doctors in the temple, at Jerusalem:—who was *He?* Hark! "Wist ye not that I must be about my *Father's* business?" *Who* is He?—the *Revealer of the Father!* But let us proceed. That young man of thirty, receiving baptism, in Jordan, at the reluctant and tremulous hands of the boldest of prophets: that faint one of the wilderness, assailed by the Tempter who triumphed in Eden: that tried and faithful one, returning to Galilee, assuming the office of a teacher, coming to Nazareth, and standing up in the synagogue, among the wondering friends of his youth, as a reader and expounder of the word of God:—who is *He?* Hark! "The Spirit of the Lord is upon *me*, because he hath anointed me to preach the gospel to the poor; he hath sent me to heal the broken-hearted, to preach deliverance to the captives, and recovering of sight to the blind, to set at liberty them that are bruised, to preach the acceptable year of the Lord:"—"*This day is this Scripture fulfilled in your ears.*" What! Is this gentle Nazarene the great subject of prophecy? But let us proceed. That meek but mighty orator, attracting to himself great multitudes from all the districts of Syria, assembling them on the mountain, seating himself in sight of all, and commanding them with ease by a voice that searches the soul as well as the ear, and never fails to reach its utmost mark: that majestic expounder of the Law of Sinai; who, though no cloud gathers round him, and no trumpet is blown, and no lightning flashes, and no thunder peals, and no rock quivers, to attest his authority, and no frightened auditors exclaim to their fellow-man, "Speak *thou* with us, and we will hear: but let not *God* speak with us, lest we die!"—does, nevertheless, beneath a smiling sky, and in the midst of a lovely landscape, and in the solemn hush of universal admiration and wonder, absolutely "*magnify* the Law," and make it more "honorable" than ever; excelling, apparently without an effort, its first proclamation, and sending it forth again, with extended powers and renewed sanctions, to all nations, and for all time—the Mediatorial Message to the Whole World—the Miracle of Morals, above all praise, irresistible in its demonstrations, and immutable as the kingdom of God:—who—I again demand—who is *He?* Hark again! "Not every one that saith unto *me*, Lord, Lord, shall enter into the kingdom of heaven; but he that doeth the will of *my Father* which is in heaven!" See! It is the Son,—revealing the Father! But let us proceed. That speaker of speakers, coming down from the mountain, and showing himself immediately as the worker of workers,—cleansing the leper, at his feet, by a word; by another word, or without a word, healing the centurion's servant, at a distance; touching the sick, and dispersing their maladies; cowering the storm into dumbness, by his rebuke; dispossessing demoniacs, and driving their tormentors, like thievish slaves, from his presence: that worker of countless miracles, on other occasions—not only remedying all the ills of life, but recovering the very victims of death—filling the cities and the deserts, the mountains and the seas, the earth and the skies, with

the proofs of his limitless control:—who is *He?*
Hark again! "Verily, verily, I say unto you,
The *Son* can do nothing of himself, but what he
seeth the *Father* do: for what things soever he
doeth, these also doeth the Son likewise." See!
Still it is the Son revealing the Father! But let
us proceed. That sufferer of sufferers, homeless,
distrusted by his kinsmen, troubled by the ingratitude of his beneficiaries, by the waywardness
of his disciples, by the dulness and even the
treachery of his apostles, and by the unrelenting
malignity of his enemies: that benevolent sufferer,
oppressed, above all, by the sorrows, and especially
by the sins, of all mankind; and so brought down
at last to the agony of Gethsemane and the crucifixion of Calvary:—who, oh, who is *He?* Hark
again! "O my *Father*, if this cup may not pass
away from me except I drink it, thy will be done!"
And again: at the cross itself,—"*Father*, forgive
them: for they know not what they do!" See!
Still it is the Son, mediating with the Father.
But let us proceed. That sleeper in the sepulchre: that first example of immortal resurrection:
that serene one, ascending in triumph to the skies:
—who is *He?* Hark again! "All power is
given unto me in heaven and in earth. Go ye,
therefore, and teach all nations, baptizing them in

the name of the *Father*, and of the *Son*, and of the
Holy Ghost; teaching them to observe all things
whatsoever *I* have commanded you: and lo, *I* am
with you alway, even unto the end of the world.
Amen." See that! Still it is the Son revealing
the Father, and providing for the proclamation of
the intelligence, under his own superintendency,
by the agency of the Holy Ghost, and the instrumentality of the ministry, through all the world,
and to the end of the world.

But it may be that all this will be admitted by
some, who, nevertheless, object to the notion that
this Revealer of the Father, in the New Testament, is the same Being who appears, and speaks,
and acts as God, throughout the Old Testament.
For their sakes, let me close this point with the
distinct and decisive testimony of "the disciple
whom Jesus loved:"—"*In the beginning was the
Word, and the Word was with God, and the Word was
God. The same was in the beginning with God.*"
What did this Word *do?* "All things were made
by Him; and without Him was not any thing
made that was made." Did this creation include
living things? Certainly: for "in Him," it is added,
"was life;" and therefore he was qualified to com-
municate life. But did it include *mankind*, in particular? Certainly: and therefore it is added,—

"and the life was the light of men:" men deriving not only their life, but their light, or intelligence, from Him. And did this "light" *continue* with men after their creation? Certainly: and therefore it is added,—"and the light shineth in darkness, and the darkness comprehended it not." It shone through all the ages preceding the Christian dispensation; but all history shows that it was not comprehended. What then? Then, as the apostle proceeds, came John the Baptist, and then came Christ,—*i.e.* the Word. Therefore it is added,—"And *the Word*"—*i.e.* of course, the same original, divine, all-creating, and all-revealing Word—"*was made flesh,* and dwelt among us, (and we beheld his glory, the glory as of the only-begotten of the Father,) full of grace and truth."

Here, then, I rest this point, having been strangely, unexpectedly, reluctantly, and even laboriously, led to protracted consideration of it, —it may be, providentially, for some appropriate and useful purpose.

According to all these scriptures, therefore, if they be rightly understood, the whole interval from the creation of Adam to the close of the first century of the Christian era was occupied, as occasion required, by the exhibition of sensible, infallible, and Divine authorities, in the persons of elect men, in the missions of holy angels, and, above all, in the mediatorial superintendency of the Christ, the Son of the living God,—"the brightness of the Father's glory, and the express image of his person,"—manifested, in various ways, *out* of the flesh, under preceding dispensations; and *in* the flesh, as Jesus of Nazareth, at the commencement of our own.

But now I must glance, at least, at the fact, that these authorities have been all withdrawn from the world, thus leaving the Bible in its sole supremacy.

II.—THE ANCIENT AUTHORITIES WITHDRAWN.

And is it not so? Where are the apostles now? Successors of the apostles are said to exist; but they are afraid of the name, and without the signs. Why do they not call themselves apostles, and prove themselves apostles? Have they seen the Lord? Have they been taught by Him, and commissioned by Him? Are they in any proper sense His personal witnesses? Where is the Saul, among them all, to whom our ascended Redeemer has returned to reveal His glory, as to "one born out of due time"? Where is the apostolic brow, with its crown of cool flame, singeing not a single hair? Where is the apostolic tongue, modulating into instant, accurate music, all the languages of the earth? Where is the apostolic shadow, at the

passing touch of which sickness vanished and
health resumed its equal and gentle pulsations?
Or where is the apostolic hand, to add a Gospel,
an Epistle, or an Apocalypse, to the volume of
inspiration?

And where are the prophets now? Where is
the prophetic eye, with its picturesque and gorgeous
visions, seeing even "the Lord, sitting upon a
throne, high and lifted up"? Where is the prophetic ear, with its frequent and familiar oracles?
hearing the six-winged seraphim responding to
each other, as they stand near the throne, "Holy,
holy, holy is the Lord of hosts! the whole earth is
full of His glory!" Where is the prophetic lip,
touched by one of those same seraphim with "a
live coal" from the altar, and then replying to the
challenge of the Lord himself, "Here am I; send
me"? Where is the prophetic spirit, let loose into
futurity, foretraversing ages, nations, and events,
and exulting in the accelerating progress and ultimate universal triumph of immortal redemption?
Where now is the Elijah, whose prayer shall be
answered by fire? Where now is the Samuel,
whose appeal shall be sustained by thunder?
Where even the priest, with the Urim and Thummim, or access to the veil that shades the Shekinah? Where even the feeble and dying patriarch,

to turn his dim eyes on "the last days," and see them flashing with the fortunes of his mighty descendants? Where, especially, is the modern Moses, to wield a shepherd's rod as the symbol of omnipotence; to smite an empire till it trembles at his feet; to smite the sea, and behold it sundered from shore to shore; and to touch the desert, and see its sands, rocks, and skies filled with daily miracles for the support of a nation of emancipated but murmuring slaves? Where now is such an one as this, who, laying his rod aside, shall stand between divinity on the cliff and humanity in the vale, and pass the law of the world from one to the other?

And where are the angels now? The light comes as ever; but where is the guest that once came with it? Down to its window among the homes of Judea, the turtle-dove glides as serenely as of old. And down to its tufted nest on the greensward of England, the sky-lark drops from his welcome to the sunrise. And down to his mountain-eyrie in our own Western wilds, the eagle sweeps from his farewell to the sunset. But where is the sky that glitters with the pinions of angels now? Or where is the landscape that gleams with their reposing beauty and living ministry? The morning star returns; but where are

the Morning Stars? The sun shakes his locks in
the east; but where are the Sons of God? Where
is Gabriel? where is Michael? where are all their
singing and shouting hosts? Heaven is open as
ever; nay, it is more open than ever; but to the
natural eye, and to the natural ear, how empty,
and how still! And yet more, infinitely more,—
Where is the Christ now? Where is the one Mediator between God and men?

Where is the Eden in which He walks? Where
the Hebron at whose tent He rests? Where the
Bethel which He brightens with visions of heaven?
Where the shining bush from which He speaks?
Where the clouded cliff from which He gives law?
Where the Joshua whom He cheers to battle?
Where the Samuel whom He calls, even in childhood, to judgment? Where the Elijah, whom He
charms by a "still small voice," more mighty than
whirlwind, earthquake, and fire? Where the priest
to whom he responds? Where the Shekinah in
which he dwells? Where the prophet whom He
inspires? Where the king with whom He enters
into covenant? But let the Old Dispensation pass.

Come to the New. Where is the Son of man?
Did He not say that His disciples would desire to
see one of His days, and should not see it? Where
is He, the contrasts of whose character and condi-

tion were so wonderfully symbolized by the manger in which He slept, and the star that watched over Him; by the shepherds who came in from the fields, and the angels who sent them with music and glory from heaven; by the dull ones around Him, who heeded Him not, and the wise men who brought Him rich gifts from afar; by the carpenter who fostered Him, as if His father, and the Architect of the universe, who was His Father; —in a word, by the cross on which He died, and the throne to which He ascended? Where is He, the weeper at the grave of Lazarus, His young and beloved friend? Where is He, the transfigured One of the mountain, with His ancient friends from Sinai and Horeb—Moses and Elias—seated by His side? Where is the Mourner of Gethsemane? Where is the Sufferer of Calvary? All we can answer is this: He is the One "whom, having not seen, we love, in whom, though now we see Him not, yet, believing, we rejoice, with joy unspeakable and full of glory, receiving the end of our faith, even the salvation of our souls."

The ancient authorities being thus withdrawn, the Bible alone remains visibly supreme.

SERMON IV.

THE CURRENT CONDITION OF THE BIBLE.

"Thou hast magnified thy word above all thy name."
Ps. cxxxviii. 2.

In the preceding sermon I noticed these facts:—
1. That there were certain authorities which combined the three distinctions of the Bible; but, 2.
That these ancient authorities have been withdrawn from the world,—still leaving the Bible in sole visible supremacy. Those authorities were Elect Men, Elect Angels, and the Messiah, the Christ, the "one Mediator between God and men."

Now, I design to indulge in various contemplations of this remarkable current condition. The past, indeed, must still receive an occasional glance; but the chief views will relate to the present. And may the Spirit of truth lead us into all truth!

66

To one surveying this whole field of the Divine administration, and observing the personal retirement of the Elect Agents from the circle of sensible, infallible, and Divine authority, leaving it all still and lonely, and the world apparently without any sufficient guide, such questions as the following, it seems, would be suggested.

What now? Is there no sensible, infallible, and Divine authority on earth? Shall God permit the two great natural systems to be impaired and obscured:—Creation to become almost unintelligible, except in expression of his power and sovereignty, and Providence to embarrass us by the innumerable inconsistencies of its results with our instinctive anticipations,—and yet do nothing to remedy these defects, or supply the wants they occasion? Shall He allow the two great social systems to be so disordered, also, as to become incompetent to the proper discharge of their high functions, and yet develop no corrective agency? Shall the State be suffered to adopt false principles, embody them in degrading and oppressive measures, and impose them, by the concentrate energies of its complicated faculties, on all nations and all generations, and nothing be done to arrest the evil? Shall the Church be suffered, as if a mere State instrument. to adopt similar

7

principles, embody them in similar measures, and impose them by similar powers and with similar results,—only modified into agreement with subtler prejudices and infinitely prouder pretensions,—and no check be imposed, either for the safety of humanity or the credit of Divinity? And, moreover, shall even the occasional reliefs of the olden time—when the earth was not a hundredth part explored, and our race was not a hundredth part expanded, and all the interests of its separate families and tribes were so divided, secluded, and inconsiderable, in comparison with the interests of society now—be withdrawn from us, every inspired man be withdrawn, and every visible angel be withdrawn, and even our most constant and unequalled friend, the adorable Mediator himself, be personally withdrawn, and the masses of mankind, in their more enlarged, and elevated, and thoughtful, and solemn, and even intensely anxious, modern conditions, be abandoned to the errors, and follies, and crimes, and cruelties of fallible, selfish, and wilful hypocrites and tyrants? In a word, shall the Highest look down on such a scene as this, and still consent that every source of true authority shall remain like a sealed fountain among inaccessible rocks?—rocks whose shadows, dry and pitiless, fall on the barren sands of a perishing camp below? Or, rather, shall God still consent that His own authority shall be like a shaded sun,—a sun obscured, not by earthly clouds, which an earthly wind might remove, but by clouds of its own, drawn closely and coldly around it, and therefore beyond the control of the dependent planet that shivers and dies for want of its beams?

The answer to all such questions must be, No, no: God is not thus careless of his intelligent creatures! He saw the end from the beginning. He knew all the exigencies of human progress, and made due provision to meet them. There is a sensible, infallible, and Divine authority on earth! There is one; but only one. There is only one; but that one is enough! And here it is!—The Bible! I look at it,—wonder at it,—cannot avoid the inclination to reverence it. If it did not itself rescue me from superstition, doubtless I should superstitiously regard it. As it is I confess that, to me, a Bible in the hand of a child is a greater marvel than the sun in mid-heaven! That, indeed, is a glorious symbol; but this is more glorious! God, himself, has magnified this above all his name.

See! It is not enough to say that the Bible is the only sensible, infallible, and Divine authority now remaining on earth. Much more than this must be said. It has a comprehensiveness, completeness, and fulness, far transcending such an announcement. The truth is, all such authorities are comprehended in this one! See! Did I say there were such authorities in ancient times and distant places, but that they are now all withdrawn? Let me correct that error; or, rather, let me more exactly distinguish the truth. Behold them! they are here,—all here! Here,—the past is present! Here,—the distant is at hand! Here,—the lost are found! Here,—the dead are alive!

Lo! the angels are here! When the Lord laid the foundations of the earth, did the morning stars sing together, and all the sons of God shout for joy? Hark! they sing yet! they shout yet! Do you not hear them? They are all here! Did an angel cheer Hagar in the wilderness? Did angels rest in the shade of the tree at the tent-door of Abraham? Did an angel restrain the sacrifice of Isaac in the land of Moriah? Did angels lead Lot out of Sodom? Did Jacob, in holy vision, see their hosts descending and ascending, from heaven to earth, and from earth to heaven? Did he meet them again at Mahanaim? Did they pitch their camp on Sinai as the Israelites pitched theirs in the plains below? Did they appear to

Balaam, to Joshua, to Gideon, to Manoah, to Elijah, to David, to Isaiah, to Ezekiel, to Daniel, to Zechariah? And, passing on to the New Testament, did they appear also to Zacharias, and to Mary, and to Joseph, and to the shepherds? Did they, indeed, when the Lord laid the foundations of the new creation,—the Church of Christ,—sing together again, and shout together again, even more gladly than at first,—glorifying Christ by their testimony, heaven and earth by their splendor, and God by their praise? Did they minister in the desert to their tempted but victorious Lord and Master? Did they bring virtue to the pool of Bethesda? Did they carry the beggar to Abraham's bosom? Did they strengthen Christ in the garden of Gethsemane? and open the door of his rocky chamber on the morning of the Resurrection? and comfort the weeping women, seeking the living among the dead? and instruct the apostles gazing from the hill-side at their ascending Lord? and then accompany Him, with their twenty thousand chariots of fire, in His triumphant transit from the tomb to the throne? Did some of them return, even after this?—to release Peter from prison? to direct Cornelius to the kingdom of God? to encourage Paul amid the dangers of shipwreck? and, lastly, and most

7*

gloriously, to open to John the Apocalypse of ages?—filling the vision with their own missions, proclaiming prophecies, sealing saints, waving censers, blowing trumpets, swearing the speedy close of time, warring with the devil and his angels, bearing the everlasting gospel through the midst of heaven, pouring out earth's last plagues from golden vials, pronouncing the doom of Babylon, binding the Dragon and casting him into the bottomless pit, and so displaying, in the close of all, the new heaven and new earth, the holy city and its happy inhabitants, the infinite grace and glory of the consummation of all things in Christ Jesus our Lord? Behold! they are here! these angels are here!—all here! Various and numerous as they are, not one is absent! Gabriel, in all his wisdom,—Michael, in all his majesty,—these, the very archangels, and all their hosts, cherubim, and seraphim, thrones, and dominions, and principalities, and powers,—all, all are living, shining, and exulting here!

And so the Elect Men, as well as Angels, are all here! The patriarchs, priests, and prophets,—the apostles and evangelists,—the princes of inspiration,—all are here! Abel, Enoch, and Noah are here! Here Abraham still sees the day of Christ, and is glad! Here Jacob still gathers his children

at his bedside, and tells them the things that shall
befall them in the last days! Here Aaron and his
successors still bear upon their breasts the Urim
and Thummim! Here Moses still trembles at the
bush, conquers in Egypt, listens from the cleft in
the rock, and rests in silence in the land of Moab!
Here Samuel still hears the God of grace whisper,
and the God of glory thunder! Here Elijah
still stands on Carmel, calling fire from heaven,
and smiting to the ground, with a single stroke,
the opposing powers of earth and hell! and here,
again, as seen on Horeb, at the searching sound
of the "still small voice" he covers his face with
his mantle, and worships the Lord of all! Here,
also, Isaiah, Jeremiah, Ezekiel, and Daniel, with
the twelve minor prophets, from Hosea to Malachi,
still hold their high positions! Here is the illumi-
nated gallery in which their pictured visions are
suspended and inclined to the gaze of the world!
Here is the embroidered shrine from within
which their unfailing oracles unerringly report
the will of God! Here is the temple-terrace, on
which they are arrayed, side by side, in immortal
beauty and rapture; their eyes still sparkling, and
their lips still glowing, as they hold aloft the
records of their foresight for the study of generations and the interpretation of time! Here,

too, the apostles still repose upon their promised
and peerless thrones! The cool glory encircles
their brows yet,—crowns without pressure of pain,
or fear of forfeiture, or shade of future dimness!
Moreover, and far more than of old, they still speak
with tongues,—many tongues, of lands and tribes
and nations then unknown! Here, too, their
very shadows still sweep, with healing virtue,
over the beds of disease and the wan eyes of
woe! Here, too, their thrilling fingers still multiply, in new forms and for new subjects, the laws
of the Church, the original, unimprovable, and
unalterable instructions and institutions of the
Holy Ghost! Here, too, they still see the Lord,
walking with Him from the beginning of His
ministry to its close; witnessing His ascension,
catching His spirit, and, in His name and power,
revolutionizing the Jewish and Gentile worlds!
Nor only so: but the evangelists, also, still supply their humbler yet highly important fellowship.
Luke is still with Paul; and the record still be-
seeches Timothy to bring Mark with him, who,
notwithstanding one old disagreement, is thus
afterward acknowledged to be profitable to the
apostle for the ministry. In like manner, Philip
still interprets the prophecies; Barnabas still dif-
fuses consolation; Timothy still illustrates the

advantages of early scriptural training; and Titus still sets the Church in order, furnishing it with elders, in every city, according to his appointment! Here, also, Stephen, the protomartyr, still bears his testimony to the Messiah, bows his shining face before the shower of stones, and springs, with loving and exulting spirit, to the outstretched arms of Jesus, at the right hand of God!

Nay,—more, far more,—Jesus himself is here,— the one Mediator between God and men! Here is the Paradise in which His voice still resounds in the cool of the day! Here are the holy walks where He converses with Enoch! Here is the ark, the door of which He shuts with His own hand, as soon as Noah has entered! Here is the summit, overlooking Sodom, to which He is conducted by Abraham, and where He still relents to the patriarch's pleadings! Here is the spot, on the border of the brook, where He still wrestles with Jacob and enriches him with His blessing! Here is the burning bush, whence He still calls to Moses! here the peak of Sinai, where He still proclaims the law! and here the Holy of Holies, where He still inspires the Shekinah! Here, also, are all the localities of Egypt, Palestine, and Assyria, where His prophetic spirit still prompts the chal-

lenge of His dauntless heralds,—" Thus saith the
Lord!" And see! Here He is, as the babe of
Bethlehem; here He is, as the fugitive child
of the Nile; here He is, as the secluded boy
of Nazareth; here He is, as the young Galilean,
baptized of John in the Jordan; and here He is,
as the Incorruptible One, still showing, by His
defeat of the tempter in the desert of Judea, the
rescue of the honor of our race, so shamefully
betrayed in the Garden of Eden! Here the whole
ministry of the Mediator is forever renewed!
Here He is, with all His doctrines, and precepts,
and parables, and prophecies, and promises, and
warnings, and personal exemplifications of the
true, and right, and good, and social institutions
and ordinances! Here He is, with all His miracles
of mercy, and wisdom, and majesty, and power,—
wrought on persons and things and elements,
without life and with life, and all through life,
and even after death,—the countless preliminary
symbols of ultimate complete salvation! Here He
is, moreover, with all His sufferings :—sufferings
occasioned by the lowliness of His lot, by the
dulness of His disciples, by the malice of His
enemies, by the subtle wrath of fiends, His rejection by the Jews, His abandonment by the
Gentiles, His temporary estrangement from the

Father, and the incalculable pressure of the burden of the sins of the whole world, from the beginning to the end of the world, on His own and only shoulders; crushing Him down, in all His sinless beauty and love, into a cold and bloody grave! And yet here He is, also, with all His triumphs!—reappearing without a broken bone; whole, sound, immortal; qualified alike for earth and heaven; wearing His wounds as seals of success, as stars of honor, as claims of reward and power; and, thus recovered, rising to the sky, returning to the bosom of the Father, reigning and rejoicing in the height of heaven, waiting for the appointed time of His second advent, and anticipating the happy moment when death, the last enemy, shall be utterly and eternally destroyed!

Nay, more,—still more,—here is the Spirit, as well as the Son; and here is the Father, as well as the Spirit! The same Spirit that originally "moved upon the face of the waters;" the Spirit that garnishes the heavens and renews the face of the earth; the Spirit that swept over Jerusalem, on the day of Pentecost, in whirlwind and fire, and concentrated its moral energies in the souls of the apostles, and diffused them again among the thousands of the people, demonstrating the Messiahship of Jesus, and installing His ever-

lasting kingdom on earth,—lo! that Spirit is
here,—moving on the waters yet, garnishing the
heavens yet, renewing the earth yet, establishing
and extending the kingdom of Christ in the souls
of men yet! And the Father,—the long-unre-
vealed Father,—the eternally self-secluded and infinitely incomprehensible Father,—lying, so to
speak, back of all, and yet who is at once above
all, through all, and in all, from whose eternal
glory the Son came when He entered the world,
and to whose eternal glory He returned when He
left the world, and in whose eternal glory He has
dwelt ever since He left the world, and now
dwells, and will forever dwell, and we, even we,
as we trust, with Him,—He also, the Father of
all, is here! Here, at last, is the effulgent un-
veiling of the exalted, incomparable, indisputable,
and inaccessible throne of His almightiness! Here
is the ineffable and pre-eminent sovereignty of His
gentle and holy and unchangeable love! In a
word, not only Elect Men and Angels, but Father,
Son, and Holy Ghost, are all here; here in a sense
of intelligible and Divine reality, sympathy, and
power, in comparison with which all other material symbols of the Deity, in all the universe, are
miserably and inexpressibly meagre and poor.

Nay, more,—much more, for all this is saying

less than half of what ought to be said,—not only is the Bible thus comprehensive of all the sensible, infallible, and Divine authorities ever known in the history of the world, but these authorities have to us no assured existence or specific character except as asserted and received through the Bible. In other terms, it has pleased God so wonderfully to magnify His word above all His name, that nothing satisfactory in relation to these authorities can be derived from any other source.

I confess for myself, at once, and with all frankness, that the question is, the Bible—or atheism, anti-theism, or Pantheism; any thing rather than deism. Take away the Bible, and you take away all the angels. Not a single cherub or seraph, not a single throne, or dominion, or principality, or power, not a single morning star, or son of God, is left. Gabriel vanishes as a phantom, and Michael melts into air and is seen no more. Take away the Bible, and you take away the elect succession of inspired men. Not a single patriarch, or priest, or prophet, or apostle, or evangelist remains, to proclaim or record a single superhuman oracle. Moses and his law, Isaiah and his visions, dissolve together. Matthew and his Gospel, Paul and his epistles, perish in the same fire. Nay, more: take away the Bible, and you take away the Lord Jesus Christ. No longer need any disputes be held in regard to the nature, person, or office of Christ, His history, condition, or destiny! All the magnificent apparatus in preparation for His coming smokes and is gone! The manger in the stable, and the star in the sky, alike disappear! The cross crumbles, the sepulchre sinks, and the throne, well symbolized by the rainbow that adorns it, like the rainbow vanishes away! His pre-existence, His current existence, His whole existence, is nothing. And so of the Holy Spirit: take away the Bible, and the Spirit becomes a ghost, indeed; or, rather, less than a ghost. Like a meteor, it flashes from darkness and falls into the blackness of darkness. And so of the Father: take away the Bible, and the Father retires into an impenetrable seclusion, infinitely more oblivious than was ever imagined before. And then, when the earth is exhausted of every thing inspired, and heaven of every thing angelic, and the universe of every thing Divine, what is left? Ay, take away the Bible, and what is left? What! Is man left? And earth, and heaven, and the universe,— are they all left? Aha! be it so. But what kind of a man is left? A man without a Maker, without a Savior, and without a soul! a man without an origin, without a purpose, and without an end! The noblest of beings, and yet the meanest and most miserable,—all sensibility, sympathy, and affection, yet sitting desolate and in sackcloth, among the graves of dead friends, full himself of living memories, ever moaning for the dead, but without hope of their return, having no hope, but that he and his children may likewise die and be no more! And what kind of an earth is left? and what kind of a heaven? and what kind of a universe? Who cares what kind! If man be a worm, if angels be the spectres of worms, if Father, Son, and Holy Ghost be mere names without substance,—who cares what kind! Let the mountains still lift their sublime and glittering peaks into the eternal solitudes of azure, silence, and frost; let the hills smooth down their tufted and flowery slopes, enclosing with many a graceful curve the still softer beauty of the green and golden vales, gurgling with shadowy fountains and sparkling with rippling streams; let the plains expand from innumerable opening ravines into broad plateaus and wide-rolling prairies, declining from all sides to the level of mighty lakes and the channels of far-flowing rivers, covering the common vastness of the warm and teeming continents with the ripe and varied richness of an

endless succession of shining and showery sea.
sons; and let the seas and oceans, more free and
ample and united than the lands they wash, still
outline the continents and ring the islands with
their foam, and freshen the world with their airs,
and mirror at once in the boundless grandeur of
their brilliant repose the whole sphere of heaven,
both day and night, sun, moon, and stars, and
the crisp and scintillant suffusion of either pole,—
ay, let the magnificent and gorgeous globe, with
all its boasted accommodations and embellish-
ments, still sweep along its ethereal path, collect-
ing and reflecting through ceaseless ages the lights
of all the orbs in space:—what is it, after all, but
a sepulchre!—not a sealed sepulchre, for there is
neither enemy to make nor friend to break a seal;
but an open, dismal, hopeless sepulchre,—ever
filling, but never to be filled, whirling through
immensity with unaccountable regularity and con-
tinuance, rattling forever with the bones of the
dead, and forever whistling with the sighs and
roaring with the curses of the living!

And heaven too,—whether near or remote,—
let it still redden the stripes of mist along its
morning horizon, and mottle its noon with cloud-
lets bright as shields of crystal and fair as shells
of pearl, and array its cliffs of snow in the yellow

haze of sunset, kindling their turreted terraces with unconsuming fire: or, expanding without a shade to its clearest and utmost scope of perfect blue, let the loftiest sun shed down the purest day, or the lowlier moon arise to illumine the cone of night, and the outer stars gleam in to show the spheres beyond, and all its inaccessible enchantments continue eternally to multiply their splendid and picturesque changes:—what is it, after all, but a cold and careless void,—a void as deceitful as it is inviting,—ever promising spirituality, immortality, and bliss, but which, in truth, is uninhabited and uninhabitable; blind,—even to its own glory,—deaf, dumb, and dead; without a refuge and without a friend!

And the universe in whole,—however immense and illustrious,—let it still stretch away on every side through all its gradations of visible stars, and through all its telescopic ranges of almost indiscernible and utterly immeasurable nebulæ, and through all the more extended amplitudes of imagination, even to the last possibilities of space: with all its separate and yet sympathetic systems perpetuating forever their radiant and reflected admixture of variegated splendors, and multiplying forever their common interchanges of subtler but all-controlling elements and powers:—what

8*

is it, after all, but a larger void and a more exhaustive contemplation, an infinite mystery of substance and shadow, of solitude and silence, of beauty without design, of order without law, of harmony without enjoyment, and of innumerable apparent effects, seeming to imply the perfections and action of a God, but, nevertheless, really existing without the slightest ascertainable cause!

Oh, no, no, no: if the Bible and all it reveals be taken away, if man be thus reduced to worse than disinheritance and orphanage, it matters not what kind of an earth or heaven or universe is left to suspend its illusions along the line of his momentary transit. Oh, my soul! or, if indeed I have no soul, still, Ah me! whatever I am: a conscious mystery in the midst of countless conscious and unconscious mysteries:—what an agony of wonder seizes, isolates, agitates, and confounds my poor dissolving being!

But bring back the Bible. Hear its first verse:— "In the beginning God created the heaven and the earth." And hear its last verse:—"The grace of our Lord Jesus Christ be with you all. Amen." See! there is the substance of it all,—God, Christ, and man, the beginning and the end, creation and redemption, heaven and earth, grace and glory.

So be it! The two verses sound like the fiat and the fact,—"Light be, and light was!"

And lo! the whole sphere of truth opens and shines! It is vaster than the earth, vaster than heaven, vaster than the universe,—immense as immensity itself, and eternal as eternity itself. The Bible is the greater sun that glorifies it all; and standing here, like an angel in the sun, I rejoice to survey it all.

See! the earth, as it rolls in this subtler and purer light, instead of resembling a dreary and wailing sepulchre, exults around all its golden circle as the chosen though chastened province of productive and distributive immortality,—letting loose, in every moment of its motion and at every point along its orbit, the redeemed and sanctified spirits whose centrally-collected and innumerable millions shall gird the throne of Omnipotence with beauty and glory, with worship and service, with music and rapture, forever and ever.

And heaven too, as here it expands, instead of gleaming upon us as a deceptive, uninhabited, and uninhabitable void,—although it exalts its zenith and enlarges its horizon until it covers a system rather than a planet,—ay, swells into the sublimity of an infinite distance above and beyond the whole universe, as easily as it shuts itself down in many-colored airs to enclose the poles of every little star,—still, this grand heaven of heavens—one heaven full of innumerable heavens—supplies its utmost scope with saints and angels, and opens to every world a gate of entrance, a host of welcoming friends, a paradise of boundless and fadeless attractions, and mansions of perfect and perpetual repose.

And now, ineffably and inconceivably greater than all,—greater than the changed earth and universe and heaven,—God Himself returns. The whole sphere of truth is the sphere of the Divine existence and government. The Father comes forth from His eternal seclusion,—not indeed to become personally visible, but to utter His voice from the sky, saying, "This is my beloved Son, in whom I am well pleased." And lo! the Son himself appears,—not indeed in the glory which He had with the Father "before the world was,"—but humbling His sinless form to the waters of baptism, and consecrating His life to the salvation of the world. And lo! the Holy Spirit also draws near, descending as if from the bosom of the Father, to adorn the brow and hallow the soul of the Son with its hovering, dove-like beauty, and its gentle, dove-like grace. And lo! with these, all truth returns. All the doctrines, all

the laws, and all the ordinances of our holy religion come back to us as familiar and trustworthy
realities. All the histories, psalms, proverbs, and
prophecies,—all the gospels, acts, epistles, and
apocalyptic symbols,—come back to us as divine
and immutable verities. Every one of us may
say, All is light. Sin is indeed sin. Redemption
is indeed redemption. By the grace of God, I
am saved. The Son is my Savior. The Spirit is
my Sanctifier. The Father is my Father. Saints
and angels are my brethren. Heaven is my home,
the universe is my range, and eternity is my lifetime.

Oh, spectacle of unparalleled sublimity!—of inexhaustible wonder! All this is committed to a
book! Not to the Church; for where is the
Church, apart from the Bible, that can show us a
single inspired man, or ministering angel, or give
us even a glimpse of the Son of God? Not to
the State; for where is the State that furnishes
such revelations as these? Not to Providence;
for where is the token of any of them all, on
land or sea, by day or night, in all the compass
of the rolling seasons? Not to Creation; for
where is the distant moon, or sun, or star, or where
the pale, evangelical comet to make its apparition
from the mysteries of space, with sign or sound

of such tidings as these? No, no: not even to the persons of the first messengers are they any longer confided. Just as God distrusts the Church and distrusts the State,—for their history, as well as his foresight, makes it needful and wise for Him so to do,—and just as He teaches providence and creation to keep their fingers on their lips and walk their solemn rounds in perfect silence, so, for reasons worthy of all concerned, He bids the saints and angels stand aloof, detains His redeeming Son close by His side, declines any visible manifestation even of His omnipresent Spirit, and, so to speak, as if to put eternal glory and majesty on the truth,—as if to show that by the seemingly feeblest instrument He can readily achieve the mightiest purposes, and as if at once to humble and elevate mankind,—He drops from heaven to earth a little book, to teach, reprove, and correct, to subdue and govern the rebellious and haughty world! And here it is!—the Bible,—the Bible, as I love to repeat it, the only sensible, infallible, and Divine authority on earth. So God has magnified His word above all His name!

SERMON V.

THE BIBLE ABROAD IN ALL THE WORLD.

"Thou hast magnified thy word above all thy name."
Ps. cxxxviii. 2.

IN the close of the last discourse, the Almighty
was represented as withholding His infallible
authority from Creation and Providence, from the
State and the Church; as bidding His saints and
angels stand aloof, detaining His Son by His side,
declining any visible manifestation of His Spirit,
and then, as dropping from heaven to earth a
little book, to teach, reprove, and correct,—to
subdue and govern the rebellious and haughty
world.

The question now arises,—Will the Bible succeed? or, what shall prove its destiny?

Brethren of the Church!—we, at least, have no
doubt of its success; no doubt of the ultimate
and eternal triumph of the truth. We accept its

assurance as our own assurance. We remember the language of our Savior in relation to the law:—"Verily I say unto you, Till heaven and earth pass, one jot or one tittle shall in no wise pass from the law, till all be fulfilled." Even the Jews should rejoice in this: for their interest in it is equal to ours. Heaven may pass away, earth may pass away,—all of heaven, all of earth, massive and glorious as they are, may pass away; but "one jot," (or *yod*,) the smallest of the Hebrew letters, or "one tittle," (or *point*,) above, below, within, or at the corner of a letter,—that is, the most infinitesimal particle of the law,—shall in no wise pass away, till all be fulfilled. In no wise shall this happen. No forgetfulness or carelessness on the part of God shall allow it; no vigilance or craft on the part of Satan shall enable him to occasion it; no art, or skill, or cunning, or might, or majesty, of any man or set of men, shall ever procure such a result. This is settled,—settled in heaven, and settled forever. So declares the Psalmist:—"Forever, O Lord, thy world is settled in heaven." The Lord, Himself, has so settled it. Even if it were practicable to burn it out on earth it would blaze abroad again in all the skies,—every jot and tittle, or every yod and point, still shining serene and uninjured in its proper place. And,

as with the law, so it is with the gospel. Here
we recall the language of Peter, quoting and applying the prophecy of Isaiah:—"For all flesh is
as grass, and all the glory of man as the flower
of grass. The grass withereth, and the flower
thereof falleth away; but the word of the Lord
endureth forever. And THIS is the word"—adds
the apostle—"which by the GOSPEL is preached
unto you." This is the verdure that never
withers. This is the bloom that never fades.
This is the life that never dies. This is the
glory that never declines. "The word of the
Lord endureth forever."

Nevertheless, let us candidly consider the matter. Here, then, is the Book. According to the
distinctive designation of it all through this discussion, it is a *sensible* authority,—the *only* Divine
and infallible authority in the world which *is* in a
sensible form. We see it, read it, hear it read,
handle it, measure it, weigh it; treat it religiously
or curiously, critically or commercially, usefully
or hurtfully; in a word, do what we please with it,
as with any other book.

It comes to us alone, relying on its intrinsic
merits, and so submits itself to our discretion.
Its authors have no more to do with it. The first
of them died some thirty-three hundred years

9

ago, and the last of them about seventeen hundred and fifty years ago. The persons it names, and the generations to which they belonged, have passed from the earth like morning shadows. Many, if not most, of its tribes and nations have ceased to exist. The cities they built, the kingdoms they established, the empires they collected and confirmed, are now no more. Some of their ruins still linger in the midst of silent deserts; but the Bible itself is the best monument of them all. In like manner, the angels, which it mentions so often, have no further visible connection with it. Death, indeed, has never touched their shining plumes; but restraint secludes them. And so the Savior, whom it is the chief object of the Book to reveal to the world as the true "Desire of all Nations," affords it no longer any visible support. Ever since its completion, He has been hidden in the heavens, like a lost star. And so the Holy Spirit has ceased to flash and flame upon our vision in attestation of the truth. And so the Eternal Father remains silent,—letting all the ages pass without a word in its behalf. In short, this asserted Supreme Authority, though itself in sensible form, has no sensible miraculous accompaniment, no supernatural magnificence or splendor, no superhuman sanction or attraction of any kind, apart from its internal character, to sustain its pretensions or give it a claim to any extraordinary respect. Here it is, in all this apparent loneliness, in the hands of men, of individuals and societies, of friends and foes,—more foes, so far, than friends,—quietly and constantly maintaining its mighty and momentous struggle.

The first remark I have to make, and a sufficient one for the present discourse, is this:—*The Bible is now abroad in all the world*,—so fairly and fully exposed that it can never again be concealed. There have been times, both before and since its completion, when, in part or in whole, it was withdrawn from society, and almost forgotten. Prior to the restoration of the law by Ezra it appears that the most of the books of the Old Testament had well nigh perished. Under Antiochus Epiphanes, all of them were ordered to be destroyed, and such persons as secreted any of them were doomed to death. Under Dioclesian, an edict was issued, requiring the whole Bible to be burnt, throughout the whole Roman Empire,—on which occasion myriads of Christians preferred death with the Book to life without it. Finally, the Church itself—that is, the Apostate Church—after long-continued neglect or abuse of the Scriptures, and consequent increasing corruption, formally forbade their use to the laity, and still more strictly prohibited the translation of them into the vulgar tongue. What was forbidden to the laity soon became useless to the clergy; and so, before the age of Luther, the Bible had nearly vanished from all observation.

But those times have passed,—never, we trust, to be renewed. The Book is abroad in all the world. Protestant Christendom is filled with it, from centre to circumference. Around all the borders of Romanism its voice is heard, like the trumpet of the resurrection. The outposts of Mohammedanism and Paganism are all startled by the same awakening music. And, "whether they will hear or whether they will forbear," it is plain that, ere long, all mankind must acknowledge its presence and its power.

See! the sensible form in which it appears includes a vast variety of modifications. As a Book, it exists, of course, either in manuscript or in print, and its records are either originals or versions.

It is a remarkable fact, that not a single autograph of the Holy Scriptures is known to be in existence. On the other hand, it is at least possible that not a single autograph has been destroyed.

And it is a pleasant thought, that He who lived from the beginning, and yet once "was dead,"—whose body lay in the grave, and whose soul entered the place of spirits,—who is now "alive for evermore," and has "the keys of hell and of death," of *hades* and of the grave,—who carries these keys at His girdle, and hands them at His will to Latrobe, or Layard, or any of His servants, to open the galleries where He has treasured the historic memorials of His reign and confirmations of His word,—may sometime direct the unlocking of a chamber within which shall be found the *real* originals of the Bible in unimpaired preservation.

Meantime, the study of extant manuscripts, especially of the accepted originals, both Hebrew and Greek, must be exceedingly interesting to those who are thoroughly qualified to pursue it. Even their external history is full of interest: their number and age, the materials on which and with which they were prepared, the extraordinary care which was taken to make them accurate and, in many instances, most richly beautiful, the veneration with which they were preserved, the costly collections and laborious collations of them, their comparative critical reputation and influence, their present local distribution and accessibleness,—these, and other points, might well claim, and would amply reward, attention. It is enough, however, for the occasion, to compile the following particulars.*

The Hebrew manuscripts are of two classes, *sacred* and *common*,—or, synagogue-rolls and private copies. "The synagogue-rolls are uniform, hardly differing one from another,—written on the skins of clean animals, prepared for the particular use of the synagogue by a Jew." The private copies "are in different forms,—folio, quarto, octavo, duodecimo,—and their material is mostly parchment, sometimes Eastern paper, and even common paper." Both kinds, of course, were wrought with extraordinary care; but of the former it may be said that it is almost impossible to exaggerate the pains that were taken to secure their accuracy and sanctity. As would be expected, the more ancient they are the more rare they are. Dr. Kennicott is said to have collated six hundred and thirty, and De Rossi more than four hundred,—the two "upwards of eleven hundred." Of Dr. Kennicott's, fifty-one were sup-

---

* See Dr. Davidson's volume, in the *new* edition of "Horne's Introduction," (1856.) The chapter on "*Hebrew Manuscripts*" may be regarded as an *improvement* of the same writer's article in "Kitto's Cyclopedia."

posed to be from six to eight hundred years old, and a hundred and seventy-four from four hundred and eighty to five hundred and eighty years old. Of De Rossi's, some were said to be of the seventh or eighth century, which would make them now eleven or twelve hundred years old. A more reliable current authority, however, not long since declared that, so far "as certainty is concerned," the "oldest Hebrew MS. at present known belongs to A.D. 1106,"—making it now seven hundred and fifty-one years old. And yet the same authority still more recently alludes to another collation, "by Pinner, at Odessa," resulting in the discovery of *one* MS. of the sixth century, (580,) two of the ninth, and two of the tenth, —the oldest, if correctly represented, being twelve hundred and seventy-seven years old. From these dates they multiply to their whole present number,—those which have been produced since the fifteenth century being reported as "very numerous."

The Greek manuscripts, the accepted originals of the New Testament, are older than the Hebrew. Their materials are vellum or paper. In the oldest of them there are none of our common divisions, but words and sentences flow on in unbroken lines of capital letters. In a brief list

which I have examined, one is attributed to the
fourth century, two are ascribed to the fifth, five
to the sixth, six to the seventh, three to the
eighth, and eight to the ninth,—the earliest of
them, therefore, being some fifteen hundred years
old, and the latest about a thousand.

Similar brief notice might be taken of the
ancient *versions*,—whether Greek, Oriental, Latin,
Gothic, Slavonic, or Anglo-Saxon. The principal of them number more than twenty; and, of
course, the design of making them was to present
the Divine Record in the living languages of the
people for common use. They were all vulgates.

It is enough, however, for my purpose to add
the remark, that the world has been searched—
and is still being searched—by Jews, Romanists,
and Protestants, and that, as the result of the
search so far, copies of the most important of all
classes of sacred manuscripts, both originals and
versions, have been largely collected and diligently collated, and are now known, located,
numbered, described, and, in common with multitudes of inferior value distributed in public and
private libraries and among the synagogues and
monasteries of all lands, are generally free to scholastic investigation.

It is in relation to *modern* versions, however, that the fact I wish to illustrate becomes most impressive, and especially as connected with the operations of the art of printing.

The first printed book was the Latin Bible,— the Mazarin Bible, as it is called, from the discovery of a copy of it, in the last century, in the library of the cardinal of that name. The date assigned to it is 1455. "We may see in imagination," says Mr. Hallam, "this venerable and splendid volume leading up the crowded myriads of its followers, and imploring, as it were, a blessing on the new art, by dedicating its first fruits to the service of Heaven." Since then four hundred years have gone by, and, to a considerable extent, they have all been employed in printing Bibles. Within the last half-century, however, an altogether incomparable work has been accomplished, in this connection, by means of Bible Societies. Since 1804, more than fifty-four millions of Bibles and Testaments have been thus distributed. The list of "languages into which translations of the Scriptures have either been made or attempted" included, six years ago, some two hundred and seventy. Doubtless the number has since increased. The versions, of course, are much more numerous, as in many instances a single language, like our own, has quite a large variety of them. In "The Bible of Every Land" may be found about two hundred and seventy "typographical specimens" of different translations. Of these, nearly two hundred have been published by the Bible Societies, and more than a hundred and twenty of this number were "never before printed." According to official statements, they have been circulated wherever practicable, in adaptation to national and provincial peculiarities, in every district of Western, Northern, Central, and Southern Europe; in Russia; in the Caucasian and other border-countries; in Persia; in India,—Northern, Central, and Southern; in Ceylon; in the Indo-Chinese countries; in the Chinese Empire; in Hither Polynesia, Further Polynesia, Africa, and America.

Meantime, as one effect of this universal charity, the Bible trade, as it may be distinctively called, instead of being checked, has been wonderfully quickened, strengthened, and enlarged. Notwithstanding the copies given away, and the readiness with which they may be almost anywhere obtained, no book in the world sells like the Bible. Within the period already alluded to, therefore, thousands of private publishers—some with state patronage, others with church patronage, but most of them without either, and all far more at liberty than the Bible Societies—have issued, it is reported, upwards of fifty millions more, *seemingly* in every possible diversity of style, and accommodated to every age and condition of life, every desire of taste, and every degree of ability to buy.* In *reality*, however, it is believed that the diversity has just begun, and that hereafter it will be greatly extended and incomparably improved.

And now, tell me,—Is not the Bible fairly and fully abroad, and beyond all possibility of reconcealment? Who can follow its flight? Every effort to do so is discouraging. Whatever centre I occupy, I see the Bible passing away—in a thousand forms, by a thousand lines—to the utmost circumference. If I follow it in one line the others are left unexplored. A sort of bird's-eye view—or rather angel's view—is all that is allowed me. To gain this, for a moment, I soar into the sky and poise myself there.

And what now? I ask for the nations and tribes who read the languages and dialects in

---

* A single Philadelphia house, as stated to the writer by one of its members, has issued for the last fifteen years, year by year, a larger number of Bibles than the American Bible Society!

which the Bible has been so far printed. I wish to see them in all their localities and other associations.

"Fold your pinions," says the angel in the sun, "and stand by my side. Instead of descending in a moment, you must wait twenty-four hours, and watch the revolution of the whole globe; for there is not a spot on its surface where some one of these languages does not reach."

And so I wait and watch, and find it is even so. I see these readers,—self-taught, mission-taught, home-taught, or school-taught,—in all natural conditions, from the equator to the poles, —enduring every climate, traversing every sea, covering every continent, and filling every island, —scaling the mountains, cultivating the plains, girding and crossing the deserts. I see them in all civil conditions,—savage, barbarian, semi-civilized, and wholly civilized: among the latter, monarchists, aristocrats, and republicans, absolutists, constitutionalists, and revolutionists. I see them in all religious conditions,—Fetichists, Foheists, Boodhists, Brahminists, Parseeists, Mohammedans, Jews, and Christians: among the latter, Romanists and Jansenists, Orthodox Greeks and Heterodox Greeks, Established Protestants and Dissenting Protestants. I see them, moreover, in all social conditions,—sovereigns, nobles, and magistrates; priests and pastors; scholars and philosophers; professors of literature, science, and art; merchants and manufacturers; mechanics and operatives; farmers and planters; herdsmen and shepherds; hunters and fishermen; soldiers and sailors; paupers and slaves; dwelling in caves and thickets, in tents and huts, in cabins and mansions, in castles and palaces, in colleges and convents, in hamlets, towns, cities, and mighty capitals,—or, again, off-shore, in canoes, in ships, on vast rafts, or in fixed fleets,—great water-capitals rivalling those on land; and, moreover, with all varieties of dress and address, ceremonies, manners, customs and usages, at births, weddings, and funerals, in private and in public, in all the stages and relations of life,— in connections quite innumerable and indescribable.

Wherever I look, I see the same visitant,—the Bible. Everywhere it bears the same message,— the same to old nations and new, to the people of yesterday and the people with a history of two or three thousand years. Moreover, in substance it is a message equally needed by all and equally adapted to all.

I ask for the motives and objects of the various

parties employed in this cause of Bible-distribution at home and abroad. Why is there so
much zeal in regard to this one book? It is not
so with the sacred books of other religions. Even
the kings and priests having them in charge do
nothing to promote their circulation. Rather,
they are careful to keep them secluded. How is
this? Why does not some one of the many Mohammedan nations form Koran Societies, to fill
the world with Korans? Why are there no Zend-
Avesta Societies among the Parsees? Why no
Veda Societies among the Hindoos? Why no
King's Societies among the Chinese? Why no
Edda Societies among antiquarian Scandinavians?
Is it not strange that there are no such Societies?
And yet stranger facts are found nearer home.
Why have the Jews no Bible Societies? Why
the Roman Catholics none? Why the Greek Catholics none? Why the Oriental Churches none?
Nay, why are Unevangelical Protestants without
them? Nay, still further, why are some of our
Evangelical churches beginning to draw off and
stand aloof from the Bible Societies? As to
Pagans, they make no pretension to the means of
a common salvation. As to Mohammedans, if
they ever had such pretensions, they have lost
confidence in them. Besides, their trust was

always in the sword rather than the book. As to the Jews, they know that the Old Testament alone is an imperfect revelation, and are waiting themselves for the consummating development. As to the Catholics, they all substitute the Church for the Bible. As to Unevangelical Protestants, they are chilled by doubt and checked by error, and can make no progress in good. And as to the withdrawing Evangelicals, they are becoming less Christian and more sectarian every day. Only the Bible Societies, and their supporters of all parties, seem to be influenced by the highest motives and devoted to the noblest objects. In contrast to Pagans, they do claim the means of a common salvation. In contrast to Mohammedans, their confidence increases rather than declines. In contrast to Jews, they possess the perfected revelation. In contrast to Catholics, they acknowledge the Bible as infallible instead of the Church. In contrast to the Unevangelicals, they are all aglow with faith and impelled by truth. And in contrast to their offended brethren among the Evangelicals, they daily become less and less sectarian and more and more Christian. In a word, with certain exceptions which it may be hoped will disappear, their motives and objects are worthy of all commendation,—immediately and exclusively connected with the one all-sufficient and incomparable work of glorifying God in the salvation of mankind. It is the just appreciation of their work in these two relations that sustains their zeal. Private publishers, in most instances, find their reward in pecuniary profits. Sectarian publishers blend personal and partisan interests in deceitful semblance of Christian sublimity. But the true sublime is with those who have nothing to do but to fill the world with the highest truth for the glory of God and the entire and eternal redemption of man. They "rejoice with joy unspeakable" that the Bible is at last abroad in all the world, and that it can never again be concealed. They are not like those who fear for its fate. "Do not send it forth without Tradition," say some. "Do not let it loose without the Apocrypha," say others. "Do not trust it without the Prayer-Book," say others. "Do not expose it without the Creed, or Confession, or Constitution, or Platform, or Discipline," say others. "We have no fear," reply the faithful ones. "We would as soon charge God with folly for issuing the sun without the pendant of a lamp to illustrate it, as for issuing the Bible without the attachment of some human authority to make it plain. No, no; let it go, even as the sun itself goes, asking no patronage of men or angels, but demonstrating its Divinity by the silent, serene, and blissful vitality of its supreme, universal, and perpetual glory."

10*

SERMON VI.

THE BIBLE RIGHTLY ABROAD IN ALL THE WORLD.

" Thou hast magnified thy word above all thy name."
Ps. cxxxviii. 2.

THE chief difficulty in the treatment of our sub-ject—especially as it opened before us in the last discourse, and now continues open—arises from the vastness and variety of the intelligence connected with it. The Bible, as in part the oldest book in the world, as a book, the successive portions of which occupied, in their composition, more than fifteen hundred years, and as one that has become in whole the most sacred inheritance of mankind, has identi-fied itself, to a wonderful extent, with all anthropo-logy, geology, and astronomy; with all chronology, history, and geography; with all government, laws, and social institutions; and with all religion, philo sophy, literature, science, and art—in a word, with

all the interests of our race. To illustrate this universal identification, by a statement of all the facts
in the case, is manifestly impracticable, within the
necessary limits of such discussions as these; and,
whatever is said, in a summary way, the remembrance of what remains unsaid leaves the statement,
at least in the consciousness of him who makes it,
painfully meagre and poor.

Still—abandoning all thought of developing the
theme according to its full capacity of expansion—I
return to it, on this occasion, in hope of exhibiting
some of the select points which are most important
to the purpose in hand, in a form which, however
condensed, may, nevertheless, prove somewhat interesting and useful, and so afford a becoming con-
tinuance, though not a conclusion of the whole discussion.

On the preceding occasion a single point was noticed, viz: That the Bible is abroad in all the World:
so fairly and fully exposed that it can never again
be concealed. It is now designed to notice two of
certain remaining points.

The first of these is—THAT THE BIBLE WAS IN-
TENDED TO BE THUS MADE KNOWN TO THE WORLD.

This is proved by its Character. There is nothing
in it that needs or asks concealment. There is no

priest-craft in it. There is no king-craft in it. There is no special class-craft of any kind in it. On the contrary, it manifestly seeks the benefit of all classes. If it show any partiality it is not for rulers either in State or Church, but for the great masses of mankind, and especially for the most poor and afflicted. It is adapted to all. Examine it; analyze it; the Old Testament, the New Testament; the covenants recorded in both; in particular the two great covenants, the Law and the Gospel; the Histories, Psalms, Proverbs, Prophecies, Biographies, Acts, Epistles, and Symbolic Visions, connected with them, and you cannot fail to perceive that the Bible is preeminently the People's Book, the Book, not of any one nation alone, but of all nations.

This intention is proved also by its Origin. It originated not esoterically or secretly, but exoterically or openly. Not a single one of its sixty-six books was written in a dead or sacred character unknown to the people. They were all written in the living and common tongues of the times and places in which they appeared. Moreover, the substance of the most of them was orally proclaimed, in some instances in the presence of the assembled nation, before it was committed to writing at all. Still further, the authors of them, with few exceptions, were neither kings or priests, courtiers or ecclesiastics, but men of the people, shepherds, herdsmen, publicans, fishermen, and others of similar classes.

The public intention is proved, also, by its own Declarations. These are exceedingly interesting, and I must dwell upon them, therefore, more at large, as connected with the Law, Psalms, and Prophets, and the Books of the New Testament.

Look, for instance, at the Law—the five books of Moses. In the 6th ch. of Deuteronomy it is written: "And these words which I command thee this day shall be in thine heart: And thou shalt teach them diligently to thy children, and shalt talk of them when thou sittest in thine house, and when thou walkest by the way, and when thou liest down, and when thou risest up. And thou shalt bind them for a sign upon thine hand, and they shall be as frontlets between thine eyes. And thou shalt write them upon the posts of thine house, and on thy gates." Such was the provision made for personal and family acquaintance with the Law. It was to be the light of every home in the land.

In the 8th ch. the Israelites were taught that all the severe discipline they had undergone in the desert, for forty years, was designed to teach them this great truth—"that man doth not live by bread

only, but by every word that proceedeth out of the
mouth of the Lord, doth man live." That is—their
Law, their Religion, their communion with God by
means of His word, was to be regarded as the true
source and support of their personal and national
life—their common daily food from generation to
generation.

·In the 11th ch., the king, by anticipation, is required to " write him a copy of this law in a book,
out of that which is before the priests, the Levites :
And," it is added, "it shall be with him, and he shall
read therein all the days of his life," &c. So that
every palace was to be illumined, and every throne
was to be established by the Law.

In the 27th ch., is the record of an arrangement,
which was also made by anticipation, for the ratification of the Law, after the entrance into the Promised Land, at Mounts Gerizim and Ebal, by the
whole assembled nation, men, women, and children,
and the strangers associating with them. In the 8th
ch. of Joshua, we learn that this ratification took
place according to the arrangement ; and certainly
it must have been one of the most grand and solemn
scenes ever witnessed. It is expressly stated, that
Joshua "read all the words of the law, the blessings
and cursings, according to all that is written in the

book of the law. There was not a word of all that Moses commanded which Joshua read not before all the congregation of Israel, with the women, and the little ones, and the strangers that were conversant among them."

In the 30th ch. of Deuteronomy, again, there is a passage, in which Moses seems to exult in the constant and universal nearness and accessibleness of the law. "For, this commandment," he proceeds, "which I command thee this day, it is not hidden from thee, neither is it far off. It is not in heaven that thou shouldest say, Who shall go up for us to heaven, and bring it unto us, that we may hear it, and do it? Neither is it beyond the sea, that thou shouldest say, Who shall go over the sea for us, and bring it unto us, that we may hear it, and do it? But the word is very nigh unto thee, in thy mouth, and in thy heart, that thou mayest do it." What a beautiful statement this is!

In the 31st ch., provision is made for the public reading of the law every seven years; in a manner corresponding with the rehearsal of it by Joshua, as already noticed. Moses commanded the Priests and Elders, saying: "At the end of every seven years, in the solemnity of the year of release, in the feast of tabernacles, when all Israel is come to appear before the Lord thy God in the place which he shall choose, thou shalt read this law, before all Israel, in their hearing. Gather the people together, men and women, and children, and the stranger that is within thy gates, that they may hear, and that they may learn, and fear the Lord your God, and observe to do all the words of this law. And that their children, which have not known anything, may hear and learn to fear the Lord your God, as long as ye live in the land whither ye go, over Jordan, to possess it." See the earnestness of his desire that this publicity of the law should be perpetual!

In the same chapter, however, anticipating the rebellions of the people against God, Moses makes still another provision to secure the law. Thus it is said :—"And it came to pass, when Moses had made an end of writing the words of this law in a book, until they were finished, that Moses commanded the Levites, which bare the ark of the covenant of the Lord, saying, Take this book of the law, and put it in the side of the ark of the covenant of the Lord your God, that it may be there as a witness against thee." See that! the reason assign-ed, by the Inspired Law-giver himself, for this sacred and secluded deposit of his autograph of the Law, was this—that, if his design, in relation to the pub-

lic preservation of the record, and its practical observance, should indeed fail, the original document
might be brought forth, in vindication of his purpose, and in rebuke of a faithless posterity.

In so far as the Law, therefore, is concerned, there
cannot be the shadow of a doubt that it was intended for universal and perpetual understanding among
all the tribes of Israel. Nor only so; but, it is
equally evident that it was intended, in no small
degree, to be understood by surrounding nations;
and so, though only preliminary to a brighter dispensation, to shine upon the heathen world, like the
sparkling ascent of the morning star. Thus Moses
himself declared—"This is your wisdom and your
understanding, in the sight of the nations, which
shall hear all these statutes, and say, Surely this
great nation is a wise and understanding people."

Look, also, at the Psalms—and you see at once
the express appeals to all the people. Thus in the
47th—"Sing praises to God, sing praises; sing
praises unto our King, sing praises. For God is
the King of all the earth." So, in the 49th—"Hear
this, all ye people; give ear, all ye inhabitants of
the world. Both low and high, rich and poor together." And again in the 50th—"The mighty
God, even the Lord hath spoken, and called the

11

earth, from the rising of the sun until the going down thereof." And so, in the 67th—"God be merciful unto us, and bless us, and cause his face to shine upon us. That thy way may be known upon earth, thy saving health among all nations. Let the people praise thee, O God; yea, let all the people praise thee." And so, in the 100th—"Make a joyful noise unto the Lord, all ye lands." And so, once more, in the 138th, the one containing our text —"All the kings of the earth shall praise thee, O Lord, when they hear the words of thy mouth. Yea, they shall sing in the ways of the Lord; for great is the glory of the Lord."

Look, also, at the Prophets—and the same fact is prominent. Isaiah commences his prophecy with the sublime challenge—"Hear, O heavens, and give ear, O earth, for the Lord hath spoken!" In like manner, Jeremiah exclaims—"Oh earth, earth, earth hear the word of the Lord." And so, in other instances.

When we come to the New Testament, we find the same distinction. Rather, the intention of publicity is still more impressively demonstrated. The openness of the Law is remembered; and the Gospel is made still more popular and common. "Search the Scriptures" was the direction of Christ,

in relation to the records of the Old Dispensation:
and, in regard to the New, it is highly important,
that we never forget such passages as the following:
When "the high-priest asked Jesus of his disciples,
and of his doctrine—Jesus answered him: I spake
openly to the world: I ever taught in the synagogue,
and in the temple, whither the Jews always resort,
and in secret have I said nothing. Why askest thou
me? Ask them which heard me, what I have said
unto them: behold, they know what I said." A
noble and glorious answer! In like manner, He
instructed his apostles to act. When He sent them
forth, during His own ministry, to "the house of
Israel" alone, He not only allowed, but commanded
them to make even His most private teachings public, and that at all hazards; saying—"What I tell
you in darkness, that speak ye in light: and what
ye hear in the ear, that preach ye upon the house-
tops. And fear not them which kill the body, but
are not able to kill the soul: but rather fear him
which is able to destroy both body and soul in hell."
And so, when the final, perpetual, and grandest of
all commissions was given them, after the resurrection of Christ, it reached the very climax of all arrangements for publicity, by saying: "Go ye into
all the world, and preach the Gospel to every crea-

ture." In short, the world itself is not more open than the Gospel. And, as it is upon the tongue; so, of course, it is in the book. The Book, indeed, was written only to make the whole revelation the more public; and to keep it so, without corruption or perversion, from generation to generation, and from age to age. "I charge you," said Paul to the Thessalonians, "I charge you by the Lord, that this Epistle be read unto all the holy brethren." And so, to the Colossians: "When this epistle is read among you, cause that it be read also in the church of the Laodiceans; and that ye likewise read the epistle from Laodicea." Hear, hear! Read, read! these are the salutations of our Holy Religion everywhere! The glad tidings are for all people. Judaism itself, with all its openness, was like a beacon on a mountain, or a light-house on the coast, in comparison with Christianity. Christianity is like the sun, detached from the earth, above it, circling all around it, and covering it with boundless and endless glory.

So much, then, for the first point—that the Bible was intended to be open to the world—as proved by its character, by its origin, and by its declarations. To these proofs, I should be glad to add the illustrations offered by its history, both among Jews and

Christians, in all the purer ages of the Church. But, enough has been said: and yet, I trust, not a word too much—for, in my own estimation, at least, it is a matter of unsurpassed importance, and especially in this age and in this country, to make it plain and impressive, and to keep it so, before all the people, that there is no secrecy, no concealment, no esoteric training in the Religion of the Bible! Here is the Book! and it is not more clear that, as already shown, it is abroad in all the world, than it is that, as now appears, it was intended to be so. It makes no provision for retreat into any hiding-places. It seeks no protection in obscurity. It asks no patronage of Church or State. It stands forth, on its own merits, and so challenges the sanction of God and the confidence of mankind.

The second point is—that the Bible DESERVES TO BE THUS ABROAD IN ALL THE WORLD. Innumerable proofs are ready to respond to any proper call for them here. One or two, however, will be abundantly sufficient for the occasion. Passing, therefore, or rather, remembering, as we pass, the various implied distinctions of the divinity of its origin, the venerableness of its antiquity, the grandeur of its doctrines, the holiness of its precepts, and the sublimity of its ordinances, the variety of its incidental intelligence,

11*

the sublimity and beauty of its style, and all similar sources of argument and illustration—we may rest, chiefly, on this fact—that the Bible interests the world: is of real, great, matchless interest to all mankind.

It interests all Historically. The origin of our race is here. The primitive and proper condition of our race is here. The cause of its present and improper condition is here. The equal brotherhood of our race is here, with its early unity, its subsequent division of tongues and tribes, and the progress of territorial discoveries, and of national migrations and settlements. In a word, the beginnings of all history are here; and, without the Bible, there is nothing worthy the name of history.

Again, it interests all Legally. The first principles of all law are here—those principles which are essential, universal, everlasting, and from which, therefore, there is, and can be no appeal or escape. The master truth is here evident, that the constitution of the universe is a moral constitution; and, of course, that all material elements and combinations, causes and consequences, are subordinate to spiritual agencies and destinies. The moral law, therefore, comes first, claiming voluntary obedience to God. The natural law comes next, securing involuntary, mechanical, and disciplinary obedience to God, according to the moral exigencies of His higher administration. Then come civil law, and ecclesiastical law, as representative modifications and adaptations of the Divine Common Law; both of them being bound by this Common Law to the due observance of all personal, domestic, and social rights—leaving all men free, first of all, to fulfil their duties to their God and to their families, and then protecting and assisting them in all proper efforts to promote their social and public elevation and improvement. In a word, the beginnings of all law are likewise here; and without the Bible there is nothing worthy the name of law.

Again, it interests all Evangelically. The consciousness of sin is universal. Whether the law of God be in the heart alone, as among the heathen; or in the heart and Book both, as among ourselves; it is not more plain that the law exists, than it is that it has been broken. But, here is the atonement for sin: an atonement made by the blood of the Son of God, acting as Mediator between God and men; an atonement designed to make God and man one again: an atonement, meeting the utmost claims of the law, and proffering its benefits, without exception of nation or respect of person, to the whole world of transgressors. Here, moreover, is provision for the regeneration of our nature—that, being renewed by the agency of the Holy Ghost, we may recover ability, in spirit at least, to keep the law; awakening to a life of holy love toward God and all our race. Here, in a word, the consciousness of sin may be exchanged for the consciousness of deliverance from sin; all remorse for the past, and fear of the future, being succeeded by perfect peace, and the gladness and glory of heavenly expectation. In all the world, without the Bible, there is nothing which it would not be an utter disgrace to call salvation.

Again, it interests all Prophetically. A better time to come, has been the presentiment of every age; the delusion, or the warranted assurance, of all generations. With the Bible before us, we have no doubt of the happier theory. God has declared "the restitution of all things"—"by the mouth of all his holy prophets since the world began." When the promise of a Saviour was first announced in the Garden of Eden, the Angel of Hope stood by the side of the Almighty, and, as soon as she heard the joyful news, began to sing the song that ever since has charmed the waiting heavens and earth. Paradise withered, indeed; and the outer world soon smoked with the curse; but, when the last leaf fell from the Tree of Life, and the first fire flashed from the volcanic peak, Hope, unalarmed, prolonged her certain chant as sweetly and serenely as ever. Then the Deluge swept from pole to pole; but, over the sea and over the storm the seraph sunned herself in the smile of the Highest, and, now looking down through the clouds at the Ark, and anon looking up through the glory at the Throne, she floated through the changeless sky with heart as calm and plumes as smooth as ever—singing as soft a strain and as sure a triumph as in any moment of beauty and bliss before. True: when Jesus died, she did, indeed, stand shuddering by the cross, hiding her face with her wings; and, when He was buried, she sat in the shadow of His sepulchre, weeping with sympathy if not with fear, and watching, wondering, for the breaking of that strange repose; but, when He rose—instantly the morning star was startled, and thrilled in its sphere, with the electric rapture of her song renewed. And still she sings, though many, now, alas! mistake her strain. "The good times coming" are all her own, and infinitely better than myriads of the friends of progress have ever imagined; but, the Angel never forgets that Christ alone can bring them! The resurrection of Christ was the pledge of our own resurrection; the ascension of Christ was the symbol of our own ascension; and

the return of Christ will be the signal of the new
creation, and the consummate enthronement of immortal joy. Such is the prophecy of the Bible;
but, without the Bible, there is nothing worthy the
name of prophecy.

So much for the second point—that the Bible deserves to be out before the world. It interests the
world—Historically, Legally, Evangelically, and Prophetically. I would like to add—Philosophically:
for the soul of all philosophy is here. I would like
to add, Poetically: for the bloom of all poetry is here.
I would like to add, Divinely: for the unveiled
splendor of the majesty and government of the
Eternal Jehovah is here. Here, and here only, is
an absolutely inexhaustible universe of reliable intelligence: personally and socially, temporally and
eternally interesting to every faculty and to every
destiny of our race. But, these hints must suffice:
where the longest and richest discourse would still
fall short of the fulness of the theme.

SERMON VII.

THE BIBLE OPPOSED.—I. ECCLESIASTICAL OPPOSITION.

"Thou hast magnified thy word above all thy name."
Ps. cxxxviii. 2.

In the preceding discourse we noticed the fact that THE BIBLE IS RIGHTLY ABROAD IN ALL THE WORLD, as it was INTENDED and DESERVES to be thus made common.

On the present occasion we advance to another fact in the same connection,—viz.: THAT THE BIBLE, BEING THUS ABROAD IN ALL THE WORLD, IS EXTENSIVELY AND VIOLENTLY OPPOSED. The proofs here are sadly numerous and prominent. Rather, they have multiplied into simple but awful illustrations of an obvious fact which no one disputes. It is only needful, therefore, to cite a few instances, and form some estimate of their force.

The ancient opposition was either Jewish or

Pagan : Jewish,—against the Christian Scriptures alone; Pagan,—against the Jewish and Christian Scriptures both. The Pagan opposition, in particular, was either philosophical, mythological, or political,—a defensive and desperate effort to repel the unarmed but mighty and irresistible aggressions of Christianity on all the forms and interests of scholastic speculation, popular idolatry, and imperial corruption and oppression. In this connection, such names as those of Celsus, Porphyry, Hierocles, and Julian appear.

The modern opposition has been, and is, either Pagan, Mohammedan, Jewish, or nominally Christian. Pagan opposition still numbers hundreds of millions of persons,—constituting a large majority of mankind; but, generally speaking, it is ignorant, rude, and inactive,—a vast, passive mass, surrounding Christendom, but apparently ready to yield to united and earnest pressure at every point. Both absolutely and relatively, it is a very feeble obstruction, in comparison with the dominant, haughty, and highly-accomplished heathenism of the olden times. Mohammedanism, also, numbers more than a hundred millions of opponents; but this opposition, in like manner, is passive, and fast yielding to pressure. It is now as nothing, when compared with its terrific magnificence in the Middle Ages. Jewish opposition numbers, perhaps, from six to eight, or even ten, millions, in all the world. But this also is passive. Broken and scattered as it is, its fragments lie hidden, or rise up lonely, in all regions of society, like so many isolated rocks in all the seas. These forms of hostility, therefore, may be passed without further consideration. There is nothing threatening in any of them. Rather, they all invite exertions to subvert and remove them. Would God there were union enough among Christians to enable them to avail themselves of the glorious opportunity!

Strange to say, however, it is within the range of nominal Christendom that active hostility to the Bible chiefly prevails. Here are the main difficulties in the way of its universal circulation, reception, and supremacy. This opposition may be sufficiently intimated, in a summary way, as Ecclesiastical, Civil, Social, and Personal.

I begin with the ECCLESIASTICAL; because, marvellous as the fact may seem, it is nevertheless instantly demonstrable that the root of the evil is here. What is the chief organic power in Christendom at the present moment? It must be either the ecclesiastical or the civil; but which of the two is it? It is a maxim that "In union there is strength." Which, then, is the more united? It it not the ecclesiastical? Do not Grecianism, Romanism, and Protestantism cover, or at least control, the whole Christian world? See the Greek Church,—in Greece itself, and throughout the tri-continental Russian Empire, to say nothing of its extra and ancient connections with Turkey, Syria, Egypt, and Abyssinia. See the Roman Church,—in Italy, Austria, France, Spain, Portugal, Mexico, Guatemala, Colombia, Peru, Bolivia, Chili, Brazil, Buenos Ayres, and other smaller states, and the colonial dependencies of all,—besides its tolerated and ambitious settlements in nearly all Protestant countries. And see Protestantism,—notwithstanding its schisms, still showing somewhat of a common sympathy, —in Great Britain, Holland, Switzerland, Prussia, Denmark, Sweden, Norway, and the United States, with the colonial extensions of all throughout the world. Now, is it not plain that either of these three great ecclesiastical systems must be stronger than any one of the civil powers within whose limits it prevails? Nay, in relation to the direction of religious affairs,—which certainly are the chief interests of mankind,—is it not plain that the ecclesiastical system must be superior to all the civil powers within its range? For instance, with regard to the attitude assumed toward the Bible: will not the civil powers be greatly influenced, if not entirely controlled, by the authoritative dictation of the ecclesiastical system, or the public sentiment excited by it? If the Greek Church shall say, I think it expedient to discourage, or, at any rate, to restrict, the circulation of the Bible, will not the states in which it is established co-operate accordingly? If the Roman Church shall say, I positively prohibit the distribution of the Bible, will not the states in which it is established enforce the prohibition? If even the Protestant Churches say, Beware of the Bible, without some one of our conflicting creeds, liturgies, or forms of government, to accompany it, will not Protestant nations, however free and enlightened, pause, and hesitate, and fear?

See! we are not without facts in the case. Rather, facts are innumerable, and of the most impressive and decisive character. A brief glance at the history of the BRITISH AND FOREIGN BIBLE SOCIETY will give us as many illustrations as we need. This institution has just celebrated its first jubilee; having originated in 1803,—fifty years ago. It had but one object,—the circulation of the Scriptures, without note or comment, throughout the world. It cordially invited to its aid all

denominations of Christians.   What was the result?   Besides other investigations, I have again
gone through *Mr. Owen's history of the first ten
years of that Society*—a book which I always read
with the greatest interest—on purpose to be able
to answer.   A few words will suffice for a summary statement.

The GREEK Church, theoretically, concedes the
right and enjoins the duty of reading the Scriptures; meaning by the Scriptures the same
Canonical books as our own,—excluding the Apocrypha.   At first, the indications of favor on the
part of this Church in relation to the Bible
Society were exceedingly encouraging.   In 1813,
a national institution of this kind was formed in
St. Petersburg, under the immediate patronage
of the Emperor Alexander, and with the most
brilliant accompaniments of princely, prelatical,
and popular approbation and rejoicing.   Indeed,
it is said that "Jews and Christians, Russians and
Armenians, Catholics and Protestants, with one
voice acknowledged that the British and Foreign
Bible Society was the wonder of the nineteenth
century, and the only adequate means ever de-
vised for civilizing and evangelizing the world."
Thus emboldened, the St. Petersburg Society resolved that its object should be " *To provide every*

family, and, if practicable, every individual in the Russian Empire, with a Bible, THAT INVALUABLE GIFT OF HEAVEN." It was expected that "the gospel of the grace of God" would be made to "sound out from the shores of the Baltic to the Eastern Ocean, and from the Frozen Ocean to the Black Sea and the borders of China, by putting into the hands of Christians and Mohammedans, of Lamaites and the votaries of Shaman, with many other heathen tribes, the Oracles of the living God." In a word, that year was to be "memorable"—on account of this Russian organization —"to the latest posterity." In like manner, the British Society was successful in Malta, Sicily, and the Greek Islands, and, in 1814, "Cyril, Archbishop of Constantinople, New Rome, and Œcumenical Patriarch," declared "the object of the Society highly laudable," approved its edition of the New Testament in particular, and gave "permission for it to be used and read by all pious, united, and orthodox Christians; to be sold in the booksellers' shops; and to be bought freely by all who wish it, without any one making the least hesitation." By such combined means, it seemed as though the utmost circumference of the Greek Church was thrown open to unhindered Bible occupancy.

12*

All this, however, was little more than apparent progress. It was like the advance of an ocean-wave,—which, let it swell and curl and foam as largely, grandly, and beautifully as it may, must nevertheless break as soon as it touches the coast, sink into the undercurrent, and retire from the scene. The Greek Church holds to the Divine authority of tradition : and tradition now, as ever, makes the word of God of none effect. Churchmen and statesmen unite in the preference of traditional institutions, notwithstanding their accumulations of falsehood and injustice, to the true and equal requirements of the Scriptures; because their personal and party interests are identified with such conservatism. Of course, as soon as the Bible wave struck upon the strand of tradition, it was turned back. In 1826, another Imperial ukase suspended the Russian Bible Society; nor has any resumption of it, I believe, ever been allowed. A Protestant Bible Society, with comparatively limited range and resources, was soon substituted, and is still in action; but nothing more is suffered. The Greek Church, with its fifty millions of members, stands aloof; nor is a single one of these members, from the prince to the peasant, at liberty to leave it for another. Referring to this change of policy, the Archbishop of Upsal, in

Sweden, remarks, in his *"Review of the Church of Christ,"* that the interest in the Bible Society "was, no doubt, not very warm, as this Church makes less account of the word of God than of external ceremonies. The will of the Emperor was almost passively obeyed, as well at the institution as at the abolition of the Bible Society." In like manner, in 1836, the Patriarch of Constantinople "published an interdict against all Protestant editions of the Bible, and translations of it into modern Greek, the Turkish, Arabic, Bulgaric, Slavonic, and other languages." In 1837, he "forbade the reading of the Bible or other writings published by the Bible Society in London," on pain of "excommunication and other punishments." Indeed, a commission seized "all books of this description" found in the city, and burned them "in the palace of the patriarch." That the same spirit still prevails is evident from the recent prosecution and imprisonment of Dr. King, at Athens, for preaching in his own house, and under the protection of the American flag, to a few people, in a way supposed to conflict with the "holy canons and the traditions of the Eastern Church." In a word, the Greek Church manifestly prefers tradition to the Bible; is afraid the Bible will overthrow tradition, and summons the

State to its aid, in guarding its interests, at every point, against the Bible. With all its documentary concessions to the Scriptures, it executively withholds them from the masses of its people, and so perpetuates ignorance and slavery together.

The Roman Church, unlike the Greek, neither enjoins the duty, or concedes the right, of reading the Bible. It teaches that the indiscriminate use of it is productive of more evil than good. The Council of Trent did, indeed, authorize bishops and inquisitors, under certain circumstances, to give written permission to read translations of it by Catholic authors; but even this, it must be remembered, when given, is not a permission to understand the Bible, but, strictly and only, to read it. No Roman bishop or inquisitor on earth is authorized to permit a member of the Church to understand the Bible for himself. In the language of the amiable Charles Butler in his "*Horæ Biblicæ,*" "Every Roman Catholic receives the Scripture from the Church, under her authority, and with her interpretation."

The standard Roman Bible is the ancient Latin Vulgate,—including the Apocrypha. This is a remarkable fact. It is remarkable that the

Apocrypha should be included in the Sacred
Canon, contrary to the testimony of the Jews
and the primitive Christians, not forgetting St.
Jerome himself. But the title of the standard,
in contrast with the practice of the Church, is
still more remarkable. The Vulgate,—*i. e.* the
Bible in the vulgar, or common tongue; for
vulgar, or common, use. Originally, the Vulgate was a Vulgate,—a version from the Hebrew
and Greek into the common language of Rome;
and that, too, at a time when the reading and
interpretation of the Scriptures were among the
most familiar exercises of the people. But now,
though this Vulgate is no longer a Vulgate, it is
still called the Vulgate, and is the standard of the
Church which is so much opposed to all real Vulgates. True, it would have been impossible to
select a standard which was not once a Vulgate;
for all the inspired books were originally Vulgates, and intended to be multiplied and perpetuated as Vulgates, among all nations, to the
end of the world. But the peculiarity of the
Roman Church is, that it supersedes the Hebrew
and Greek originals by the dead Latin Vulgate,
and then fulminates wrath against the free use of
Italian, German, French, Spanish, English, and
all other living Vulgates. Doubtless, the hie-

rarchy wishes that these were as dead as the Latin.

Under such circumstances, it was a matter of great surprise and great pleasure to the British and Foreign Bible Society to find its early movements, in many instances, most heartily responded to by Roman Catholics. In answer to the inquiry, "Whether the Bible was still prohibited to the Catholics?" a Suabian priest declared, "Properly speaking, the Bible has never been prohibited to the Catholics." This priest appeared to be delighted with the new institution, and promised "some attempts" toward "the formation of a similar Bible Society among the Roman Catholics." At Ratisbon, such a Society was formed, under the care of the "Director of the Ecclesiastical Seminary in that place." By this Society the New Testament was "largely and most acceptably distributed in Austria, Bavaria, and Switzerland: many Catholic clergymen publicly recommended the perusal of them from their pulpits;" and one of them declared, "The Bible is now read by students, by the people, and even by children." A Bavarian priest addressed the British Society in these terms:—"United to Christ, we are united to each other: neither continents nor seas, neither various forms of govern-

ment, nor different outward confessions of religion, can separate us: all these things pass
away, but LOVE ABIDETH." The Catholic Pro-
fessor of Divinity in the University of Marburg
"described the solicitude of the people to obtain
the Scriptures as exceeding not only his means
of supplying them, but almost any conception
which the most sanguine mind could ever have
entertained." "The prejudices of our clergymen," said he, "against laymen's reading the
Bible are gradually disappearing: many begin
even to promote its dissemination." Similar encouraging intelligence was received from Ireland, France, Sicily, Malta, and other points in
Europe; from Madras, and the coast of Malabar,
in the East, and from North and South America.
Several bishops, a vicar-general, a director of an
ecclesiastical seminary, professors, priests, and
people, united in these demonstrations. True,
there was no Roman Catholic monarch to imitate
the Emperor Alexander in the foundation of a
National Bible Society; nor did the Pope of
Rome follow the example of his brother of Constantinople, in commending the object of the
London Institution and allowing the sale and distribution of its publications. But, nevertheless, the
indications were far more favorable than had been

anticipated,—sufficient to suggest, if not to justify, the thought that even Rome itself might, at last, somewhat abate its hostility to the word of God.

Vain hope! Rome is fast bound, fast as fate, by its own infallibility. It cannot change. It must either triumph or be destroyed,—triumph over the Bible, or be destroyed by the Bible. Therefore its speedy and violent uprising against the Bible Society. "We have been truly shocked" —said Pius VII. in a Papal brief issued in 1816— "we have been truly shocked at this *most crafty device*, by which the *very foundations of religion* are *undermined*." See that! How much better the Pope understood the matter than the innocent and charitable subordinates to whom I have referred! He saw, and rightly enough too, the Vatican, St. Peter's, all Rome, ready to be fired and consumed, and felt the preliminary tremor of the seven hills. "We again and again exhort you"—he continued—"that, whatever you can achieve by power, provide for by counsel, or effect by authority, you will daily execute with the utmost earnestness." Nor was this enough. Hear the appeal of Leo XII., in 1824, to all "the Roman Patriarchs, Primates, Archbishops, and Bishops:"—"You are aware, Venerable Brethren, that a certain Society, commonly called the Bible

Society, strolls with effrontery throughout the
world; which Society, contemning the *traditions* of
the *holy fathers*, and contrary to the well-known *de-*
cree of the Council of Trent, labors with all its might,
and by every means, to translate—or rather to per-
vert—the Holy Bible, into the *vulgar languages of*
every nation; from which proceeding it is greatly to
be feared, that what is ascertained to have happened
as to some passages may occur with regard to
others; to wit, "that, by a perverse interpretation, the gospel of Christ be turned into a human
gospel, or, what is still worse, into the gospel of
the devil." See! there it is again!—the old opposition of tradition to the Bible! Alas! that very
tradition, which the Pope was so anxious to save,
—that is the "human gospel," that is the "gospel of the devil;" and the great relief is that the
Bible has come forth to save mankind from it.
But—the Pope concludes—"Again, therefore, we
exhort you, that your courage fail not. The
power of *temporal princes* will, we trust in the
Lord, come to your assistance, whose INTEREST, as
reason and experience show, is *concerned* when the
authority of the *Church* is *questioned*," &c. "A
very *intelligible intimation*," adds Mr. Mendham,
from whose work on the "*Literary Policy of the*
Church of Rome" I have copied these Papal sen-

13

tences, "and, in favorable times, well fitted to produce a *crusade*."

So much for the Roman Church; and, to show its controlling influence over the temporal princes to whom it appeals for aid, it may be added that there is not a Papal state in the world from which the Bible Society is not utterly excluded, or within which its progress is not met at every step by the sternest hostility. At least, I know not of a single exception. I find the Society rejoicing, indeed, in some of its latest reports, in certain successes in Belgium and France; but even these have been hardly won. In Italy, it is acknowledged that "stern despotism restrains the freedom of opinion:" in Austria and Hungary, "difficulties are in the way:" "Spain and Portugal," it is said, "are still, for the most part, closed against the general dissemination of the Scriptures:" and so in other cases. The recent persecution of the Madiai, by the Grand Duke of Tuscany, illustrates the spirit of Romanism everywhere,—an instance in which the intercessions of all Protestant Christendom could scarcely procure the liberation of two humble Bible-readers, husband and wife, from separate, interdistant, protracted, and almost fatal, imprisonment. Doubtless, if the hierarchy had the power, every faithful

Bible-reader on earth would be shut up in a prison from which there should be no release,—except by death. I say this, because, as already stated, it is a death-struggle. Rome, or the Bible, must perish.

But now let us turn to the PROTESTANT Churches. These profess to reject the authority of tradition, and unite in asserting the Bible as the only rule of faith and practice. Of course, they both theoretically and practically concede the right, and enjoin the duty, of reading the Scriptures. Indeed, the principles which originated and justify their existence imperatively demand that the whole world shall be filled with Bibles and Bible readers.

The Hebrew and Greek originals form the standard Protestant Bible,—excluding the Apocrypha. These originals, and all versions of them, ancient and modern, authorized and unauthorized, correct and incorrect, are held to be of right open to all who can read them,—the responsibility of treating them properly resting upon those who receive them, and who must account to God for the use they make of them.

When the British and Foreign Bible Society commenced its operations, Protestants generally hailed it with gratitude, joy, and hope. To give the facts which illustrate this statement would require a large volume. Suffice it to say that in about ten years the London Institution was surrounded by more than five hundred auxiliary associations, in Great Britain, Ireland, and the adjacent islands; fifty other Societies, with various auxiliaries, had been established in different countries on the European continent, five in Asia, two in Africa, two in the West Indies, and one hundred and twenty-nine on the American continent. Some $500,000 had been expended; and nearly 1,500,000 Bibles and Testaments issued, in sixty-three languages and dialects. Sixteen years later, —that is, in 1833,—the interest in this great work had increased to such a degree that it was seriously proposed to the Bible Societies of this and other countries, by one of our Presbyterian clergymen, "to attempt to supply, within twenty years, the entire reading-population of the world with the Holy Scriptures." Although the proposition was warmly encouraged, more than twenty years have elapsed, and the world is yet far from being thoroughly supplied. Nevertheless, as was noticed in a preceding discourse, the printed versions now number two hundred and seventy; and the Bibles and Testaments issued amount to more than 54,000,000. So far, at least, Protestantism has sustained its professions; to say nothing of all it has accomplished in illustration, publication, and circulation of the Bible through a thousand other agencies.

But here, also, certain great drawbacks appear, which cannot be conscientiously disregarded. The Greek and Roman Churches are not the only ones that oppose the Bible. It is a sad truth, patent before heaven and earth, that the Protestant Churches also, to a great extent, are inconsistently involved in the same censure.

Protestantism is remarkable for its sectarianism. The Bible opposes sectarianism, and sectarianism, therefore, opposes the Bible. The Bible, however, acts in God's name; but sectarianism reacts in despite of God's name. That is, so far as this opposition goes, Protestant sectarianism, just like Grecianism and Romanism, prefers its own inventions, with their accompanying dignities, powers, and emoluments, to the supreme claims of truth and charity; and so, like its antique rivals, though not so grossly or grotesquely as they, " makes the commandments of God of none effect."

Protestant sectarianism is either Established, Dissenting, or Independent. Cranmerian Episcopalianism is established by the State in England

and Ireland; Calvinian Presbyterianism in Scotland, Holland, and Switzerland; and Lutheranism, whether Episcopal or Presbyterial, in Prussia and throughout Northern Germany generally, in Denmark, Sweden, and Norway. In England and Ireland, dissenting sects are numerous; so in Scotland, and so in Holland; but in Switzerland, and in several of the Lutheran States, dissent is scarcely tolerated. In Sweden, a native quitting the National Church for another becomes liable to imprisonment or exile. Where no Establishment exists, there, of course, are no Dissenters. Thus, in our own country, notwithstanding the frequent abuse of the term, we have, and can have, no Dissenters. Here all sects are alike independent.

Now, what I affirm is this: that nearly all Protestant sects, whether Established, Dissenting, or Independent, are involved, to some extent, in the censure chiefly applied to the Greek and Roman Churches: that is, they are constitutionally and practically opposed to the use of the *Bible alone*. The Greek Church will admit the Bible, *with tradition*. So will the Church of Rome. The sin of both churches is, that they prefer tradition to the Bible, and are afraid the Bible will destroy tradition. So, in their lesser measure, it is with most of the Protestant Churches. *They* have traditions,—authoritative traditions,—traditional creeds, governments, ordinances, and interests; and they prefer these traditions to the Bible. They accept the Bible with the traditions, but refuse the Bible without the traditions. True, this is a great inconsistency; but, nevertheless, it is a fact, as already stated, patent before heaven and earth. If I be referred to the distribution of the Bible, by means of the Bible Society, as conflicting with this statement; I answer, that is just exactly the difference between the Bible Society and the sects: the Bible Society sends the Bible alone, without note or comment, into all the world, while the sects invariably send their traditions with the Bible. If it be further objected, that nearly all these sects encourage and assist the Bible Society; I answer, that is because Protestantism, unlike Romanism, holds that the Bible alone will do more good than evil, even among the masses outside of the sects; and, besides this, that it is the best weapon, by itself, that can possibly be employed for the overthrow of Romanism, and all other anti-Protestant systems: but let any of the Bible converts, outside of the sects, come to the sects for admission to membership and the advantages of Christian communion, and instantly it appears that, not the Bible alone, but the Bible and tradition together guard the gateways, and, moreover, that when the Bible is satisfied, tradition still insists on terms which the Bible does not warrant, and from the imposition of which it sadly retires, waiting in patience for God's own time of its proper and exclusive supremacy.

This Protestant opposition to the Bible is impressively evident in the history of the Established sects; and more particularly in the conduct of the Church of England toward the British and Foreign Bible Society. Indeed, it might be remarked here, that the very existence of an Establishment, either with or without the toleration of Dissenters, is an organic and continuous opposition to the Bible. It is the intrusion of human authority into the house of God; dividing His family; cherishing and enriching one part, and dispossessing and disinheriting another. It excites pride, vanity, and all corruption, on one side, and envy, hatred, and bitter denunciation, on the other. Not the Bible, but the Church, becomes the primary interest; and the circulation of the Bible by itself must be hindered, for fear of endangering the Church.

For instance, to return to the case specified,

there are two institutions, older than the Bible Society, connected with the Church of England, and controlled, exclusively, by its members. One is *"The Society for Promoting Christian Knowledge;"* the other, *"The Society for the Propagation of the Gospel in Foreign Parts."* Now, is it possible to imagine any thing more incongruous than that two Societies, with such titles as these, should be arrayed against the Bible Society? Yet they have been, and especially the former, ever since the Bible Society was organized! They are the mediums through which the hostility of the higher powers of the Establishment is, in part, manifested. But why is this? Is not the end of all these institutions the same? Does not the Bible Society promote Christian knowledge? Does not the Bible Society propagate the gospel in foreign parts? Certainly, and in the purest form. And yet, their end is not the same. The Bible Society is a great Protestant Institution,—nay, a great Christian Institution,—above all sects. But the others are sectarian Societies,—Societies that prefer sectarianism, within the Establishment, to Christianity throughout the world. See! the old Societies distribute the Bible and Prayer-Book together; the new Society circulates the Bible alone. The old So-

cieties send out the Bible, accompanied by the
Creed, Liturgy, and Government to guard it; the
new Society issues the Bible, without note or
comment, trusting its defence to the God who
gave it. The old Societies seek to subject men
to human authority; the new Society urges only
Divine authority. The old Societies would make
men sectarians; the new Society strives to
make them Protestant and Evangelical Christians. Surely, here are reasons enough for opposition: and it is almost incredible to what an
extent, especially in the beginning, this opposition was carried. "Supply these men with
Bibles," said one, alluding to Dissenters, "and
you supply them with arms against yourself."
"Some of these books," said another, "are exclusively fit for the meditation of the learned."
"Out of sixty-six books which form the contents
of the Old and New Testaments, not above seven
in the Old, nor above eleven in the New, appear
to be calculated for the study or comprehension
of the unlearned." The most distinguished com-
batant against the new cause insisted upon the
danger "to the Established Church from the
practice of neglecting to give the *Prayer-Book*
with the Bible." Even Romanists congratulated
their Anglican brethren on the adoption of the

Roman principle, "that true religion cannot be found by the *Bible alone*," and on their consequent opposition to the distribution of the Bible alone. This early and strange warfare, I regret to add, is perpetuated to this day; though it should not be forgotten that the Evangelical party is free from this High-Church reproach.

In regard to the Dissenting sects of Protestants in Europe, I am not aware that any one of them has ever exhibited this kind of hostility. Their general, if not universal, co-operation in the Bible cause is the great relief in the case, and one of the chief excitants of the hope of a better future. The only opposition to the Bible here charged upon them is, their *maintenance of the principle of false authority*, by which, to a great extent, the Bible is nullified. That is, the Bible plainly and positively requires CHRISTIAN UNION, UNIVERSAL CHRISTIAN UNION, the ONENESS OF CHRIST'S MINISTRY and PEOPLE throughout the world. The Greeks have broken this union by their traditions. Romanists have broken it by their traditions. Protestant State establishments have broken it by their traditions. And Dissenters multiply the fractures and the fragments by their traditions. The principle, in all parties, is precisely the same. The only difference is in its practical applications.

It is false authority added to, or substituting, true authority.   It is the authority of man embarrassing or annulling the authority of God.

So it is with the Independent sects of our own country.   Though the Greek Church has no existence here, though the Roman Church is merely represented by a small minority, and that exposed to the full blaze of the open Bible, and though there is no domineering Protestant Establishment to overshadow our States and give just occasion to dissent, still, free and equal and enlightened as we are, old prejudices continue to haunt us with such an awe and majesty to whatever is superstitious within us, that even we too bow down to false authority; even we too consent that tradition shall supersede the illustrious symbol which God himself has magnified, not only above all our names, but even above all His own name; above all the radiant and reflected splendors of all the circling spheres in immensity, and all the living glories that veil their faces at His throne, or gild the outline of His empire with the golden beauty of their love-commissioned and untiring flight.

The results of this general Protestant deflection from the right course are sadly evident.   For instance, *sects have multiplied beyond all former example.*   In the Greek, Roman, and Parliamentary

Churches, tradition may be said to have changed its office. It no longer divides, but compacts. Not so among dissenting and independent Protestants. If old traditions displease them they are at liberty to make new ones. Instead of casting away the whole system, they have used this liberty. Now, therefore, instead of constituting, as they ought, one great Bible communion, their separate denominations outnumber, I presume, all Protestant State Establishments, and all organic Greek and Roman diversities, put together.

I am aware that the attempt is often made to form a parallel of Roman and Protestant divisions. Vain effort! Roman divisions are all subject to a supreme Union. The Pope employs them as he pleases. It is not so with Protestants. They have no controlling centre. They acknowledge, indeed, the Bible; but, in regard to Christian union, they do not obey it. The Bible is not a pope. It is not a living agent, with power to enforce its decrees. It claims rational, voluntary, and happy obedience. So far, Protestants are not fully prepared for this. They are approaching it, but have not reached it. For the present, therefore, unlike Rome, they are disunited.

But, some may ask, should all true Christians

14

be fused into one great ecclesiastical amalgam? Not at all! That is the effort of the Greek Church, —of the Roman Church,—of the Parliamentary Churches,—of all Churches with visible and controlling centralizations. I understand it, as "the mind of Christ," that there shall be no visible and controlling centre but the Bible; no pope, either man or council; no pope, at Constantinople, Rome, or London; no pope, in any province or district, however small; no pope, over any circle of congregations, or in any particular congregation. "Call no man your father upon the earth; for one is your Father, which is in heaven." Christian union is the opposite of all popery, from the lowest to the highest. Christian union is the union of Christians,—union on the basis of the Bible alone, and for the promotion of the purposes of the Bible alone. It may be beautifully exemplified by a single congregation. It may be grandly extended, so as to convene, for sympathetic but unauthoritative co-operation, the representatives of all the congregations of a city, a state, a nation, or the world. Wherever it prevails, it is voluntary, cordial, and free.

But, others may ask, What should be done with the traditions?—the creeds, canons, liturgies, forms of worship, forms of administering the ordi-

nances, forms of government, &c. &c.? I believe
the Christian answer to be, substantially, this:—
Deprive them of their authority—their false,
divisive, Bible-supplanting authority—and you
may do almost any thing you please with them.
Without authority, they would sink into their
proper relations. They would constitute a curious
class of ecclesiastical literature, and might be
used or not used, modified or even multiplied,
preserved or destroyed, at pleasure.* What is

---

* The author thinks it no inconsistency to acknowledge here a
special attachment to what is commonly called *The Apostles' Creed*.
It is not speculative, not metaphysical, not philosophical, not in
any way scholastically presumptuous or vain, but simply, briefly,
beautifully, solemnly, scripturally, and satisfactorily narrative and
doctrinal. He loves to recite it in fellowship with living Christians
and the remembered ages. Moreover, he has sometimes imagined
that there is an important prophetic recognition of it in the *Apocalypse* in connection with the latter-day glory of the Church. He
is not in the habit, however, of yielding to imagination where
truth and right are in question. Especially, he would make no
concession to false authority in any relation. He would not suffer
the Apostles' Creed or any other to be *imposed* upon him.

It may not be idle to add, that the SWEDISH CHURCH reads, in
one clause, not *the holy* CATHOLIC *Church*, but *one holy* CHRISTIAN
Church. See the *"Review of the Church of Christ,"* page 143, by
the late Archbishop of Upsal.

Similar qualified acknowledgments might be made in respect of
the beauty and dignity of many ecclesiastical formularies, but, as
instruments of division, they are mournful inventions.

here insisted upon is this:—That it is a subversion of the authority of our Lord and Savior Jesus Christ—and that in relation to a point in which he most pathetically manifested a special interest—to allow these traditions to break up the unity of his ministry and people; and therefore, let what will become of the traditions themselves, that they ought to be, must and will be, divested of the power to perpetuate and multiply schisms.

But not only have sects multiplied beyond all former example, in consequence of this Protestant preference of tradition to the Bible. Other evil results are obvious; two of which may be briefly stated. For instance, *sectarianism has disabled and endangered the whole cause of Protestant and evangelical Christianity, within the limits of Christendom itself.* What insulting and menacing attitudes are assumed, in opposition to the religion of the Bible, by Romanism and its allies, on the one hand, and by infidelity, socialism, fanaticism, sensualism, and all manner of charlatanism, on the other! Would this state of things continue, if the professed friends of the Bible were all united on the basis of the Bible alone, and all devoted to the promotion of the purposes of the Bible alone? Nay, verily, on every hand, these haughty antagonists would cower in the glance of truth, and shrink from the sword of the Spirit. The Lord would *consume them by the breath of his mouth, and destroy them by the brightness of his coming.* This gracious result is now kept in abeyance by the idolatry of tradition. The Lord will never give his glory to idols. When Bible Christians become willing to trust the Bible alone, then, and not till then, we shall cease to hear so many lamentations from abroad, and Romanist prelates at home will forbear to lecture on "The Decline of Protestantism."

In like manner, as the other evil result alluded to, *sectarianism has perplexed and hindered the progress of Protestant and evangelical Christianity beyond the limits of Christendom.* It exhausts nearly all its ministerial and pecuniary resources in maintaining its own interests within its own limits; and the little that it spares for the conversion of the world is expended in diffusing among the heathen the same diversities which we so much deplore among ourselves. My brethren, I may mistake error for truth in these connections; but, whether I mistake or not, I must be honest to my convictions. They have not resulted from narrow and hasty researches. I must say, therefore, that, in my judgment, the world will never be converted in this way! Never! Still, I would not withhold my hand from helping. According to my ability and opportunity, I would aid every sect and society on earth sincerely and earnestly engaged in the great work. But I verily believe that the Bible Society deserves more aid than all the traditional institutions put together. And, if there were a Missionary Society corresponding with it, sending forth true ministers of Christ to use the Bible alone, without note or comment, as their only rule of faith and practice, the only authority to be urged upon mankind, the only sensible, infallible, and divine authority on earth,—the one which God himself has magnified above all his name, and which therefore we are bound to magnify infinitely above all our poor, little, insignificant names,—then I at least would be content that the Bible Society and this Missionary Society should share the wealth, and the worth, and the prayers of the world between them. Twenty years! Why was not the whole world supplied with Bibles during the twenty years? Because sectarianism hindered. And why may not the whole world be supplied within the next twenty years? Because sectarianism still hinders. Let Christianity supersede sectarianism, and there will be a shower of the stars of inspiration all over the globe equal to the fall of the meteors in 1833, and every one of them shall touch the land-scape, and abide, and burn, and blaze, until all the dark places of the earth shall shine like the streets and glitter like the palaces of the New Jerusalem. But, as things now are, we can only say, the cause is perplexed and hindered; and we must wait in patience and hope for better times.

Oh, if the Greek Church would give up tradi-tion for the Bible,—if the Roman Church would give up tradition for the Bible,—if the Protestant State Churches would give up tradition for the Bible,—how the whole world might rejoice! Not against the persons of patriarchs, popes, or metro-politans, archbishops, bishops, or priests, or of any of the emperors, kings, princes, nobles, and magistrates connected with them,—much less of the oppressed people subject to them,—can there be any humane or Christian objection. Nothing is objectionable among them but the traditions that oppose the Bible, and, by so doing, corrupt the high, desolate the low, and retard the king-dom of God. Away with tradition, and the Bible brotherhood will fill the earth.

But, if those old parties are too rigid to be reformed, at any rate, let the Dissenting Pro-

testants of Europe and the Independent Protestants of America give up their traditions for
the Bible.   Or, if even this be too much to
ask at present,—if our transatlantic brethren are
yet too much enthralled for such a movement,—
still, at least, let the free Christians of our own
glorious land unite in setting the high and holy
example.   Oh, if this alone could be accomplished, we might be content to ask no more.
If this alone could be accomplished, all else
that is desirable would surely and speedily succeed.   And may not our countrymen be persuaded to this desistance?   Why persist in opposing the Bible?   Were these "new heavens"
and this "new earth" intended to be ruled by
tradition, or by the Bible?   Were they intended
for the heritage of sectarians, or of Christians?
—of a thousand parties in conflict they know
not why, or of one peaceful and enterprising
fraternity, enlightening and renovating the world?
What drove our fathers hither? Was it not tradition?   What brought them hither? Was it not
the Bible?   To what are their errors chargeable,
and the errors of their descendants?   Is it not
tradition?   And to what are their virtues to be
ascribed, and the virtues of their descendants?
Is it not the Bible?   Surely, of all lands, this

ought to be, pre-eminently, the land of the Bible. And yet we have more traditions, and more sects, in this country, than can be found in any other! We have imported the old ones from nearly all nations, and have manufactured, and are still manufacturing, many new ones. True, it is not to be wondered at that old ones should come from abroad; but it is a reproach to our intelligence and moral sense, a dishonor to our liberty and dignity, to fabricate new ones here. We ought to be prepared to welcome all immigrants to the religion of the Bible alone, and to make them instantly one with us in freedom from all traditions. It is our glory that we are free; but, we should use our liberty as not abusing it. We are just as much at liberty to lay aside false authority as we are to cherish it; and we ought to lay it aside. We are just as much at liberty to reject tradition as we are to retain it; and we ought to reject it. We are just as much at liberty to choose the Bible alone as our bond of union, and instrument of government, as we are to connect any other bond or instrument with it; and we ought to choose the Bible alone.

I rejoice that a good work, of this kind, is already in progress in our country. Indeed, the supremacy of the Bible is the doctrine, though

not the practice, of all the Protestants among us,
—that is, of the greater mass of our population.
Some of them, it is true, fall far short of the
practical requirements of this doctrine. Others
come nearer, but still fail to fulfil them. A few
sects come very near,—failing, perhaps, only in
one point; as where, for instance, immersion is
made a term of membership. One of these
parties professes to adopt the principles of the
Bible and private judgment fully, boasts of
them, and opposes sectarianism on the ground
of them,—without apparently being aware that
it is itself involved in the same evil, through the
suppression of private judgment by Church
authority in that imposition of immersion. It
is marvellous how tenacious and exclusive this
particular tradition is! If it were not for this,
I suppose all the immersionists in the world
would immediately take their stand on the
ground of the Bible alone. As it is, in addition
to the maintenance of close-communion Churches,
—they are now actually engaged, in part at least,
in the promotion of a sort of close-communion
Bible-Society,—so threatening some serious confusion, both at home and abroad, even in this
most catholic department of Christian enterprise.

But, besides all the parties so nearly on the

right platform, and which might so easily step upon it, there are quite a number of Churches in our country—and they are likely to multiply hereafter with much greater rapidity than they have done heretofore—which do, literally and strictly, humbly but boldly, quietly but successfully, reject the false authority of tradition in whole, and are governed entirely by the true authority of the Bible alone. This is one of them. True, it has been recently divided; but it was not the Bible that occasioned the division. It was tradition. The Bible, on the contrary, saved it; and now nothing is necessary to its continued and enlarged prosperity but honest and earnest obedience to the Bible. The God who gave the rock on which to build it and gave the man by whom it was built, if it still be kept free from idols, will, in time to come, as He did in time past, hallow it as His own temple, and cause its walls to glow with His glory, and its roof to reverberate with His praise.*

These Bible Churches are at the true starting-

---

* The Church here alluded to is the independent "Associate Reformed Presbyterian Church" of Baltimore, Md.,—better known in connection with the name of the late Rev. Dr. John M. Duncan, a faithful pastor, whose cenotaph most aptly describes him as "An eloquent man, and mighty in the Scriptures."

point.   What an immensity of traditions the
Christian world generally must clear out of the
way in order to assume the same position! Still,
this difficulty is not so great as it seems.   Let
them drop, and they are gone.   As it regards
new churches, there is no difficulty.   Here are
God's book, God's preacher, and God's people.
Is any thing else wanting?   Nothing under
heaven, but God's blessing.   And will this be
withheld?   Never,—if only His people and
preacher prove faithful to His book.

But, besides internal faithfulness, every Bible
Church is bound to take part, according to the
calls of Providence, in the salvation of the world.
Every Bible Church must remember that its position is only a starting-point, and so contemplate
progress.   Other Bible Churches must be raised
up, to sympathize with each other and encourage each other, and in every way establish and
extend the work.   And let me say, as the result
of no careless contemplation, that this time at
least appears to be the "accepted time," and this
country the accepted country, for the accomplishment of this purpose.

"Behold!" cries one, "the provision for a new
sect!"   "God forbid!" is our instant and reverent reply.   This objection, however, is so often

heard, and does so much harm, that I will state the distinction which utterly destroys it. What is a Christian sect? It is a section of professed Christians distinguished by holding the authority of both the Bible and tradition. But what is a Christian Church? It is a congregation of Christians distinguished by holding the authority of the Bible alone, without tradition. Can any distinction be more strongly marked? Surely not. It is an impossibility, therefore, to form a new sect by multiplying Bible Churches. If the whole world were filled with Bible Churches, the effect would be the annihilation of all the sects in existence. Let no timid member of a Bible Church, therefore, be alarmed by this stale and worthless objection. It is a shame and a grief that the wheels of the gospel chariot have been delayed so long by such a pitiful clog.

In conclusion, I cannot but hope that a fairer vision than ever yet has charmed the eyes of men has been reserved, in the wisdom and goodness of God, to illustrate our beloved Union! Union! That is the watchword! Thank God for its meaning, its music, and its power! Union!—civil and religious!—the oneness of humanity, and the oneness of Christianity! A religion worthy of our liberty!—a religion that may be as much a light to the Churches of the world as our liberty is to the States of the world!

If Canadians, Mexicans, and South Americans, if Irishmen, Englishmen, Welshmen, and Scotchmen, if Swedes, Danes, and Norwegians, if Portuguese, Spaniards, and Frenchmen, if Belgians, Hollanders, and Germans, if Swiss, Italians, Poles, Hungarians, Russians, and Greeks, if even Turks, and Arabs, and Persians, and Hindoos, and Siamese, and Chinese, and Australians, and Polynesians,—if, in a word, all the varieties of humanity—except the poor Africans, and even some of them in some of our States—may be here assembled, and made, to all intents and purposes, civilly one,—then, I ask, may not even Greek Catholics, if they should come among us, and Roman Catholics, here at least if nowhere else, and Protestants from all the State Establishments, and Dissenting Protestants of all classes, and our own Independent Protestants of all parties,—in a word, may not all the varieties of Christianity be made ecclesiastically one? If all the obstructions of distance, danger, poverty, language, habit, manners, and social customs, have been overcome in the civil union, may not the single obstruction of tradition be overcome for the accomplishment of the ecclesiastical union,—a simple Christian union,—a Holy Bible union? Here we are, by the good providence of God, one mighty brotherhood, gathered from all nations. Here we are, with the grandest seas of the globe tossing all their billows between our happy shores and the haughty tyrannies of the Old World. Here we are, as citizens, already one. Why not also be one as Christians? Have we not already thrown off a thousand political traditions? And are we not equally at liberty to throw off all sectarian traditions? Then let us use our liberty. Away with the false authority of all divisive traditions! Away with this ecclesiastical opposition to the Bible! The Bible belongs to all! The Bible is acknowledged by all! Let the Bible be obeyed, and it will unite all! If, however, in this as in the former case, it shall seem that there must be some exceptions, let us pity and pray for them. But let all who can come make haste to come. Let the union be consummated! The tidings of it will electrify the world! Popery, like Lucifer, having ascended to the highest heaven in all the pride of the Son of the Morning, shall suddenly drop into the deepest depth of mockery and scorn! Infidelity, like Satan, having covered itself with a cloud and slowly exalted its front against the throne of God, shall fall again like lightning to the marsh from which it rose! Paganism, like Mania, worshipping it knows not what, shall be startled by the quickening voice of truth, and, clasping her brow at the thrill of returning reason, shall stand before the Highest, illumined, enraptured, and restored! Judaism, weeping by the Temple-wall, shall hear strange news from the land where her children have never found cause to weep, and confess that Jesus is indeed the Christ! A second and more sacred national flag shall attend the first in all its flights from pole to pole,—a flag flashing with the stars of prophets and apostles, and glowing with the stripes of the Savior's painful but blessed and beckoning atonement; and the United States of America, and the United Churches of America, magnifying the Bible and the God of the Bible, and magnified in turn by the benediction of both, shall become and remain "the joy and the praise of the whole earth."

SERMON VIII.

THE BIBLE OPPOSED.—II. CIVIL AND SOCIAL OPPOSITION.

"Thou hast magnified thy word above all thy name."

Ps. cxxxviii. 2.

In the preceding discourse we entered upon the subject of Opposition to the Bible, — confining our attention then to the one form of Ecclesiastical Opposition. On the present occasion I design to notice two of the three remaining forms of it,—the Civil and Social. It is not necessary, in either of these connections, to be very elaborate. A brief statement will suffice for each; and so, without inconvenience, we may pass through all.

Civil opposition to the Bible, as previously represented, is generally, if not always, occasioned by ecclesiastical opposition. The priest deceives

the king, and the State becomes the dupe of
the Church. "The Church is in danger!" is the
cry of the crafty prelate; "and, if the Church
fall, the State will fall. Let the State, therefore,
if only to save itself, hasten to the rescue of the
Church." This is the substance of the significant
sentence already cited from the Encyclical Letter
of Leo XII.:—"The power of *temporal princes*
will, we trust in the Lord, come to your assistance,
WHOSE INTEREST, as *reason* and *experience* show, is
concerned when the *authority* of the *Church* is
questioned," &c.

Now, there is a certain sense in which this
statement is true. Reason and experience *do*
show that the *interest* of princes who are *like* the
prelates, of States which are *like* the Church,—*i.e.*
of civil usurpers and tyrants corresponding with
the ecclesiastical usurpers and tyrants,—"*is* concerned when the authority of the Church is
questioned." And just so it might be said, with
equal truth, that the interest of the *Church* is concerned, as reason and experience show, when the
authority of such *States* is questioned. The simple
fact is, *both* authorities are *false* authorities; and
it becomes them to sustain each other. The
people whom they have so long degraded and
oppressed are likely now to call them both into

judgment and doom them to perdition.   In this
sense their interest is indeed one.

But, in regard to any justly-constituted and
justly-administered civil government, it is *not* true
that its interest is concerned when the authority
of the Church is questioned,—*i.e.* the authority
of the Papal or any other ecclesiastical despotism.
Rather, it is the interest of such a government to
have the authority of the Church questioned, or
to question it *for itself*.   It is its interest to dis-
prove and put down this authority.   Reason
shows this; for the Papal theory is, that the State
is subject to the Church.   Experience also shows
it; for the Papal practice has been, according to
its ability and opportunity, to trample upon the
rights of the State.   Moreover, it is a plain matter
of fact that Protestant States—the very States
which do question and reject the authority of the
Church—are at this moment the best-established
and most prosperous States in the world.

Even Protestant States, however, generally
speaking, are not so well established and prosperous as they might be if they held and acted
upon the *true* Church and State theory.   See!
there are *three* of these theories: first, the Roman
Catholic theory,—that the State is subject to the
Church; secondly, the Protestant National theory,

—that the Church is subject to the State; and, thirdly, the Bible theory,—that neither is the State subject to the Church, nor the Church to the State, Church and State being separate from each other and independent of each other. The great practical exemplification of this Christian theory is found in our own happy and beloved country.

The condition of other countries—except in so far as the influence of the Bible theory is now extending among them and modifying their estate—may be represented, in a summary way, as follows:—

1. The Voice of the State to the Church:—*No Church, no State!*

2. The Voice of the Church to the State:—*No State, no Church!*

3. The Voice of the King to the Bishop:—*No Bishop, no King!*

4. The Voice of the Bishop to the King:—*No King, no Bishop!*

5. The Voice of the King to the People:—*No Bishop, no Church!*

6. The Voice of the Bishop to the People:— *No King, no State!*

7. The Voice of the People to the King and Bishop:—*All hail, King and Bishop!*

8. The Voice of the King and Bishop to the People:—*All hail, Subjects and Laics!*

9. The Voice of the People again:—*Long live the King! Long live the Bishop!*

10. The Voice of King and Bishop again:—*Receive our Royal and Apostolic Benediction!*

11. The Voice of the Bishop to the King:—*All right, your Majesty!*

12. The Voice of the King to the Bishop:—*Venerable Father in God, All right!*

And so the king and bishop return to their palaces, and the people to their fields and factories and mines, their stores and shops and ships.

Not so in our country. Here Church and State are separate, and mutually independent. Here the Bible alone is supreme. Here the people, under the authority of the Bible, establish free States and free Churches to suit themselves. These States and Churches are not yet indeed entirely conformed to the excellency of the Bible models, and, therefore, need further changes and improvements. The people, however, have no reason to fear the Bible on this account, but rather to honor and obey it; for, just as they succeed in meeting the requirements of the Bible, so will they progress toward the perfection of civil and religious liberty. The Bible here, instead of being an apparition of terror, is the angel of all grace, — the divinely-magnified symbol of all greatness and goodness, all majesty and power.

Whatever civil opposition to the Bible is manifested in any country may, therefore, be regarded as consequent on the unjust organization of the State, or its oppressive administration, or its unholy alliance with some form of ecclesiastical apostasy, corruption, exclusion, and extortion. It is *not* the *interest* of any State that *ought* to flourish —any more than it is of any *Church* that ought to flourish—to oppose the Bible. On the contrary, the Bible embodies in itself all the interests of mankind.

As a matter of fact, civil opposition to the *circulation* of the Bible exists only in States under the influence of the Roman and Greek Churches,—as was shown on a previous occasion. Protestant States are all open to this good work. In regard to the *application* of the Bible, however, to both State and Church affairs, there is some Protestant obstruction, as might be expected. For instance, in England, the friends of the voluntary system urge the Bible theory of the separateness of Church and State against the established union of Church and State. On the other side, the friends of the union resist the influence of this Bible theory to the utmost. Some of them have even proposed reunion with Rome, if necessary, in order to guard against it. But it must be remembered, in this and in all similar instances, that the controversy is a *free* one. So far it is worthy of Protestantism. The State does not authoritatively interfere with it to foreclose or suppress it. It is going on, and will go on; and, as soon as the Bible theory shall obtain its proper hold on the convictions and consciences of the people, it will accomplish its recognition and acknowledgement by the State.

So in our own country. The application of the Higher Law — as the law of the Bible is styled—to the correction of certain legislative and social evils among us has been very strenuously resisted in some quarters. But here, again, the controversy is a *free* one; and no person can reasonably doubt its result in so far as the *authority* of the Bible is concerned. Only let the true meaning of the Bible, in this relation, be fairly and fully made out; only let the practical requirements of the Bible be clearly and surely demonstrated; and the Bible must triumph. Let the question be simply, The Bible, or Social Customs? — The Bible, or State Laws? — The Bible, or Congressional Laws? — The Bible, or State Constitutions?—The Bible, or the Consti-

tution of the United States?—and it will soon be
seen, I am profoundly persuaded, that the Bible
is indeed the Higher Law,—higher than all customs, statutes, and constitutions in our land, put
together! It is not the *authority* of the Bible that is
questioned by the American people in general.
This is admitted as supreme, universal, and eternal.
The interpretation and application of it are the
grounds of disagreement. With us, not even the
voice of the people, but the *voice of the Bible*, is the
voice of God!

Social opposition to the Bible opens a wide field.
Its main points, however, may be indicated by a
few words in relation to each of them.

Social opposition—at least, generally speaking—
is *not* occasioned by ecclesiastical opposition. It is
independent of the Church. It is independent
of the State. In some instances, it abhors the
Church as much as it does the Bible, and abhors
the State as much as it does the Bible. Nay, in
some instances, it identifies the Bible with the
Church and the Church with the State, and
hates and opposes the Bible chiefly or only because it supposes the Bible to be the support of
the Church and the State. This identification of
the Bible with apostate Churches and oppressive
States is the greatest mistake that social reformers

or revolutionists have ever made. In this mistake is the secret and solution of many of their failures,— indeed, of all their failures, when they have attempted any thing really good. It has turned their forces aside from civil and ecclesiastical tyranny—which, as a matter of human origin and merely human resources, they might have overcome—to battle against the impenetrable bulwarks and irresistible thunders of eternal Omnipotence. I can easily imagine that the popular conspirators, the indignant insurrectionists, of any country desolated by regal and sacerdotal imposition and misrule, should succeed in scattering princes and prelates to the end of the earth, in pounding to powder their ancient and illustrious altars and thrones, in turning their palaces and temples into hospitals and asylums, their parks and gardens into paradises for the poor,—in a word, in changing, at once and forever, any and every thing of man's making alone; but, when they assail the Bible, I can no more expect them to be successful than I could if they were to shake their swords, and point their bayonets, and fire their cannons, and fling their bombs, at the seraphim of the tempest, or the higher, serene, and untroubled beauty of the angel of the sun.

This social opposition is embodied in certain

16

schools or classes, certain confederative or independent, open or secret, institutions or fra-
ternities,—various formal or informal groupings,
occasioned by special sympathetic affinities. It
involves speculative philosophy, natural science,
natural theology, Biblical criticism, popular literature, business pursuits, benevolent associations,
semi-benevolent associations, public amusements,
fashionable religion, &c.

Speculative philosophy, to a great extent and
in various ways, opposes the Bible. Indeed, the
very notion of it and name of it, occurring in
the presence of the Bible, seem to intimate somewhat of insult and hostility. True, there may be
speculation merely as additional to revelation, or
even in defence or support of revelation; but the
history of speculative philosophy, within the limits
of Bible-distribution, is rather a history of opposition. It is speculation against revelation! It
generally presumes, in the beginning of its researches, to ignore the existence of the Bible, and
seldom recurs to it, except, perhaps, to exercise
a kind of condescending patronage, by showing
how wonderfully some "inspiration of the Almighty" coincides with the more infallible de-
ductions, the transcendental ascertainments, of its
own theoretical or practical reason, or else to

sneer at it for the ineffable folly of some apprehended ground of difference. It is difficult to imagine any form of opposition so proud, so audacious, so offensive to Heaven, as this. It starts from skepticism and returns to skepticism. The Bible assumes the existence of God; but speculative philosophy disdains such an assumption. The Bible acknowledges, without dispute, the existence and immortality of the human soul; but speculative philosophy scorns such an easy acknowledgment. The Bible concedes, without thought of questioning it, the existence of the earth, and of sun, moon, and stars,—or the whole material universe; but speculative philosophy is not to be duped into any such concession. Nay, verily, this philosophy must hold God, man, and the universe all in doubt until it shall find time and reason to determine whether to let them exist or not. In some cases, by one of its faculties, and for its own peerless honor, it deliberately undertakes to annihilate the Deity, and then, by another faculty, in pity for the unphilosophical mass of mankind, it re-creates and re-enthrones Him. In some cases, it decides that man has no soul; in others, that he has no body; and in others, that it makes no difference whether he has either, or both, or neither, inasmuch as there is no world for him to inhabit and no God for him to love, serve, or adore. I know not how many thousands of pages of this boasted but empty wisdom I have taken pains to read, with the closest attention, in hope of some ultimate good; but this I do know,—that a large part of it, as it now exists, is utterly subversive of the claims of the Bible as God's own magnified word.

Natural science also, though scarcely to so great an extent, and certainly with much less impudence and much more evidence, takes part in this general opposition to the Bible. Natural science is more worthy of respect than speculative philosophy. Philosophy is attractive to the pride of the intellect. Its lofty abstractions, its subtile discriminations, its comprehensive generalizations, and its pretentious phraseology, promise such sublimity and delicacy and masterly sweep of thought, that a sharp and earnest spirit can hardly resist the temptation to engage in its culture. But science is more soberly inviting. It appeals to one's love of fact and truth and law. It challenges observation and reflection, and prompts invention and discovery, by the submission of material elements and powers, combinations, processes, and results, actual, obvious, palpable, apparently demonstrable and indisputable.

It gives a more practical character to the mind, and, so, to the life. It is incomparably more satisfactory,—especially in its present positive and seemingly reliable developments.

I need not name its vast variety of subordinate departments. The three great ranges of it, which include all its interests, are anthropology, geology, and astronomy,—or the science of man, of the earth, and of the universe.

As it respects anthropology, I allude chiefly to such results of it as are employed in sustaining the notion of the mere materialism of our nature. With the denial of a spirit in man, the doctrines of immortality, responsibility, and retribution all pass away. Sin has no existence; death, of course, is not the consequence of sin; our accidental physical organization is the whole of our being, and this being acts by some inexplicable and uncontrollable necessity, and expires utterly with the dissolution of the organism itself. That all this tends to make the Bible a fable is too plain for remark.

As it regards geology, I allude to similar but more numerous and various results. It is surprising how many anti-Biblical statements may be collected here. Let me sketch the consecutive errors:—No God; no Father, Son, or Spirit; no spirit of any

kind; no creation; no providence; no sin; no fall;
no redemption; no miracle; no history; no prophecy;
no revelation; no moral agency or purpose in
natural changes; nothing of higher promise than
some supposed law of progress, by which, from the
rudest beginnings, all things have been brought
to their present condition, and in virtue of which
also they are all supposed to tend toward final
perfection in the far-off future.   Even Christian
geologists, it appears to me, have been greatly
too much in haste to concede to their new and
favorite science unwarranted advantages over the
Bible.   For instance, one of the most eminent of
these—a gentleman of learning, station, and influence—abandons the time of creation as ordi-
narily computed, and accepts millions of years or
ages for the existence of our planet, instead of
some five or six thousand years.   In like manner
he abandons the notion of an aqueous chaos,
abandons the creation of sun and moon on the
fourth day of the week, abandons the notion that
the animals were all created at any one centre or
in pairs, abandons the notion that death is the
effect of sin, and abandons also the notion that
the Deluge was universal,—confining this catas-
trophe, as he had previously restricted the Adamic
creation, to the vicinity of the Caspian Sea.   Now,

it may be very properly admitted that the Biblical
text in all these connections is capable of mis-
construction; that it is possible it has been mis-
construed; that the popular understanding of it
is perhaps a misunderstanding; and that it may
be a part of the providential mission of science
to correct such errors and illustrate the true
meaning of the record. But the admission of
these possibilities is not a sufficient apology for
hasty concessions to the claims of the new science,
or hasty reversals of old interpretations of the
Scriptures. All haste is inappropriate here. The
Bible has waited thousands of years for correction, and remains pretty much as it was at first:
while thousands of its supposed corrections have
become obsolete infatuations. Such, I have no
doubt, will be the fate of many of what are now
considered, by some, geological demonstrations—
demonstrations contrary to the commonly-received
understanding of the Bible.

As it regards astronomy, I allude to the same
class of results again. Indeed, anthropology,
geology, and astronomy, thus considered, are only
three forms of one great evil whose results are
identical. That is, they are all forms of materialism; and materialism, in its consummation, is
the exclusion of all spiritualism, and, of course,

of all moral government and of all immortal retribution. Nothing but matter, on this theory, exists; and therefore the assumptions of the Bible, from its first chapter to its last, of a Spirit-God, and spirit-angels, and spirit-saints, and a spirit-world, sinless, deathless, and happy,—all these assumptions are mere assumptions, without any substantial realizations. No wonder, therefore, that it should be said, by one of the princes of astronomy, that, according to the progress of discovery, the doctrine of final causes is pushed farther and farther away, even to the boundaries of knowledge; for, if there be no first cause, and that cause an intelligent spirit, there can, of course, be no final cause, no design, no adaptation, in any thing. The universe, thus contemplated, becomes an infinitude of chances, to which the Bible has no application.

I am aware, indeed, that the whole range of natural science has been greatly affected by the progress of Christianity. In fact, science has become tributary to Christianity in no small degree, and often supplies many beautiful and impressive exemplifications of revealed truth. It may still be affirmed, I presume, that the greatest names in science are Christian names. "Even the scientific speculations which are hostile to Scrip-

ture," in the language of a recent reviewer of the
last half-century, "are seldom presented as such."
But, after all such grateful acknowledgments, it
still remains a sad truth—at least, in my humble
judgment — that Christians, in many instances,
for the sake of securing an apparent harmony of
science and revelation, have made concessions to
science which are exceedingly injurious to the
Scriptures, and, by so doing, have encouraged
the covert hostility of the prudent class of infidels
just alluded to, and made still more violent the
open opposition of those who boast that science
is absolutely destructive of the Bible and of all
its spiritual powers and destinies.

Natural Theology it may seem strange to mention in connection with opposition to the Bible.
Still, there is reason for it on one account,—if not
more. Revealed religion, it may be said, rests
upon natural religion. For instance, the Bible
rightly assumes the existence of God; because
nature previously demonstrates the existence of
God. Now, I acknowledge the demonstration of
the divine existence by the natural world; but it
seems to me that a *book* may demonstrate this as
well as a *world*, and that the Bible does demonstrate it, and therefore is not quite so dependent
on nature, even in this relation, as is generally ·

supposed. But, the chief point to which I here refer is this: natural theologians have conceded too much to natural instruction in relation to the *moral character of God*. They have agreed that nature illustrates the *goodness* of God as well as His intelligence and power. They have allowed infidels to descant, without check, on the moral perfections of the Deity, as though they had really collected the proofs of these perfections from material contemplations. Now, all this seems to me just so much in opposition to the Bible. Nature, in its *present condition*, is a revelation of *wrath*. Every man is an eye-witness of this fact. I do not mean, of course, that there is nothing but wrath revealed. The relics of original goodness are all around us; but wrath has come down upon the whole scene of peace and filled it with desolation. All the evils in the world are forms of wrath. The proper logical deduction from this fact would be, were there no additional intelligence to prevent it, that God Himself is a Being of wrath. It would be impossible, under such circumstances, to make out His moral perfections. This I insist upon as the true Bible view of the subject. "For we are consumed by thine anger," says the Psalmist, "and by thy wrath are we troubled." "All our days are passed

away in thy wrath: we spend our years as a tale
that is told." Therefore the Bible was given to
correct the current indications of nature; to assure
mankind of the essential *goodness* of God, as it
was manifested, without any sign of wrath, before
sin entered the world, and is now manifested in
the world where there is no sin, and will hereafter be manifested again in our own world when
sin shall be destroyed. Therefore nature and revelation—wrath and mercy—are so strongly con-
trasted in the Scriptures. "For the *wrath* of
God," says St. Paul, "is revealed from heaven
against all ungodliness and unrighteousness of
men;" but, in regard to the GOSPEL, he declares
that he is not ashamed of this,—"for it is the
power of God unto *salvation*;" *i.e.* the same *power*,
but manifested in *mercy* instead of *wrath*. In a
word, the *natural* attributes of the Deity, as their
title implies, are revealed by nature; but His
moral attributes are not so revealed. It is not
upon sky or landscape that we read the inscription, "The Lord is good to all, and His tender
mercies are over all His works." It is not upon
the morning or the evening star, upon the moon,
or even upon the golden globe of the sun, that
we find the infinitely more glorious words, "God
is love!" No, no! these are Bible disclosures, and

it is by such disclosures that God has magnified His word above all His name. Deists, in my judgment, have no right to avail themselves of these representations of the Deity in their opposition to the Bible; and Christians make a sad mistake in encouraging them to do so by their improper and undiscriminating concessions. If Deists will reject the Bible, let them content themselves with the God of Nature apart from the corrections of the Bible. Their God is not our God! Their God is the God of wrath, the Creator, and yet the Punisher, of a miserable and helpless race of sinners, an almighty Tyrant over endless fugitive generations of His own sighing and dying offspring. Our God is the God of mercy,—just, indeed, and therefore incapable of clearing the guilty as though they were *not* guilty, but, at the same time, as He declared to Moses, and, through him, to Israel and the world, He is "merciful and gracious, long-suffering, abundant in goodness and truth, keeping mercy for thousands, forgiving iniquity, and transgression, and sin."

Other points might be noticed in this connection, showing that natural theologians, in their zeal for a favorite system, have frequently placed themselves in a false position in relation to the

Bible, and aided rather than checked the efforts of its opponents. It is requisite, however, not only to omit these, but to hasten, with still greater brevity, through the topics yet in waiting.

Biblical Criticism it may seem still more strange to introduce so formally in connection with opposition to the Bible. I allude to it, of course, merely as the instrument of degenerate and apostate professors, previously corrupt in morals, and therefore ultimately so degraded, impaired and perverted in intellect. The principal historic reference is to the neologists, rationalists, and accommodationists of Germany, and their sympathizers and imitators in other countries. These are the agents who have wrought most of the disasters to Protestantism on the Continent of Europe, and whose influence has been most threatening, according to the extent of its diffusion, in Great Britain and in some sections of our own land. *Nothing contrary to reason* is the apparently reasonable principle on which they proceed; forgetting, if I may so speak, that the reason needs to be converted as much as any faculty of our nature—needs to be renewed, to be enlightened, and to be sanctified, that it may rightly fulfil its office in the study, appreciation, and improvement of revelation. Revelation is often *above* reason,

17

but never *contrary* to right reason. It invites reason to soar into the empyrean, to contemplate a wider scope than it ever thought of before, to understand higher, holier, happier, mightier, and more permanent relations than nature alone ever presented. In all this, right reason may find a divine harmony that will not only satisfy but charm and delight it forever. The rationalist, however, comes to the Bible in his natural condition, with all his selfishness, sensuality, corruption, and consequent skepticism, and finds it, as might be expected, full of repulsions. Miracles!—no such things; miracles are impossible. Tricks may be played; natural events may be mistaken for miracles: but, as to real miracles, there never were and never will be any. And yet, when the reason is illumined, there is no necessity in the universe more obvious and impressive than the necessity for miracles. There can be no redemption without miracles. The very notion of revelation implies a miracle. Repeated revelations are repeated miracles. A volume of revelations is a volume of miracles. Revealed history is the history of miracles. Revealed prophecy is the prophecy of miracles. The resurrection of Christ was a miracle. The resurrection of our race will be a miracle. The re-creation of heaven and earth will be a miracle. There is no hope of personal or social perfection or immortality without miracles. All power in heaven and in earth is in the hands of our Savior on purpose to qualify him to redeem us by miracles. And yet, to get rid of miracles, the most absurd attempts at explanation that were ever known have been rationalistically applied tó the Scriptures ; and, where even such attempts could not be made successful, the books themselves, in whole or part, one or many, have been rashly and utterly rejected. What makes all this the more deeply and memorably mournful is the reflection that it has occurred within the limits of the Church itself, and among those who ought to have been its exemplars, guardians, and guides. "Certainly," it has been said, "no body of Christian ministers, so large, so learned and influential, in any age or period of the Church, ever before fell" into such "a depth of falsehood and blasphemy." Another specially grievous fact in this connection is that, although this evil, by the grace of God, is at last declining in the country where it originated, it is nevertheless, by the malice of the devil,—like some fashion that has grown old in Paris and is now perhaps actually laughed at there,—spreading itself among our own people, and seeking to renew its horrors in this fairer field.

From all such terrible importations there is abundant reason why we should earnestly pray, "*Good Lord, deliver us!*"

But how shall I even intimate the remaining topics? See! Popular Literature! What a world of opposition is here! Books, reviews, magazines, pamphlets, newspapers, in every form, in every style, at every price, in endless succession, in boundless multiplication and circulation, in every house, along every thoroughfare, in all languages and among all nations,—the most accessible, the most obtrusive, and perhaps the most influential and mischievous, instrumentalities of iniquity now in action. Of all literary productions, novels in particular, contrary to their name, are now the least novel; and, among all the varieties of human character, perhaps there is not one which may not find a thousand tempting fictions adapted to attract and corrupt it. Every appetite has its excitant, every passion its provocative, every vice its encouragement, and every crime its embellished example, its seductive apology, its sufficient sanction. "Satanic literature" is the name very properly given to a vast mass of the issues of the press; and satanic purposes, certainly, are promoted by it to an immeasurable extent. How this whole development operates against the study of the Bible and the performance of the duties it enjoins, I need not stop to describe.

Again: Business Associations:—in regard to which I allude chiefly to two things,—the *matériel* of trade, and the manner of conducting it; or the too frequent want of conscience, first, in relation to the personal or social influence of the products or fabrics distributed in the community, and, secondly, in relation to the arts and terms of barter and sale. In too many instances the Bible is only a Sunday book, even among those who profess to regard it as the word of God,—a book in place, at home or in the sanctuary, on the one day of rest, but not applicable to the management and interests of the counting-room and exchange during the six days of employment and of gain. All this is a sad obstruction to the progress of pure moral principles.

Again: Benevolent Associations. Even these, so far, by constraint of circumstances, if they do not hinder the good work to which they are devoted, at least fall short of the requirements of the Bible. For instance, the Bible Society, the Tract Society, the Sunday-School Union, and similar institutions, are often successful, through their agents, by the grace of God, in the con-

17*

version of sinners. But they have no homes for their converts, no plan of Christian communion, no way, when they have persuaded men to become Christians, of keeping them Christians, no pastorate, no ordinances,—in a word, no provision for the establishment of simple, unsectarian, Bible-Churches. On the contrary, their converts are discouraged from remaining Christians alone, and are distributed among the different sects according to their family or other affinities, and so become liable, at least, against their wish and will, to sink, little by little, from the great catholic position of mere disciples of Christ—one with all other disciples all the world over—into the divided partisans of all the numerous, various, and conflicting forms of false authority. The circumstances which for the present constrain the societies to this mode of action arise from their dependence upon denominational contributions. If they should attempt the organization of simple Bible Churches, doubtless they would speedily lose the patronage that now chiefly sustains them. Still, we may hope that they will prepare no small amount of material which others may employ in more liberal Christian associations.

Again: Semi-Benevolent Associations. By this title I refer chiefly to the various popular socie-

ties—some old, some new, all more or less secret—
the most or all of which use the Bible in whole,
the New Testament as well as the Old, as the symbol of their character and an ostensible bond of
their union. The only apology for the existence
of these societies, it seems to me, is the fact that
the Bible in other connections, where it is right-
fully expected to be fairly and fully honored and
obeyed, has been allowed to lose its proper control; in consequence of which a sort of separation
has occurred between natural and spiritual interests,—the Church devoting itself chiefly to the
spiritual, and leaving the natural, even in relation
to its own members, to be provided for by worldly
expedients or to perish in the want of them.
Now, if the new societies, while they use the Bible,
would also illustrate it by thorough fulfilment of its
requirements, they would accomplish a mighty
reformation. But, in my humble judgment, they
treat the Bible—perhaps unintentionally, or, rather,
without due consideration—with infinitely greater
disrespect than do the Churches. That is, the Bible,
pre-eminently, is the Book of Christ! Old Testament and New are alike Christ's Testaments!
Without Christ, the Bible is as utterly empty as
would be the sky without air or the sun without
light. Christ is the original of the Bible. The

Bible is the manifestation of Christ, as Christ Himself is the manifestation of the Father. The Bible is the brightness of Christ's glory, and the express image of His person, just as He is of the glory and person of the Father. But these societies, many or most, if not all of them, for the sake of including Jews, infidels, and others, *omit Christ!*—omit His name from their forms and ceremonies; omit it in their very prayers; offer Jewish prayers, Deistical prayers,—any kind except Christian prayers. "Ask in *my name*," said Jesus; and no Christian, without sin, can ask in any other way. But these Societies, in this respect, virtually deny Christ,—virtually say, We will not ask in thy name; which is equivalent to a rejection of His whole mediatorial character and office. True, I was informed, on a certain occasion, that *one* of these institutions allows its lodges to pray as they think right,—a very great improvement, and one which, it is to be hoped, will be imitated by others. This, however, is the only instance of the kind I have met; and it is very obvious that the general introduction of such a change would occasion quite a revolution in every Order referred to. At present, of necessity, they are without *true life.* Their sky has no air, their sun is without light.

Again: Public Amusements. It is not necessary to do more than make a passing allusion to these, as among the main sources of opposition to the Bible. It is unspeakably grievous to find that professors of Christianity, instead of holding themselves and their families more firmly and sacredly aloof from these reviving and multiplying treacheries, show, in many cases, a disposition rather to yield to their temptations and indulge in their pleasant wiles. Some years ago it appeared as though higher tastes and nobler principles were gaining supremacy in society; but now there are evidences all around us of some relapse, at least, toward the low and vile.

Finally, it would be well, if it were practicable, to dwell somewhat at large on the opposition to the Bible arising from Fashionable Religion. Fashionable religion!—not a holy religion; not an intelligent religion; not an experimental religion; not a practical religion; not the religion of faith, hope, and love; not the religion of doctrine, reproof, correction, instruction in righteousness, personal perfection, and social good works; not the religion of the Bible; not the religion of Christ: but, the religion of Fashion! I mean the religion of *Selfishness!*—of personal selfishness and social selfishness; the religion of opulent and exclusive selfishness; the religion that delights in splendid church architecture, however ill adapted to gospel purposes; that delights in splendid musical appointments, however costly, irreverent, or even profane; that delights in splendid oratory, however destitute of the pulse of spiritual life or the electric power of the Holy Ghost; that delights in splendid drapery and array, dress and address, attendance and equipage, and is equally facile in honoring the distinguished, in contemning the obscure, and in watching the ranks of rivalry with prejudice, circumvention, and scorn.

But—it must be so.   The time is out.   Let social oppositions pass.   They are innumerable and indescribable.

SERMON IX.

THE BIBLE OPPOSED.—III. PERSONAL OPPOSITION.

"Thou hast magnified thy word above all thy name."

Ps. cxxxviii. 2.

NONE but a minister of the gospel can fully express the solicitudes of such a mission; and it is not always wise for him to do it. On the present occasion, however, I trust that the following discrimination will be received as both prudent and appropriate.

The Ministerial Charge reads thus:—"Go ye into all the world, and preach the gospel to every creature." The gospel, therefore, has two relations: first, to the whole world; and secondly, to every individual. Now, the minister may get so much into the habit of contemplating the vast range of social interests, as to become comparatively negligent of personal interests; or, on the

other hand, he may so exclusively devote himself
to the cultivation of private piety, as to become
improperly careless of the important claims of the
public sphere. Of the two errors, I think the
former the greater. That is, it is a greater evil
to neglect personal interests, than it is to neglect
social interests : for personal interests constitute the
basis on which social interests rest, and without
which they would fall into ruins. Still, the true
plan is to bear both classes of interest in mind,
and give due attention to each.

My previous discussions of this subject have
been of a general character. Sometimes I have
feared, that while I was conducting these in the
manner which you have witnessed, some immediate
personal demands of the congregation might be
unmet; something, in particular, more intimately
connected with the welfare of the young, with the
conversion of sinners, with the consolation of the
afflicted, might be too long omitted. It is, therefore, with special readiness, and zeal, and prayer,
and hope—if not with special pleasure—that I am
brought, this morning, by the order of topics
before me, to a consideration of our personal connection with this great subject of the authority of
the Bible—a view of it which ought to be impressive and useful to every one of us; and pre-

eminently so, in the presence of these sacred and solemn memorials of our Saviour's sufferings and death. May the Holy Spirit aid us in all our services!

Personal Opposition to the Bible! See! The Bible itself anticipates this. Doctrinal and practical statements, historical and prophetical examples, abound in it—showing that it has entered upon its great struggle with a due estimate of the resistance to be overcome. Indeed, its whole treatment of this subject is plain proof of the omniscience of its inspiration.

Look at a few of its Doctrinal Statements. "The carnal mind is enmity against God, for it is not subject to the law of God, neither indeed can be." Again:—"The natural man receiveth not the things of the Spirit of God, for they are foolishness unto him: neither can he know them, because they are spiritually discerned." Again:—"The old man"—*i.e.* the natural or carnal man—"is corrupt, according to the deceitful lusts." Again: —"Out of the heart proceed evil thoughts, murders, adulteries, fornications, thefts, false-witness, blasphemies." And again:—"The works of the flesh are manifest, which are these: adultery, fornication, uncleanness, lasciviousness, idolatry, witchcraft, hatred, variance, emulations, wrath,

18

strife, seditions, heresies, envyings, murders, drunk-
enness, revellings, and such like; of the which,"
says the apostle, "I tell you before, as I have also
told you in time past, that they which do such
things shall not inherit the kingdom of God."

These passages, as you perceive, relate to the
constitutional condition of our race. Certainly,
no one can object that they are not plain enough,
positive enough, decisive enough. Such a condition must teem with the elements of opposition
to all holiness, and especially to the Book which
is the chief visible symbol of holiness. Moreover,
as our natural condition, it is our common condition. Not a single individual is exempt from
it. It may exist in different degrees of virulence,
and with different modes of manifestation, in
different persons. Nay, it is plain that it does
thus exist. But this is the only mitigation
that can be allowed. Even in the fairest specimens of natural character, the essential and malignant evil prevails to some degree, and in some
form. Sin, as both hereditary and voluntary, is
literally universal.

Look, also, at a few of the Practical Statements
alluded to. "Ye ask, and receive not, because ye
ask amiss, that you may consume it upon your
lusts. Ye adulterers and adulteresses, know ye

not that the friendship of the world is enmity with God? Whosoever therefore will be a friend of the world, is the enemy of God. Do ye think that the Scripture saith in vain, The spirit that dwelleth in us lusteth to envy?" Again:—"Love not the world, neither the things that are in the world. If any man love the world, the love of the Father is not in him. For all that is in the world, the lust of the flesh, and the lust of the eyes, and the pride of life, is not of the Father, but is of the world. And the world passeth away, and the lust thereof: but he that doeth the will of God abideth forever." Every kind and degree of this yearning after the world is a manifestation of the natural opposition of the heart to God and all goodness. "How can ye believe," said Jesus to the Jews, "which receive honor one of another, and seek not the honor that cometh from God only?" St. Paul, also, speaks of some who are "lovers of pleasure more than lovers of God." Again, he declares—"The god of this world hath blinded the minds of them which believe not, lest the light of the glorious gospel of Christ, who is the image of God, should shine unto them." And St. James, in an exceedingly impressive admonition, says:—"Let no man say when he is tempted, I am tempted of God: for

God cannot be tempted with evil, neither tempteth
he any man. But every man is tempted when he
is drawn away of his own lust and enticed. Then,
when lust hath conceived, it bringeth forth sin:
and sin, when it is finished, bringeth forth death."
A terrible statement this, and especially the last
clause of it! Sin may seem pleasant; nay, doubtless, in every personal instance, it does seem
pleasant in the commencement of its development
and influence. It is selfishness in unchastened
excitement, in prosperous and joyous action. But
oh! how treacherous this pleasant sin is! Like
the vampire, while it fans the form it exhausts the
blood of its victim. Or, to use a Scriptural and
surer figure, like "the wine when it is red, when
it giveth its color in the cup, when it moveth itself
aright, at the last it biteth like a serpent, and
stingeth like an adder." "Sin, when it is
finished"—Oh! remember this, all ye upon whom
it is even now exerting its charming but destructive influence—"Sin, when it is finished, bringeth
forth death." Like the vampire, again, when it is
full, it leaves its prey in the paleness and coldness
of a sleep that none can break. In view of this
deplorable natural condition, and the necessity of
a new and higher life to counteract and overcome
it, well might our Saviour declare, as to the Jewish

ruler, with so much solemnity He did declare:—
"Verily, verily, I say unto thee, except a man be
born again, he cannot see the kingdom of God."

Glance, also, at the Historical Statements. Infidels have sometimes reproached the Bible on
account of its narratives of the wickednesss of
mankind, and particularly because of its record of
the errors, faults, and occasional crimes of the
professed servants and people of God. Strange
reproach! Why, all this is demonstration of the
consistency, fidelity, and candor of the inspired
writers. Their consistency is demonstrated by
the accordance of their theory with the great
mass of facts in all the world; their fidelity, by
the acknowledgment of the facts in cases which,
but for their love of truth, they would have preferred to conceal; and their candor, by the un-
equivocal concession of guilt in all such instances,
and, generally, by the appendage of its proper
punishment also. The sooner it is understood,
that the Bible both exposes the turpitude, and
opposes the indulgence and commision of all
kinds of sin, the better; for this is the fact, and
all men ought to agree upon it.

Here, indeed, is the secret of all personal
opposition to the Bible. The Bible hates sin;
but men love it. The Bible opposes sin, and

therefore men, in behalf of sin, oppose the Bible.

It is exceedingly painful to remember how invariably this stupid and impure perverseness has set itself against all God's gracious designs and redeeming interventions. Had it not been for this, the Deluge might have been withheld, and the lingering beauty of the Paradisaical dispensation might have been spared to enchant us still. The Deluge was not a natural event. It was the reluctant renewal of primitive judgment. It was a supernatural and disciplinary visitation. "God saw that the wickedness of man was great in the earth, and that every imagination of the thoughts of his heart was only evil continually. And it repented the Lord that he had made man on the earth, and it grieved him at his heart." "The earth also was corrupt before God, and the earth was filled with violence. And God looked upon the earth, and, behold, it was corrupt, for all flesh had corrupted his way upon the earth."

Be pleased to pay special attention to this closing statement. I have seen it explained as meaning that man had corrupted his own way upon the earth,—his customs, manners, and habits. But, surely, this is not the meaning. The meaning is, all flesh had corrupted God's way upon the earth; and, thus understood, this passage becomes one of the key-notes of the whole Bible oratorio, or, rather, one of the master-symbols of its great philosophy.

See! God has always had a "way upon the earth," *i. e.* a plan of government; and this way, as the very embodiment of His infinite goodness, wisdom, and power, modified to suit the circumstances of the chief eras of time, is the way, of course, in which our race ought to have walked. Had we walked in God's way, what a path of glory and joy it would have proved to be! "As for God,"—says the Psalmist,—"His way is perfect; the word of the Lord is tried; He is a buckler to all those who trust in him. For who is God, save the Lord? or who is a Rock, save our God?" It matters not how God's way is announced, whether by His own voice, by His angels, by inspired men, or, as at present, by the Inspired Record; it is substantially the same way, and the right way, and, let men make as many experiments as they will, the only right way. His ways—like those of wisdom—are "ways of pleasantness," and all His "paths are peace." For want of willingness to pursue the proper course thus divinely prescribed for us, we have stumbled upon the mountains and fainted in the valleys, wandering among rocks and pits, and filling the world with vain lamentations.

Why did the Almighty at first impair the human estate by the severe judgment pronounced in Eden? Because Adam had corrupted His way, violated His government, and so made such a change absolutely necessary. Just so it was that the Deluge was occasioned. All flesh followed the example of Adam. After long trial, God found His modified administration so utterly perverted and abused that nothing remained but to change the whole physical system again, and, by means of a new stock, to make a new trial, securing if practicable greater obedience, and so exhibiting a happier succession of generations.

The result was much the same as before. During the comparatively brief interval between the flood and the call of Abraham, it would seem that the new race had all lapsed into idolatry. By the agency of Abraham, however, God again revealed His way; and again, in a few hundred years, it was generally corrupted. Then came the great national manifestation of it, by the miraculous mission of Moses, and the cloud-wrapt presence, and frequent audible superintendency, of Jehovah himself. Exceedingly solemn and imperative were the requirements of obedience to this new revelation. "Ye shall observe to do, therefore, as the Lord your God hath commanded you; ye shall not turn aside to the right hand or to the left. Ye shall walk in all the ways which the Lord your God hath commanded you." "Thou shalt also consider in thine heart that, as a man chasteneth his son, so the Lord thy God chasteneth thee. Therefore thou shalt keep the commandments of the Lord thy God, to walk in his way, and to fear him." Notwithstanding, however, all the wonders and solemnities of that grand governmental disclosure, it was not long before, to a great extent, it shared the fate of its predecessors. Human nature was seen to be as unmanageable as of old.

True, the Mosaic economy in whole was stamped too deeply on the fortunes of Egypt, of the tribes hovering along the borders of the Desert, and of the Canaanites and their conquerors, ever to be effaced from the history of the world. In particular, it so permeated the personal, domestic, social, national, and international life and action of the Israelites themselves; so identified itself with every step of their progress through the ages, whether in weal or wo, at home or in exile; so multiplied its monuments, and verified its rewards and penalties among them, holding them, whether

obedient or disobedient, under a manifestly omnipresent, omniscient, and omnipotent control,—that
it was utterly impossible it should ever fall into
such desuetude as to be forgotten. It was divinely
emblazoned on sky and landscape. It shines there
still. Nay, it burns there still, burns in wrath,
waiting for mercy. It is, at this moment, the most
imperishable thing among the rocks of Sinai.
The mosque of Omar, overshadowing Moriah, is
but a mist to the firmament, when compared to
the endurance of the Law. "Till heaven and earth
pass, one jot or one tittle shall in no wise pass from
the law, till all be fulfilled."

Still, God's way was corrupted again, as in preceding instances. I often think of the solicitudes
of Moses, in this connection; of the aggregate of
personal oppositions which he was called to bear
every day for so many years, and especially
of his clear, sure, sad prophetic contemplations
of continued and increased rebellion after his
decease. Though the meekest of men, he was
provoked into offences which prevented his own
entrance into the promised land; and when he
drew near his last hour, after depositing the Law
in the Ark as a witness, he mournfully declared,
"I know thy rebellion and thy stiff neck; behold,
while I am yet alive with you this day, ye have

been rebellious against the Lord, and how much more after my death? Gather unto me all the elders of your tribes, and your officers, that I may speak these words in their ears, and call heaven and earth to record against them. For I know that after my death ye will utterly corrupt yourselves, and turn aside from the way which I have commanded you; and evil will befall you in the latter days, because ye will do evil in the sight of the Lord, to provoke Him to anger through the work of your hands." Indeed, the Lord Himself refers to the same trial, in one of the Psalms, saying, "Forty years long was I grieved with that generation, and said, It is a people that do err in their hearts, and they have not known my ways; unto whom I sware in my wrath, that they should not enter into my rest."

But that was only the beginning. Come down to the time of Solomon—a conspicuous example. After the gifts made to him of wisdom, understanding, riches, and honor, almost beyond parallel, God said to him, "If thou wilt walk in my ways, to keep my statutes and my commandments, as thy father David did walk, then I will lengthen thy days." That is, I will grant thee the longest life for the enjoyment of the greatest prosperity. On the memorable day of the dedication of the temple, that same Solomon, in his noble supplication, thus, in part, besought the Lord:—"Then hear thou from heaven, thy dwelling-place, and forgive, and render unto every man according unto all his ways, whose heart thou knowest; (for thou only knowest the hearts of the children of men;) that they may fear thee, to walk in thy ways, so long as they live in the land which thou gavest unto our fathers." And yet, that same Solomon proved himself perhaps the greatest corrupter of God's ways whom the Israelites ever knew. Therefore it is written, "And the Lord was angry with Solomon, because his heart was turned from the Lord God of Israel, which had appeared unto him twice." Therefore, also, the adversaries which were raised up to vex him, and therefore, too, the threatened, and finally the actual, disruption of his kingdom, "because,"—said "the Lord, the God of Israel,"—"that they have forsaken me, and have worshipped Ashtoreth, the goddess of the Zidonians; Chemosh, the god of the Moabites; and Milcom, the god of the children of Ammon; and have not walked in my ways to do that which is right in mine eyes, and to keep my statutes and my judgments, as did David his father."

Hear the prophet also:—"Who gave Jacob for a spoil and Israel to the robbers?" inquired

Isaiah. "Did not the Lord, He against whom we have sinned? for they would not walk in his ways, neither were they obedient unto his law." "Thus saith the Lord," exclaimed Jeremiah, "Stand ye in the ways, and see, and ask for the old paths, where is the good way, and walk therein, and ye shall find rest for your souls. But they said, We will not walk therein." Again:—"Since the day that your fathers came forth out of the land of Egypt unto this day, I have even sent unto you all my servants the prophets, daily rising up early, and sending them: yet they hearkened not unto me, nor inclined their ear, but hardened their neck; they did worse than their fathers." Therefore followed the captivity, with all its humiliations and sorrows. Ezekiel represented the Jews as worse than the Samaritans and Sodomites, saying, "Yet hast thou not walked after their ways, nor done after their abominations; but, as if that were a very little thing, thou wast corrupted more than they, in all thy ways. As I live, saith the Lord God, Sodom thy sister hath not done, she nor her daughters, as thou hast done, thou and thy daughters." And so it continued, until the close of that dispensation: the very last verse of the Old Testament intimating that, but for the change of dispensation, God would smite the earth with another curse.

Then came the Christian dispensation. "God, who at sundry times and in divers manners spake in time past unto the fathers by the prophets, hath in these last days spoken unto us by his Son, whom he hath appointed heir of all things, by whom also he made the worlds; who, being the brightness of his glory and the express image of his person, and upholding all things by the word of his power, when he had by himself purged our sins, sat down on the right hand of the Majesty on high; being made so much better than the angels, as he hath by inheritance obtained a more excellent name than they." "Therefore," says the same apostle in the same connection, "we ought to give the more earnest heed to the things which we have heard, lest at any time we should let them slip. For if the word spoken by angels was steadfast, and every transgression and disobedience received a just recompence of reward, how shall we escape, if we neglect so great salvation; which at the first began to be spoken by the Lord, and was confirmed unto us by them that heard him; God also bearing them witness, both with signs and wonders, and with divers miracles, and gifts of the Holy Ghost, according to his own will?"

But there is too often a great difference between

our duty and our conduct; between even our interest and our conduct. We have seen what ought to have been done; what a superior welcome ought to have been given to this greatest of all dispensations: but what was done? what kind of a welcome was extended? The New Testament history is not like the Old. Instead of extending through more than a thousand years, it closes with the first century. Still, it is sufficient to show, as far as it goes, a result in this case corresponding with that of every preceding case. "Prepare ye the way of the Lord," cried the Baptist in the wilderness, "make his paths straight." And so they did. "Then went out to him Jerusalem, and all Judea, and all the region round about Jordan, and were baptized of him in Jordan, confessing their sins." But, when the Lord himself came, in the way thus prepared for him, and in the path thus made straight for his feet, the very people who had so carefully prepared His way and straightened His path, "despised and rejected" Him! What though he was the "Son" of God? What though He was "the heir of all things"? What though He did "make the worlds"? What though He was "the brightness of the Father's glory and the express image of His person"? What though He did "uphold

all things by the word of His power"? Did He
not know better than to take upon Him "the
form of a servant," and be "found in fashion as a
man"—"a man of sorrows and acquainted with
grief"? Did He not know that they expected Him
to appear in transcendent pomp and power; subduing the Gentiles to His royal sceptre, and elevating Israel to the dominion of the world? How
dared He to disappoint their just expectations?
Such a Messiah, indeed! Nay, verily, they "hid,
as it were," their "faces from Him. He was despised, and" they "esteemed Him not." That is,
in few words, in this, as in all other instances,
they preferred their own way to God's way. Even
some of those who became convinced, at last, that
Jesus of Nazareth was really the Christ, soon
began to corrupt God's way, endeavoring to blend
the works of the law with the grace of the gospel; so that this history also, brief as it is, shows
the continued and accumulating strength of the
same old spirit of natural, sinful, opposition, even
to the wisest and most merciful of all the divine
instructions in behalf of our race. The Apostolic
Epistles, in particular, are full of illustrations of
this opposition.

As it was with the Jews, so was it with the
Gentiles. The gospel differed from the law, in

the universality of its appeal. No commission was ever given to a group of prophets like that which Christ gave to his group of apostles. It was never said, "Go ye into all the world and preach Judaism to every creature." The world was reserved for the inheritance of the "new and everlasting covenant." Peter opened the gate of the Gentiles at Cæsarea. Afterward, Paul opened a hundred gates,—one of them at Rome itself. What, then, was the result among the Gentiles? The gospel found them in an awful condition. It is written that, "as they did not like to retain God in their knowledge, God" had given "them over to a reprobate mind," and they were "filled with all unrighteousness." They "walk," said their own apostle, again, "in the vanity of their mind, having the understanding darkened, being alienated from the life of God, through the ignorance that is in them, because of the blindness, or hardness, of their heart, who, being past feeling, have given themselves over unto lasciviousness, to work all uncleanness with greediness." As a matter of course, the preaching of the gospel to such nations was an enterprise of imminent peril,— prosecuted always at the risk of life, and often with the loss of life. True, everywhere, to some extent, the encouragement of success was secured:

churches were established in the chief cities
of the Roman empire; and Christianity, though
generally regarded as a new superstition, became
known throughout the world. Among the Gentile Christians, however, as well as among the
Jewish, signs of corruption soon appeared. God's
way was thought capable of improvement, and the
rival philosophies of the East and of the West, the
Persian and the Grecian, both attempted the task
of making it what it ought to be. These results
also find their confirmation in the various Epistles.
The cause was the same,—the old inveteracy of
human malignity against the purity and wisdom
of the Divine compassion.

Turning, however, from the historical statements of the Bible in this connection, the view
must be completed by a glance at its Prophetical
statements.

Our Lord himself anticipated, even more clearly
and certainly than did Moses, the character and
extent of future opposition. Not only His own
sufferings and death, but the martyrdom of His
apostles, the persecution of His disciples generally, the whole fate of His cause prior to the
destruction of Jerusalem, and its subsequent progressive struggles in all the world, to the end of
the world,—all this range was open to His con-

templation, and more or less fully described in His literal and parabolic predictions. When Christ had closed His personal ministry and ascended to heaven, His Spirit, as was promised, took his place. And so said St. Paul:—"Now, the Spirit speaketh expressly that, in the latter times, some shall depart from the faith, giving heed to seducing spirits and doctrines of devils; speaking lies in hypocrisy; having their conscience seared with a hot iron; forbidding to marry, and commanding to abstain from meats, which God hath created to be received with thanksgiving of them which believe and know the truth." This, you perceive, is the foresight of a great Christian apostasy,—a departure from the faith. Again says the same apostle:—"This know also, that in the last days perilous times shall come; for men shall be lovers of their own selves, covetous, boasters, proud, blasphemers, disobedient to parents, unthankful, unholy, without natural affection, trucebreakers, false accusers, incontinent, fierce, despisers of those that are good, traitors, heady, high-minded, lovers of pleasure more than lovers of God,—having a form of godliness but denying the power thereof." This is supposed by some to relate to Infidelity, as the other to Romanism; but the latter part of the description connects it with a religious profession, whether honestly made or not. Infidelity is more plainly anticipated by Peter, in this language:—"There shall come in the last days scoffers, walking after their own lusts, and saying, Where is the promise of His coming? for since the fathers fell asleep all things continue as they were from the beginning of the creation." And so, in the Epistle of Jude:—"But, beloved, remember ye the words which were spoken before of the apostles of our Lord Jesus Christ: how that they told you there should be mockers in the last time, who should walk after their own ungodly lusts. These be they who separate themselves, sensual, having not the Spirit." That is, materialism against spiritualism, —the great strife, indeed, of all ages, in some form.

But the last book of the New Testament is the one which contains the most numerous, various, and impressive anticipations of opposition. The most interesting theory in relation to the Apocalypse is, that it was designed to complete the cycle of revelation by filling up with prophecy the whole interval from the Christian era to the end of the world; so that, by means of the history and prophecy of the Bible conjoined, we may hold in one view the entire course of human affairs, from the creation of Adam to the final establishment of the

city and kingdom of God, and the glorious inheritance of the saints in the full enjoyment of
everlasting life.

I cannot enter upon the particular predictions
of this wonderful book. It answers my purpose
to notice the fact that they involve a series of
oppositions—natural, sinful, malignant oppositions—to all God's works and ways; ending,
indeed, in the triumph of immortal holiness and
joy, but continued to the very latest moment of
practicable resistance, and only destroyed at last
by the Omnipotence that can tolerate them no
longer. As long as shall be possible, this poor,
miserable, foolish nature of ours will summon
whatever specimens of its hatred remain, to array
them against all the manifestations of the infinite
perfections of Jehovah.

Such, then, is the Bible anticipation of opposition,
—of personal opposition, assuming in its progress
all varieties of social opposition. Its doctrinal and
practical statements are strictly, truly, and satisfactorily philosophical. Its historical and prophetical
examples—corroborated and confirmed by the observation, experience, and literary and other monuments, of all mankind—are exactly such as would
be expected to accompany and illustrate such a
philosophy. The lesson which combines all the

elements we have collected is this:—That there is a constitutional opposition of man to God,—of man's selfishness to God's benevolence, of man's supposed wisdom to God's real wisdom, of man's sensualism to God's spiritualism, of man's foulness to God's holiness, of man's madness to God's mercy, of man's wretchedness to God's happiness; and that this natural, common, personal hostility has manifested itself, from the beginning of the world, in the instant rejection or gradual corruption of every plan of government and every covenant of redemption which God has ever introduced into the world; or, in one word, has manifested itself in the perpetual preference of our own way to the way of the High and Lofty One that inhabiteth eternity, —the only wise God and our Savior.

It is with all this reason to anticipate continued opposition that the Bible comes to us this day. It comes to us, knowing that we naturally dislike it. It comes to us, knowing that in many instances, at least, we have dishonored it, and still dishonor it. It comes to us, knowing that on thousands of occasions we have preferred the merest trash of bigots, fools, and skeptics to the rich infinitude of its redeeming and Divine intelligence. It comes to us, knowing that, although God has magnified it above all His name, we have presumed to pass it with neglect or repel it with scorn. Still, it comes to us with a pity as great as its glory. It comes to us to plead with us,—to plead with us in the spirit of one of its own prophets,—nay, in the Spirit of the God who sent him.

"Wherefore I will yet plead with you, saith the Lord, and with your children's children will I plead. For, pass over the isles of Chittim, and see, and send unto Kedar, and consider diligently, and see if there be such a thing. Hath a nation changed its gods?—which yet are no gods? But my people have changed their glory for that which doth not profit. Be astonished, O ye heavens, at this, and be horribly afraid, be ye very desolate, saith the Lord. For my people have committed two evils: they have forsaken me, the fountain of living waters, and hewed to themselves cisterns, broken cisterns, that can hold no water." No wonder the heavens were called to darken and shudder over such a scene of ineffable folly and woe!

But we have committed the same evils. And yet the Bible comes to us still, pleading with us, and with our children, and with our children's children, beseeching us to return to our God.

Surely it is an unspeakable condescension for the Almighty to assert his own superiority to such worms as we are; and yet, unless He do it, we are lost.   Never can we cast off the case of our worm-hood and soar away upon the pinions of angelic immortality, until, by some means, God succeeds in getting the notion and the belief and the ad-miration of His own infinite excellency into our souls, to annihilate the insolence of self and sin and quicken us with the sympathies of universal truth and love.

Hearken, then, to the gracious challenge:— "Seek ye the Lord while He may be found; call ye upon Him while he is near.   Let the wicked forsake his way, and the unrighteous man his thoughts, and let him return unto the Lord, and He will have mercy upon him, and to our God, for He will abundantly pardon.   For"—see! here is the divine condescension,—"for my thoughts are not your thoughts, neither are your ways my ways, saith the Lord.   For as the heavens are higher than the earth, so are my ways higher than your ways, and my thoughts than your thoughts."

Oh, the goodness of God! to stoop to assure us of such a truth as this!   And yet we need such stooping; for, though no language in heaven, earth, or hell can declare the absurdity of the thing, still, it is the fact of all time, the demon-stration of every age and of every generation, that we think our thoughts higher than God's thoughts and our ways higher than God's ways. Thank God, therefore, for condescending to assure us that this is an error! Thank God for the hope that the world will yet confess and abandon this error! Thank God for the number of those who have abandoned it, and who now sit, in their right mind, clothed with humility, at the feet of Jesus, with the open Bible on their knees, and the light of their Master's countenance shining upon it!

Oh, my brethren, it was always so, though the world knew it not! Before the first book of the Bible was written, the voice that proclaimed the ways of God was the sublimest voice on all the air. When the first book of the Bible was written, that book was the sublimest vision in all the light. As book after book was added to the first, it was like the opening of heaven over heaven, revealing new forms of truth and good, of beauty and bliss. When the whole development was complete, it was like the telescopic expansion of a boundless universe before contracted or concealed. And now, pleased with His work, God hallows the Sabbath of revelation, and magnifies His word above all his name. It is full of His thoughts and ways,—full of thoughts of wisdom and ways of mercy, full of thoughts of pardon

20

and ways of salvation, full of thoughts of grace and ways of glory. As the heavens are higher than the earth; as the meteoric heavens are higher than the earth; as the starry heavens are higher than the earth; as the third heavens are higher than the earth; as the heaven of heavens— transcending the utmost amplitudes of all astronomy, overarching and comprehending all other heavens; as that heaven—the heaven of innumerable and immeasurable heavens, the Lord God Almighty's own intensely-illumined, inaccessible, and imperishable heaven—is higher than the earth, if any one can remember what the earth is,—so are God's thoughts higher than our thoughts, and God's ways higher than our ways! The Bible is the spiritual immensity in which the thoughts of God are suns and the ways of God are systems. There they shine forever, there they roll forever,—every thought more radiant than our noonday fire, and every way more beautiful than Saturn with all his rings and moons, and with a wider sweep than Neptune through all his tremulous range of outer gloom. There they shine forever and roll forever,—some in sight, and some out of sight, ever multiplying through the penetrating power of more spiritual instruments, and still stretching away and away and away, as if to invite the continually-extending explorations of our most earnest and delighted immortality.

But all efforts are vain to tell the true difference between the thoughts and ways of God and those of man. God is infinite, man is finite; and we can say no more. Let us therefore descend to simple and more practical views. Let us resolve that we will return to God; that we will endeavor to improve the gift of the Bible; that we will take from it God's thoughts and try to make them our own thoughts, and take from it His ways and try to make them our own ways.

If Adam had not preferred his own way to God's way, Paradise might have been blooming yet. If the antediluvians, generally, had not corrupted God's way upon the earth, the fountains of the great deep might have remained sealed until this very hour. If the postdiluvians had not fallen into the same sin, the confusion of tongues and division of nations might never have been necessary. If the Israelites had not followed the sad example, they might have enjoyed the dew of heaven and the fatness of the earth in their own holy land even to this day. If the early Christians had been true to their trust, Romanism, Grecianism, and Protestantism might never have disturbed the world, and all other evils might long ago have vanished from the realms of truth and peace. If we ourselves had not, "like sheep, gone astray," had not "turned every one to his own way," it would not have been requisite for us to remember, with shame and grief, that the "Lord hath laid upon" Jesus "the iniquity of us all."

Alas for the series of unspeakable humiliations! Behold the consequences of this miserable wilfulness of our race! Adam exchanged the sonship of God for the servitude of the devil. The antediluvians rebelled against their Maker for the privilege of murdering each other and destroying the world. The postdiluvians forgot the rainbow Redeemer to worship brutes and reptiles. The Israelites forsook the Mighty One who smote Egypt, sundered the sea, shaded the desert, shook the mountain, parted the river, and rolled the thunder of His omnipotence from the palm-covered wells of Beersheba to the cedar-crowned peaks of Lebanon, to bow down to the meanest idols of the tribes they conquered and enslaved. The Christians abandoned their allegiance to the Son and Heir of the Highest to kiss the slipper of the Pope, exchanged the authority of the Bible for the authority of the miscalled Church, and renounced the spiritual merits of the blood of atonement for the transubstantiated mysteries of a wafer. And we ourselves,—what have we gained by this marvellous preference of our own way to God's way? Is there man or woman here who does not know that all the degradations and remorseful remembrances of life are consequences of selfish opposition to the purity, wisdom, and benevolence of Jehovah? Who is there among us, that, having used the Bible as the lamp to his feet and the light to his path, has gone astray?

Oh, let the time past suffice wherein we have wrought folly. Have we ardent affections? Let us purify them with the love of God as revealed in the Bible. Have we an indomitable will? Let us devote it to the promotion of the cause of the Bible. Have we genius? Let us quicken it with the inspirations of the Bible. Have we learning? Let us humble it before the unerring truthfulness of the Bible. Have we wealth? Let us consecrate it to the benevolent promptings of the Bible. Let our character, in whole, be a Bible character. Let our homes be Bible homes. Let our churches be Bible churches. Let us remember that the glory is not in the house, not in the style, not in the cost, not in the material magnificence or splendor of any

20*

external connection, but in the gospel,—in the man-subduing gospel; in the God-glorifying gospel; in the gospel which is the "power of God unto salvation unto every one that believeth."

SERMON X.

THE TRIUMPH OF THE BIBLE OVER ALL OPPOSITION.

" Thou hast magnified thy word above all thy name."
Ps. cxxxviii. 2.

PART I.

THIS last sermon of the series brings us to our proper culminating topic. In preceding discourses we have noticed, briefly—What the Bible is in itself; What it is as compared with Creation and Providence, with the Church and the State; What it is as preeminently the Book of Christ; What its current condition is as the only sensible, infallible, and divine authority on earth; How it is abroad, and rightly abroad, in all the world; and, How, being thus abroad, it is extensively and violently opposed. Now, therefore, as just intimated, I propose to conclude with the culmination of the whole subject in the triumph of the Bible over all opposition.

The only argument required in the case may be

presented in the form of a simple inference from the text. That is—As God, from the beginning, has magnified His word above all His name, so He will continue to magnify it even unto the end. This inference commends itself to my judgment as all-sufficient for the occasion, and is the more acceptable because of its harmony with all that has gone before. It will be found, however, more than a mere infer-ence—a doctrine confirmed by numerous, explicit, and decisive testimonies.

See! The chief forms of opposition to the Bible, as heretofore stated, are—Pagan, Mohammedan, Jew-ish and nominally Christian. The Pagan, Moham-medan and Jewish forms of it are *comparatively* passive; the nominally Christian alone being earn-estly and widely active. This active opposition was described as Ecclesiastical, Civil, Social, and Personal. The Ecclesiastical was found, in different degrees, in the Greek, Roman, and Protestant Churches; the Civil in all countries where Church and State are united; the Social in connection with speculative philosophy, natural science, natural theology, biblical criticism, popular literature, business pursuits, be-nevolent associations, semi-benevolent associations, public amusements, and fashionable religion. To these might have been added the grosser forms of infidelity and such delusions and impostures as Mormonism and Spiritualism. The personal opposition was traced to the natural corruption of the heart, as witnessed in its historic and prophetic developments. This indeed prevails not only within the limits of Christendom, but among all our race.

Now, therefore, the affirmation is, that over all this opposition the Bible is destined to triumph! Do you ask—How? when? where? Do you say, It requires strong faith to assure one of this? For lo! the vast, passive, stolid, ignorant, superstitious, vicious, obstinate opposition of Paganism, Mohammedanism, and Judaism! And lo! the zealous, active, widespread, various, subtle, searching, insidious, unrelenting opposition within our own Christian borders! Can it be that all this shall be overcome? Certainly: all this, and more than this, if there be any more, both can and will be overcome: more certainly than that the sun shall rise to-morrow.

Remember how, from the beginning, God has magnified His word above all His name. Remember that there was a time, more than three thousand years ago, before the first book of the Bible was written. Whatever was known of God, then, was learned from His works, or received by tradition from such of the patriarchs as had held oral communication with Him or His messengers. The intelligence thus accumulated was incidental and imperfect. Something was necessary, more correct and complete, and in a form better adapted to perpetual preservation. Then it was, that, to begin at least the supply of this necessity, Moses, by divine inspiration, composed the book of Genesis. Think of it!—that first inspired record! There alone it existed, a single, autograph volume, in an encampment of emancipated slaves, in the Arabian desert. And yet, even of that one manuscript, it might have been said, God has magnified His word above all His name; for never before was He so gloriously revealed to mankind, either by natural symbols or in personal interviews. Next, by the same author, followed Exodus, Leviticus, Numbers, and Deuteronomy, so perfecting what has ever since been styled the Law of Moses. Then, after the entrance into Canaan, succeeded Joshua, Judges, Ruth, First and Second Samuel, and First Chronicles. Perhaps the book of Job was written in the early part of the same period. So far we have twelve books. Then came the Psalms, chiefly, indeed, by David, but in part by other authors, and occupying, in whole, some five hundred years. The one containing our text is entitled, A Psalm of David. If David was its author, he must have referred, in the text, to the twelve books just mentioned. Thou hast magnified Thy word, as found in these twelve books, above all Thy name. Notwithstanding its title, however, this

Psalm is assigned, by some chronologists, to a later date—even so late as the dedication of the second temple, on which occasion they supposed it was sung. If this be correct, then, in the interval, about twenty other books had been added, and the text must be regarded as applying to thirty-two in all. Seven books of the Old Testament, and all the books of the New Testament, are thus omitted from the original application of the text. That is, the Psalmist, whoever he was, and whenever he lived, is not to be understood as affirming, primarily, of the whole Bible, just as we have it—the sixty-six books of the Old and New Testaments both—that God has magnified His word, in *this* form, above all His name; but, as a matter of course, he affirmed this only of the inspired records which were then extant, unless prophetically, whether twelve, twenty or more. At most, they were only a part of the Old Testament; and yet, just as they stood, they were crowned by Jehovah, in the presence of the universe, with this incomparable honor. It will appear, on a little reflection, that this contemplation is of importance in the progress of our discussion.

See! Before the production of those books, and during the ages in which they were produced, heaven and earth were as full of the natural symbols of the Divine existence, character, and government as they are now. Creation and providence everywhere displayed their permanent and changeable wonders—sun and moon, stars and comets, continents and oceans, day and night, and the rolling seasons. Nay, more, society had already assumed organic forms, more or less resembling Church and State, and claiming the right, by Divine authority, to impart instruction and enforce obedience in the high relations of religion and law. Still further, as already intimated, amidst the abounding false pretensions, there was a traditional line of true revelation, which had come down from the beginning, though not designed as continuously adequate to the growing wants of the world. But when, in after ages, the Almighty would direct attention to His grandest disclosures of truth—to the noblest means He had employed to accelerate and improve the progress of mankind—whither did He point? To sun or moon? star or comet? earth, air, or sea? day or night? spring, summer, autumn, or winter? Had He spent the centuries in embellishing with new and more splendid significance the immensity of creation? or in giving clearer voice and juster harmony to the innumerable instrumentalities of providence? Had He ever appeared in our noonday sky, teaching the nations in tones reverberating from pole to pole? Had He ever taken His stand among the stars and written His will, in sight of the

world, with his own right hand, on the smooth firmament, in lines of indelible lightning? No, no; the
vast circles of creation, providence, and society, remained as they were. God had done more than all
this, and was content to point to the few parchment
records among His chosen people, in. their little sea-
coast heritage, and proclaim to men and angels that
He had magnified His word, as thus given to them,
above all His name! There the Sun of the Law, and
the Moon of the Prophecy, far more magnificent than
the lights of nature and the miracles of providence,
at the command of our greater Joshua, stood still,
not for a day only, but for ages on ages, shining on
Zion and all the realm around it, with a glory and
beauty nowhere else disclosed, and with results of
victory.

It is astonishing how men are imposed upon by
the material, even by matter without life. There is
a bowlder; here is a grain of wheat. The bowlder
weighs a thousand tons; the grain scarcely anything.
But the bowlder is a great thing, and the grain a
little thing. Bowl the bowlder around the globe,
east and west, north and south. Try every soil with
it, and every climate. Let it rest a century for each
experiment. And what is the result? 'Tis the same
bowlder still, only worn by the abrasion and exposure.
Meantime, some one has planted the grain of wheat

in the centre of the Mississippi valley; and while you are vainly bowling the bowlder, he sees the wheat run eastward to the Alleghanies, westward to the Rocky Mountains, over both to the Atlantic and the Pacific, and northward and southward toward both poles, annually whitening into a universal harvest. What difference can it make whether the truth be revealed *on* a world, or *in* a word? The word is nothing, and the world is nothing—the truth is all. What is the truth? *that* is the question. Would you understand, more perfectly, *how* it is that God has magnified His word above all His name?—how He did thus magnify even the part of it to which the text originally referred? Behold, how easy, and how satisfactory, the answer! It was—by the truth He put in it: that truth which is spirit and life. And what truth did He put in it? Take Genesis—the first book. Take the first chapter. Take the first verse. And hark!—"In the beginning God created the heavens and the earth." What now? May I not ask, with equal reverence and confidence, could God himself improve that? Would it be any improvement to make the first heaven, the second heaven, the third heaven, or the heaven of heavens, all ablaze with it? Would it be any simpler or sublimer in itself, or could we understand it any better? Is it not complete? Take the third verse: "And

God said, Let there be light; and there was light."
Is not that absolutely perfect? Is it not next to the
creation of the light—the one God's act, and the other
just as evidently his own declaration of the act? If
all the light in the universe were employed in re-
peating the record to the utmost reach of immensity,
it would be no plainer or grander than it now is.
Take the twenty-sixth and twenty-seventh verses:
"And God said, Let us make man, in our image,
after our likeness; and let them have dominion over
the fish of the sea, and over the fowl of the air, and
over the cattle, and over all the earth, and over every
creeping thing that creepeth upon the earth. So, God
created man, in His own image, in the image of God
created He him; male and female created He them."
Was it possible for the Almighty to give greater
dignity to humanity than by such a revelation as
that? Who can even imagine a truth more exalted, or
a form more fit for its conveyance to our race? And
so with the whole chapter. Its Divine intelligence is
worthy to be embodied in the amplest and most illustrious symbols of the universe; but it has pleased
God the rather to enshrine it in His word, and so He
has magnified His word above all His name.

This, however, is merely the beginning: the first
chapter of the first book. And what shall I say
of the additional truth in the forty-nine other chap-

ters of this same book, narrating, as they do, the controlling events of the world, from the creation to the death of the patriarch Joseph—an interval of more than twenty-three centuries? Think of the original condition of moral and physical perfection in Paradise. Think of the introduction of sin, and its awful consequences, universal and perpetual. Think of the promise of redemption. Think of the world before the Flood. Think of the Flood itself, and its effects in all the earth. Think of the world after the Flood. Think of the covenant with Noah. Think of the division of the earth. Think of the confusion of tongues. Think of the separation of the nations. Think of the prevalence of idolatry. Think of the call of Abraham, and of the covenant with him and his seed for ever. Think of the descent of the Israelites into Egypt; and so come again to the close of this first book. Within this range, we have the history of more than a third of the duration of the world: the history both of nature and society, and of the manifestations of God Himself, personally and by His angels, in government of both. Moreover, prophecies are interspersed through all the record, taking hold on all time and extending into eternity. This is the truth in the case; truth of vital importance to the honor of our Maker and the welfare of our race. God has magnified this part of His word by committing this truth to its keeping; and magnified it above all His name, inasmuch as it is truth which can be found nowhere else, and which, notwithstanding all opposition, ancient and modern, has been sacredly maintained, in this form, free from any fatal error, through the vicissitudes of all generations. Does God uphold the universe? Not more certainly than he guards, sanctions, and sustains His own authority in the Book of Genesis.

It is a common thing for preachers to make frequent reference to the beginning, as described in this book. Some complain of this. The complaint is unjust. Such references are inevitable. The prophets made them. The apostles made them. Our Saviour Himself made them. They are essential to the understanding of our Holy Religion, and of most, if not all, of the greatest problems which agitate modern society. To say the least of it, the Book of Genesis is as important this moment, as it ever was. "Thy word is true from the beginning," said the Psalmist: "and every one of Thy righteous judgments endureth forever." So of this particular book. Like Christ Himself, whose works of creation it narrates, and whose works of redemption it predicts, it is "the same, yesterday, to-day, and forever." It is styled *Breshith*—"In the beginning," and is designed to connect the beginning with the end.

And what now? It is obviously impracticable to notice, even thus briefly, each of the books originally alluded to in the text. But, the next in order, the book of Exodus, must not be passed without some special attention. I need not describe the servile sufferings of the Israelites in Egypt, nor the mission of Moses, nor the smiting of the oppressors, nor the deliverance of the oppressed, nor their subsistence in the desert, nor the great variety of minor statutes and judgments enjoined upon them. When I ask, How did God magnify the book of Exodus, in particular, above all His name? What truth did He put into this part of His word?—the first grand and mighty answer comes: He committed to it, from His own vocal rehearsal, and from His own stone-wrought autograph, the perfect purity of the Moral Law—the transcript of the Decalogue—the Ten Command-ments, as though numbered upon His fingers, to show their completeness; the Two Tables, as though the stretching forth of His hands, all thrilling with omnipotence, to grasp the palpitating conscience of the world, and hold it fast forever.

In this instance, God did manifest himself person-ally: not among the stars, indeed, nor yet in the zenith of our own sky, nor to all the nations of the earth, but on the top of one of the noblest mountains of the globe, in open day, and in the presence of the twelve tribes; not visibly, indeed, except as to the clouds which enshrined Him, but more distinctly audible than trumpet or thunder, searching the souls of all with overpowering solemnity, and causing them to shrink from the terrible glory in fear of instant death.   Hark! and as you hearken, think—think how little would be gained, if such words were inscribed on the firmament or sounded from the planets, "And God spake all these words, saying:"

"I am the Lord thy God, which have brought thee out of the land of Egypt, out of the house of bondage.

" Thou shalt have no other gods before me.

" Thou shalt not make unto thee any graven image, or any likeness of any thing that is in heaven above, or that is in the earth beneath, or that is in the water under the earth: thou shalt not bow down thyself to them, nor serve them; for I the Lord thy God am a jealous God, visiting the iniquity of the fathers upon the children unto the third and fourth generations of them that hate me; and showing mercy unto thousands of them that love me, and keep my commandments.

"Thou shalt not take the name of the Lord thy God in vain; for the Lord will not hold him guiltless that taketh his name in vain.

" Remember the Sabbath-day to keep it holy.   Six

days shalt thou labour, and do all thy work : but the seventh day is the Sabbath of the Lord thy God : in it thou shalt not do any work, thou, nor thy son, nor thy daughter, thy man-servant, nor thy maid-servant, nor thy cattle, nor thy stranger that is within thy gates : for in six days the Lord made heaven and earth, the sea, and all that in them is, and rested the seventh day : wherefore the Lord blessed the Sabbath-day, and hallowed it.

" Honour thy father and thy mother ; that thy days may be long upon the land which the Lord thy God giveth thee.

" Thou shalt not kill.

" Thou shalt not commit adultery.

" Thou shalt not steal.

" Thou shalt not bear false witness against thy neighbour.

" Thou shalt not covet thy neighbour's house, thou shalt not covet thy neighbour's wife, nor his man-servant, nor his maid-servant, nor his ox, nor his ass, nor any thing that is thy neighbour's."

Who can imagine the awful sublimity of such scenery, such a voice, such commandments, and such a conscious nearness of God ! No wonder that the people, witnessing " the thunderings, and the lightnings, and the noise of the trumpet, and the moun-

tain smoking"—"removed and stood afar off!" No
wonder "they said unto Moses, Speak thou with us,
and we will hear: but let not God speak with us, lest
we die!" How amazingly did Jehovah then "magnify" His "word" above all "His name!"

But there is another instance in this book, of similar grandeur. True, it is a revelation, made directly
to Moses alone; but, through him, it was made to
Israel and the world. It is of the utmost importance.
I allude to the proclamation of the name of Jehovah;
with its moral significance; as recorded in the thirty-
fourth chapter. You may remember, that in the 6th
chapter, "God spake unto Moses, and said unto
him, I am the Lord; and I appeared unto Abraham,
unto Isaac, and unto Jacob, by the name of God
Almighty; but by my name Jehovah was I not
known to them." And yet, in Genesis, the name of
Jehovah occurs, frequently, from the time of Adam
down. Critics have been greatly perplexed by this
fact; and many theories have been proposed to account for it. Some of these may be satisfactory
enough; and yet, it seems to me that there is another
perhaps more satisfactory. I mean this:—that, ad-
mitting that the *name* of Jehovah *was* known to the
patriarchs, they did *not* know the *nature* of God *by*
this name, for, the *meaning* of it was not particularly
revealed to them. *They* needed to know the *power*

of God more than his other attributes; and therefore
he manifested himself unto them by the name of God
Almighty."   In his covenant with Abraham, for instance, he said :—" I am the Almighty God : walk
before me and be thou perfect.   And I will make my
covenant between me and thee, and will multiply
thee exceedingly."—" And I will make thee exceeding faithful, and I will make nations of thee, and
kings shall come out of thee."—"And I will give
unto thee, and to thy seed after thee, the *land* wherein thou art a stranger, all the land of Canaan, for an
everlasting possession; and I will be their God."
All this, as you perceive, addressed to a man nearly
a hundred years old, required special confidence in
the creative and proprietary omnipotence of him who
gave the promise, and therefore it was introduced by
the declaration, "I am the Almighty God."   But,
now, to Moses, and to the Israelites in whole, it was
desirable, and not only desirable but necessary, that
there should be a more complete revelation of the
Divine nature—a revelation, not only of his natural
attributes, but more particularly, of his moral character.   And this more complete revelation, as we
shall see, was granted, by making known, for the
first time, what the patriarchs had not known, the
meaning of the name Jehovah.   They may have
known the *name*, but, if they did, *that* was all, or

nearly *all*. Its *meaning* was either *not* known or
very imperfectly known, until, as we shall see, it was
revealed unto Moses: and, through him, to Israel
and to the world, fully and forever.

Moses was oppressed by the responsibility of his
office as the Leader of Israel, and, having no trust but
in God, he was exceedingly anxious to know the prevailing dispositions, or moral principles of the Divine
Nature, in relation especially to such a sinful, ignorant, rebellious set of people as these emancipated
slaves were. He seems to have feared that God would
abandon them, as utterly unworthy his further protection and care, and so that the whole enterprise
should fail. He had seen proofs enough of the
strength of God's *arm*, but what was the controlling
feeling of his *heart?* *This* was what he wanted to
know; and, therefore, when God had assured him
that he would *not* forsake them, Moses added this
one more prayer—" I beseech thee, show me thy
glory;" or, as it has been rendered by some, " I beseech thee, show me thy *heart*"—thine essential and
controlling nature. And the Lord said—" I will
make all my *goodness* pass before thee, and I will
proclaim the name of JEHOVAH before thee; and
will be *gracious* to whom I will be gracious, and will
show *mercy* on whom I will show mercy." So, at
the appointed time and place, while Moses stood in

the cleft of the rock on Mount Sinai, Jehovah descended in the cloud, and stood with him there, and proclaimed the *name* of Jehovah. And Jehovah passed by before him, and proclaimed, JEHOVAH, JEHOVAH God, *merciful* and *gracious, long-suffering*, and *abundant* in *goodness* and *truth, keeping mercy* for *thousands, forgiving iniquity* and *transgression* and *sin*, and that will by no means clear the guilty; visiting the iniquity of the fathers upon the children, and upon the children's children, unto the third and to the fourth generation!"

No wonder that when Moses heard this, he " made haste, bowed his head toward the earth, and worshipped." He had been favored with the grandest disclosure of the Divine character ever made; and under circumstances never to be forgotten. And, not only as regarded previous history, but, also, for fifteen hundred years afterward, or for more than four thousand years in all, this continued to be the grandest proclamation of the nature of God. There can be no doubt that it was intended to be the standard representation, for remembrance and reference, especially among the Israelites, through all the ages of their national existence. It was a kind of argument, or plea, with which Jehovah purposely provided them in advance, to encourage them to come to his throne, and assure them that, notwithstanding their sins, they would always, as penitents, find it to be a throne of Grace, a Mercy-Seat, where they might "obtain mercy, and find grace to help" them, in every "time of need." It was a revelation never surpassed until the personal advent of Christ.

It has often been in my heart to trace the influence of this Standard Proclamation of the meaning of the name Jehovah, as manifest in the later books of Scripture: for, in reading these books, I have often met the indications of this influence. In the present instance, particularly, I thought of doing this; but, having made the examinations necessary to such an exhibition, I find that the illustrations are entirely too numerous for such an occasion. A selection of these, however, it may be desirable to notice.

I begin with Moses himself. No sooner was the proclamation made, than he proceeded, with grateful and humble boldness, to take advantage of it, in behalf of the sinful tribes around him. Having bowed his head and worshipped, he immediately offered this prayer: "If now I have found grace in thy sight, O JEHOVAH, let JEHOVAH, I pray thee, go among *us;* for *it,* (or *this*) is a stiff-necked people; and pardon *our* iniquity, and *our* sin, and take *us* for thine inheritance."

Again, in the 14th ch. of *Numbers,* JEHOVAH is represented as about to *destroy* the Israelites, utterly,

22

for their great *provocations;* and then MOSES pleads
with him again on the same ground, saying: " If
thou—kill all this people as one man, then the nations which have heard the fame of thee will speak,
saying, Because JEHOVAH was not *able* to bring this
people into the land which he sware unto them, *therefore* he hath slain them in the wilderness. And now,
I beseech thee, let the *power* of my Lord be great,
according as thou hast spoken"—See !—" saying, JE-
HOVAH is *long-suffering,* and of *great mercy, forgiving
iniquity* and *transgression,* and by no means clearing
the guilty, visiting the iniquity of the fathers upon
the children unto the third and fourth generation.
Pardon, I beseech thee, the iniquity of *this* people,
according unto the greatness of thy mercy, and as
thou hast forgiven this people, from Egypt even until
now.   And JEHOVAH said, I *have* pardoned according to thy word : but, as truly as I live, all the earth
shall be filled with the glory of JEHOVAH."   So, instead of instantly destroying them, he turned them
back into the wilderness, to pass their lives there, and
afford an opportunity to raise up a braver and hardier
generation.   So when DAVID brought up the *ark,* he
ordered Asaph and his brethren to sing : " O, give
thanks unto JEHOVAH, for he is *good,* and his *mercy*
endureth forever."

So, when SOLOMON dedicated the temple to the

worship and glory of JEHOVAH, he prayed, again and again, that, as the NAME of JEHOVAH was to abide there, whenever his people, however sinful, should turn to him, and " *confess his name,*" in time of *war,* or of *drought,* or of *famine,* or of *pestilence,* or of far-off *captivity,* and *pray* unto him, and make *supplication* unto him, he would *hear,* and *forgive,* and *forgive,* and still *forgive, remembering* his *covenant* with their fathers, and cherishing them still as his chosen inheritance.

So, at the restoration of worship, under NEHEMIAH, in connection with the *second* temple, the Levites, after confessing the transgressions of the nation, added—" But, thou art a God ready to pardon, gracious and merciful, slow to anger, and of great kindness."

So, in the prayer of DANIEL :—" O LORD, to us belongs confusion of face, to our kings, to our princes, and to our fathers, because we have sinned against thee "—but—" to the LORD, our god, belong *mercies* and *forgiveness.*" And again : " We do not present our supplications before thee, for *our* righteousness, but, for thy great *mercies.* O LORD, hear ; O LORD, forgive : O LORD, hearken and do ; defer not, for thine own sake, O my God, for thy city and thy people are called by thy *name*"—that is, by the name of JEHOVAH.

So, in the exhortation of HOSEA—"O Israel, return unto JEHOVAH, thy God; for thou hast fallen by *thine iniquity.* Take with you *words*"—what words but the old words of Sinai?—"and turn unto JEHOVAH, and say unto him, Take away *all iniquity,* and receive us *graciously.*"

So, also, in the prophecy of JOEL—"Therefore also now, saith JEHOVAH, Turn ye to me with all your heart, and with fasting, and with weeping, and with mourning; and rend your heart, and not your garments, and turn unto JEHOVAH, your God: *for*—he is *gracious,* and *merciful, slow* to *anger,* and of *great kindness,* and *repenteth* him of the evil."

So, likewise, in the prayer of JONAH—the impatient prophet, if I may so style him. And here I may glance, in passing, at a strange mistake made by one of the most learned and celebrated of modern Biblical critics, in this connection. Looking at his remarks on JONAH, especially in relation to JONAH's anger, I was surprised to find it said:—"*That God* is *merciful* to the *penitent,* wherever they are found, he *did not know.*" And yet the passage in his prayer, which I was just about to cite, *proves* plainly enough that he *did* know all about it:—for—"He prayed unto JEHOVAH, and said, I pray thee, O JEHOVAH, was not this my saying, when I was yet in *my* country? Therefore I fled unto Tarshish: *for I knew* that thou art a *gracious* God, and merciful, slow to anger, and of great kindness, and repentest thee of the evil."

So, again, in MICAH. "Who is a God like unto thee, that *pardoneth iniquity*, and passeth by the *transgression* of the remnant of his heritage? he retaineth not his *anger forever*, because he *delighteth* in *mercy*. He will turn again, he will have compassion upon *us;* he will subdue *our* iniquities; and thou wilt cast all their sins into the depths of the sea. Thou wilt perform the truth to JACOB, and the *mercy* to ABRAHAM, which thou hast sworn unto *our fathers* from the days of old."

In like manner I might refer to the PSALMS— many, many thrilling passages, but a very few will be enough :—

Thus in the 86th—"Rejoice the soul of thy servant; for unto thee, O JEHOVAH, do I lift up my soul. For thou, JEHOVAH, art *good*, and ready to *forgive;* and *plenteous* in *mercy* unto all them that call upon thee."

So in the 103d—"JEHOVAH made known his *ways* unto MOSES, his acts unto the children of ISRAEL. JEHOVAH is *merciful* and *gracious*, *slow* to *anger*, and *plenteous* in *mercy*."

So in the 130th—" Let Israel hope in JEHOVAH: for with JEHOVAH there is *mercy*, and with him is *plenteous redemption.* And he shall redeem Israel from all his iniquities."

So in the 145th.—"JEHOVAH is *gracious*, and full of *compassion*, slow to *anger*, and of great *mercy*. JEHOVAH is *good to all*, and his *tender mercies* are over all his work."

As for the 136th Ps.—it both begins and ends with thanksgiving for mercy—"O give thanks unto JE-HOVAH: for he is good; for his *mercy* endureth for-ever." "O give thanks unto the God of heaven, for his mercy endureth forever." And *every one* of its *twenty-six* verses, closes with this glad refrain—"for his mercy endureth forever."

It seems as if *Christ*, or JEHOVAH, on Sinai, were speaking not only to Moses, or to Israel, but to the whole world, his voice, of divinest music, sounding down through all the ages—JEHOVAH, JEHOVAH GOD.

PART II.

And, what now? To pass through all the Scrip-tural books, after the manner in which Genesis and Exodus were noticed, is manifestly impracticable. Two books, thus reviewed, on each occasion, would require thirty-three sermons for the whole sixty-six. The questions, in relation to each one, would be—*How* did God magnify *this* book above all his name? What *special* truth did he commit to *this portion* of his word? And these would be very interesting questions too, with very important answers: but, we have not time for them.

Instead of that course, I propose the following: to remind you, as readers of the Scriptures, and in a summary way, of these great facts—that God magnified those parts of his word which were extant in the time of the Psalmist; and afterward magnified the later books of the Old Testament; and finally magnified the books of the New Testament, also, thus completing the whole canon of Scripture, by committing to them certain HISTORICAL truth, and DOCTRINAL truth, and LEGAL truth, and COVENANT truth, and PROMISSORY and PROPHETICAL truth, infinitely transcending any thing elsewhere to be found in nature or society.

First, as to the twelve books extant in the time of the Psalmist, and to which, of course, he alluded in the text. Of these, we have already sufficiently noticed Genesis and Exodus.

Glance, then, at the *Historical* truth committed to the others. From MOSES to DAVID was an interval of some four hundred and fifty years. The history of this period is found in these books. "LEVITICUS," indeed, is chiefly occupied with laws. "NUMBERS" continues the history of the wanderings of the Desert:

bringing the Tribes from Sinai to the land of Moab, and recording the transactions in the plains of Moab, until the appointment of JOSHUA as the successor of MOSES, and the provision made for the partitioning of the Promised Land, when its conquest should be sufficiently completed. "DEUTERONOMY" repeats the history of the four preceding books, and exalts the whole idea of its importance.—Then, leaving the five books of MOSES, we come to that of "JOSHUA;" in which we find the history of the occupation of the Promised Land, its division, and the ratification of the Law at Ebal and Gerizim—with the last address of JOSHUA to the people, his death and burial. Next comes the book of "JUDGES," giving the history of the ISRAELITES in the interim from the death of JOSHUA until the death of SAMSON, and near to the time of ELI and SAMUEL; with all the vicissitudes of war and peace, conquest and captivity, under the twelve or thirteen JUDGES, when there was no king in Israel, and comparatively little authority was exercised by any one: "every man," as it is written, doing "that which was right in his own eyes." Next comes that beautiful little gem of the Old Testament —that elegant and pathetic sketch of rural life—the book of "RUTH"—with its important genealogy of the house of DAVID, Gentile as well as Jewish. Next come the two books of "SAMUEL," chiefly devoted to the reigns of SAUL and DAVID; and the first book of "CHRONICLES," containing a sort of genealogical and historical review, from the creation to the commencement of the reign of SOLOMON. The book of "JOB," probably, finds its origin somewhere during the production of the books already named; and the "PSALMS," in part, occupy the same interval. These make twelve complete books, with a portion of the thirteenth—including the *text*. "JOB" and the "PSALMS," indeed, though comprising many historical facts, are mainly poetical compositions. Whoever shall reflect upon the historic range thus referred to, will soon be convinced that the truth thus recorded, notwithstanding its connection with many things at first sight of a merely national and transient character, is elevated into extraordinary, superhuman, and even Divine dignity, by its manifest close relation to the whole plan and progress of the world's redemption. It is this, which makes the great difference between this and all other history—as we shall see more clearly hereafter.

Glance, next, at the *Doctrinal* truth committed to these books. Here, in addition to what has already been said, of both God and man, it is necessary only to refer to one grand point. I mean—the MOSAIC CREED. This creed consisted of only one article— but that was infinitely sublime, all-comprehensive, and peculiarly distinctive—cutting off, at a stroke, in design, though not in actual practice, all communion of the Israelites, in religious matters at least, with the idolatrous nations around them. I allude, of course, to the proclamation made by MOSES, to the Chosen People, as recorded in the sixth chapter of " Deuteronomy : "—" Hear, O Israel, the Lord our God is one Lord : " or, Hear, O Israel, JEHOVAH, our God, is one JEHOVAH !—This was the foundation doctrine of the *Jewish* Church—just as one other article is the foundation doctrine of the *Christian* Church : for it may be affirmed, with entire assurance of truth, that both these Churches are founded on creeds, consisting each of only *one* article, and that one is enough. How did God magnify His word above all His name? by enshrining within it forever the essential truth of the Unity of His Nature ! The untaught heathen collected the nation of *many* gods from the diverse forms and forces of the natural world ; and the Israelites might have done the same. Indeed, they did frequently yield to this notion, consenting to the idolatrous temptations and enchantments about them. But the challenge to the Chosen People was : Hear, O Israel, the Lord our God is one Lord !—just as the challenge *might now be* —Hear, O Christians ! JESUS is the CHRIST ; the SON of the LIVING GOD ! Therefore said our Saviour, for this was all it was necessary to say—" Ye believe in GOD, believe also in ME." As *Jews*, ye believe in *God;* now become Christians by believing in *me*.

Glance, next, at the *Legal* truth embodied in these books. On a former occasion, we noticed the *Moral* law; but now it is in place to remember, also, the *Ceremonial* and *Civil* laws. As to the *Ceremonial* law, that related to the Tabernacle, with its Holy and Most Holy Places, its Furniture, and Priesthood, and Sacrifices, and Offerings, all of which were important as preservatives against the false religions of the heathen nations; and, moreover, symbolical of better things to come—the spiritual distinctions of the Gospel dispensation. By studying the Epistle to the Hebrews, in connection with the book of Leviticus, the spiritual significancy of the Mosaic ritual becomes exceedingly plain and impressive. As to the *Civil* law, that maintained the most intimate relations to the *Moral* law, and seems, indeed, to have been designed to apply and enforce the *Moral* law, in all personal, social, and national affairs. Its adaptations were to a great extent *local;* and, of course, the whole system, as a literal formulary, like the *Ceremonial* law associated with it, was intended only for temporary prevalence. Still, this I presume may be affirmed, without the slightest hesitancy, that, for the time, there were no laws in the world, either Ceremonial or Civil, to compare with these for a moment. Their wisdom was manifestly Divine.

Glance, also, at the *Covenant* truth recorded in these books. This is a highly interesting contemplation. For instance, the two covenants with Adam— first, the covenant of works, before the fall; and secondly the covenant of Grace, after the fall. As to the first, "The Lord God," as it is written, "took the man, and put him into the Garden of Eden, to dress it and to keep it. And the Lord God commanded the man, saying, Of every tree of the garden thou mayest freely eat; but of the tree of the knowledge of good and evil thou shalt not eat of it; for in the day thou eatest thereof thou shalt surely die"—or— "dying thou shalt die"—that is, beginning to die thou shalt continue to die until the process of death is complete. As to the second, the covenant of Grace, that, of course, followed the fall, and is distinguished, chiefly, by the assurance that the Seed of the Woman should bruise the serpent's head—though with this is connected the painful doom of woman, and the toilsome doom of man—both, though seemingly severe, really gracious. Next comes the *Covenant* with NOAH—when the LORD said, in his heart:—"I will not again curse the ground any more for man's sake; for the imagination of man's heart is evil from his youth: neither will I again smite any more every living thing as I have done. While the earth re-maineth, seed time and harvest, and cold and heat, and summer and winter, and day and night, shall not cease." Then came the more extended and expressive annunciation of it, with the appointment of the Rain-bow Seal of it, sanctioning and sustaining it, forever.

Next came the covenant with ABRAHAM: as-suring him that his seed should be as numerous as the stars of heaven, and the sands upon the sea-shore; that the land of Canaan should be given to his descendants in the line of Isaac, for a pos-session; and that in his seed all the nations of the earth should be blessed. This, in various forms, but the same in substance, was several times repeated, and most solemnly confirmed. It was succeeded, also, by similar covenants with ISAAC and JACOB, personally, and even with JUDAH, indirectly, in their day and generation.

Next came the great National Covenant with MOSES: set forth in the four last books of MOSES, as well, indeed, as in the Old Testament generally: with all its sanctions, and all its rewards for the obedient, and all its punishments for the disobedient.

Then, finally, so far as this present section of our subject is concerned, came the covenant with DAVID, himself, the supposed *author* of the *text*. And, in-deed, it may be that the Psalmist has some *reference*, in this Psalm, to *this covenant:* though it is more plainly alluded to elsewhere. In the 132d, for instance, it is said—"The LORD hath sworn in truth unto DAVID, he will not turn from it: Of the fruit of thy body will I set upon thy throne. If thy children will keep my *covenant,* and my *testimony* that I shall teach them, their children also shall sit upon thy throne, forevermore."

These covenants, as we may see more fully hereafter, reaching, as they do, from ADAM to NOAH, and from NOAH to ABRAHAM, and from ABRAHAM to MOSES, and from MOSES to DAVID, are altogether without parallel in any other history: and pre-eminently on this account, or for this reason, that they are all connected with the incomparable work of the world's redemption. They magnify the word of God above all His name.

But, glance also at the *Prophetic* truth embodied in these books. The *strength* of this point is to be developed in another connection: but, even here, in view of the books extant in the time of DAVID, it may be affirmed that God had wonderfully magnified His name by the *prophetic* truth entrusted to them. The *Prophets* predicted many things in relation to prominent *persons,* both of their own and of other times and countries; and, in like manner, they foretold the destinies of foreign nations, both near and

remote—especially of those most adjacent to their own
land, or most frequently brought in contact with their
own people. But, as it was with the miracles of
Christ, during his ministry on earth—miracles not
constituting the object of His mission, but being
merely incidental to His progress as He passed on
toward the Cross, and the One Great Purpose of His
Coming, the making of an atonement for the sins of
the world by His sufferings and death: so with the
Prophets—their predictions in relation to mere men,
and their transient kingdoms, were only the *incidents*
of their course—illustrations of the reality and power
of their Divine inspiration, rather than the fulfilment
of the One Grand and Distinctive Object of their
Office. *That* Object was—to bear their testimony to
the coming of Christ—to foreshow the advent and
work of the Son of God and Saviour of the world.
Therefore, it is written—that "the testimony of
Christ is the spirit of prophecy;" and again, that
"to Him give *all* the prophets witness." Of course,
even *before* DAVID's *time*, as well as *in* his time, and,
indeed, in part, by his *own* agency, as *one* of the
prophets, Christ was foretold. The coming of Christ,
indeed, was already the great burden of prophecy,
and had been from the beginning of the world. The
PATRIARCHAL dispensation, as well as the MOSAIC,
was full of types of Christ, and promises of Christ.

Histories, Doctrines, Laws and *Covenants*, all had prophetic relations to Him.   But, *specific declarations* were not wanting: some of them, indeed, not made by the prophets, but by the LORD himself.   So to the *Serpent*—" *He* shall *bruise* thy head, and *thou* shalt *bruise* his " *heel.*"   So to ABRAHAM : " In thy Seed, shall all the nations of the earth be blessed ; because thou hast obeyed my voice."   In other cases, *human agents* gave the utterance: So with JACOB, just before his death :—" The Sceptre shall not depart from JUDAH, nor a lawgiver from between his feet, until SHILOH come ; and to Him shall the gathering of the people be."   So with MOSES—not long before *his* death—" The Lord said unto me,—I will raise them up a *Prophet* from among their brethren, like unto thee, and will put my words in his mouth; and he shall speak unto them all that I shall command him."   So with DAVID himself—or, rather, with the writer of the 2d Psalm, whoever he was—" Thou art my SON, this day have I begotten thee."   And so with the 110th Psalm, which is ascribed to DAVID, even by our Saviour himself : " The LORD said unto *my* LORD, Sit thou at my right hand, until I make thine enemies thy footstool."   Such passages, taken together, and in their connection with the whole system of typical sacrifice and worship, were even then significant of the promised Redeemer.

But now, *see!* This is the way our argument runs —accumulating strength as it passes from point to point. If, in review of the HISTORICAL truth, and DOCTRINAL truth, and LEGAL truth, and COVENANT truth, and PROPHETICAL truth, all connected with the great scheme of Redemption ; and all found in the twelve or thirteen books supposed to be extant in the time of our Psalmist, the author of the text, it was true and right to affirm, so solemnly and decisively, "Thou hast magnified thy word above all thy name :" what shall be said, in view of the fact, that, *after* this time, *twenty-six* other books were added to the canon of the OLD Testament, and that, to *all* of them, God committed *further* revelations of truth, richer and richer, brighter and brighter, illuminating with surpassing splendor the centuries heralding the advent of His Son.

See! Of these *twenty-six* additional books, *six* are HISTORICAL—viz: 1st and 2d KINGS: 2d CHRONICLES: EZRA, NEHEMIAH, and ESTHER: *three* are POETICAL—PROVERBS, ECCLESIASTES, and the SONG OF SOLOMON : and *seventeen* are PROPHETICAL—including the *Major* prophets from ISAIAH to DANIEL, and the *Minor* prophets, from HOSEA to MALACHI. And what now? Who can think of this varied, beautiful, and sublime range of inspiration, even for a moment, without being overpowered by the remem-

brance of the grandeur of the truth committed to
these books, and of the glorious manner in which
God has thus magnified his word above all his name!
Why the one book of ISAIAH alone, would furnish
themes for the eloquent and joyful expatiation of an
angel for a thousand years. And then—to think of
DANIEL's succession of human kingdoms, and ultimate establishment of the Kingdom of God! But,
there is no time to dwell on any of these topics.

Still the cumulative argument advances: for, if
God so wonderfully magnified his word above all his
name, by committing such truth as that to which I
have alluded to the books of the *Old* Testament;
then, again, what shall be said in regard to the fact,
that, *after this* time also,—*i.e.*, some four centuries
later, *twenty-seven* other books, constituting the whole
of the *New* Testament, were added to the Old—so
completing the *entire* canon of Sacred Scripture. And,
such books! Not occupied by types and shadows,
rites and ceremonies, brief promises and prophecies
sometimes mystical or vague; not telling over and
over again, from age to age, the old story, and
the old hope, that the time was coming, when the
Divine Redeemer, first declared in Eden, and afterward waited for through thousands of slow-rolling
years, should actually and personally come: but, an-
nouncing, once and forever, the good news, the glad

tidings, the transcendent and omnipotent verity, that
HE HAS COME! the four great witnesses, MATTHEW,
MARK, LUKE, and JOHN, turning toward the four
quarters of the world, and, like the *North* wind, and
the *South* wind, and the *East* wind, and the *West*
wind, with all their gales and thunders blowing their
angel trumpets, as though just handed down to them
from the throne of God, startling the *poles* and shak-
ing the *equator* with the indubitable demonstrations
of the visible, audible, palpable presence, and ministry, wisdom and power, grace and glory, of the Only-
Begotten and Dearly Beloved Son of the Highest;
Eve's Comfort, Abraham's Seed, Jacob's Shiloh,
David's Heir, Isaiah's Prince of Peace, Jeremiah's
Lord our Righteousness, and Haggai's Desire of all
Nations, the One Peerless Object of the Whole
World's Hope—working miracles, preaching and
teaching, eating and drinking, sleeping and waking,
journeying and resting, humbling Himself to the
lowest, forgiving the vilest, cherishing the poorest,
exalting the most abased, and passing steadily on to
the grand consummation, for which he left the Bosom
of His Father and the Palace of the Universe, even
to the Garden of Gethsemane, and the Cross of Calvary, and the Tomb of the Arimathean, and the
Summit of Olivet, that He might agonize for us, and
die for us, and be buried for us, and rise again for us,

and ascend to heaven for us, and take His place at the right hand of the Father again for us, "ever living to make *intercession* for us," and so promote our final, and perfect, and everlasting triumph, over all our adversaries, and over all our adversities, in the inheritance of the blissful kingdom that shall never pass away. Eighteen hundred years have gone by, and still there is no music in any wind of heaven, like the music of the Gospel of our Lord and Saviour Jesus Christ. And not only do MATTHEW, and MARK, and LUKE, and JOHN, rehearse this music still, but PAUL, and PETER, and JAMES, and JUDE, take part with them, and the whole

"Sacramental host of God's elect,"

Ministers and people, men, women, and children, the possessors of the fruits of the oldest Civilizations in the World, and the New Tribes, just converted from the abominations of the most degraded barbarism, and cleansed and clothed, and adorned, and sanctified, and saved, and made instruments of salvation to others, by the agency of the Spirit and Truth of Jehovah, unite in the hosannas and hallelujahs that hail, and welcome, and bless, and celebrate, and in every way magnify the *first* advent of the Mediator; and, also, still further unite in the waiting, and watching, and wishing, and praying, for His *second* advent—the *Only* Hope now left to our poor, deceived, disap-

pointed, and almost ruined and despairing world—
evermore responding to His own most gracious assurance—"Behold! I come quickly!"—with the
ready, and instant, and common, and happy acclaim,
"Even so—Come, Lord Jesus!"

> "Come, then, and added to Thy many crowns,
> Receive *one* more, the crown of all the earth,
> Thou who alone art worthy."—So shall it be—

> "*One* song employ all nations, and all cry,
> Worthy the Lamb, for He was slain for us!
> The dwellers in the vales, and on the rocks,
> Shout to each other, and the mountain tops,
> From distant mountains, catch the flying joy,
> Till, nation after nation taught the strain,
> Earth rolls the rapturous hosanna round!"

And what now? If it be true, that God has thus
magnified his word above all his name during the
last three thousand years, and does so magnify it at
this very moment; is there not an irresistible logic
in the inference that He will continue to magnify it
even unto the end?—not now, indeed, by adding
other books to the sixty-six already in existence, but,
in causing these, just as they stand, to triumph over
all opposition?

What does He himself say, in regard to this? I
wish I had time to answer fully—but, without time
for this, I must nevertheless give some answer.

What does God say of *Himself?* Hark!—"The

LORD said to MOSES, I AM that I AM." Again, in
various places: "Beside me, there is *no God*, I know
not any." "*Before* me, there was no God formed."
"I *am God*, there is no God *with* me." Therefore,
the precept against idolatry—"Thou shalt know no
God *but me*." It is the consciousness of Divine All-
ness, of Infinite Comprehensiveness and Exclusiveness, that thus speaks out of its own Essential and
Eternal Solitude. Can any man believe that there
is any *other* God than *this* God; or that any kind of
opposition can ever make Him less than God, or prevent the fulfilment of His *designs* as God? As sure
as He is God, must He not triumph over all opposition?

Of His character as *King*, it is said:—"The
Lord is King, *forever and ever*." So in many other
passages.

Of His *Throne*, in like manner, it is said:—"Thy
throne, O God, is *forever and ever*." So in other
passages.

Of His *Reign*, it is said: "The Lord shall *reign,
forever and ever*." So in other passages.

Of His *Kingdom* it is said:—"Thy kingdom is an
everlasting kingdom, and thy *dominion* endureth
throughout all generations." So in other passages.

So, in particular, of His *Truth* it is said—"His
truth endureth to *all generations*." And again: "The

truth of the LORD endureth forever." And again:
"Happy is he that hath the GOD OF JACOB for his
help, whose hope is in the *Lord* his *God;* which
made heaven and earth, the sea and all that therein
is; *which keepeth truth forever.*"—And so, in other
passages.

So, still *more* particularly, of His WORD, as the
embodiment of His *truth.* "The voice said, *Cry.* And
he said, *What* shall I cry? All flesh is grass, and
all the goodliness thereof is as the flower of the field.
The grass withereth, the flower fadeth," "but—the
word of our God shall stand forever." And so, again,
"*Forever,* O Lord, thy word is *settled in heaven.*"
And again, "Thy word is true from the beginning,
and every one of thy righteous judgments endureth
forever." So in other passages.

So, still more particularly, of His *law*—as *one*
from His word. "Think not"—said our Saviour
Himself—"that *I* am come to *destroy* the *law,* or the
prophets: I am *not* come to destroy, but to fulfil.
For, verily I say unto you, Till heaven and earth
pass, one jot or one tittle shall in no wise pass from
the *law,* till *all be fulfilled.*"

So, of His *covenants*—as constituting *another* form
of His *word.* For instance, in that with NOAH, the
Lord said—"And the bow shall be in the cloud; and
I will look upon it, that I may remember the *ever-*

lasting covenant between God and every living creature of all flesh that is upon the earth." As long as you see the Rainbow no fear of this covenant. So with the ABRAHAMIC covenant: "God said, SARAH thy wife shall bear thee a son indeed; and thou shalt call his name ISAAC, and I will establish my *covenant* with him for an *everlasting* covenant, and with his seed after him." As long as you see a Jew, no fear of this. So with the Covenant with DAVID. "My covenant will I not break, nor alter the thing that is gone out of my lips. Once have I sworn by my holiness, that I will not lie unto DAVID. His seed shall endure forever, and his throne as the sun before me. It shall be established forever as the moon, and as a faithful witness in heaven." As long as Psalms are read and sung, no fear of this. JEREMIAH seems to *allude* to this, when he says,—" Thus saith the LORD, If ye can break my covenant of the day, and my covenant of the night, and that there should *not* be day and night in their season, *then* may also my covenant be broken with David my servant, that he should not have a son to reign upon his throne." As long as you see day and night, no fear of this. So with ISAIAH, looking more plainly forward to the Christian Dispensation, and the ingathering of the Gentiles under it—"Incline your ear and come unto me, hear and your soul shall live; and I will make an *everlasting* covenant with you, even the *sure mercies* of DAVID. Behold, I have given him" (or his Greater Seed) "for a witness to the people, a leader and commander to the people. Behold, thou shalt call a nation that thou knowest not, and nations that knew not thee shall run unto thee; because of the Lord thy God, and for the Holy One of Israel; for he hath glorified thee." As long as missions prosper, no fear of this. And so, once more, of the *New* covenant, as announced in that beautiful benediction, at the close of the Epistle to the HEBREWS: "Now the God of peace, that brought again from the dead our Lord JESUS, that great Shepherd of the Sheep, *through the blood of the everlasting covenant,* make you perfect in every good work to do his will, working in you that which is well pleasing in his sight, through JESUS CHRIST, to whom be glory forever and ever. Amen." As long as the blood of Christ is better than that of Abel, and of the Law, no fear of this.

In like manner, I might speak again of the PROPHECIES—as another form of His word. For instance, when the ISRAELITES doubted the Divine promise in the wilderness, "The LORD said unto MOSES, Is the LORD's hand waxed *short?* thou shalt *see* now, whether my word shall come *to pass* unto thee or *not.*" And, of course, it *did* come to pass.— So, even in the mouth of BALAAM, the LORD put the message to BALAK—"God is not a *man* that he should lie; neither the son of man that he should repent; hath *he* said, and shall he not *do* it? or hath *he* spoken, and shall he not make it good?"—So, when SOLOMON blessed the people, at the dedication of the temple, he lifted up his voice, and added— "Blessed be the LORD, that hath given rest unto his people ISRAEL, *according to all that he promised:* there hath not failed *one word* of all his good promise, which he promised by the hand of MOSES his servant."— So, but more generally, said our Saviour—"The *Scriptures must* be *fulfilled."* And again:—"All things *must be fulfilled,* which were written in the law of MOSES, and in the PROPHETS, and in the PSALMS, concerning *me."* And again—"The Scripture *cannot be broken."* And again—for His own words in particular—"Heaven and earth shall pass away, but my words shall not pass away;" and *all* are *His* words. As long as heaven and earth stand, there need be no fear of this.

And what now? Is not *all—forever?* Certainly, according to its own testimony, the *Bible is all forever!* Its *History* is *history forever:* its *Doctrine* is *doctrine forever:* its *Law* is *law forever:* its COVENANTS are *covenants forever:* and its PROMISES and PROPHECIES are Promises and Prophecies *forever.* Is there any other Book with such *Records* as these? or with such

Claims as these? Is there even a *pretence* to anything of the kind, in all the world? Surely, God *has* magnified His word above all His name!

But, what does the WORD itself say, in relation to its *triumph over all opposition?* its final and perpetual *success?* I wish I could tell you a *hundredth part* of what it says! But, is it not in your own hands? Is it not open before your own eyes? Does it not constantly appeal to your own mind, and heart, and conscience?

Hark!—the Voice and Harp of the Sweet Singer of Israel:—"All the ends of the world shall remember and turn unto the Lord; and all the kindreds of the nations shall worship before thee. For the kingdom is the Lord's, and he is the governor among the nations!" And again—"O let the nations be glad and sing for joy, for thou shalt judge the people righteously, and govern the nations upon earth! Let the people praise thee, O Lord: yea, let all the people praise thee!" And again: "Blessed be the Lord God, the God of Israel; who only doeth wondrous things. And blessed be his glorious name forever: and let the whole earth be filled with his glory. Amen and amen." The prayers of David, the son of Jesse, are ended.—Beautiful ending: like that of the Prophet of the Apocalypse—"Even so: Come, Lord Jesus!"

But, hearken—to the Silver Trumpet of ISAIAH, also. "The earth shall be full of the knowledge of the Lord, as the waters cover the sea"—or, rather, as they cover the *deep*—the great and mighty deep—with all its profound plateaus, and profounder ravines, deeper and still deeper, but little by little, covered over, filled in, and smoothly filled up, and then rolled into tide-waves, blown into billows, and cast like a world-full of breakers on a thousand rock-bound shores. So, the knowledge of the Lord shall fill up, and overflow the earth.

Hearken also to the glad response of ZECHARIAH —"The Lord shall be king over all the earth: in that day, shall there be one Lord, and his name One."

Hearken to HABAKKUK, also, in the same words as ISAIAH—"For the earth shall be filled with the knowledge of the glory of the Lord, as the waters cover the sea."

PART III.

But, what is the present state of this opposition? So long a time has elapsed since the preceding sermons were prepared, and so much delay has occurred in their appearance, that, notwithstanding the best recent revision which has been given them, I am anxious, in this new composition, completing the series, to conduct the record of facts as near as practicable to this date (1864), that it may be more exactly evident what hostilities are yet to be met, and what may be expected in the process of Bible conquests.

First, therefore, I invite attention to the following condensed classified survey of the greater part of the world—a careful abstract from the latest Reports of the British and Foreign, and American, Bible Societies.

I. PRESENT STATE OF PAGAN OPPOSITION.

1. CHINA. Opposition to the Bible, in that great empire, is modified by the Civil War, and the complications of the government with foreign nations. Christianity finds freer access than formerly. Still, allusions are made to the—"stiff and ignorant prejudices of those in authority"—to the "contempt and scorn" of the learned men—and to the "extreme indifference" of the people. It is said, that—"the Atheism, the Materialism, the Apathy of the Chinese mind in regard to religion, coupled with its intense ignorance, peculiar exclusiveness, and Satanic prejudices on the subject, are more and more felt to be *terrible difficulties* in the way of our success. They are all in active exercise on every side, and are the

24*

better understood the closer we come in contact with them." The colporteurs are represented as "exposed to the full brunt of argument, ridicule and scorn, at the hands of those they meet." In some cases, the Book is abused or destroyed, its distributors arrested by jealous officials, and the few disciples subjected to severe persecution. Notwithstanding such facts, however, the Agents report various encouragements, and seem to be cheerful in prospect of favorable changes.

2. JAPAN. Here the opposition is described thus: "The jealousy of the Japanese is on the alert in reference to efforts for the introduction of Christianity; and as the Missionaries are confined by the authorities within very narrow limits, the opportunities of circulating even the Chinese Scriptures, which can be read by the better educated classes, are comparatively few. Efforts to disseminate the Scriptures in Japanese would, it is feared, call forth decidedly hostile action on the part of the government." When the Japanese Ambassadors were in Washington, it was proposed to supply them with the Scriptures—but the gift was declined. It seems that, more recently, while the Ambassadors were in England, the British and Foreign Bible Society made a similar effort, and with the same result. "Three copies of the Chinese Bible were specially prepared for presentation" to them, and "transmitted to their Excel-

lencies, accompanied by a suitable address on behalf
of the Society. Immediately, however, before they
quitted England, the copies were sent back, with po-
lite acknowledgments, and the intimation that the re-
tention of the gift might involve these functionaries
in a misunderstanding with the Government on their
return to Japan."

3. INDIA. There, opposition is indicated by reference to—"prejudice, stern and bitter"—to "fatalism
and infidel philosophy," as abounding, and enchain-
ing "The intellect of multitudes"—and, to " the po-
tency of caste," as presenting "a formidable barrier
against the reception of the humbling doctrines of
the Cross." Allusion is made, also, to "heathen
vices," to "ignorance, superstition, ancestral customs" and "pharisaic pride." There too the Colporteurs occasionally meet " violent" repulsions, and are
"laughed at as engaged in a hopeless enterprise."
New converts have to endure "household" persecution, holiness and humility are assailed with "hatred
and scorn," and "pantheistic theories and diabolical
idolatries" are wielded against the Word of God.

4. OTHER SECTIONS. In Malaysia, the majority
are said to be "sunk in ignorance and wretchedness."
In Australia, the reports refer to the Colonists rather
than the natives. In New Zealand, the War is a
difficulty. In the South Seas, at Tauna and Error-

manga, the savages are in arms against the Missionaries. In the Mauritius' the Brahmins are trying to
"check the spread of Divine truth" by temples and
schools of idolatry. In Madagascar, the terrible
persecutions were closed by the advent of the new king
—though much slumbering or suppressed heathen
hatred is supposed to exist still. In South Africa,
the "unhappy effects" of Bishop Colenso's movements are noticed—"the recent notorious attempt to
invalidate the historical truth of the Pentateuch, and
so to shake all faith in Divine Revelation." And so
the sketches of Paganism are concluded. Let us
turn, therefore, to :—

II. THE PRESENT STATE OF MOHAMMEDAN
OPPOSITION.

"The work among the Mohammedans is not without interest, even in these days of severe animadver-
sion and criticism from some of the highest officials
of the Government." "The cause has to contend with
differences of faith, nationality, and language, as well
as with the Oriental custom of female seclusion, which
renders access to the family circle almost impossible."
In Algiers, the authorities forbade the circulation of
the Bible, and "put its Colporteur on a level with
criminals;" but, afterward, the circulation was allowed, except of copies in the Arabic language. So

some generosity was assumed, while the False System remained well guarded. "Bigotry and fanaticism" are represented as "characteristic of Mohammedans;" with "intense prejudices—against the Gospel." In the "interior parts of Arabia," especially, "Mohammedan fanaticism runs high." An Agent was desirous of venturing to "Mekka, itself; but he was prevented doing so by the British Consul, who, in explanation, assured him that certain death would await him, if he entered the 'holy city of the Mohammedans' as a Christian." Arabia, indeed, is described, as "that country of the world, which, all things considered, is probably least accessible to a Christian agency." From these partial glimpses, of Mohammedanism let us now pass to :—

III. THE PRESENT STATE OF JEWISH OPPOSITION.

Here, however, there is a lack of material. Occasionally, a case is mentioned, like that in which a dying Jew forced his daughter to "promise never to enter upon any conversation, or read any book, relating to Jesus." But, strange to say, the Jewish cases, in most instances, are those of submission rather than of opposition. Indeed, it is not in Paganism, Mohammedanism, or Judaism, separately or jointly, that the chief opposition to the Bible is found, but, within the limits of nominal Christianity. We must proceed, therefore, to such notices as occur of opposition by the Greek and other Oriental Churches; by the Roman Catholic Church; by the States with which these Churches are connected, and which, in this relation, they seem to control; and, finally, by certain forms of Protestantism itself.

IV. THE PRESENT STATE OF NOMINALLY CHRISTIAN OPPOSITION.

In the Armenian districts of Asia Minor, "great opposition" has been met, with "threats to kill" the Bible readers, and "terrible persecution" only falling short of murder: though some improvement begins to appear. In Egypt, "the great stumbling-block in the way of doing good"—even to the Mohammedans —"is the Coptic Church;" the members of which have not "the means, at present, of knowing what true Christianity is." In Eastern Turkey, allusion is made to the "thick darkness which for so many centuries has been brooding over (the) land." Among the Armenians, "the universal inability to read is a serious obstacle." "The ignorance and mercenary character of the Ecclesiastics is another serious obstacle. A priest who was "questioned as to his knowledge of the Scriptures, could not tell a single command of the Decalogue." "The most trying hinderance to the introduction of the Bible is found in the opposition of the priesthood. In one case, a vartebad (or monk) sought an opportunity to assassinate a Bible distributor." In Georgia, also, the converted Armenians are greatly persecuted by the Old Orthodox Church.

The Greek Church, as so much mightier, is alluded to more frequently. In Russia, the inability to read, among the serfs, is still a difficulty—though emancipation is likely to be followed by education. In the Southern Provinces, Government restrictions are in the way. "Prevailing distress and religious apathy," also, are impediments. In Bulgaria, the ignorance of priests and people is the great obstacle. In Greece, the "superstition—bigotry—abuses and errors" of the establishment are referred to. In the island of Crete (or Candia), the Metropolitan would not allow the school-teachers even to accept the Scriptures as a gift. The hostility of the Patriarch of Constantinople, joined to that of the Metropolitan, is represented as very injurious; more than counterbalancing the liberal policy of the Government—the State, in such cases, being manifestly overruled by the Church. In Servia, and especially at Belgrade, the Greek archbishop, and others like him, are reported as having "endeavored to crush the operations" of the Society.

But, after all, as would be expected, the chief

opponent, everywhere, is the Roman Catholic Church. Even in our own country this is evident—though the reports are very defective. In Michigan, for instance, of 251 Romanist families visited, only 56 had courage to receive the Bible. In Minnesota, the priests refuse the privilege of reading it, and will not hear confessions of those who do read it. In Rhode Island, of 1754 destitute families, more than 1100, as Romanists, declined the Bible. In our army, the prohibition of the priests is a restraint upon the Catholic soldiers. In Mexico, Bible circulation has been stopped by the war with the French. There, however, it has been "always resisted—by the dominant influence of the Romish priesthood, which holds the people in abject bondage." In Brazil, the archbishop suspended the sale—though it was afterward resumed. In South America generally, allusion is made to the "sad degradation" consequent on "the rankest superstitions of Rome"—the "dark systems of error which have so long crushed the energies and demoralized the population of one of the finest regions in the world." In Buenos Ayres, "Popish fanaticism" is said to be less "rampant"—than in the other Republics of South America. Chili is described as having "an intensely Popish character." In New Granada, mention is made of "the supremacy of Jesuitical intrigues." In the West Indies, the chief

difficulties arise from ignorance and poverty, with occasional Romish interference. In Dominica, the Romish Prelate has " publicly denounced the action " of
the Bible Society. Coming North again, in Canada
we read of " the cruel tyranny of the Romish Priesthood, who are determined, if it can be done, that the
Bible shall have no currency amongst the members
of their flocks, and are ceaseless in their inquiries to
ascertain where the Scriptures have been received."
" Striking facts are mentioned, showing the wretched
spiritual thraldom in which the people are held, and
the dread entertained of priestly anathema." A Colporteur states that " the Curé tells the people they will
be lost if they read (the books), and that it is not
right even to touch them. Accordingly the Curé
tries to burn or to destroy the Scriptures." In some
cases, they have been seized and burnt. Crossing the
Atlantic, we find such statements as the following.
In France, " the Bible is branded (by the Romish
Priesthood) as the symbol of anarchy and misfortune,
and the offer of it through the agency (of the Bible
Society) has been resolutely declined by those who
are taught that the admission of it into their dwell-
ings would be a fruitful source of misery, and entail
upon them the dreaded anathema of the Church."
" The blind partisans of the temporal power of the
Papacy—have represented to those who will still lis-

25

ten to them, that those falsified Bibles and Testaments, as they are pleased to designate our copies of
the Scriptures, are circulated with no other object
than to dethrone the Holy Father, and with him to
destroy the Catholic, Apostolic, Roman religion ; that
those so-called Bible Colporteurs are nothing better
than the Socialists, without faith and without law,
who are in the pay of foreign Protestant nations, and
with whom, in view of the Government of France,
it is most perilous to enter into connection." So
strong is this opposition, especially as added to the
commercial distress, that, in certain parts of the
country, the prosecution of the Bible work has been
rendered absolutely impossible.   There is a Protestant Bible Society in Paris, authorized by the Government, but only on condition that it should not operate
among Roman Catholics ! Another Society, independent of the Government, is in existence, but too weak
to do much.   In one of the Northern Departments,
a Curé bought up and collected all the copies he could
get, and burned them in a large fire.   In Belgium,
which is described as " one of the most intensely
Popish and bigoted lands of the Continent," the Romish opposition appears to be still greater.   It is
styled "active and persevering hostility."—In some
of the provinces, the priests threaten those who have
purchased a Testament, and do not burn it, with not

being allowed to confess, and with "eternal damnation."
In some cases, they "go from house to house to take
away the Testaments." One Colporteur says—"I do
not think there is in Europe a country so full of
darkness, and where the clergy have such power."—
Even in Holland, in some districts where Romanists
reside, they oppose the "diffusion of the Scriptures,"
and resort to acts of cruelty as the most summary
method of carrying out their designs—stoning the
Colporteurs—cursing and scoffing at them—denying
them accommodations—threatening to kill them. In
Volkenburg, it is said, "the priests are continually
visiting the houses in search of our books; if they
find any they take them away and burn them." In
Germany, again, we find "the priests denouncing the
books, and warning the people against buying them:"
occasionally buying them up, themselves, and burning them. In Austria, especially, the opposition,
even on the part of the Government, continues unrelenting. There, is another instance of the Church
overruling the State—Civil opposition prompted by
Ecclesiastical. It is reported that "every effort to
induce the Government formally to allow the introduction of the Bible has had no effect." The Agent
"has repeatedly visited Vienna, and had interviews
with official persons," but, "it would seem as if the
Bible must be as rigorously shut out of Austria as

ever." Even the privilege of distribution among the Protestants of the empire is withheld : "a cruel wrong," as it is justly styled. In 1861, the Government issued a decree promising better things ; but it appears that the Church has restrained the Government. The question is very properly asked : "Is the Government not strong enough to carry out its own plans ; is it obliged to bend to the dictates of a hierarchy which has always opposed the dissemination of the Scriptures?" In Spain and Portugal, matters are still worse. Of the former, the Report says : "Spain, ever the abject vassal of the Papacy, still retains her intense aversion to the Bible and Protestantism, and will relax none of the penal restrictions which forbid the circulation of the Scriptures amongst her subjects. The indignant protest which has been uttered by Protestant Europe, against the atrocities perpetrated of late by Spain, in the dishonored name of religion, has had no effect in mitigating the relentless cruelty with which the Government persecutes the noble men, who will brave loss of liberty rather than abjure the Bible." The Report well stigmatises the whole process as "a revival of the old spirit of the Inquisition, which revelled in cruelties and horrors, the recollection of which makes the boldest heart shudder." For the present, therefore, Bible operations in Spain "are impracticable." It is added :

" Indeed—there is reason to believe that a more rig-
orous surveillance than ever is practiced to shut out
the Scriptures, and that a Secret Society has been
formed amongst the most bigoted Romanists, with a
view of aiding the police in detecting those who are
suspected of leanings toward Protestantism." So
much for Spain. That is another State overruled by
the Church. So, if possible, Rome would overrule
all States. As to Portugal, that is represented as
" likewise closed against the entrance of the Bible"—
but, still, as in a more hopeful condition than Spain.
In Italy it is observed that there "are retarding
causes still operating with prodigious force, in many
parts, which cannot fail to have an adverse influence
on the circulation of the Scriptures. In some districts, the power of the priests is supreme, and the
people are held in a state of profound and abject submission to the ecclesiastical despotism which has so
long ruled with irresistible sway. The dread of
priestly power and anathema deters many a timid
spirit from any attempt to burst the shackles, which
Popery ever seeks to impose upon its deluded victims; and the fear of the consequences which might
result from reading the Scriptures, on the fact becoming known to the priest, often leads to a rejection
of the Sacred Volume even when there is a strong
desire to possess it." Ignorance also is a great diffi-

culty. Large masses, in both town and country, are
unable even to read. Political excitement, also, is an
obstacle; and likely to continue so at least, until the
city of Rome be secured as the capital of the Kingdom. In Milan, Genoa, Florence, Bologna and
Naples, the opposition of the priests is mentioned.
Bologna, in particular, is described as " one of the
strongholds of the Papacy, where priestly influence
has long been in the ascendant. Every effort to
spread the truth here has encountered fierce hostility."
In Sicily, it is said the majority of the people " are
too blindly attached to Romish superstition to give
much heed to the teachings of the Bible." Proceeding to Malta, the same adversary appears again.
" The strict surveillance exercised by the priests has
a tendency to check any effort on the part of the people to obtain possession of the Scriptures." This
influence follows them abroad. At Tunis, on the
African coast, it is said of the Maltese, that "they
spend their days in the most profound ignorance,
manifest the same blind and servile submission to
their spiritual guides, and are as difficult to be ap-
proached by Protestant truth as when in their native
island of Malta." In Turkey, we meet again the
open opposition of the Roman Clergy. And now,
sweeping away with the Reports to the South Seas,
we find in the Georgia Islands " the seductive influ-

ences and the superstitious charms of Popish error—
seeking to plant its standard on the spots where pure
Christianity has achieved such glorious triumphs."
In the Fiji Islands, also, we are told that " Popery is
making special efforts among these people, and it
gains a few converts from *us*, but mainly such as are
noted for being troublesome; and some from heathenism, in various parts of this extensive group of islands." In the Mauritius, also, the Romanists are
active; and in Madagascar it is said that " unscrupu-
lous intrigues " have been used, though vainly, to influence the king "in favor of Popery;" while other
efforts have been made "to foster the suspicion in the
minds of the people, that the Protestant Missionaries
are giving them a mutilated and imperfect Bible,"
well knowing that the entire Scriptures, if placed in
their hands, would demonstrate the Divine authority
of the Papacy. In West Africa, also, particularly
at Fernando Po, the Protestant Missionary has been
excluded by the intolerance of the Spanish Government; there, as at home, the mere tool of the priests.
So much for Romanism. If it had been the main
object of the Reports to illustrate the range of this
opposition, doubtless they would have multiplied instances in connexion with all parts of the globe—Pagan, Mohammedan, Jewish and Christian, and every
point of contact within every part. Popery and the

Bible are the same everywhere, and must contend until one shall conquer. Even in the island of Ceylon, where violent heathen opposition is now rarely encountered, it is said—"Whenever hostility *is* experienced, it is manifested by the priests and adherents of the Church of Rome, who seek to prejudice the minds of the people against the reception and reading of the Word of God." So in China, "the Romish Propaganda is seeking to establish its mission on a scale of imposing grandeur, and is setting up claims which, if admitted, will invest it with large resources and extended influence." As a Protestant superintendent of Colportage remarks : "The spread of Roman Catholic dogmas is perplexing the minds of many, without satisfying them." It is stated, that, "to the present time, no Protestant Missionary has been permitted to reside at the Capital (Pekin), with a view to the active prosecution of his Christian labors, amongst the teeming population. In this respect, an obvious advantage has been secured by the Roman Catholic priests, who are freely tolerated in their work, by express stipulations, contracted through the Representative of the French Government." See that, again !

But, what is to be said of the Protestant Churches? In our former review of Ecclesiastical Opposition, these Churches were found to be somewhat inconsistently involved. Are there any traces in the Reports of such opposition now? Not many. Had it been the object of the Reporters to ascertain more, doubtless they might have done it. In Germany, it appears,—"considerable opposition has arisen of late on account of the omission of the Apocrypha"—so retarding the sales. On this account, also, some of the German Bible Societies have ceased from "intimate co-operation" with the British and Foreign Bible Society. So in Holland, "the opposition thrown in the way by superstition" is noticed. By the State-Church party, or the Rationalists connected with it, the Bible Society is "violently opposed;" its work being regarded as a wanton outrage against the Sovereign authority of the Church. The Schools, "sustained by the Government—deny all entrance to the Bible, and abjure the religious element in the education that is imparted." In Norway, allusion is made to "the enemies of the great and precious truth, that Jesus alone is our righteousness:" enemies who would rejoice in the discontinuance of Bible distribution. In England, itself, references are made to certain "vexatious controversies" and "ecclesiastical discussions," which it was feared would "seriously interfere" with the work, but which appear to have passed so far without doing much harm. Such, only, are the current allusions to anything in the way of

Protestant opposition to the Bible. As already intimated, much more than this might be said.

Other forms of opposition, or obstruction, are occasionally introduced; as ignorance, inability to read,
poverty, infidelity, &c. But, as the most of these
have already incidentally been mentioned, it is enough
to add a few words here in relation to the last—infidelity. The American Report refers to some of our
own States, in which both the old skepticisms and
the new form of spiritualism are frequently met. In
Michigan, it is said that "the Bible is gaining
largely upon skepticism." Still, there is much hostility. Those who were most violent against the
Bible called themselves spiritualists. One man
"burned his wife's Bible;" another "refused to let
his dying wife have the Bible in her possession." It
is said that "at New Ulm—in Brown County—Minnesota: practical atheism characterized the people;
and it has pleased God, by the hands of savages, to
blot out that place as thoroughly as He did Sodom
and Gomorrah." Leaving our own country again, we
observe, in Holland, "the increased spirit of infidelity, which prevails throughout the country:" the
fact that "the mission of the Bible—is by many
rudely and ignorantly scoffed at, as an impotent crusade against the increasing enlightenment of a philosophic age;" and the statement that "the spirit of

infidelity is still in the ascendant, and spreading its blight over the professed Protestant Church." In Germany, in one case, the Colporteur was told : "The man who believes the Bible is two centuries behind the age." In another,—"the Bible was pronounced to be false, and the reading of it an absurdity." The condition of the German Protestants in the Danubian Provinces of Turkey is alluded to, as one of "deplorable practical infidelity and heathenism." In England, "while some were looking at the books, and seemed disposed to buy, one man remarked that it was of no use to ask him to buy, as he did not believe in the Bible; nor in the existence of God or devil, heaven or hell." (This man, however, was soon after converted.) In South Africa, "reference is made to the unhappy effects produced by the recent notorious attempt to invalidate the historical truth of the Pentateuch, and so to shake all faith in Divine Revelation;"—that is, the foolish Colenso assault upon the Bible.

Such then is this opposition, so far as it came within the province and thought of the American, and British and foreign, Bible Societies, in their most recent Reports, to specify and illustrate it. At least, it is sufficient to give us a passing glimpse of both the massed and scattered foes of the Bible in all parts of the world. This opposition, whether of Pagans, Mohammedans, Jews, or merely nominal or heretical Christians, is all to be overcome.

Before quitting these peaceful Reports of Religious and Benevolent Institutions, it may not be without some suggestive interest to observe to how great an extent *war-terms* are used by them in describing the progress of their Bible work. Thus, on one hand, we have "the power and device of the adversary;" the "difficulties to be combatted, prejudice and bigotry to be assailed; and hostility and resistance encountered;" the "enemies now commenced a different mode of attack;" and they "fought furiously to the last, and ceased only when tired and conquered." On the other hand, we find such phrases as these:— the "Conquests of Truth;" the "defeat" of the Priests; "Divine truth has vanquished it (*i.e.* prejudice), and can vanquish it again;" and "marvellous has been the triumph of God's Word." In connexion with India, the Society, it is said, does not despair of "ultimate triumph in the East." And again: "No cause can so well afford to abide its time; no cause is so sure of perfect victory." Meantime, "the Word of God is the only effectual weapon to wield" in this great war.

So it is—a universal and perpetual war; a war that must continue until the Rebellion of the World is subdued, and "the kingdoms of this world are become the kingdoms of our Lord and of his Christ; and he shall reign forever and ever."

ADDITIONAL INDICATIONS OF PRESENT OPPOSITION.

The foregoing abstract, as already variously intimated, is of necessity very defective—because of the character of the documents from which it has been made. An exhaustive treatment of the subject would require a very wide range of reading, and a very careful methodical elaboration of collected materials —especially those from recent antagonistic literature. Neither time nor space remains for this.

The most painful fact connected with present opposition to the Bible is, that, here at home, within the limits of Christendom itself, it has assumed so many plausible and captivating disguises, theological, scientific, and literary, and invaded, to so great an extent, all departments of mind, from the highest to the lowest, everywhere claiming even self-sacrificing honesty, and professing to appear and act only in the interest of truth.

ADDRESS,

Originally delivered at the Anniversary of the Young Men's Bible Society, Cincinnati, November 21, 1848; and revised for the Anniversaries of the Philadelphia and New York City Bible Societies, November 27 and 30, 1856.

THE Bible is distinguished from all other books by two grand characteristics:—I. It is the Book of God: II. It is the Book of Man.

I. THE BOOK OF GOD.

As the Book of God, the Bible, certainly, is an incomparable production. The contemplation of God as an Author, in a literary sense, is wonderful. The notion of human authors is common enough. There is no history of the first, and no prophecy of the last. Thousands of years ago it was said, "Of making many books there is no . end." Ten thousand times as many, I suppose, are now made as were then; and yet the end seems as far off as ever.   Among all the titles of our poorly-rich old world, one of the most impressive is this:—the World of Books!

But the Bible is not of human authorship. True, its contents have been committed to parchment, paper, and various other materials, by human hands; but those hands were under infinitely higher direction than that of the human spirit.   Even human authors frequently dictate their thoughts to amanuenses: sometimes, because of physical defect; at others, because of mental impatience; and for many different but sufficient reasons.   In a word, authorship, like every thing great, is of the soul.   There originate the

"Thoughts that breathe and words that burn,"

of which Gray so sublimely sings.   Thence spring the living lightnings of the eye and the living thunders of the tongue.   Without the soul, the eye,—how dull! the tongue,—how still! the hand,—how awkward and inapt! Homer and Milton, therefore, are not less the authors of their immortal poems, nor Thiers and Prescott of their applauded histories, for want of autograph manuscripts.   Neither is the God of Nature any less the Author of the Bible, because we have no sacred vellum to unroll from its golden rod, full of starry symbols traced by His own thrilling fingers.

It were a marvellous thing for an angel to appear as an author,—for Gabriel or Michael, for instance, to favor the world with some duly-attested composition, as a fair expression of his genius and intelligence; some history, law, or psalm; some proverb or prophecy; some doctrinal and practical epistle, or apocalypse of things unseen and unknown. And yet this were nothing in comparison with God's appearance as an Author. He, whose absolutely-perfect infinitude is the source and support of all the subjective and objective intellect in the universe, has condescended to assume this humble form in our midst. Here, in the Bible, He reveals Himself in all the relations just alluded to,—as a Historian, Lawgiver, and Poet; a Proverbialist and Prophet; a Doctrinal and Moral Preceptor; a graphic Delineator of the symbolic apocalypse of the future.

It may be that this is at once the first and last appearance of our Maker in this way. He has created millions of worlds, but composed only one book. What a contrast! The worlds,—how magnificent they are! Even the planets are magnificent: how much more the suns! and, still,

26*

how much more the systems! How infinitely magnificent the universal system of systems! To the all-comprehensive eye of their Creator, with what a blaze of glory they light up immensity! To the all-comprehensive ear of their Creator, with what a concert of music they enliven eternity! How much of His perfections He has diffused among them all! And yet, after all, —for this is the point of these remarks,—He has enclosed more of His perfections in this little Book than He has spread abroad over all the creation! His mind opens here as it never opened there. His heart throbs here as it never throbbed there. Nay, more,—to finish the figure and tell the whole truth,—His eyes weep here, His tongue falters here, and His hand trembles here. No wonder He resigned the pen to steadier nerves. He might indent the Law on tables of stone; but He could not record the story of the Cross!

It is enough! One sun in heaven, one Bible on earth!—one the light of the natural world, the other the light of the spiritual world! Where is natural day? Wherever the sun shines! And where is spiritual day? Wherever the Bible shines! In either case, day is nowhere else. True, the moon gives light when the sun has set;

and so the church may give light when the Bible is withdrawn. But, in both cases, it is night-light, not daylight. Besides, the sun is not set to the moon, but only to the earth: the moon sees it still, though the earth does not, and the moon shines because she sees it. And so the Bible is not withdrawn from the church, but only from the world. In all such instances the church sees it, though the world does not, and the church shines only because she sees it. If all the moon be dark except half its edge-line, even that is proof that the sun is still in sight; and so, if all the church be dark save some small segment, even that, however small, is proof that the Bible has not quite passed away. Still, the moon rejoices most when the sun returns and she is allowed to hide herself in his glory; and so the church triumphs most when the Bible returns and she is permitted to fade in its excelling splendor!

I know not how others feel in this connection; but in my own heart there is a desire that the Bible may not perish with this poor sinful world,—that the Book of God may not be consumed with the productions of men. The Caliph Omar has been reproached, for more than a thousand years, for consigning the Alexandrian Library to the flames; and it may be that the warming of four thousand baths for six months was but a paltry recompense for the loss suffered by literature in that barbaric incident. Still, it can scarcely be supposed that any human writings will survive, or deserve to survive, the conflagration of the last day. The constitutions and laws of states and churches, and all the annals of protected and progressive civilization connected with them, will mingle their ashes with the ruin and refuse of all things, and, it may be, no reason remain to deplore their fate. But the Bible,—God's own and only Book!—surely it would seem that one copy of that at least—one perfect and imperishable transcript,—in its texture and inscription purer than the firmament and brighter than its fires; attested, moreover, in behalf of Father, Son, and Spirit, with the seal and signature of our Lord Jesus Christ—should adorn forever the mercy-seat in heaven, as once the Shekinah adorned the mercy-seat on earth.

II. THE BOOK OF MAN.

But the Bible is the Book of man as well as the Book of God. In this relation, also, it is an incomparable production. Schools of literature, art, science, and philosophy,—all have their text-books. Ecclesiastical sects and political parties,—

all have their text-books. Nations have their text-books. But where is the text-book of our common humanity? Where, but in the Bible, can any thing be found in the slightest degree worthy to bear the title of the Book of Man?

And now, tell me, who could have expected a Book for mankind to come forth from the Jews? Remember, they were a small nation, an isolated nation, an exclusive nation, regarded by others as malignant, and denounced, in so many words, as the haters of mankind. How came they to commence and consummate a work so complex in its structure, and yet so simple in its adaptations to the character and condition of our whole race; a work so early begun, so long continued, so gradually developed, and so happily completed; a work so changeable in its scribes, so various in its style, so consecutive in its subjects, so comprehensive in its relations, and so transcendent in the importance of its contents; with occasions so grand, with objects so stupendous, and with means so mighty and sure; recovering the past, occupying the present, and anticipating the future; filling heaven and earth; possessing time and eternity; discoursing of God, angels, devils, and men; unfolding creation, providence, and redemption; disdaining nothing, however little; despairing of nothing, however great; and yet so selecting its facts, so inculcating its principles, so urging its obligations, and so exercising its authority, as to constrain — absolutely constrain, reluctantly but inevitably—all art, all science, all philosophy, and all literature,— all schools, all sects, all parties, and all nations,—all ages of time and all kingdoms of nature,—to bow down to it and confess its supreme and separate claims as the one and only Law of the world; enthroning itself in inaccessible pomp, and power, and glory, with the spoils of all genius, and all learning, and all invention, and all advancement, laid down in lowly homage at its feet?

Is there not something more than the majesty of the Jewish mind in all this? Why, then, has not the Jewish mind produced other Bibles? A longer interval has elapsed since the completion of the Sacred Canon than occurred during all its progress,— fifteen hundred years before, and eighteen hundred, since! If, during the fifteen hundred years, sixty-six Books of Glory originated there, why not one from the same source during the eighteen hundred years which have since gone by? Such questions are the more pertinent because of the fact that, while the greatest nations of antiquity, in the providence of God, have been destroyed, the Jews, by the same providence, have been preserved. Here they are, at this day, standing among us as a perpetual social miracle. Nor only so; but they have existed, to a great extent, as colonists of genius and learning, in all lands and ages. In all probability, they are as numerous now as they ever were; and their national mind has lost little, if any thing, of its merely natural majesty. Therefore I press the question,—If there be nothing more than Jewish mind in the Bible, why has not this same mind produced other and equal Bibles?

I take the more interest in this topic, because of the folly of some who declare, even in the sanctuary, that if men now living, whether Jews or Gentiles, would lead holy lives, corresponding with those of the inspired writers, they might prepare new Scriptures, as full of inspiration and as high in authority as the Bible of the prophets and apostles of old. Alas, that the wisdom of God is so misunderstood! More than holiness is requisite to inspiration. There must be a purpose with God, as well as principle in man, to prompt the gift.

Why cannot such persons see that the Bible was written to meet the demands of great occa-

sions,—to perpetuate the controlling facts of the
divine administration,—to register the creation,
the fall, the promise, the curse, the deluge; the
covenants with Noah, Abraham, and Moses; the
first advent of Christ, the organization and destiny of the church, and the second advent of
Christ, without sin, unto salvation? Are there
any such occasions to require the aid of inspiration now? Have we any new creation to record?
Has any new Adam fallen?—any new Paradise
been forfeited?—any new curse been pronounced?
—or any new deluge drowned the world? Has
any new Noah, or Abraham, or Moses, appeared?
Has our Savior renewed His first advent, and are
new evangelists needed to prepare new memorials? Are the crucifixion, burial, resurrection,
and ascension, recent events, still unrecorded?
Is Pentecost just over? Is the church just opening its gates to Jews and Gentiles? Are new
Epistles, or is a new Apocalypse, wanted? Can
any thing be brought down from heaven more
beautiful than the New Jerusalem? Or, as the
last inspired book, from which nothing can be
taken away and to which nothing can be added
without incurring the most fearful wo, now closes
with the benediction:—"The grace of our Lord
Jesus Christ be with you all. Amen!"—is not

that enough? Let men find occasions, great
occasions, demanding inspiration, before they
speak so pertly of securing and employing it.
Even the old localities, sacredly as they are
cherished, have lost their old occasions. As to
the world before the flood, that seems to be still
under the flood. But go to Ararat: how its lifeless pinnacles glitter in the lofty realms of perpetual snow! Go to Sinai: how still the cliffs
which once sounded and resounded with the
trumpets of angels and the voice of God! Go to
Bethlehem and Jerusalem, to Gethsemane and
Calvary, to Ephesus and Patmos, to Athens and
Rome, and, whatever may remain, you will find
that the grand occasions for inspiration no longer
exist. How could it be otherwise? They passed
with the times to which they belonged. We
find them, not where they occurred, but in the
Bible itself, their appointed and proper de-
pository. Open the Bible, and Ararat shows its
ark, and altar, and rainbow, yet. Open the
Bible, and Sinai trembles beneath the footsteps
of Jehovah yet. Open the Bible, and Calvary
not only trembles, but breaks its heart, though
stern as rock, in shuddering sympathy with the
dying Son of God.

But, leaving this topic, let us look at another.

27

There is a wonderful resemblance between the
Bible itself and Him whose story it tells and
whose spirit it embodies. Like our Lord himself, the Bible was long surrounded by envious
and malignant foes, and for much the same
reason. If it would have ministered to worldly
ambition, they would have made it the king
of books, as the enemies of Christ, on the same
condition, would have made Him the King of
men. But, like Him, it spurned the bribe. Like
Him, it uttered its instructions and wrought its
miracles for nobler ends. Like Him, therefore,
it was derided and denounced. Its enemies,
like His, took counsel against it in private, and
assailed it by concert in public. They questioned it on every subject which they hoped
would entangle it. They sought, with all cunning, to secure matter of accusation against it;
but its answers silenced them so completely,
that they became afraid to question it further.
Still, they plotted its destruction; bought over
not only one, but many, of its professed friends;
and then arrested it, mocked it, spit upon it,
smote it, tried it, condemned it, crucified it,
buried it, sealed its sepulchre, set a guard there,
and then triumphed in the power of their wrath:
ay, triumphed, until that guard, all pale and

quivering, hurried in and alarmed them with
the tidings of its resurrection! Then fast they
fled to the horns of the altar; but only to find
that the veil of their temple was rent in twain,
that their protection and glory had forever departed, and that their Victim, radiant with immortality, had ascended to the throne of universal
and perpetual dominion!

And what now? Eighteen centuries have gone
by since the ascension of Christ,—since "the
Father of glory" "set Him at His own right
hand in the heavenly places, far above all principality, and power, and might, and dominion,
and every name that is named, not only in this
world, but also in that which is to come;" and
determined to "put all things under His feet,"
and, in the mean time, "gave Him to be the
head over all things to the church, which is His
body, the fulness of Him that filleth all in all;"
ordaining that, ultimately, "at the name of Jesus
every knee shall bow, of things in heaven, and
things on earth, and things under the earth; and
that every tongue shall confess that Jesus Christ
is Lord, to the glory of God the Father." Now,
however, we are all in waiting for this. "We
see not yet all things put under Him;" but this
we see:—"We see Jesus, who was made a little

lower than the angels, for the suffering of death,"
or as the reward of His suffering, "crowned with
glory and honor, that He, by the grace of God,
should taste death for every man;" that is, that
His very crown and glory, given to Him in
proof of the favor of God, should demonstrate
to the world that He died, not for His own sins,
but for the sins of mankind,—to redeem them
from death and the grave, and exalt them to an
everlasting participation in the ineffable grandeur
and felicity of His own destiny.

And what now? Is Christ, therefore, now
without enemies? Has the world learned at
last to admire and adore the infinite dignity of
His mediation? Does it lift up its voice, and
exclaim, "We bless and magnify thy name,
O Christ, that thou didst not bow down to the
littleness of earthly ambition! We thank thee
that when Satan tempted thee with the proffer
of all the kingdoms of the world and the glory
of them if thou wouldst bend the knee to him,
thou didst straighten thy stature, and darken
thy countenance in awful rebuke, and drive him,
confounded, from thy presence! We thank thee
that when the people, charmed by thy sympathy
and benevolence, would have taken thee by
force to make thee a king, thou didst hide thy-

self in the mountain-seclusion, preferring to be alone, with the thought of redemption, rather than to sway the sceptre over the proudest empire of sin! We thank thee that when the 'chief priests, and scribes, and elders' mocked thee, and said, 'He saved others, himself he cannot save: if he be the king of Israel, let him now come down from the cross, and we will believe him,'—thou didst still prefer the cross, even when thy Father himself seemed to turn away from it and from thee,—preferred it to all that earth and heaven could give besides! We thank thee that after thy resurrection, when thy disciples, still infatuated with sensual delusions, inquired of thee, 'Lord, wilt thou at this time restore again the kingdom to Israel?' thou didst answer them only with the promise of spiritual gifts, and then ascended to heaven to receive them of the Father and distribute them unto men! We thank thee, moreover, that, ever since, thou hast consecrated to the same work of entire and eternal salvation the concentrate sympathies of thy humanity and energies of thy divinity, and art now conducting it, with infinite patience and perseverance, toward its decreed, and certain, and ineffably-illustrious triumph!"

27*

Does the world at last thus lift up its voice, and bless and magnify the name of Christ? Nay, verily. True, He has more disciples now than He had in the beginning; but so has He more enemies,—enemies, if possible, more crafty and malicious than those of old. He was sneered at on the cross; He is blasphemed on the throne!

And, my friends,—friends of the great and glorious cause now before us,—just so it is with the Bible. What though it has been raised from the dead? What though it has ascended to the very zenith of spiritual pomp and power? What though it is the mightiest agent now in action in all the world? What though its God-like objects are still prosecuted as benignantly and beneficently as ever? At this very moment it is as much as ever, if not more than ever, abhorred and abominated by its multiform foes.

But what of that? Can they pluck it down from its sublime sphere of majesty and glory? What! Can they kill it again, and bury it again? As well might they attempt to crucify and entomb the Lord Jesus Christ again! Here is the point of the resemblance I have drawn. As well might they attempt to crucify and entomb the Lord Jesus Christ again!

What then? I appeal to them. Where is your Judas? Bring him out. Where are your officers? Summon them hither. Where are the elements of your mob? Collect them all. Give them staffs; for they have a long journey before them. Give them swords; they need keener blades than human hands have ever wielded. But, as to lanterns, let them leave these behind; for there is "no night there; and they need no candle, neither light of the sun: for the Lord God giveth them light." Now, therefore, if your bands can bear that light, let their motley ranks march on. First, let them try their steel against the lightning-scimetars of the twelve legions of angels whom Jesus held in restraint in Geth-semane. Next, let them drive back and over-turn the twenty thousand chariots of fire which escorted Him from earth to heaven, when He "ascended on high, and led captivity captive, that He might receive gifts for men; yea, for the rebellious also, that the Lord God might dwell among them." Then let them force open the gates and batter down the everlasting doors, which would not lift up their heads even to the King of glory, without due challenge and answer, —would not allow even the Lord strong and mighty, the Lord mighty in battle, the Lord of hosts, to come in, until His victorious retinue had shouted the password to their faithful and fearless sentinels. This done, let them press their way through the. whole population of the New Jerusalem,—saints, angels, and archangels; cherubim and seraphim; thrones, and dominions, and principalities, and powers; the morning-stars and the sons of God;—press their way to the height of Zion and to the palace of the King,—press their way through portal, and hall, and all their flaming guardians,—press their way to the very chamber of Presence and to the throne and person of Him who is "God over all, and blessed forever." Then let the Arch-Traitor draw near and kiss Him, saying, "Hail, Master!"—and then let the captains seize Him, —and then, amidst countless millions of silent harps and trumpets, let them raise the shout of Satanic triumph,—and then let them return to the earth again, leading with them, through all the weeping orders of the helpless hierarchy, their pale and placid Victim, down from the throne, and crown, and sceptre of eternity, to the reed and thorns of Pilate's hall, and the nakedness, nails, and cross of bloody Calvary! Then let them seal his sepulchre again; set around it a guard which no angel can frighten, and make all dark, and still, and sure forever! Let them do all this; for then—and not until then—they may do the same to the Bible!

Let *them* do it? *Who* do it?—*who?* Really, the very contemplation of their presumption involves the oblivion of their persons! A flock of bats may endeavor to overshadow the world with their wings, when the sky reddens and flames, and the morning leaps from peak to peak among the mountains, and the whole ocean flashes from pole to pole in the sunrise; but who that happens to notice their crooked pinions, and leather membranes, and zigzag flight, even for a moment, does not, the next moment, forget them all forever? If they cannot but hate the light, let them content themselves with obscuring their own cavern,—hanging close together in its entrance, hook by hook and claw within claw, with their eyes shut and their faces turned inward,—leaving all the world without to exult in its noontide blaze of heavenly splendor.

No, no: the Bible is enthroned on earth, as Christ is enthroned in heaven, for the salvation of souls, for the redemption of mankind. As Christ is the Son of God, so the Bible is the Book of God. And as Christ is the Son of man, so the Bible is the Book of man. And as God is in Christ, reconciling the world unto himself, so He is in the Bible, reconciling the world unto himself,—not imputing their trespasses unto them, but, for Christ's sake, forgiving and saving all who believe in Him, and in the Book which testifies of Him.

God knows what man is; Christ knows what man is; and the Bible—the Book of God, and of Christ, and of man—shows what man is.

Some of the enemies of the Bible reject it altogether,—are ready to throw it into the fire and spit upon its ashes. These are the selfish ones,—sensual, or cruel, or both: rioters of passion, or tyrants over the bodies and souls of the people.

Others reject only what the Bible relates of the life to come. In relation to the life that now is, they have recently discovered that the Bible is a fine Book; that it teaches universal brotherhood, liberty, and equal rights; that it furnishes the best shield in the world against the spear of the oppressor, and the best sword in the world wherewith to cut him down. These are the vain reformers of our race,—the dove-hearted dupes of the tiger-hearted devil.

The Bible rises, and will continue to rise, above them all. "For my thoughts are not your thoughts, neither are your ways my ways, saith the Lord. For as the heavens are higher than the earth, so are my ways higher than your ways, and my thoughts than your thoughts." The Bible is the Book of man,—not of a herd of brutal sensualists. It is the Book of man,—not of an alliance or convocation of tyrants. It is the Book of man,—not of the body only. It is the Book of man,—not of the soul only. It is the Book of man,—not of a few bodies and a few souls only. It is the Book of man, —not of a sect or party in either church or state. It is the Book of man,—not of the state in whole, nor yet of the church in whole. It is the Book of man,—not of state and church combined. It is the Book of man,—not of all states and churches on earth combined. It is the Book of man,—of every man, body and soul, —of all men, in all relations and throughout all generations,—"having promise of the life that now is, and also of that which is to come." "This is a faithful saying, and worthy of all acceptation."

Can any man suppose that God would give His Son to the cross, or His Book to the press, for a part of the world only? No more than He would give rain, or sunshine, or air, for a part of the world only! He values spiritual life more highly than natural life, and is not less free in the gift of means to sustain it. But, strange to say, these means are committed to a few for the benefit of all. The Book — unlike the rain, and sunshine, and air—must be sent abroad by human hands. Herein is our elect honor. Herein is our most solemn responsibility. God help us to act worthily!

It is well, sir, to hold such anniversaries in National Halls. It is well to claim the support of Cities of Brotherly Love. It is well to challenge the help of the noblest representatives of church and state. But "who is sufficient for these things?" As the Bible itself is the Book of God and the Book of man, so the circulation of it is the cause of God and the cause of man. In such a work, the rarest human energy is nothing without the richest divine blessing.

What then? Let us all say, deliberately and reverently, Down with state authority, down with church authority, down with all authority, —on land and sea, at home and abroad, now and forever,—in so far as it opposes the authority of the Bible! The Bible is not only the higher Law, but the highest Law; not of one country

only, but of all countries; and not for one age
only, but for all ages. Up, therefore, with individualism; not, however, the individualism of
infidelity, but the individualism of the Bible;
not the element of anarchy, but the regenerating
conservatism of society,—the best basis of common order and peace; the individualism of evangelical repentance, faith, hope, and love; the
individualism of true manhood; the individualism
of the image of God impressed on the soul and
shining in the very countenance-of the redeemed.
The Bible and private judgment!—the Bible and
liberty of conscience!—the Bible and personal responsibility!—the Bible and social progress in
church and state, here and everywhere, now,
henceforth, and forever. Amen!

CORRESPONDENCE.*

"House of Representatives,
"Washington, March 19, 1860.

"Rev. T. H. Stockton.

"Dear Sir:—The undersigned, Members of the House, would respectfully request a copy of your salutatory Sermon, delivered yesterday in the Hall of the House. We wish it for publication, that its influence may be widely extended by the circulation we shall give to it. If it comport with your inclinations and convenience, a compliance with this request will greatly oblige

"Your friends,

"S. S. COX,	G. W. SCRANTON,
JNO. HICKMAN,	W. HOWARD,
E. JOY MORRIS,	THOMAS B. FLORENCE,
THOS. A. R. NELSON,	JNO. G. DAVIS,
A. A. BURNHAM,	JAS. C. ROBINSON,
JOHN McLEAN,	J. W. STEVENSON,
JNO. A. BINGHAM,	ROGER A. PRYOR,
ROBERT McKNIGHT,	C. L. VALLANDIGHAM,
JAS. B. McKEAN,	J. K. MOORHEAD,
E. B. FRENCH,	C. B. SEDGWICK,
JOHN HUTCHINS,	WM. PENNINGTON."

"Washington, March 22, 1860.

"Gentlemen:

"Your request was as much a surprise as my election. Humbly trusting, however, that there is a vindicating and progressive Providence in these incidents, and wishing, most devoutly, to be enabled to answer its purposes, I respectfully commit my discourse to your disposal.

"As you appropriately intimate, it is a simple *salutation*,—prepared hastily, but not without prayer or care,—designed to announce certain main principles and connect them with suitable reminiscences and exhortations. If, in looking at the manuscript (containing a few verbal corrections and additions of personal names), you still deem it likely to do good, I shall be grateful for the use you may make of it.

"With all respect, I remain
"Your servant, for Christ's sake,
"T. H. STOCKTON.

"Hon. Wm. Pennington, Speaker of the House of Representatives.
" John McLean, Judge of the Supreme Court.
" S. S. Cox; Hon. Jno. Hickman;
" E. Joy Morris; and other Members of the House."

---

* Copied to indicate co-operative sentiments then prevalent.

SERMON FROM THE CAPITOL.

THE IMPERISHABLE AND SAVING WORDS OF CHRIST.

Delivered in the Hall of the House of Representatives, on Sabbath morning, March 18, 1860.

"Heaven and earth shall pass away, but my words shall not pass away."—MATTHEW xxiv. 35.

WE need elevation. As men, Americans and Christians, we need elevation. In our persons and families, states and churches, we all need elevation. Properly speaking, it is impossible to desire too great elevation. The woe of the world is the want of a true ambition.

To prevent us from taking unjust advantage of this truth, it is enough to remember the Gospel maxim:—"*For whosoever exalteth himself shall be abased; and he that humbleth himself shall be exalted.*" This maxim both commends the object and directs the pursuit.

321

And now,—see! One day, a young Galilean
carpenter, followed by a few lake-shore fishermen, entered the Temple at Jerusalem; as a
company of our countrymen, from any rural
district, on any day, enters this Capitol. Soon
after, as they left the Temple, some of the
young man's friends invited his attention to
certain fine ornaments and massive stones, characteristic of the general and incomparable richness and strength of the buildings. But he
replied to them, "*See ye not all these things?*
Verily I say unto you, There shall not be left here
one stone upon another, that shall not be thrown
down."

What did they think of that? What would
we think of a rustic visitor, who should leave
this Capitol, saying to his companions,—and in
a manner implying imminency of the event,—
Not one stone of it shall be left upon another!

Strange as it may seem, that Galilean group
had no little confidence in their leader; and,
therefore, when they had come with him, out
from the city, down the hill, over Kedron, and
up Olivet, until they reached a suitable position
for a wide resurvey of the scene, no sooner was
he seated than they drew near to him with the
question, "*Tell us, when shall these things be?*"

What then? Did he withdraw what he had said, or make light of it, or intimate any possibility of mistake? Not at all. Rather, he gave them a prolonged and specific answer; in the course of which, ascending, with infinite ease, to an infinitely sublimer assumption, he did not hesitate to declare, *"Heaven and earth shall pass away, but my words shall not pass away!"* It is as though he had said, There reposes the Holy City; girt about with all the defences of art and nature; and glittering all over with the concentrate wealth and power and pride of a great nation, during a long succession of royal and priestly ages. There expands, pre-eminently and most impressively, the peerless magnificence of the venerated and impregnable Temple. To you, it seems marvellous that I should predict the destruction of all. But to me, that olden glory is only as the fading pageant of a summer sunset. Look away from the city, beyond and above it. Behold the mountains round about it! Behold the firmament bending over it! Nay, let your thought exceed your vision. Think of the fulness of heaven and earth; of continents, islands, and seas; of sun, moon, and stars; of the divine origin, grandeur, perpetuity, and government of all. Think well of these things, and then remember,—that my words are mightier and more enduring than all. Not only shall Jerusalem pass away, but heaven and earth shall pass away; and yet my feeblest word, the faintest sound of my voice, the gentlest breath from my lips, shall never pass away.

Did they believe him? Yes; and with good reason. They witnessed, to a great extent, the power of his words. Attracted by those words, cities were emptied and deserts filled. At his word, the "common people," who "heard him gladly," grew wiser than the wisest of their teachers. At his word, the hierarchs of genius and learning, of law and religion, blushed and trembled,—darkening with rage or paling with affright. At his word, his humble disciples were qualified and commissioned to supersede "the wisdom of the world," and become themselves the apostles of nations and instructors of mankind. At his word, every scene of his presence became a circle of divine enchantment: where deaf men listened, and dumb men spoke, and blind men looked, and lame men leaped, and the paralytic stood still, and the leper was clean, and the maimed made whole, and the withered restored, and the sick revived, and the lunatic calmed, and the demoniac dispossessed, and the

dead—just risen from their tombs—exchanged
new greetings with the pressing multitudes of
the living. True, their faith was sorely tried:
chiefly, when their youthful leader expired on
the cross. But he soon rose from the dead,
ascended into heaven, and thence "gave gifts
unto men." Thus, their faith was renewed and
confirmed, forever. Then they repeated and recorded his words; committing them, in trust, to
all nations and ages. In fulfilment of the prediction specially referred to, before that generation passed away, the Temple was destroyed, and
Jerusalem with it; and the people were scattered
and their institutions overthrown. The carcass
of Judaism lay stretched along the hill-side, and
from the whole cope of heaven the eagles of
Rome hurried to the festival. Since then, the
words of that young man have become the law
of the world; and miracles, corresponding with
those of his transient ministry, have been multiplied on a larger scale and in more enduring
relations. At his word, deaf nations have listened, and dumb nations spoke, and blind nations looked, and lame nations leaped, and paralytic nations have been strengthened, and leprous
nations cleansed, and maimed nations made
whole, and withered nations restored, and sick

nations revived, and lunatic nations calmed, and demoniac nations dispossessed, and dead nations brought forth exultant from their graves. Even these miracles are "as nothing, less than nothing, and vanity," in comparison with others which are yet to come,—miracles in behalf of all nations, and of our whole race, and of the world itself. And still, with the same easy, natural, infinite sublimity as at first, he assures us all, "*Heaven and earth shall pass away, but my words shall not pass away.*"

Now, therefore, rises the all-important question:—Do *we* believe him? We live more than eighteen hundred years after his advent. We live in a new world; unknown to the old, in which he lived, until within less than four hundred years ago. A new soil is under our feet, and a new sky over our heads. We show, on a vast area, free and unembarrassed, the best results of a thousand social revolutions. To us, the most of the old things of the old world have passed away: old governments, old mythologies, old philosophies, old sciences, old arts, and old manners, customs, and usages. To us, nearly all things have become new. But have the old words of that young Nazarene passed away from us? or has any new master superseded his authority over us? Not in the slightest degree! His authority is still supreme, and every syllable of his utterance as sure as ever. As it has been, and is, so it always shall be. With gratitude for our history, in vindication of our honor, and in acknowledgment of the true and only source of our power,—in due remembrance of our fathers, with due respect for ourselves, and due regard for our children,—I here arise, on this highest height of the nation, as a representative, however humble, of our people at large of every State in the Union, and of the United States in whole; and thus, with lifted hand, repeat our solemn, national affirmation,—our official and perpetual proclamation to all mankind,—that HEAVEN AND EARTH SHALL PASS AWAY, BUT THE WORDS OF OUR LORD AND SAVIOR JESUS CHRIST SHALL NOT PASS AWAY!

I contemplate the heaven and earth of the old world: the overrulings of Providence and changes of society there. I think of the passing away of the whole circle of ancient Mediterranean civilization. I think of the dark ages of Europe. I think of the morning of the Reformation, and the fore-gleamings of "the latter-day glory." I think of Art, and her printing-press; of Commerce, and her compass; of Science, and her globe; of Religion, and her Bible. I contemplate the opening of the heaven and earth of the new world: the overrulings of Providence and changes of society here. I think of the passing away of savage simplicities, and of the rude semblances of civilization in Mexico and Peru, and of earlier and later declensions. I think of the gracious reservation of our own inheritance for present and nobler occupancy. I think of our Revolution, and its result of Independence. I think of our first Union, first Congress, first prayer in Congress, and first Congressional order for the Bible; and of our wonderful enlargement, development, and enrichment since. And, in view of all,—of the whole heaven and whole earth of the whole world; and of all changes, social and natural, past, present, and future; profoundly and unalterably assured, as I trust we all are, that the truth as it is "in Jesus" is the only stability in the universe,—I feel justified in invoking, this day, your renewal of our common and constant confession, that Heaven and earth shall pass away, but the words of Christ shall never pass away. And, standing where we do, on the central summit of this great Confederacy, unequalled in all history for all manner of blessings, if we did not so confess

Christ; if we did not cherish the simple confidence of His primitive disciples, and hail the coming of our Lord with hosannas; if we could ignobly hold our peace; the very statues of the Capitol "would immediately cry out;" the marble lips of Columbus, Penn, and Washington; of War and Peace; of the Pioneer and of Freedom, would part to praise His name; and the stones of the foundation and walls, of the arcades and corridors, of the rotunda and halls, would respond to their glad and grand acclaim.

But we do confess Him! From Maine to Florida, from Florida to Texas, from Texas to California, from California to Oregon, and from Oregon back to Maine; our lake States, gulf States, and ocean States; our river States, prairie States, and mountain States; all unite in confessing and blessing His name; beholding His glory, surrounding His throne, high and lifted up; and ever crying, like the six-winged seraphim, one to another, far and near, from the North and the South, from the East and the West, "*Holy, holy, holy, is the Lord of hosts: the whole earth is full of his glory.*"

But *where* are the words of Christ? and *what* are they? He did not write them; but merely spoke them, and that during a brief ministry.

Nevertheless, they were recorded; and not only such as were uttered in the flesh, but others with which the writers were inspired by His spirit, both before and after His advent,—the revelations of the prophets and apostles. All alike are His words; and here they are,—in the Bible! The Bible, from beginning to end, is the book of Christ. And, therefore, affirming of the whole what is true of every part, I hold up the Bible, and, in the name of Christ, proclaim to the country and the world, HEAVEN AND EARTH SHALL PASS AWAY, BUT THE BIBLE, THE HOLY AND BLESSED BIBLE, SHALL NOT PASS AWAY!

What, then, are the words of Christ? or, as the Bible, the whole Bible, and nothing but the Bible, is the inspired and authoritative record of them,—*what is the Bible?*

We hear much of the Higher Law; and the application of the phrase to civil affairs has excited great prejudice and given great offence. But what is the Higher Law? It is said to be something higher than the Constitution of the United States. Can there be a law, within these United States, higher than the Constitution of the United States? If there can be, and is, such a law, what is it? I need not, and will not, recite inferior, questionable, and inappropriate answers here. But is there not one unquestionable answer? Suppose it be said, that, in relation to all subjects to which it was designed to apply, and properly does apply, the Bible is a higher law than the Constitution of the United States. Will any man, unless an utter infidel, deny this? Surely not. Waiving its practical operations, certainly, as an abstract proposition, this must be admitted as true. It may be extended, so as to include all our State constitutions, and all our Church constitutions, and all our more Social constitutions. Put them all together, magnify and boast of them as we may, not only is the Bible a higher law, but it is an infinitely higher law. For thus saith the Lord: *"As the heavens are higher than the earth, so are my ways higher than your ways, and my thoughts than your thoughts."* Therefore, also, the universal and perpetual prophetic challenge:—*"O earth, earth, earth, hear the word of the Lord!"*

If this be not true, my mission, at least, is an entire mistake, and my commission ends. But it is true; and, if there were no other argument to prove it true, this one were all-sufficient. All human constitutions—social, ecclesiastical, and civil—are changeable, and contain provisions for change; but the Bible is unchangeable. Instead of any provision for change, it is guarded, at all points, against change. The writer of its first five books declares, in the last of the five, " *Ye shall not* ADD *unto the word which I command you, neither shall ye* DIMINISH *from it, that ye may keep the commandments of the Lord your God, which I command you.*" And, in like manner, the author of its last five books declares, in the last of the five, "*If any man shall* ADD *unto these things, God shall add unto him the plagues that are written in this book: and if any man shall* TAKE AWAY *from the words of the book of this prophecy, God shall take away his part out of the book of life, and out of the holy city, and from the things which are written in this book.*" And so Isaiah, standing midway between Moses and John, exclaims, "*Lift up your eyes to the heavens, and look upon the earth beneath; for the heavens shall vanish away like smoke, and the earth shall wax old like a garment, and they that dwell therein shall die in like manner; but my salvation shall be forever, and my righteousness shall not be abolished.*" Therefore, it is only in accordance with the testimony of all His witnesses, that Christ himself avers, "*Think not that I am come to destroy the law, or the prophets: I am not come to destroy, but to fulfil. For verily I say unto you, Till heaven and earth pass, one jot or one tittle shall in no wise pass from the law, till all be fulfilled.''* And so again, in the text itself, *"Heaven and earth shall pass away, but my words shall not pass away."*

Thank God for one book above amendment! *"Forever, O Lord, thy word is settled in heaven."* And here, in our place and day, we respond to the psalmist on Zion,—Forever, O Lord, thy word is settled *on earth.* No man or set of men; no king, priest, or scribe; no popular convention, ecclesiastical council, or national congress, would dare to erase one letter from the record. Let our own countrymen, in particular, treat other books as they think they have a right to do, or feel it their duty or make it their interest or pleasure to do,—by amendment, abridgment, or enlargement; by interpolation or expurgation,—not one among them, North, South, East, or West, would presume to touch, with any such purpose, the sacred ark containing the Higher Law of God. Here is our shrine of worship, the oracle of our wisdom, and the glory of our power.

But a higher Law implies a higher Judge, and a higher Administrator. And who is the higher Judge? The HOLY SPIRIT! the Spirit of truth, promised unto us to guide us into all truth; making us spiritual and giving us spiritual apprehension; aiding us in the comparison of spiritual things with spiritual; searching the deep things of God, as contained in the Bible, and revealing them unto us. And who is the higher Administrator? CHRIST Himself! into whose hands the Father has committed all power "in heaven and in earth," to qualify Him fully for the duties of this sovereign office. Does any one object to the higher Administrator? Does any one object to the higher Judge? Then why object to the higher Law? They go together, are all divine, and all supreme forever. So that we may say with the prophet, "*The* LORD *is our judge, the* LORD *is our lawgiver, the* LORD *is our king; he will save us.*"

"*He will save us!*" Blessed conclusion! without which all else were in vain, and worse than in vain. He deigns to become our judge, lawgiver, and king, only that He *may* save us; and, if we do not thwart Him by our iniquities, *because* He is our judge, lawgiver, and king, He *will* save us.

Tell me, oh, tell me! what is it we need? Do we need health, or genius, or learning, or eloquence, or pleasure, or fame, or power? Do we need wealth, or rank, or office? Does any one of us need to be chaplain, or clerk, or representative, or senator, or speaker, or vice-president? an officer of the army or navy? a member or head of any department? a foreign minister? a cabinet officer? or even a successor in the line of presidents of the United States? Is such our need? Ah, no! we need salvation.

What did I say in the beginning? Did I not say we need elevation? As men, Americans and Christians, we need elevation: in our persons and families, states and churches, we need elevation. Certainly I did thus speak, and meant all I said.

O my friends! all the distinctions alluded to, such as we know them here, are comparatively little things. Greater things are in prospect; but these things, though they seem great, are really little. Pause, think, recall what life has taught you,—what observation and experience have combined to impress most deeply upon your consciousness,—and begin your review with the sad words, *after all!* After all, health is a little thing, and genius is a little thing; and learning, and eloquence, and pleasure, and fame, and power, and wealth, and rank, and office, all earthly things, are little things. How little satisfaction they yield while they last, and how soon they pass away!

Ask the most successful around you, in these relations, if they have yet supplied their highest need? As the general rule, the more successful they have been, the older you will find them. They have not attained their coveted posts of honor by a single leap. They have risen gradually, through years of earnest toil. And the soberness of reflection is now about them. And the anticipation of a hastening end is with them. Ask them, and they will answer:—After all, we have spent our lives in little things. We yet need true elevation.

I would tell you, more particularly, of whom to inquire,—were it not that you would prove it in vain to seek them. Twenty-six years ago, at the age of twenty-five, I was first called to this office. Two years afterward, I served again. I now compare, though briefly and imperfectly, the present with the past. I find a new Hall and a new Senate-Chamber; but the old Hall and the old Senate-Chamber are still here. I find also a new House and a new Senate; but where are the old House and old Senate? How many reminiscences crowd upon me!—forms, and faces, and voices, and gestures, and elaborate speeches, and casual debates, and social remarks, and current incidents: all impressed on youthful sensibilities, and not yet effaced. But I cannot describe them. Where are JARVIS, of Maine, and CUSHMAN and HUBBARD, of New Hampshire? Where are ADAMS, CALHOUN, and CHOATE; DAVIS, JACKSON, and LAWRENCE; LINCOLN, PHILLIPS, and REED, of Massachusetts? Where are ELLSWORTH, HUNTINGTON, and JUDSON, of Connecticut? Where BURGES and PEARCE, of Rhode Island? Where ALLEN, EVERETT, and SLADE, of Vermont? Where BOKEE, CHILDS, and CRAMER; GRANGER and LANSING; LEE, MOORE, and WARDWELL, of New York? Where is PARKER, of New Jersey? Where are BEAUMONT, CHAMBERS, and DENNY; HUBLEY, McKENNAN, and MANN; MILLER, MUHLENBERG, and WATMOUGH, of Pennsylvania? Where is MILLIGAN, of Delaware? Where are DENNIS, HEATH, and JENIFER; McKIM and STEELE; STODDERT and WASHINGTON, of Maryland? Where BOULDIN, COLES, and DROMGOOLE; JONES, MASON, and MERCER; PATTON, STEVENSON, and TALIAFERRO, of Virginia? Where CONNER, DEBERRY, and McKAY; SHEPPARD, SPEIGHT, and WILLIAMS, of North Carolina? Where are BLAIR, CAMPBELL, and DAVIS; GRIFFIN, McDUFFIE, and PINCKNEY, of South Carolina? Where GLASCOCK, GRANTLAND, and HAYNES; HOLSEY and WILDE, of Georgia? Where are WHITE, of Florida; and LEWIS and MURPHY, of

Alabama? Where are BULLARD, GARLAND, and RIPLEY, of Louisiana? Where is SEVIER, of Arkansas? Where are CARTER, CROCKETT, and DUNLAP; FORRESTER and HUNTSMAN; POLK, POPE, and STANDEFER, of Tennessee? Where ALLEN, BOYD, and FRENCH; GRAVES, HARDIN, and HAWES; JOHNSON, LYON, and WILLIAMS, of Kentucky? Where is ASHLEY, of Missouri? Where are DUNCAN and MAY, of Illinois? Where BOON, DAVIS, and HANNEGAN; KINNARD, LANE, and McCARTHY, of Indiana? - And where are HAMER, LYTLE, and SLOANE; SPANGLER, THOMPSON, and VANCE, of Ohio? All these, if my quest has been rightly answered, have passed away, not only from this House, but from the world; and, doubtless, many of their colleagues, if not already gone, are just about to follow. At least, they are not here. Scarcely a relic is left! And so of the Senate. Where are CLAYTON and CUTHBERT; GOLDSBOROUGH, HILL, and HENDRICKS; KENT, KING, and KNIGHT; MOORE and PORTER; SOUTHARD and SPRAGUE; TIPTON, TOMLINSON, and WALL? Where the venerable WHITE, and the good-natured GRUNDY, and the sharp POINDEXTER, and the learned ROBBINS, and the handsome LINN, and the graceful FORSYTH, and the sagacious WRIGHT, and the indomitable BENTON, and the gentle-tongued LEIGH? Where is the easy, all-elate, sonorous, and majestic eloquence of CLAY? Where the calm, cool, clear, and massive magnificence of WEBSTER? Where the affable dignity, the intellectual and moral loftiness, of CALHOUN? Passed away,—all passed away! Or, will you leave the Halls of Congress? Do you think of the Army?—Where, then, are MACOMB and GAINES? Of the Navy?—Where, then, are RODGERS and BARRON? Will you enter the Supreme Court?—Where is MARSHALL, Chief of the Judges? and where is WIRT, Chief of the Attorneys? Or, will you at last repair to the Presidential mansion? Where, then, is JACKSON, Chief of the Heroes? Passed away,—all passed away! How many of their companions, how many of their successors, have also passed away, I have neither time nor knowledge to declare. It is but a little while and a limited area of which I speak, and yet—what a scene of honored dust, in sacred silence, alone remains!

Oh, if I could direct you to them, and you could find them, and should ask them,—After all, what is human need? would they not say, It is elevation, it is salvation,—salvation by humiliation, in accordance with the life, and death, and triumph of the meek and lowly Nazarene?

Hearken to me this day, men, brethren, and fathers! Christianity is the most practical thing, the most immediately and substantially important thing, in the universe. Visionary! fanciful! impractical! The occupation of dreamers, enthusiasts, and fanatics! Aha! Did I not tell you that we need elevation? How can any, how dare any, prate thus of our faith?

Hearken to the truth! If we need health, it is perfect health, and that forever! If we need genius, it is perfect genius, and that forever! If we need learning, it is perfect learning, and that forever! If we need eloquence, or pleasure, or fame, or power, or wealth, or rank, or office,— whatever we need, it implies constitutional and conditional perfection, and that forever!

Let me speak for you, one voice for humanity. I need a perfect soul. I need a perfect body, to contain, identify, and obey my soul. I need a perfect home. I need a perfect society. I need perfect employments. I need a perfect government. I need the fulness of eternal life, with God, in heaven. I need the attainment of my true destiny; to stand, as a perfect man, before the perfect God, acknowledged as His child, His image, and His heir.

The Son of God knew this need, and therefore

became the Son of man, that He might supply it.
Therefore He appeared as the young Galilean carpenter, despised and rejected of men, but loved
and accepted of the Father, making peace by the
blood of the cross. Therefore, already overlooking the place of His crucifixion, He uttered the
memorable prediction, *"Heaven and earth shall
pass away, but my words shall not pass away!"*
His words are words of pardon, words of purity,
words of triumph over death, words pertaining to
the resurrection of the dead and the inheritance
of life everlasting. Did the stones of the Temple
understand Him? Did the palaces of Jerusalem
catch His meaning? Did the mountains around
the city, and the sky above it, startle at the
sound? Did heaven and earth, anywhere or in
any way, show the slightest consciousness of His
utterance? Senseless, all senseless, utterly senseless, these are the things that pass away. But something was there, nobler than all these,—something
destined to outlast all these; to flourish only the
more, and still more forever, when heaven and
earth shall vanish like the dream of a night. I
mean the immortal soul! Jesus of Nazareth, the
Son of God, the Saviour and Sovereign of the
world, committed His words of redeeming and

sanctifying truth to the immortal soul of man, and therefore in form, as well as in essence and authority, they remain imperishable.

And so, my friends, in conclusion, I this day commit these words to your immortal souls, that, by God's blessing, they may abide with you in saving virtue forever. Only four months ago, by these same fingers, the eyes of my dear little JESSIE were closed in death. That was a more important event to me than the rise, progress, and fall of a thousand empires. Pity me,—oh, pity me! I speak not for myself alone, but for all humanity,—one voice for humanity. Think of your own homes; of those you love, and have loved, and love only the more in death. We are all alike in these relations. And where is our hope of reunion with the lost? Ah, never would the Lord Jesus have uttered the words of the text had He contemplated merely a series of social changes. But He knew and sought our true interest. He fulfilled His humble ministry, and suffered and died that He might secure for us entire and eternal personal redemption,—an elevation above all earthly things, and the enjoyment of the fulness of His grace and glory in heaven. Let us cherish His spirit and imitate

His example. Let us take due advantage of His mediation, and humble ourselves before God in all penitence and faith, that in due time we, with Him, may be truly and forever exalted.*

---

* This last paragraph is an effort to recover the substance, at least, of a purely extempore close,—a half-restrained yielding to natural impulses in hope of spiritual profit.

ADDRESS,

Delivered in the Hall of the House of Representatives, on the Day of National Humiliation, Fasting, and Prayer, Friday, January 4, 1861.

I.—THE OCCASION.

On this day of national humiliation, fasting, and prayer, recommended by the President and accepted by the people, I desire, from this official position, to address to my countrymen, with equal frankness and reverence, a few words, in the name and by the blessing of the Father, and of the Son, and of the Holy Ghost, to whom be all glory, as it was in the beginning, is now, and ever shall be, world without end, Amen.

Two months ago, the Governors of our States, with unexampled richness of occasion and unanimity of grateful joy, invited their fellow-citizens to unite in the celebration of a day of thanksgiving and praise. Then there was no section of the sky, suspended over any section of the globe,

344

within whose cloudless horizon lay such a domain of grandeur, beauty, plenty, and peace; or such a society of personal, domestic, civil, and religious freedom, wisdom, purity, power, and glory; as glittered upon the vision of men, and saints, and angels, and Christ, and of God Himself, the Father of all, within the golden circle of the American Union. It might well have been anticipated that, on the opening of the appointed and hallowed festival, there would go up, through the serene and benignant brightness, to the very throne and heart of the Highest, such a concert of hallelujahs as no nation on earth ever offered before. But was it so? Alas! though the day was so fair, and the feast so bountiful, and so many divided families re-collected in old homesteads, and the laugh of childhood was clear as the tinkling of a cymbal, and the songs of youths and maidens were merry as the chimes of a wedding, still, among all the mature and thoughtful and over all the elders of the land, there was a chilling gloom of shame, sorrow, and fear, and in all the temples of religion the cheerful tributes for Divine mercy in the past were checked, if not subdued, by lamentations over present human folly, and deprecations of future wrath and woe.

And what now? Two weeks after Thanksgiving, another proclamation was heard,—not made by a Governor and limited to a State, but proceeding from the President and extending "throughout the Union." "Numerous appeals" had been made to him, "by pious and patriotic associations and citizens, in view of the present distracted and dangerous condition of our country, to recommend that a day be set apart for Humiliation, Fasting, and Prayer," and, "in compliance with their request, and (his) own sense of duty," he designated this day, "Friday, the 4th day of January, 1861, for this purpose."

Marvellous revolution! Hark! "The Union of the States is at the present moment threatened with alarming and immediate danger!" Two months ago, how different! Again: "Panic and distress of a fearful character prevail throughout the land!" Two months ago, how different! Again: "Our laboring population are without employment, and consequently deprived of the means of earning their bread!" Two months ago, how different! Again: "Indeed, hope seems to have deserted the minds of men. All classes are in a state of confusion and dismay, and the wisest counsels of our best and purest men are wholly disregarded!" From all this, how different, only two months ago!

And so, in solemn haste, we are turned back to "the God of our fathers," as our only "resort for relief" "from the awful effects of our crimes and follies." Instead of coming for thanksgiving,—though we have still infinitely more to be thankful for than we are worthy to enjoy,—we come in self-abasement, with self-affliction, and to pour out our souls in most penitent and earnest supplication. Well may we thus come; for, this day, there is no section of the sky, suspended over any section of the globe, within whose clouded, flashing, and muttering horizon such scenes are witnessed of ingratitude toward God, disparagement of blessings, dishonor of national and universal brotherhood, intent madness of fanaticism and pride, and terrific imminence of all possible, unspeakable, and perhaps endless evils, as those which disgrace and threaten to destroy, from centre to circumference, in sight of all mankind, this same American Union.

Let us humble ourselves, is the exhortation of our Chief Magistrate; let us confess our sins; let us implore the removal of false pride; let us beseech God to restore friendship and good will; to save us from the horrors of civil war, and not desert us, but "remember us as He did our fathers in the darkest days of the Revolution, and

preserve our Constitution and our Union, the
works of their hands, for ages yet to come."
Amen! and let all the people say, Amen!

II.—THE ANTI-CHRISTS OF THE AGE.

But, just here, I come to a more timely, more
important, and most imperative duty. Some
may regard it as a divergence from the proprie-
ties of the occasion. But I know that it is not.
I know that the day, the place, the interests of
the auditory, and of the outer auditory, even
though it be of the continent or the world, demand such an utterance. In making it, I only
attempt, by gracious assistance, to reach

> "The height of this great argument,
> And justify the ways of God to men."

See! Now, as of old, "there are many Anti-
Christs in the world:" persons, parties, powers;
infidel, artistic, scientific, philosophic, economic,
—from the merest skeptics to the sheerest deists,
atheists, and anti-theists,—these, with their inventions, theories, systems, and instruments of influence. Constitutionally, educationally, by proud
and vain self-culture, and by the clique venom
of mutual flattery and impious pretension, these
enemies of God and man, taken just as they
stand, in sum total of life, are haughty, con-

temptuous, narrow-minded, ignorant, shallow to
simple shimmering, incapable of appreciating or
even apprehending the highest truth; blind, deaf,
dumb, thoughtless, and heartless to the whole
spiritual universe, and yet captivated by innumerable brilliant but deceptive idealities, hallu-
cinations of super-loftiness, with all manner of
unequalled sublimities and elegancies of intellectual and moral contemplation. These are the
Anti-Christs. They do not know Christ. They
despise Him. They hate Him. They oppose
Him. They say,—Any thing but Christ! I need
not call them fools. But one who was inspired
of God did style them fools, and therefore, on
Divine authority, which is decisive, they are
fools.

These Anti-Christs, like their master, are imitators,—meagre and miserable imitators. Reject-
ing Christ's redemption, they fashion a substitute.
Redemption? Certainly. What! human perfec-
tibility true? Unquestionably. And actual perfection in prospect? Most assuredly. In a word,
say they, we too have an Evangel, a glorious
Evangel; and our Evangel is, "There's a good
time coming!" But where is it coming? To
all the world. And how will it be marked?
Well, the soil will be more fruitful, the air more

healthful, social conditions more equal, and life, nearly or quite exempt from disease, will be greatly prolonged. And when shall this good time come? Within the lapse of the innumerable and immeasurable ages. And by whose miraculous advent will it be introduced? Oh! we have nothing to do with advents or miracles: we have long since discarded the fables of our childhood. It will happen so. It will be the natural result of the common and magnificent progress of our race. It will be the final triumph of the march of mind. And so, to the demoniac music of such a march as this, tramp, tramp,—tramp, tramp,—the hosts of Anti-Christ push through the darkness of time to the blackness of darkness in eternity. Sin in the past, sin in the present, and sin in the future; sorrow in the past, sorrow in the present, and sorrow in the future; death in the past, death in the present, and death in the future: sin, sorrow, and death,—all utterly and forever unredeemed! This is "the good time coming," the Evangel of Satan, the salvation of the world without a Saviour!

And so, at this stage of human progress, when it is inquired, What does the world need? these enthusiasts of superficial enchantments reply:— Let Japan be thrown open to commerce; let

China dust her buttons at the feet of the allied barbarians; let Russia annex Turkey; let France annex Syria; let England annex Egypt; let Hungary humble Austria; and let the unity of Italy be completed by the subjugation of Venetia and the submission of Rome. But is this what the world needs?

And just so at home! Here, therefore, under all this pressure of the burden of national humiliation, fasting, and prayer, in the very crisis of our civil destiny, I justify this pause, this broader view, this introduction and consideration of interests still superior, and infinitely superior, to those which we deplore as so awfully imperilled. Hear me, therefore, this day, O my fellow-men, fellow-citizens, fellow-Christians! hear me this day, if ye never hear me again, and remember my teaching of this hour, if all my other teaching shall be forgotten forever. Especially, ye disciples of Anti-Christ, listen this once to one of Christ's disciples, — a disciple not without hope, however unworthy,—listen and think, if ye can think, and feel, if ye can feel, and pray, even though ye never prayed before, that ye may think wisely, feel truly, and after all be saved.

What, then, do we need? Does the Highest behold, from His throne in heaven, that this day is observed with due sincerity and solemnity throughout all our land? Is our humiliation acceptable? our fasting acceptable? our prayer acceptable? Are all our exercises acceptable, through Jesus Christ our Lord? And is the heart of our Father moved in our behalf, and does He incline to answer our petitions? Then lift up thy hoary hairs, thou aged and anxious President! Lift up your heads, ye Governors of all our States! And ye, O prostrate people! North, South, East, and West, arise, and stand in the presence of God, and receive His blessing.

Let the "distracted and dangerous condition of the country" be suddenly changed into its former estate of harmony and peace. Let the "Union of the States" be recovered and confirmed. Let the "panic and distress" subside. Let our "laboring population" abound in work and wages. Let the "false pride of opinion" be removed. Let "friendship and good will" be restored. Let the "horrors of civil war" be averted. Let God "remember us as He did our fathers in the darkest days of the Revolution, and preserve our Constitution and our Union, the works of their hands, for ages yet to come." Let all we are thus prompted to pray for be granted unto us. Nay, more; being thus reconciled to

God and to each other, renewed in all our pros-
perities, and exalted among the nations to greater
power and glory than ever, let the admiring and
sympathetic authorities of Europe—Denmark,
Sweden, and Russia; Portugal, Spain, and France;
Holland, Great Britain, and all others concerned
—commend to our protection and resign to our
rule all their American possessions; and Mexico,
Central America, and even Hayti, learn to con-
fide in us, and claim our kindness and care, until,
from the smallest mission in Greenland to the
rudest fort near Behring's Straits, and all around
by the shining isles of the Gulf and the smoking
mountains of the Isthmus, the whole northern
continent, with all its appurtenances, from the
Bermudas to the Sandwich Islands, shall have become ours,—peacefully, honorably, happily ours,
—with no desire or dream of secession or dis-
union within all its bounds. What now? Is this
what we need? Would this be enough for us?
Could this satisfy us?

Ay, ay! shout the Anti-Christs. That is what
we need! That would be enough for us! That
well might satisfy us, whether God or man should
work the change!

But cease your shouting, ye witless Infidels!
Be dumb as death, ye silly Anti-Christs! This is

not what we need. This would *not* be enough for us. This could *never* satisfy us. All this, and infinitely more of the same sort, were "nothing, less than nothing, and vanity," in comparison with our true want. "For what shall it profit a man, if he gain the whole world and lose his own soul? Or, what shall a man give in exchange for his soul?" A man is more than South Carolina. A man is more than the United States. A man is more than the whole world. Since South Carolina determined to secede, how many hundreds of her citizens have died! Since the President issued his call for this day of national humiliation, fasting, and prayer, how many thousands of the citizens of the United States have died! Since the report of our dissensions went forth to other lands, how many myriads of mankind, in all the world, have died! And, before these dissensions shall be settled, how many millions more—some here, some there, some everywhere —will have died! What did they want? What do their survivors want? What, as one with them, do we want? A change in the civil government? or, the perpetuation of the government as it is? Alas! for the Anti-Christs!

And so it has been for six thousand years! The earth, smitten, ravaged, broken, parcelled out among the nations; the nations, relatively, increasing and diminishing; empires, rising and falling; governments, forming, flourishing, failing; but, under all circumstances, at all times, and in all places, man—sinning, sorrowing, dying! Such a world, O ye Anti-Christs! if purposely made so, and hopelessly kept so, were a shame, a disgrace, a curse, to its Maker. And do ye still bespeak for it the innumerable and immeasurable ages? Aha! God knows better and will do better!

There is a Being, hidden from us, though not we from Him, clothed in our own nature perfected and glorified, sitting and reigning at the centre and zenith of this universal circle of light and life, of whom it is declared: "In the beginning was the Word, and the Word was with God, and the Word was God." And again, "In the beginning God created the heavens and the earth:" for "all things were made by Him; and without Him was not any thing made that was made:" over whose creations, all perfect like Himself, "the morning stars sang together, and all the sons of God shouted for joy." This is He "whose goings forth have been from of old, from the days of eternity;" even "Jesus, the Christ, the same yesterday, and to-day, and forever:"

31

into whose hands the Father has committed "all power in heaven and in earth;" "in whom dwelleth all the fulness of the Godhead, bodily;" "whom, having not seen, we love; in whom, though now we see Him not, yet believing, we rejoice with joy that is unspeakable and full of glory, receiving the end of our faith, even the salvation of our souls;" and waiting for the end of our hope, also, even the salvation of our bodies, in the beauty and glory of the resurrection. From the fall of Adam until now, not a year, or day, or hour, or moment has passed, but His eye has watched our planet, and His heart been intent on the redemption of our race. By the sufferings of His first advent He made an atonement for sin itself, and by the miracles of the second He will set us free from its consequences. At the close of His last prophetic interview with His latest surviving apostle, He declared:—"Surely I come, quickly; Amen:" to which the apostle replied, in behalf of the church and the world, "Even so, come, Lord Jesus!"

I profess no skill, or assurance, in determination of prophetic times and seasons. I simply wait on the Lord. Nevertheless, I cannot but understand that we are now nearly eighteen centuries nearer the fulfilment of the promise than when it was given. Neither can I forget that many lines of prophecy, relating to the same great event, appear to converge about the present era. And neither can I be unobservant of the facts, that the world is now open from pole to pole,—that the Gospel has already performed its office, to a great extent, as a witness for Christ among all nations,—and that the condition of nature and society, everywhere, seems to invite Divine intervention for the resurrection of the dead, the transformation of the living, the judgment of all, the renovation of heaven and earth, the establishment of everlasting righteousness, and the universal development and triumph of the kingdom of glory and of God.

All we can say, is,—and this must be said with infinite reverence,—"the sooner, the better:" the sooner Christ's time comes, the better for all who wait for His coming. If, amidst the conflict of empires, the revolution of kingdoms, the crumbling of republics, and the consequent amazement and alarm of all mankind, we seem to hear a repetition of the promise, as just about to be realized,—"Surely I come quickly!"—let our hearts leap within us as we answer, "Even so come, Lord Jesus!"

Here is our want,—Christ! "Thou, O Christ!

art *all* we want!" He, essentially and truly, whether known or unknown, is "the desire of all nations." Let the Anti-Christs say what they will, the only hope of the world is in Jesus Christ. *1 shall gain my chief object, if I can only persuade you duly to remember this.* Whatever personal dangers, or social dangers, may at any time press upon us, —however we may humble ourselves before God, and fast, and pray for deliverance from them; and even though our prayers be heard and answered, and the dangers which threatened us be removed,—still, in all conditions and at all times, our own supreme and most urgent want, and that of the whole world quite as well, is— CHRIST — CHRIST'S PERSON, CHRIST'S SPIRIT, CHRIST'S ADVENT, CHRIST'S MIRACLES, CHRIST'S KINGDOM, CHRIST'S GOVERNMENT, CHRIST'S PEOPLE, AND CHRIST'S PERFECT AND EVERLASTING SALVATION!

III.—THE NATIONAL CRISIS.

Now, therefore, having borne this humble testimony in behalf of our highest interests, I return, for a brief interval, to this solemn crisis in our civil affairs.

If what I have hitherto said be true, the best condition in which any nation can be placed is that in which the people, personally and socially, have the best opportunity and facilities to understand, appreciate, obey, enjoy, and extend our Holy Religion.

Here, therefore, I affirm, that—since the hour in which the Lord Jesus declared, "And I, if I be lifted up from the earth, will draw all men unto me,"—His cross has never been planted in any land, or His redeeming attraction exerted upon any people, whose advantages, in these highest of all relations, bore any comparison with our own.

The only difficulty in demonstrating this, is the want of time. But you do not need the demonstration. While I speak, the globe revolves in the light of thought, and you see that there is no other land like ours,—no land at once so ample, so varied, and yet so completely one,—no land so interlocked, north and south, through the whole range of both coasts, by indestructible mountains, —no land so interlaced, on both shores, and all over the interior, by innumerable rivers, ever lengthening their matchless courses by endless curves, as though they would leave no ravine unclaimed, and no hill unclasped, in all the common heritage,—no land so washed all around by lakes, gulfs, and oceans, sharply defining its

31*

own bounds, but still holding it adjacent or opposite, open and accessible, to all the world besides,
—no land, in a word, where the lay of the soil is
so like the lift of the sky, immense, unbroken,
and inseparable forever. Inseparable forever!
What! Would any divide it? Let them make
the Mississippi a hundred miles wide and a thousand fathoms deep,—an impassable line of perpetual storms. Would any divide it? Let them
turn the Alleghanies and the Rocky Mountains
east and west, and unite them in a Missouri com-
promise that cannot be abolished. "He that sit-
teth in the heavens shall laugh, the Lord shall
have them in derision." As easily might they
fracture the firmament from sunrise to sunset,
and from the north star to the equator. And so
with our people. They, too, while I speak, expand before you in the clear thought-light. The
cross of Christ has drawn them together from all
countries, and made them one. In the beginning a few Italians, a few Spaniards, a few Englishmen, a few Frenchmen, a few Germans, a few
Swedes; but now, more than thirty millions, representing nearly every nation under heaven!
In their little, isolated, native states and provinces, they lived side by side for centuries,—
estranged, embittered, hostile; diverse in lan-

guage, government, religion; in arts, customs,
and usages; shut up, apparently, to the bloody
necessity of everlasting strife. But here, on this
vast, and equal, and happy area,—free from local
traditions of prejudice, hatred, and war,—they
have already mingled, and are still more perfectly mingling, in one homogeneous mass, incomparable in all the history of man. Remember, they have not been driven hither, but drawn.
By the attractions of religious liberty, and of that
true civil liberty which flows from it, and by the
long reserved plenty and quiet of a natural heritage worthy of both, Christ has drawn them
hither. They have come, not as exiles, but as
immigrants. They have come of grateful choice.
They have come with impulsive admiration.
They have come with tender sympathies and
glowing affections. They have come on purpose to love us, and to be one with us. And so,
their native lands, and governments, and govern-
ment-religions, lose their interest; and, little by
little, their languages decline, and their habits
become assimilated to our own; and presently
our homes are their homes, and our churches
their churches, and our States their States; and
we are all, and only and all we desire to be, men,
Americans, and Christians,—the best situated of

all the nations on earth for the performance of the highest duties and the attainment of the highest destiny of our race.

And here let me proclaim anew our one greatest glory. I remember, indeed, that we are fond of boasting,—too fond of boasting. We have many apologies for it, but no sufficient apology. Perhaps this is one of the chief sins, in confession of which we should this day humble ourselves before God. And yet, the one great glory to which I refer can never be remembered, and ought never to be remembered, without the most earnest rejoicing. The materialist boasts of the mineral, vegetable, and animal opulence of the country. The intellectualist boasts of its arts and sciences, its literature and philosophy. The philanthropist boasts of its institutions of benevolence. The statesman boasts of its Constitution and laws, its freedom, equality, and power. And the religionist boasts of its churches and societies, and all its endowments of piety and zeal. But it is not by any or all of these distinctions that we are elevated to the best position on earth for the understanding, appreciation, and practice, the enjoyment and extension, of our Holy Religion. We owe this to one distinction alone. I mean, THE BIBLE,—the free and open Bible,—the uni-

versally circulated Bible,—the commonly accepted, confessedly supreme, and divinely authoritative Bible,—the only light in the gloom which
now environs us, the only hope in the despair
which presses on us! When I speak thus of the
Bible, I do not idolize a book,—but allude, of
course, to its living and active connections with
the omnipotent agency of the Spirit of God, and
the inspirations of that Spirit, as witnessed in the
noblest motives, energies, and exertions of mankind. Let the materialist go South with all his
natural treasures. Can he buy back affection,
union, and peace? Alas! pride is too strong for
him. Let the intellectualist try it, and they will
burn his books and break his instruments. Let
the philanthropist try it, and he will need a hundred philanthropists to return him safe home.
Let the statesman try it, and they will scoff at
the Declaration of Independence, and trample
the Constitution of the Union under their feet.
Let the religionist try it, and he will find the
fragments of broken churches and societies in all
his path, his influence forfeited forever, and his
former brethren praying against him, that God
may confound his counsels and prevent the success of his devices.

But, thank God! from the centre to the circumference of our confederacy, the Bible is still supreme. Its meaning may be disputed, but its divine authority is admitted. It is absolutely and inviolably sacred. No man, or set of men, would dare to add one word to it, or take one word from it. Here it stands,—the Book of Christ; the Brightness of His Glory; the Express Image of His Person; the Visible and Audible Angel of His Power; the Higher Law of the Nation, and the Highest Law of the World!

The South reads it historically; and, as though there were no progress, sanctions the present by the past. The North reads it prophetically; and, as though all progress were consummated, demands of the present the improvements of the future. Both parties mistake its current applications. Oh, when I think of the inexhaustible and yet constantly accessible intelligence of this Book; its sublime and comprehensive philosophy of God and man; of Creation, Providence, and Redemption; of Nature, Grace, and Glory; of Earth and Heaven; of Time and Eternity; its innumerable adaptations to all classes and conditions of mankind; and its invariable tendency to enlighten, purify, elevate, and, in every way, save and bless persons and families, States and Nations; I am ready to exclaim,—Withhold your reckless hands, and spare, O spare, our Union, if only for this unequalled privilege, that all our millions, over all our continent, with none to hinder, but all to help, may study together, and yet understand alike, and then exemplify alike, the love and truth and purity of God, as revealed in the Holy Bible!

And can it be, that South Carolina is determined to destroy this Union? And can it be, that other States encourage her rebellion? And can it be, that, suddenly as the evil has come upon us, it is already too late by any means to arrest it?

And now shall our enemies rejoice over us? Our enemies! Who are they? Where are they? By the blessing of God, the world is full of our friends! By the greatness of our Union, we have become a chief power among the nations; and by the fairness of our conduct, we have won their respect and affection. There was a time when Columbus vainly sought, along our southern borders, the golden roofs of Zipangu; but now, by a voyage three times as long, the Princes of Zipangu, excited by its fame and confiding in its honor, come to pay their respects to the richer world of Columbus. There was a time, and a second time, when Great Britain sent fleets

and armies to subdue our Colonies and ravage
our States; but now she too sends her Prince
and his train to mingle as equals with our people,
and to stand with bare brows, and tearful eyes,
and reverent hearts, at the hallowed tomb of
Washington. No, no,—even China and Japan
will mourn for the rent in the flowery flag!
Even Africa, far from indulging a feeling of re-
venge, will stretch forth her hands unto God,
and pray for us! And as for the nations of
Europe, gradually changed, even more than we
hoped, by the grandeur of our progress and the
value of our friendship, from revilers to admirers,
—identified with us by ceaseless immigration and
interchange of travel and intelligence; inspired
by our spirit, and inclined rather to imitate our
example than desire our injury,—England and
France, Switzerland and Germany, Italy and
Hungary, and many a generous and sympathetic
power, will weep over us! But, here at home,
how shall we restrain our own tears, or who shall
bind up our broken hearts? Alas for us! "O
that my head were waters, and mine eyes a fountain of tears, that I might weep day and night
over the slain of the daughter of my people!"
Ah! prophets of Judah and Israel, little did ye
dream of our greater grief! Ye only lamented

the desolation of Zion, and of the hills and vales around it. But here is a vast and varied world, which Jehovah reserved through thousands of years, and has now disclosed, enriched and adorned, as the crowning beauty and glory and wonder of all time! And shall such a heritage as this be sundered and destroyed? Clasp thy broken staff with shame, O flag of stars! superseded and dishonored by the pitiful palmetto! Start from thine eyrie, thou eagle of the morning! shake from thy pinions the dews of the night, and relume thy vision in the splendor of the sunrise,—lest the rattlesnake, crawling up the cliff, shall steal on thy slumber and strike thee unaware. God be merciful unto us!—and has it really come to this? Vacant seats in the Senate; vacant seats in the House; vacant seats in the Cabinet; resignations in the Army; resignations in the Navy; resignations in the Judiciary; a secession convention; a secession ordinance; a new oath of allegiance; Sabbath sessions; secret sessions; commissioners from a foreign State; warlike preparations; seizure of forts and arsenals; seizure of betrayed ships; obstruction of the port-channels; slaves throwing up earthworks along all the coasts; freemen leaving their homes, camping out on the

32

wintry strand, marching and counter-marching, in instant readiness for bloodiest conflict! How shall we account for this universal enthusiasm of utter madness?

SLAVERY! The liberty of twenty-six millions imperilled by the servitude of four! It is said that the South loves slavery, and that the North abhors it: that the South is determined to maintain it forever, and that the North is resolved to abolish it as soon as possible. It is an "irrepressible conflict!" The States must be all slave States, or all free States. Therefore, the North hates the South, and the South hates the North. We are mortal enemies!

It is false! all false! utterly false! In the name of God and man, I pronounce it essentially and eternally false. There is not now, there never was, in all the history of the world, an equal territory, with an equal population, so diverse in origin and in minor interests, where, because of the attraction of the supreme interests of religious and civil liberty, and of all forms of material prosperity, the people have so perfectly melted into one loving mass, as within the limits of this glorious and blessed Union. The country is too great for us. We do not comprehend it. We must rise higher and look wider. We have

mistaken the noise of sectional fanaticism for the
common feeling and judgment of the mighty but
silent nation. This day the whole land is in surprise and astonishment. I do not mean among
our sensation cities, always excited and multiplying excitements; but hundreds and thousands of
miles away, among the honest and quiet millions
of the interior.

Hark! Does this sound like hatred? "Our
Southern brethren are in arms! South Carolina
has seceded. Other States are about to follow.
They think we hate them, and are determined to
oppress them. But it is not so. Are they not,
equally with ourselves, men, Americans, and
Christians? We love them,—purely and fer-
vently love them. What do they want? Slavery
in the States? Let them have it: not because we
approve it, but because it is their Providential
allotment, for the time being, and they alone are
responsible for it. What do they want? Slavery
in New Mexico? Let them try it: if they fail,
the fault is their own, not ours. What do they
want? The enforcement of the fugitive-slave
law? This is the duty of the General Government; let it be performed. What do they
want? The repeal of the personal-liberty bills?
If the States were ill-advised in their passage, let

them be repealed. What do they want? The privilege of slave-service at the national capital, and in their current transits through the land? Let them have it, without molestation, at their own unavoidable risk. What do they want? Any thing less than a sacrifice of principle, conscience, and honor; any thing reasonable, proper, and expedient; any thing that God may command and humanity yield? Let them have it, and our true love with it, and our prayers with our love, that the God of the Bible may overrule all events for His own glory, and the welfare of the nation and the world!" *Does all that sound like hate?*

Pause, then, ye States preparing for secession! Reconsider thy course, thou lonely State that hast seceded! Come back, SOUTH CAROLINA! come back to the circle of honest and earnest affection; come back, with God's blessing; come back, with the nation's welcome; come back in peace; come back before a single drop of blood shall be shed! Blessed be JAMES BUCHANAN! if only for this one thing: that he will not, if he can help it, consent to the shedding of a single drop of blood. If he cannot help it, then be it remembered, that the Ruler "beareth not the sword in vain: for he is the minister of God, a revenger to execute wrath upon him that doeth evil." Let his skirts be clear. Let the skirts of the Army and Navy be clear. Let the skirts of the still United States be clear. But, O LORD JESUS, thou who hast promised to "come quickly," come now. At least, in all the healing love and pity of Thy Holy Spirit, come now. "Even so, come, LORD JESUS!" So shall all nations praise Thee, and, looking from afar, exulting in our restored, confirmed, and perfected Union, "BE-HOLD!" they will cry, as with one heart, and one voice, and one hope, "BEHOLD, *how good and how pleasant it is for brethren to dwell together in unity!*"

"The grace of our Lord Jesus Christ be with you all. Amen."

AMERICAN SOVEREIGNTY.

A SHORT SERMON

Delivered in the National Hall of Representatives, Sabbath morning,
July 28, 1861.

"Let every soul be subject unto the higher powers. For there is no power but of God: the powers that be are ordained of God."
—ROMANS xiii. 1.

I DO not intend, on this occasion, a long, formal, or elaborate discourse. But I desire, with the blessing of God, to state, clearly and impressively, certain elemental truths of our Holy Religion, important to be remembered always, but especially so in the current crisis of our affairs.

By the "higher powers," the text plainly alludes to political sovereignty and its authorized representatives. Political sovereignty is not of human origin. It is a divine institution.

372

In this country, we say much of State sovereignty and of United States sovereignty. But,
strictly speaking, our sovereignty is the sovereignty of the people. The people of the United
States existed before the States were united. The
people of every State existed before the State
itself. When, in the course of God's providence,
the due time came, and, with it, the due natural
and social conditions, He brought the people to
these shores as dependent colonists. Again, in
due time, by the Revolution, He made them independent,—a simple, elemental, popular, sovereign power. In this capacity, He committed to
them two great trusts,—the construction of the
two great institutions, without which no community can perpetuate a prosperous existence,—
one civil, the other religious; one the State, the
other the Church. In the execution of these
trusts, there was no external human authority to
control or direct them. So far as other men, on
all the earth and under the whole heavens, were
concerned, they were absolutely free,—were at
liberty to do all they would and could. God virtually said to them, "Behold, my people! the
continent is before you. I made it for you, and
you for it. Here none shall molest or make you
afraid. Build ye a State for yourselves. Build

ye a Church for yourselves. Build ye a State and Church worthy your own dignity and destiny, worthy the imitation of the world, and worthy my progressive and redeeming dispensations."

But, while thus set free from human authority, were they left destitute of Divine guidance? Not at all. There was a visible representative of Divine sovereignty among them, commissioned and qualified to superintend and modify the performance of their appropriate work, and to which they humbly acknowledged their own sovereignty to be subordinate and subservient. I mean, of course, God's book,—the Holy Bible. As the people existed before the Union, before the States, and even before the Colonies, so the Bible existed before the people,—thousands of years before them; the angel in the cloud, to all the tribes of their ancestry, in all their wanderings through the wilderness, from the earliest recorded ages of time.

What then? By the instrumentality of the Bible, God prompted them to come hither. When they came, they brought the Bible with them. It was their highest distinction, their richest treasure, and their purest joy. It was to them, as it is to us, or ought to be to us, the

highest law in all the world of the Highest
Power over all worlds. Their twofold obligation was, to found the State and found the
Church, on the Bible; to make their State a
Bible-State and their Church a Bible-Church.
This was not because any human authority had
any right or power to command them to do so;
but simply because God Himself, by His marvellous providence, so commanded them. No
human authority would even have attempted
such intervention. All human authorities had
more or less dishonored the Bible. It was held
under the foot of the State, and under the thumb
of the Church. Therefore God, with a high hand
and an outstretched arm, had conducted His
people from the Old World to the New. It was
He who thus exalted the Bible in its new sphere,
and from the beginning exacted obedience to its
precepts. He made His people free on purpose
that they might thus honor His book.

But what is the history, what are the facts?
Did they build up a Bible-State? Did they build
up a Bible-Church? Is the Bible supreme, this
day, in both State and Church? If not, then I
insist upon it that the people have been, and yet
are, unfaithful to their trusts. And, if unfaithful, then I further insist upon it that it is not too

late to repent, not too late to reform; and that
it is still their imperative duty to fulfil the task
at first assigned them,—to conform both State
and Church to the doctrines and morals of the
Bible.

If any thing be plain, this gradation of sovereignty is plain. The *first* sovereignty in our
land is the sovereignty of the Bible,—representing the sovereignty of God. The *second* is the
sovereignty of the people,—representing the sovereignty of the Bible. The *third*, in view of superior numbers, though inferior interests, is the
sovereignty of the State,—representing the sovereignty of the people in secular affairs. And the
fourth, relating to smaller numbers but greater
interests, is the sovereignty of the Church,—representing the sovereignty of the people in religious affairs. Below all these are the divisions
and diversities of popular sovereignty, exhibited
by particular States and Churches, and all minor
voluntary social institutions.

It is greatly to be regretted that this gradation of sovereignty is not more generally understood, remembered, and practically acknowledged.
There are men among us who deny, or doubt, or
in some way habitually ignore, the sovereignty
of the Bible,—as representative of God. In like

manner, they deny, or doubt, or ignore, the sovereignty of the people,—as representative of the
Bible. ˏAnd so, coming within the State sphere,
as though there were no God and were no Bible,
they treat the sovereignty of the people, in secular affairs, as a natural right, a birthright, a right
to be exercised without responsibility except to
the will of a majority of their own number as ex-
pressed by a legal vote, or the will of a minority
as enforced by revolutionary violence.   Therefore we so commonly hear it said, by zealous but
ill-informed advocates of national sovereignty,
that the Constitution of the United States is the
supreme law of the land: as though this were an
absolute and not a relative truth; as though it
required no qualification; as though there were
nothing beyond and above it; as though the
national Constitution were the highest symbol of
popular sovereignty; as though there were no
other to compare with it; as though it had become unchangeable; as though it had got to
be superior to the people themselves, and were
wholly independent of the Bible, and the God
of the Bible.

How strange all this is!   What is the national
Constitution?   It is *one* of the people's institutions; *one* of their political institutions; and their

highest political institution: so much, and no more. Hark! "WE, the people of the United States, in order to form a more perfect union, establish justice, insure domestic tranquillity, provide for the common defense, promote the general welfare, and secure the blessings of liberty to ourselves and our posterity, do ordain and establish *this* Constitution for the United States of America." That is, this is *one* thing, and politically the *chief* thing, that we, the people, choose to do, in exercise of our sovereignty: not presenting it as an unchangeable instrument, but providing for suitable amendments of it, and remembering that the same sovereignty which now ordains it will always remain superior to it, and hold it in entire control.

But what are the relations of this Constitution? Here it is, especially, that the want of correct knowledge, or just appreciation of facts, already alluded to, becomes painfully evident. Hark again! "This *Constitution*, and the *laws* of the United States which shall be made in pursuance thereof, and all the *treaties* made, or which shall be made, under the authority of the United States, SHALL BE THE SUPREME LAW OF THE LAND." Here the zealous advocates of absolute constitutional supremacy are accustomed to stop.

The Constitution is the supreme law! This sovereignty is the only sovereignty in the land! Christians, Jews, infidels, men of the world, we, in whole, are the people, and the national Constitution is our supreme law. Away with every other! Away with the heretics who assert any other! We intend to abide by this alone, and be governed by this alone. From all it prohibits, we will carefully refrain; but all it allows we will do at our pleasure, and none shall hinder us. To this extent, we are absolutely free. We confess no higher responsibility.

Now, what nonsense all this is, and how unspeakably deplorable it is! The sovereignty of the national Constitution is *not* absolute, but *relative*. It is only a midway sovereignty. Above it are other sovereignties, to which it is subordinate; and below it are other sovereignties, which are subordinate to it. The sovereignty of the people themselves is above it, and the sovereignty of the Bible is above the people, and the sovereignty of God above the Bible. Why, the relations of this constitutional sovereignty are not left in doubt. They are plainly declared in the very section a part of which I have just cited. And what are they? Does the article, after saying that this "shall be the supreme law

33

of the land," proceed thus: "And the judges in every State shall be bound thereby," any thing in the sovereignty of the people, or of the Bible, or of God, "to the contrary notwithstanding"? Not a word like it. These are superior relations, —relations beyond and above it, over which it has no control, but on which it is entirely dependent. The specified relations are, of course, inferior; and therefore the article reads thus: "This Constitution, &c., shall be the *supreme law* of the land; and the judges in every State shall be bound thereby, any thing in the *Constitution* or *laws* of any STATE to the contrary notwithstanding." The article is directed, not against popular sovereignty, or Bible sovereignty, or Divine sovereignty; but against the monstrous error, the awful heresy, the bloody dogma, as it has turned out to be, of State sovereignty,—either in opposition to, in secession from, or in rebellion against, the sovereignty of the Union.

That was the design of our fathers. They never dreamed of superseding the higher sovereignties by this merely political national sovereignty. When they had ordained and established the Constitution of the United States, they regarded and confessed themselves as completely subject to the Bible and the Bible's God as they

were before. Had it not been for the Bible, the
Constitution could never have been ordained and
established. If it embody true principles of human rights, and sure promises of honorable perpetuity, its principles and promises are alike derived from the Bible. It has no value except as
the Bible sanctions it. And if, in any respect, it
is in conflict with the Bible, it should be made to
conform to it.

But now let us turn, for a little while, to the
Church sphere,—representing the sovereignty of
the people in religious affairs. Here we are at
once struck by a great difference between our
State and Church arrangements. We have even
a greater number of separate denominations or
churches than we have of individual States. But
we have no general union of churches, no general
ecclesiastical government, no common Christian
constitution, not even "Articles of Confedera-
tion." Instead of a great national document,
commencing,—"WE, the *Christians* of the United
States, in order to form a more perfect union,
establish truth, insure tranquillity, provide for
common prosperity at home, promote the conversion of the world abroad, and secure the blessings of our Holy Religion to ourselves and our
posterity, do ordain and establish this Constitu-

tion for the United *Churches* of America:" instead
of any thing like this, and an article providing for
amendments of such constitution, and another declaring it to be, under God and the Bible, the supreme law of the Christians in the land, and that
the office-bearers in every church shall be bound
thereby, any thing in the constitution or laws of
any church to the contrary notwithstanding: instead of all this, or any thing like it, we have a
promiscuous assemblage of separate and diverse
ecclesiastical sovereignties, not divided by State
or other territorial lines, but intermingling their
forces, interests, rivalries, and courtesies all over
the continent. Historically, the most of these,
and especially the most powerful of them, are
descendants of Old World colonists, with Old
World creeds, rituals, ordinances, and usages.
There has never been an AMERICAN ECCLESIAS-
TICAL REORGANIZATION, to bring the churches into
closer conformity with the Bible and greater
unity and harmony among themselves. For
want of this, in my humble judgment, there has
been great loss of Christian influence.

But, without stopping to notice any supposed
imperfections, I wish to remark here that the
American Church, under God and the Bible, is
an institution of popular sovereignty as much as

the American State; that the great mass of its members are evangelical Christians; that they are the main dependence of the nation for all the elements of moral and intellectual, if not, also, even physical power; and that they deserve to be better represented, and ought to be better represented, and must be better represented, and when they become fully awake to their powers and privileges, and learn how to exercise and improve them most efficiently, will be better represented in the administration of State affairs,—which are their own affairs just as much as church affairs are their own. Pre-eminently they are the people. The concentration of sovereignty is within their circle. They hold it in their hands, almost without knowing it, certainly without rightly using it.

The theme is far, far too large and important for such an occasion as this. I merely teach, as already intimated, a brief primary lesson.

For instance, what is the Christian doctrine of war? May the Church declare war, and prosecute war? Not at all. May it even encourage war? I doubt this,—as a direct measure. The Church is a peace institution. It should preach peace, and in every way promote and encourage peace. The Church, so to speak, is not the

33*

people's proper war organ. It was designed for redeeming, and not destructive, purposes. But they have a proper war organ. It is the State. As citizens, they are joint possessors of State power, and responsible for the exercise of it. The State may declare war, and prosecute war. But what is its justification? May it commence and carry on war at its own pleasure? Not at all. It is the most solemn performance of a sacred ministerial office, and must be fulfilled in the name and with the sanction of God. The context illustrates the whole subject. Let me read the text again, in its connection with subsequent verses:—

"Let every soul be subject unto the higher powers: for there is no power but of God: the powers that be are ordained of God. Whosoever, therefore, resisteth the power RESISTETH THE ORDINANCE OF GOD; and they that resist shall receive to themselves damnation (or condemnation). For rulers are not a terror to good works, but to the evil. Wilt thou then not be afraid of the power? Do that which is good, and thou shalt have praise of the same: for he is THE MINISTER OF GOD to thee for good. But if thou do that which is evil, be afraid, for he BEARETH NOT THE SWORD IN VAIN; for he is the MINISTER of God, a revenger to execute wrath upon him that doeth evil. Wherefore ye must needs be subject, not only for WRATH, but also for conscience sake. For, for this cause ye pay tribute also; for they ARE GOD'S MINISTERS, attending continually upon this very thing. Render, therefore, to all their dues: tribute to whom tribute is due; custom to whom custom; fear to whom fear; honor to whom honor. Owe no man any thing, but to love one another; for he that loveth another hath fulfilled the law."

In ordinary cases,—cases concerning a single criminal, or a few criminals only,—war is not necessary. Punishment of evil is easily accomplished, under such circumstances, by ordinary methods. But in extraordinary cases,—cases of extended treason and all-threatening rebellion,—war, in some form, becomes a necessity. Yet the nature of the act remains the same. It is an official duty. It is a ministerial punishment of evil-doers. There is no pleasure in it on the part of the magistrate, any more than there is on the part of God,—that is, if the magistrate act in the true spirit of his office. It is an awful, but imperative, obligation, and derives all its propriety and dignity from this fact. The more blood on the sword, the more tears also; and happy is the day when its blade may be restored to its brightness and returned to its sheath.

What then? If war is to be thus justified by Christianity itself, as, for the time being, an indispensable State power and office, how shall it be conducted? Who shall be chiefly represented in its management? The worst part of our population? wicked men? ignorant men? wild, rash, and cruel men? men who take pleasure in rapine and violence? men who fight for the love of fighting, and care not what amount of distress they create? men who laugh at the Bible, and scoff at God? Are they to be chiefly remembered and respected by our authorities, and allowed to fill our camps with profanity, Sabbath-breaking, intemperance, and all manner of iniquity? Surely these are not the people. They are the rabble. The great masses of evangelical Christians, and all who sympathize with them in reverence of divine institutions, *they* are the people, the strength and beauty and glory of the nation. *They* are to be chiefly represented in the management of war, as in all other connections; the best part of our population; good men; intelligent men; prudent men; just men; benevolent men; men who deplore the necessity of war; men who believe the Bible and adore and worship God. They are to be remembered and respected, and such a discipline established and enforced in the council, in the camp, and in the field, as they can approve and sustain; such a discipline as will preserve in the army the highest moral tone, the majestic sense of law, and the solemn and immovable might of a good conscience.

There is no Sabbath in war. Who says so? Has God ever said so? Does the Bible say so? Do the people say so? Does the Church, or even the State, duly representing the people, say so? Or is it an unauthorized assumption,—an arbitrary and infidel desecration? The Jews regarded the law of the Sabbath as prohibiting war. In their later ages, indeed, they so construed it as to admit the propriety of a *defensive* battle. And, so far as I have noticed, they always made their defence good. But an *onset* was not allowable on the Sabbath. Neither, in my judgment, does Christianity allow it. Nor can I hope for success under such circumstances.

Our late battle was a Sabbath battle. It is said to have been specially ordered so, to provide a spectacle for civilians who could most conveniently attend that day! Can this be true? If so, who can wonder at the result?

Some forty regiments were there. Were there forty chaplains also, representing the Christian ministry of the country? And were there hundreds or thousands of soldiers also, representing the membership of the churches of the country? Why, then, was not the Christian sentiment of the country remembered and respected? Was that *onset* a work of *necessity?* Not at all. Was it a work of *mercy?* Not at all. Rather, it was a work of *cruelty.* The necessity was for *rest,*— for *sleep,*—for *food,*—for *religious instruction* and *worship.* Had the Sabbath been observed, as it ought to have been, in all probability,—that is, so far as we can see and judge,—the result would have been different. As it was, there was no defeat, properly speaking. Never was greater bravery exhibited, in the history of the world. And victory was almost assured.. But then, for wise purposes doubtless, the *innocent were allowed to suffer for the guilty.* Then came the *punitive panic,* —the *judicial disappointment.* And the civilians, for whom, it is said, the battle was ordered, became the instruments of overthrow. The "NATIONAL INTELLIGENCER"—perhaps the most trustworthy of all journals, in an editorial, headed "THE TRUTH OF HISTORY," issued on last Friday —distinctly declares, "The *panic, begun* with some *amateur warriors,* was *communicated* to the *teamsters,* and affected only a *portion* of the troops, who had been wearied by a *ten hours' struggle* without *food* or *refreshment* of *any kind.* The great body of the army maintained good order."

Well would it have been for these civilians, and for their country also, if, instead of attending this Sabbath battle, they had been quietly assembled in the sanctuaries of the city, adoring and worshipping God in the beauty of holiness. And well would it have been for our army, as for our country also, if that Sabbath had been kept as a holy day, throughout all the encampments; if the bodies of the soldiers had been refreshed by food and rest, and their spirits refreshed by hymns and prayers, and the thousand conscience-cheerers of the Word of God.

If there were no commandment to remember the Sabbath-day and keep it holy, the very beauty of it, and blessedness of it, should make it regarded as the most charming of all human inventions or institutions. And surely, if six days out of seven be enough for working, six days out of seven are enough for fighting. I would that we might hope that *henceforth there shall be no more Sabbath fighting*,—at any rate, *no setting of the battle*, on our part, on this hallowed day.*

---

* The sermon closed with some extempore remarks on the importance of attending, in the midst of all this uncontrollable strife, to the great work of *personal salvation*.

WHY COULD NOT WE CAST HIM OUT?

A SERMON

Delivered in St. John's (Rev. Dr. Seiss's) Lutheran Church, Philadelphia, on the National Fast-Day, Thursday, April 30, 1863.

"Why could not we cast him out? And he said unto them, This kind can come forth by nothing but by prayer and fasting."
—MARK ix. 28, 29.

ALL the miracles of Christ are interesting, but this one is of peculiar interest. The record begins with the intimation of a very impressive contrast. Our Lord had just come down from the Mount of Transfiguration; and, from the amazement of the people at His appearance, it would seem that somewhat of the glory which distinguished Him on the height was still glittering among the folds of His garments, and gleaming in the beauty of His countenance. Strange to say, gentle and glowing and loving as He was, He was immediately met by the dark scowl and bitter malice of His old and unrelenting enemy, the prince of devils! That is, the first sufferer brought to Him for relief was this poor youth, possessed by an evil spirit. But Satan is no match for the Son of God. On any cloud, on any mountain, or in any valley, the night may meet the morning; but how easily the morning dispossesses heaven and earth, and fills the world with the splendor of common and perfect day!

Our Saviour took three of the apostles with Him when He ascended the mountain; but the nine others remained below with the waiting multitude. It was during the absence of Christ that the young demoniac was brought to the place; and the father, being oppressed by anxiety in his son's behalf, and finding that nine of the apostles were there, hoped that they might suffice, in want of their Master, and therefore besought them to cure him. It may be that the apostles thought they could cure him; for previously to this occasion they had been sent forth on purpose to perform such works, and had performed them. Moreover, it is plain that in this case they tried to expel the demon, but failed. The reason of their failure seems to have been the subject of the great questioning that was in progress when our Lord came to them. The scribes may have taunted them

34

with their want of success:—You say you have
wrought such miracles in other places. How is
it that you lack the power here? Surely this is
a case that appeals to all your sympathies. If
you can relieve him, why not do it? Aha! Vain
boasters are ye all! We do not believe you ever
wrought a miracle!

In this condition Christ found them. It seems
appropriate that He appeared to them with more
than usual majesty, so as at once to encourage
His disciples and overawe their opponents. Ad-
dressing Himself directly to the scribes, He asked,
"What question ye with them?" And just here
is one of the most pathetic points in the narrative.
The scribes did not answer. Neither did the
apostles make any reply. Probably they would
have spoken soon after; but *one* was there whose
heart was too full of sorrow and solicitude to
wait for any of them. This was the almost broken-
hearted father. Falling on his knees before the
gracious and glorious Redeemer, he cried out,
"Lord, I have brought unto thee my son, mine
only child. Have mercy on him, for he is lunatic
and sore vexed; he has a dumb spirit, and wherever he taketh him he teareth him; and he foameth, and gnasheth with his teeth, and pineth away;

and I spake to thy disciples, that they should cast him out, and they could not."

The case being thus pathetically stated, and the fault, not of one party only, but of all parties, being so manifest to the all-searching Spirit of divinity, "Jesus answered and said, O faithless generation, how long shall I be with you? how long shall I suffer you? Bring him unto me." As though He had said, My disciples, indeed, have shown a great want of faith, and therefore a want of power, and so have exposed themselves to the reproaches of their enemies: but the fault is not theirs alone. It is the fault of the father also, and of all who sympathize with him and bear him company. The poor sufferer lingers in his agony because ye are all faithless. And here, my friends, is a great lesson,—a lesson relating to all Christian operations, and especially to all church enterprises. It is, indeed, important that the ministry shall believe, but it is no less important that the people shall believe also. Without faith on the part of both classes, it is impossible to please God as a church, or to succeed in the true mission of a church. Faith must be the co-operative social law. Moreover, it was even then necessary, and now it is still more so, to exercise faith in Christ though personally absent. He could not long remain with those who were then about Him; and, as to ourselves, He has never been present with us except by his Spirit. It is the unseen Saviour whom, as Christians, we love, in whom we believe and rejoice, and by whom we are saved ourselves and made the instruments of salvation to others. It is all a matter of faith; and without faith we are as weak as the men of the world.

"Bring him unto me." As though He had said, While I am with you, I cannot neglect you. I must feel for you, and will show my sympathy by helping you.

Then they brought the poor, miserable youth into the Saviour's presence. But, as soon as he saw Christ, the malignant spirit that possessed him "tare him, and he fell on the ground, and wallowed, foaming." Notwithstanding His tenderness, Jesus remained calm. "And he asked the father, How long is it ago since this came unto him? And he said, Of a child. And ofttimes it hath cast him into the fire, and into the waters, to destroy him; but," he cried, as if it was impossible for him to dwell longer on the mere history of the case while his dear boy was thus violently convulsed at his feet, "if thou canst do any thing, have compassion on us, and help us." As though he had said, Oh, I do not know thee; I have heard of thee; it is said that thou canst work such miracles; and if thou canst,—if thou art, indeed, superior to thy disciples, and hast power to help us,—have pity on our sorrow, and grant us help at once. Look at my poor boy, and do not wait a moment. But Jesus, of course, knew all that was right and proper in the case, and acted according to the suggestions of His own infinite wisdom. "If thou canst believe," said He, "all things are possible to him that believeth." As though He had said, The delay is not occasioned by any lack of either pity or power. The responsibility is thine, rather than mine. It is needful for thee to believe. Canst thou believe? It did not take long for the father to decide. And, yet, how finely his honesty is developed, as well as his love and anxiety! Great as was the pressure upon all his sensibilities and affections, intensely as he longed for the deliverance of his son, he could not pretend to more than he felt. Oh, the struggle in his soul! I would, if I could. I would do any thing for my son. What shall I do? Then, it may be, looking up into the face of Jesus, seeing the serene and shining countenance, so full of grace and glory, and so expressive of willingness and readiness to save, he was instantly subdued, and, bursting into tears, straightway cried out, "Lord, I believe; help thou my unbelief." As though he had said, Oh, yes, yes! I will, I do believe: only I fear that my faith is not as perfect as it should be! Lord, strengthen me, and help me to believe with all my heart! Hearing his agonizing cry, the people came running together, and Jesus, satisfied with the answer, rebuked the foul spirit, saying unto him, "Thou dumb and deaf spirit, I charge thee, come out of him, and enter no more into him." Ah, that, indeed, was more than His disciples, in all probability, could ever have said! Not only, Come out of him; but, also, Enter no more into him! A perfect cure, at once and forever! No wonder the spirit cried, and rent him sore, and *so* came out of him; leaving him as dead, insomuch that many said, He is dead. It may be that he was dead, or so nearly dead that, if the disciples had tried to resuscitate him, they would have failed again, even though the devil was gone. "But Jesus took him by the hand,"—oh, the thrilling virtue of that touch!—"and lifted him up, and he arose." Then Jesus "delivered him again to his father. And they were all amazed at the mighty power of God." I wonder if the father

ever doubted after that! Methinks he must have
been a whole-hearted believer as long as he
lived.

But the disciples, the nine apostles, how mor-
tified they must have been! A most painful state
of feeling; but often very profitable, notwithstanding the pain, or, rather, because of the pain.
According to the fuller record by Matthew, who
was one of them, they came to Jesus apart, and
said unto him, "Why could not we cast him
out? And Jesus said unto them, Because of your
unbelief; for verily I say unto you, if ye have
faith as a grain of mustard-seed, ye shall say
unto this mountain, Remove hence to yonder
place, and it shall remove; and nothing shall be
impossible unto you. Howbeit, this kind goeth
not out but by prayer and fasting." The gradation here is this: 1. Fasting; 2. Prayer; 3. Faith.
Comparatively, fasting is important; prayer, more
important; faith, most important. Philosophically,
fasting tends to the increase of prayer, and prayer
tends to the increase of faith. The desirable
result is, that we may be made strong in faith,
and so, by good works, be enabled to glorify God,
in the promotion of all human interests. Without fasting, or rather without prayer, or rather
without faith,—the sum and substance of all, the

spirit in the absence of which all forms and efforts
are nothing,—without this faith, we may attempt
a thousand needful and excellent things, but fail
in all; spend our whole lifetime in toil and sacrifice, and exhaust our resources utterly in vain.

And what now? Is there any thing in this
history applicable to the peculiar demands of this
occasion?—any thing in our national affairs ana-
logous to the conditions of the parties here described? What a tempting opportunity for the
exercise of oratorical ingenuity—what a fine
opening for the exhibition of dramatic skill!
Alas for every thing contrary to the simplicity
of the Gospel! Yet see:—

Our Lord himself, where is He? Is He not
personally absent from us? Is He not enthroned
on the height of heaven, transfigured and illustrious, seated in the immediate presence of His
Father, and rejoicing "in the midst of His an-
cients gloriously"? Are not many of His disciples, elect statesmen and churchmen, some of
whom we ourselves have known, and all of whose
names are dear to our country, assembled with
Him there, and do they not prove it to be good
to be there? and do they not desire above all
things to remain there?

But who are these on earth, waiting for our

Lord's return? What great multitude is this, and why is it so greatly excited, and why is there so much questioning and disputation among the people? Is there not some case of great difficulty or trouble pending here?—some case of social lunacy? of demoniacal State possession? Who is the victim? Is it not the South? Who is the father? Is it not the National Government? Who are the disciples? Are they not represented by the Border States and Free States of the East, West, and North? And who are the captious scribes, and the great concourse of spectators? Are they not England and the world at large?

And see how the matter, so far, has proceeded. The South has been possessed with an evil spirit, the devil of slavery; a foul spirit, foul beyond all utterance of foulness; a dumb spirit, stifling all words of complaint, all groans of pain, and demanding silence even of the commiserating world around it; a deaf spirit, deaf as the adder, and as deadly too, stinging and poisoning and destroying black and white alike, hearing the shrieks and heeding the agony of neither.

At last, after long-continued affliction and mourning, the fatherly Government seeks relief for the lunatic son; brings him, in purpose, to Christ Himself, but, failing to find Him, implores

the help of His disciples.   The North—speaking
now of all the free sections as one—looks upon
the South with true sympathy; detesting, indeed,
the devil that works the woe, but pitying the
victim who endures it.   Calm in the assurance of
its own sanity, confident in its great strength and
ample resources, it has at first no doubt of its
ability to do all that is required.   With certain
expectation, therefore, and with a clear, loud
voice, the command is given to the evil spirit to
quit the sufferer and depart.   But, as in the case
of the Jewish exorcists of Ephesus, especially of
the seven sons of Sceva the chief-priest, the
attempt is a failure;   the adjuration is scarcely
pronounced, when the evil spirit exclaims, "Jesus I know; but who are ye?" and the South,
inspired with demoniac fury, leaps upon the North,
overcomes it, prevails against it, and the North
flees from it, naked and wounded.   Then England
cries out, "Aha! disappointed, are you? Not so
easy as you thought!   More mettle than you
looked for!   The chivalry has better blood than
you imagined!"   And every scribe connected with
her press, and every Pharisee pampered by her
Church, all ranks of her social, civil, and ecclesiastical hierarchy, exult in the Northern reverse,
and join in the haughty taunt, "You conquered

us, did you, in two wars? And you conquered
Mexico, did you, since then? And you were
quite sure you could quickly conquer the South,
were you? Why don't you do it? You can't!
You see you can't! There's no use in trying!
You had better give it up!"

Alas for the poor North! How every true-
hearted patriot and Christian laments the result!
But it would never do to abandon the case at this
juncture. The very song of the children becomes
a quickening prompter, "Try, try again!" And so
another trial is made, and another, and another,
and yet another; nay, such trials are continued
for weeks, and months, and even years. True,
sometimes the North appears to succeed. For a
while the violence of the demoniac is subdued.
But it is only for a little while. Soon the resistless paroxysm returns. And who can hope in
such a contest? Now the South flees, "naked and
wounded;" and again the North flees, "naked
and wounded." Both parties stream with blood,
and still the evil spirit retains his possession.
Still, also, the scribes and Pharisees multiply their
cutting sarcasms. "'Tis all in vain!—worse than
vain. You are as mad as the South. Why don't
you stop, and let the devil hold his own in peace?"

And what now? How did the apostles act

after their failure and in the midst of their shame? We are not told. The record is silent on this subject. But we may suppose that they said, each in his heart, and perhaps openly one to another, Oh that our Lord and Master would come down from the mountain! We have almost forgotten Him. We have trusted too much to our own strength. Therefore we have failed, and exposed ourselves to all these insults. Perhaps they looked up toward the height, and breathed a prayer for His return.

So with us of the North. We have been ready to say, as indeed the Israelites in the Desert said of their great leader while secluded in Sinai, "As for this [Jesus], He who brought us up from the land of our captivity, we know not what has become of Him." Christ has been in heaven so long that, to us, He has become as one dead, or, at least, as one lost. We have forgotten Him. But now we see our sin and confess it. So, in the form of the President's proclamation, we say, "We have forgotten God." This is the burden of the national confession. We have forgotten God! We have assumed the place of God ourselves. We have arrogated to ourselves His attributes, claimed as our own His achievements, substituted our law for His law, and presumed thereby to determine our future destiny. More successful than Adam, while he merely sought divinity, we have secured it! So we persuaded ourselves. But now we see our folly. Now we feel our folly. Now we deplore our folly. Alas for us, of ourselves we are "nothing—less than nothing—and vanity!" Oh that we might see one of the days of the Son of man! Oh that Christ would come back to us! Without Him, as He himself forewarned us, we "can do nothing." We have attempted more than we can accomplish. Oh for His help, to rescue us from failure and make us successful!

Well, now suppose that the Redeemer graciously appears in our behalf. We are more amazed than was the multitude of old. He inquires, first, Why all this questioning? The North says nothing. England says nothing. But the Government, father-like, cries out, Lord! I have brought unto thee my son. Have mercy upon him. He is lunatic and sore vexed. He has a dumb spirit. Wheresoever he taketh him, he teareth him; and he foameth, and gnasheth with his teeth, and pineth away; and I brought him to thy disciples that they should cast him out, and they could not. Jesus answers, "O faithless generation! how long shall I be with you?

35

How long shall I suffer you? Bring him unto
me." So the South is presented to Christ And
what a pitiable spectacle it is! Did Jesus Himself ever see a case so sad? And, lo! as soon
as the South looks into the face of Jesus, the
demon tears his poor victim. He falls to the
ground, and wallows, foaming. Jesus speaks to
the Government, "How long is it ago since this
came unto him?" And the Government answers,—
oh, so sorrowfully!—"Of a child! And ofttimes
it hath cast him into the fire, and into the waters,
to destroy him; but"—more earnestly still the
fatherly cry continues—"if thou canst do any
thing, have compassion on us, and help us!"
Jesus saith again unto the Government, "If thou
canst believe, all things are possible to him that
believeth." And straightway the Government
cries out, with tears, "Lord, I believe; help thou
mine unbelief!" So bitter is this cry, that all
within hearing hasten toward the scene of interest.
And Jesus, not wishing any further embarrass-
ment of the case, promptly rebukes the foul spirit,
and commands him, saying, "Thou dumb and deaf
spirit, I charge thee, come out of him, and enter
no more into him." And the spirit fairly shrieks
with malice and spite, and sorely rends his wretched
subject, and comes out of him; and he lies upon

the ground as one dead, and some say, He is
dead; but, lo! Jesus takes him by the hand, lifts
him up, helps him to stand, and so delivers the
poor South to the Government again, restored
and in his right mind, never,—for here is the
beauty of it, the glory of it, the everlasting joy
of it,—never to be repossessed by the devil, free
from slavery at last, and certain of remaining so
forever! And what has England to say now?
What say her scribes? What say her Pharisees?
Do they say, It was a great mistake to expel the
devil, with so much pain? It would have been
better to let the poor South remain as he was?—
What! remain as he was! Subject to renewed
attacks forever! Falling into the fire still! Falling into the water still! Near being destroyed
every moment still! Oh, no, no, no! rather let
England say, and the world say, "It is the Lord;
let him do what seemeth him good!" And as
for the disciples, what do they say? What can
they say, except simply to inquire, "Lord! why
could not we cast him out?" And what can the
Lord answer, but this, "Because of your unbelief;
for verily I say unto you, if ye have faith as a
grain of mustard-seed, ye shall say unto this
mountain, Remove hence to yonder place, and
it shall remove; and nothing shall be impossible

unto you.   Howbeit, this kind goeth not out but
by prayer and fasting."

And what now?   Will this do?   Is such an
analogy sufficient for the occasion?   Not at all;
not at all!   The case is not as thus represented.
We have no reason to expect a miracle.   Christ
is in heaven; and there He will abide until the
time appointed for the accomplishment of a far
greater work than this shall require His personal
attention.   The difficulty is left to our own management, under ordinary earthly circumstances.
The Government and the North must settle it,
under God, themselves.   Besides, the representation of the South as the only child would not be
correct; neither would it be just, without qualification, to describe it as lunatic and possessed
with a devil, especially if in contrast to a sane
and wise and innocent North.   Allowance would
have to be made for much individual piety, intelligence, and general good character in the South,
however for the time perverted and misled.
Similar allowance would have to be made for
individual examples of ignorance and corruption,
of wickedness and worthlessness, in the North;
notwithstanding the array of much of all, as a
fighting force, on the side of what we esteem to
be right.   As for England and other nations, the

allusion to them, perhaps, might stand, as not seriously amiss. But, upon the whole, I could not work such an analogy efficiently, for fear of doing injustice to some of the parties in the case. And there is nothing under heaven that so completely takes the soul out of an orator, and makes him speak like a mere automaton, as a doubt of the truth of his utterance, or a fear that what he says is not just. If you would have an orator all soul,—a pure, celestial fire, burning and blazing gloriously as an archangel fresh from the throne of Omnipotence,—fill him with the truth, and assure him of the justice of his cause. Then, if he ever knew what genius and passion are, their real divine virtue, he will set sky and earth and sea in flames, if necessary to the accomplishment of his patriotic, philanthropic, and Christian purpose. Even I, therefore, discarding, of course, all pretension, must drop this analogy for simpler, plainer, purer doctrine. And what is that? Why, leaving all circumlocution, and pressing straight onward in my speech, it is this:—We may fast as much as we will, and pray as much as we will; but, unless our fasting increase the fervency of our praying, and our more fervent praying increase the might and majesty of our faith, all our efforts will end in irreparable and everlastingly disgraceful failure.

35*

Unless we go forth to the battle in the fulness of a true, pure, trustworthy, equalizing, elevating, and almighty faith,—the faith of a holy Christian democracy,—as opposed to all the blandishments and all the selfish, degrading, and destructive tyrannies of an infidel and insatiable aristocracy,— our sacred Union is dissolved forever; our sacred territory is divided forever; our sacred liberties, if not destroyed, are impaired, imperilled, and shorn of half their glory forever; our sacred example is darkened and dishonored forever; and our sacred mission in behalf of all humanity, for all lands and all ages, is basely and ruinously forfeited forever.

The two sections assert opposite systems. It is impossible for both to be true. We must decide which is true, and give our faith, and our life with our faith, to that, and that alone, and that forever.

The South asserts slavery. Slavery is right. Slavery is a good. Slavery is sanctioned by the Bible and by the God of the Bible. Slavery is constitutional. State sovereignty is constitutional. Secession is constitutional. While the Union lasted, slavery gave us inestimable advantages. Slavery enabled us to rule at our will four millions of black people. Slavery enabled us to rule at our will seven millions of poor white people.

8*

Slavery enabled us to divide the ·North, and so rule at our will twenty millions more of white people. Slavery enabled us to secure and hold the General Government, and so rule at our will, in whole, more than thirty millions of people. And so fond are we of rule, that *we would not belong to a government which we could not control.* Now that the Union is dissolved, and we are an Independent Confederacy, though our rule will be more limited, it will be more complete and less disturbed. Free from the everlasting annoyance of the contemptible hypocrites and fanatics of the North, we will keep the black man under one foot, and the poor white man under the other, and there shall be none in heaven or earth to say, Remove your feet, and let the down-trodden arise. We will re-open the slave-trade, and, at our pleasure or according to our interest, multiply its horrors a hundredfold. We will cultivate sympathy with all the aristocracies and monarchies of Europe. We will encourage and strengthen them. We will give the lie to all our former professions of republicanism; and, making slavery the corner-stone of our institutions, we will put the Bible in that corner-stone, seal it up, bury it, build upon it, and so proceed, cementing every layer of stone with blood and tears, until we

reach the top-stone, shouting over that, at last,
Democracy is a humbug! Republicanism is a
failure! Cotton-lords are we! Cottondom is our
kingdom! Cotton is our king! And the God
of cotton is our God, and the God of our children,
and our children's children, for ever and ever!

What now? Can we pledge our faith and devote
our allegiance there? Impossible! Essentially,
formally, utterly, eternally, unspeakably impossible! We must antagonize the whole theory. We
must assert liberty! Slavery is wrong; liberty
only is right. Slavery is evil; liberty only is
good. Slavery is not sanctioned by the Bible.
As with all other evils, so with this, the Bible
suffers it, but provides redemption from it. Liberty only is sanctioned by the Bible and the God
of the Bible. State sovereignty is not constitutional; but liberty only. Secession is not constitutional. While the Union remained, slavery deluded and blinded the nation. Its least mischief
was wrought among the blacks. It corrupted and
perverted the aristocrats themselves; changed
them from witnesses for God and humanity into
witnesses for Satan and self, and, practically, by
their agency, nullified the constitutional guarantee
of a republican form of government for every
State, and, within its own limits, trampled repub-

licanism in the dust. At the same time, it ate
out every thing vital in the Church. Instead of
educating, elevating, enriching, and encouraging
the Christianization of the non-slaveholding population around it, it made that population perhaps
the most ignorant, irreligious, embruted, and
wretched white population on the face of the
earth. Its influence on the North was the haugh-
tiest and vilest, the proudest and meanest, the
most seductive and the most contemptuous, that
ever divided, demoralized, and humbled a free
people. It made our general Government, against
all the instincts, traditions, and professions of our
history, against every pulsation of every honest
heart in the land, the hypocrite of nations!—the
protector of pretended lovers of freedom, who in
reality were the most arrogant despisers of fraternity and equality, and chief swindlers of the
rights of mankind. And, since the attempt to
sunder the Union,—which, thank God! is yet
only an attempt, and destined, I trust, to speedy
and perpetual disappointment,—all this, and more
than this, has come out, and is boldly emblazoned
on every rebel banner, and everywhere flaunted
in the vision of heaven and earth. How they
hate and persecute to the death the comparatively
few Union men of their own States who have not

yet been cowed into submission! How they hate
the multiplying Union men of the half-rescued
Border States, and how ready they are to plunder
and murder them! How they hate the more
numerous Union men of the wholly-rescued Border States, and denounce their preference of
liberty and Union to slavery and secession! How
they hate the freemen of the Middle States and
Eastern States and Western States, classing them
all as Yankees and Hessians, cursing them with
bitterest curses, and spurning every thought, even
the gentlest and kindest, of any thing like reunion with us! How they disown and despise
us, as all of another and inferior race,—baser than
they, both in blood and spirit! And where are
their embassadors? Are they anywhere, in any
land, among the people? Or, as strangers to the
people and scorners of the people, do they seek
shelter and warmth under the wings of foreign
aristocracies, and peep from the shade of such
patronage, and mutter in the ears of such audi-
ence?

Body and soul, with life, fortune, and sacred
honor, in the name of God and man,—of the
Fatherhood over all and the brotherhood among
all,—we go for liberty, true liberty, honest, earnest, equal, open-hearted, open-handed liberty!

Ah! how well I remember the exclamation of a
Virginian, at the ratification of the nomination
of General SCOTT for the Presidency, in Monument Square, Baltimore! "Our heroes remain,"
said he, "but our orators have departed!" Even
then I thought, No wonder! for, as LONGINUS declares, "No slave can be an orator;" and we may
still more truly affirm, No advocate of slavery can
be an orator! Ten thousand advocates of slavery
would fail to make one real, genuine orator. The
soul of the true orator is not a compound of such
selfish atoms. No, no; it is the great breath
of the Almighty, the inspiration of divine liberty.
This it was that made PATRICK HENRY an orator:
never more so than when he clasped his hands,
and looked up toward the God from whom his free
spirit descended, and cried from earth to heaven,
"Give me liberty, or give me death!"

Yes, my friends, my brethren, my Christian
brethren, we go for liberty! We go for liberty
even for the aristocrats themselves. We do not
hate them; cannot hate them; would not hate
them if we could. We are infinitely too happy
in our own nobler, broader, and sublimer faith, to
hate even the proudest, bitterest, and worst of them
all. All we want is to see them converted; or,
if that cannot be, to see them transported to their

transatlantic kith and kin, to the European paradises of aristocracy, to the palaces and gardens of
all who prefer self to the redemption of the world.
Whatever comfort such exclusiveness can give
them,—and, doubtless, they would scarcely ask
any better,—let them have it!

But, next, we go for liberty to the poor blacks;
not an insurrection, but a resurrection. And,
next, we go for liberty to the poor whites,—a still
wider and more glorious resurrection. And, next,
we go for liberty to all the Union men of the
South,—another resurrection. And, next, we go
for liberty to the whole sweep of the continent,—
north, south, east, and west, from lake to gulf,
and from ocean to ocean,—one heritage for all
people. "Liberty *and* Union, one and inseparable,
now and forever," for ourselves and our children,
our race and the world, as long as time shall last
or even immortality endure!

What then? Is this right, or wrong? Is this
true, or false? Is this good, or evil? We must
decide, or, rather, we have decided. This *is* right,
is true, *is* good. This is our faith. With this
faith, we go forth to the battle; sad, indeed, that
there must be any battle; loving our enemies,
praying for them, and yet pressing on them,—not
so much because they are *our* enemies, as that

they are the enemies of truth, right, and good;
enemies of liberty, fraternity, and equality; enemies of civilization and Christianity; enemies of
God and man: even if honestly so, still only the
more efficiently so because of their honesty, and
therefore the more resolutely to be met, and opposed, and subdued, and put down, and kept
down, for ever and ever. Either this, or we ourselves must be put down; and republicanism
must be put down; and aristocracy exalted; and
liberty destroyed; and slavery rattle its chains,
and utter its groans, and drop its blood, through
all the ages; and our holy religion itself be crucified between thieves, with little hope of its ever
living again. We may fast, but this is not enough;
we may pray, but this is not enough: we must
believe, or we can do nothing. We must sacrifice
every thing we have to our faith. There is no
room for treason here; no room for divided sympathy here; no room for timid shrinking here;
no room for hesitating and vacillating caution
here; no room for equal matching and chivalrous
duelling here; no room for jealousy and self-
seeking here; no room for partisan plottings and
counter-plottings here; no room for invidious
distinctions between the Government and the
Administration here; no room for any thing

under God's heaven or on God's earth but the immense, simultaneous, outnumbering, overpowering progress of a GRAND, NATIONAL, JUDICIAL PROCESS, solemn as death, sublime as eternity, and, by the grace of God, resistless as Omnipotence: the necessity of love; the recompense of hope; the magnificent march of faith, in triumphant vindication of all that is noble in man and worthy of his Maker.

www.ingramcontent.com/pod-product-compliance
Lightning Source LLC
Chambersburg PA
CBHW021337110726
47900CB00005B/1510